DIAGNOSIS:
SMALLPOX

"Ladies and gentlemen," Kay Erwin said, her voice cracking. "I'll get straight to the point. We've got a seriously ill patient in our isolation ward." She paused to draw a breath. "He's got smallpox."

A qualm rattled through me. *Had she really said smallpox?* I jotted the word down, although I wasn't likely to forget it. A medieval scene flickered across my mind—pockmarked, dead bodies piled high on oxcarts. I felt a crawling sensation at the back of my neck.

I wasn't the only one with the creeps. Murmurs passed among the other reporters like a spreading epidemic. Nobody had expected anything so sinister. The terse public information e-mail hadn't even vaguely hinted at this. A minute before, the video cameras and sound booms of two TV crews had seemed like two too many. But Kay had just reset all our thinking. Now, seasoned press people whispered like bad mannered schoolchildren. Smallpox wasn't something you could mention without causing a stir.

Smallpox. I scribbled the word on my notepad and noticed I had written it twice.

THE
SMALLPOX
INCIDENT

A Peyton McKean Mystery

THOMAS P. HOPP

PART ONE

DARK DAYS IN SEATTLE

THOMAS P. HOPP

surgical scrubs. Occasionally a patient in a blue hospital bathrobe would be wheel-chaired in to show off a remarkable recovery. But these guys wore standard business attire, like most of my colleagues in the press corps. I glanced at the hefty man sidelong as he settled into his chair. There was something familiar about his chubby-cheeked face. He hunkered forward, apparently ready to hang on Kay's every word. The other guy sat beside him and spoke to him in low tones.

Kay moved near the microphone to deliver her first line. But before she did, her face pinched up like she had caught a whiff of formalin from the autopsy room. She balked in front of the microphone for a second. Knowing she was normally cool in front of a crowd, I thought it all quite odd.

"First of all," she blurted. "I want to assure you there is nothing to be alarmed at."

My eyebrows went up at that one—quite a statement from the public health lady. Right away I wanted to raise my hand and point out all the things that caused me plenty of alarm: Ebola, West Nile virus, polio, avian flu, tuberculosis.

"Ladies and gentlemen," she went on, her voice cracking. "I'll get straight to the point. We've got a seriously ill patient in our isolation ward." She paused to draw a breath. "He's got smallpox."

A qualm rattled through me. *Had she really said smallpox?* I jotted the word down, although I wasn't likely to forget it. Kay had added a whole new entry to my list of alarms. A medieval scene flickered across my mind—pockmarked, dead bodies piled high on oxcarts. I felt a crawling sensation at the back of my neck, as if a big hairy wolf spider had run across it.

I wasn't the only one with the creeps. Murmurs passed among the other reporters like a spreading epidemic. Nobody had expected anything so sinister. The terse public information e-mail hadn't even vaguely hinted at this. A minute before, the video cameras and sound booms of the two TV crews had seemed like two too many. But Kay had just reset all our thinking. Now, seasoned press people whispered like bad mannered schoolchildren. Smallpox wasn't something you could mention without causing a stir.

Smallpox. I scribbled the word on my notepad and noticed I had written it twice. I was in a totally unsettled mental space.

Kay Erwin waited until the whispered echoes of her bombshell died down. "Let me give you some details," she said. "The patient is a fifty-five-year-old male named Harold Fenton, F-E-N-T-O-N." She spelled the surname to avoid misprints. "Last Tuesday morning he was referred to us from a community clinic in Sumas, Washington, near the Canadian border. Mr. Fenton arrived here with symptoms including fever, congestion, and the early stages of a pustular rash that has since spread over his body. In the three days Mr. Fenton has been with us we have used a DNA test to confirm his clinician's initial diagnosis of smallpox.

"We notified the Centers for Disease Control in Atlanta on the first day and sent them a blood sample by special military jet transport from Boeing Field. Sumas, as you may know, is a small border-crossing town between Seattle and Vancouver, British Columbia. Mr. Fenton is a U.S. Customs inspector there. That adds a significant wrinkle to this case."

She paused. The sounds of scribbling and typing on laptops increased to a fever pitch, including my own notepad scrawling.

"The border between Canada and Washington State has been on heightened alert for terrorists ever since Ahmed Ressam, the would-be Los Angeles Airport bomber, was apprehended with explosives at Port Angeles. I just want to emphasize we've seen nothing that establishes a terrorist connection."

She paused again to let another ripple of concerned whispers die down.

"Now, regarding Mr. Fenton. He is seriously ill, but we are working diligently on his case. No one else is ill, and we consider the disease confined at this time, along with its only victim." She ended the statement with a note of finality, as if she had said her piece.

There was a brief moment of near-silence, punctuated by someone whispering into a cell phone. Then a spray of hands went up. Kay nodded in the direction of the first and most eager. Arran Fisk, a local TV reporter down front asked, "Can you tell us more about where the virus came from?"

"Unknown at this point," Kay replied. "Possibly an immigrant traveling across the border."

"An immigrant from where?"

"Unknown."

She nodded toward another waving hand. Victoria Tanner, an old Seattle Times Newspaper reporter in a hot pink skirt suit asked, "How big a threat does Mr. Fenton represent?"

"Minimal," Kay replied. "Assuming we confined him before he spread the disease to others." The audience was buzzing. A couple more cell phone calls went out. Kay put up her hands in a slow-down gesture. "I want to emphasize again that the situation is under control." She looked around for nods of understanding and agreement. She didn't get any. "Mr. Fenton's physician, Ronald Adams, made a quick, accurate diagnosis of smallpox and moved to contain it before there was any chance for it to spread. Dr. Adams said he had recently read a smallpox-awareness article in a medical journal, written by Mr. Northwest Casual, up there in the back." She pointed at me with the flat of her hand. By Northwest Casual, she meant my less-than-well-heeled look: an untucked T shirt in marrionberry purple, khaki cargo-pocketed pants and silver-and-Day-Glo-green jogging shoes, one of which was parked on the chair back in front of me. I took the foot off the chair, smiling self-consciously at her acknowledgement. My smallpox article had been the lead story in *Clinical Practice* web-magazine.

"That article," Kay went on, "was a refresher on the CDC's recommended response procedures. Dr. Adams followed them and reacted quite effectively. On the same day he transferred Mr. Fenton to our isolation ward, he called Fenton's family and close contacts at work. He advised them to isolate themselves at home until they had stayed free of symptoms for three weeks. A CDC field team has since arrived to monitor their compliance. The team will also institute a ring vaccination protocol. That's where the immediate circle of contacts receives doses of smallpox vaccine. Thanks to Dr. Adams' swift action, we have every expectation that this incident has been halted at its start.

"In the intervening two days since Mr. Fenton was transferred to our facility, both the CDC and the Army's laboratories at Fort Detrick, Maryland have confirmed the diagnosis. They also identified the strain of smallpox. It's a familiar one, referred to as the Bangladesh strain, isolated in the mid-twentieth century when the last naturally occurring strains were analyzed. Subsequently, as most of you should know, smallpox was eradicated by worldwide vaccinations in the nineteen-eighties. More recently, concern about bioterror has led the U.S. Government to vaccinate military and health care personnel. I myself got a dose several months ago."

Down front, a hand went up from a reporter from the *Seattle Post Intelligencer Online*. Melinda Coury, a newbie of the young, female, pretty, and unmarried kind, with shoulder-length dirty blond hair and an appealing spangle of freckles across her nose, asked, "For our readers' information, could you go over the symptoms of smallpox?"

Kay's mouth crimped like she would rather not dwell on the subject. But she dished it up. "Smallpox starts with head- and chest-congestion like a common cold. It then progresses to a high fever accompanied by white, pustular sores that cover the victim from head to foot. Many patients die from lethal effects of the fever, but some victims recover after a month or so of incapacitation."

A chilling thought crept into my mind as I jotted down Kay's description. I waved my pen to catch her eye. She nodded.

"Most younger Americans haven't been vaccinated against smallpox," I said. "So quite a few of us aren't immune. How big a threat are we facing? What's the worst case?"

Kay's jaw tightened, letting me know this question was not on her preferred list of topics. But she knew from past encounters that I would ask tough questions and stick to them.

"That's a very good question," she said, pausing to take a sip of water from a glass on the podium. She swallowed hard. "You have your facts straight, Fin Morton. Because the vaccine causes some side effects, including rare fatalities, the U.S. stopped routine vaccinations after 1977. And as you said, most Americans under age thirty have never received smallpox shots. So they're naturally more susceptible than older Americans who got vaccinated as children. You're talking approximately half the U.S. population. Is that enough to satisfy you?"

It wasn't. "What about the availability of the vaccine? If the virus gets loose in Sumas, is there enough vaccine on hand to protect everybody in the U.S.?"

Kay raised both her hands. "As I mentioned, we already have the situation under control by isolating Mr. Fenton and vaccinating his contacts. And Sumas is a very small town in a dairy farming community. There are more cows there than people. But if additional vaccine is needed, there are stockpiles nationwide that can be rushed to the area in plenty of time."

"Now, just a minute," I said, struck by a thought. "You said Mr. Fenton is fifty-five years old. That means he received the original vaccine as a child."

"You're good with math, Fin," Kay replied. She shrank behind the podium and that deer-in-the-headlights look came back. She knew it was dawning on me that the implications of Mr. Fenton's case went on and on. Her knuckles went white where she gripped the sides of the podium, making me almost want to let up on her.

But a story is a story. "So why is he sick?"

"That's a mystery," she croaked. "And we're still grappling with it. We checked Mr. Fenton's immunization records and found he was indeed vaccinated as a child. Not only that, but as a border officer, he was entitled to a shot of new vaccine, which he got just last month. That dose should have been effective against the Bangladesh strain. However, immunity takes time to build. So we're left wondering whether Mr. Fenton's immunization was too late."

My spine began to tingle. "Or," I said, "the virus made him sick *despite* his immunizations." A thought was shaping up in my mind, a scary one. "Is it possible it's a new strain of virus?"

She sighed, realizing I was going to drag it all out of her. "Yes,

Phineus Morton, I'll admit that your concept may fit the facts in this case. Still, I'm surprised Mr. Fenton has such a fulminant case."

"Fulminant?" Melinda asked.

"A rapidly developing course of disease," Kay responded to Melinda, no doubt relieved to break the lock that had developed between her eyes and mine. "You would expect at least a slight protective effect from Mr. Fenton's two vaccinations. But he is in bad shape. His fever is high and he is comatose. That's something we would normally expect only in a non-immunized subject. It suggests there is something different about the virus, though our preliminary tests haven't distinguished it from the old Bangladesh strain."

"But if it *is* a new strain," I chimed in, snapping Kay's head my direction again, "or a mutant for which the vaccine isn't effective, then—"

"Let's not go there," Kay stated flatly. She stared at me hard, signifying I had taken the idea as far as she was willing to go. "Now, if there are no further ques—"

My hand went up again. Kay's eyes flashed and her head tilted angrily, warning me. My hand stayed up. I supposed I had better delete her name from my imaginary date book. When she nodded at me, I unleashed the worst question of the batch.

"Is the virus natural or man-made? You know, a bio-warfare agent?"

Kay let out a short, derisive laugh. She shook her head slowly. "That is pretty far fetched, Fin. Way out there. The concept of a deliberately altered virus has crossed my mind, and my colleagues' minds. But so far there is not the remotest hint suggesting anyone has tampered with this virus's genes. Until we have proof otherwise, we're going to assume this is just an isolated, anomalous case, coming from a natural source. Don't forget, the immigrant population in Vancouver B.C. has grown dramatically over the past few years. It's possible an infected individual brought the virus from one of the former endemic areas—Bangladesh, perhaps. Right now, nothing suggests foul play of any kind. If we thought that were the case, I would tell you so. And you can bet Fort Detrick's Biological Warfare people would take up the matter, as would the White House, the Pentagon, the CIA, and the FBI. Everyone I just mentioned is aware of the situation and none of them has declared an emergency. They all feel we have things under control here."

"Amen," whispered Cameron Phipps, a colleague sitting one row ahead of me. Sweat dotted the umber skin of his forehead. He took out a handkerchief and daubed his face.

"Please, folks," Kay Erwin said, raising her hands again. "Sometimes my job is a balancing act between informing the public and scaring them. I want to emphasize that this single case is not a cause for public alarm.

When you report it, I hope you will use a balanced approach and avoid sensationalism. Our isolation unit here at Seattle Public Health, the Northwest Regional Infectious Disease Isolation Facility, is a wonderful, ultra-modern operation. It was funded by a consortium of Microsoft, Google, and Starbucks billionaires and several well-to-do individuals, including the gentleman seated at the front of the room, who has been waiting very patiently to speak. He has some reassuring words for you." She pointed the flat of her hand toward the bald guy. "I'd like to introduce Dr. Stuart Holloman, President and Research Director of Seattle's Immune Corporation. Dr. Holloman."

Stuart Holloman! Not a guy I should have had trouble identifying. He rose and turned toward the audience and I got a better look at him. His round, pink-cheeked face was suddenly familiar. I wondered how I hadn't identified the most eminent biotechnology mogul in town. Perhaps it was just that I hadn't expected such a prominent man to attend what I had thought was a routine press conference.

Kay Erwin went on. "As you all know, Immune Corporation is a powerhouse of research on viruses and immunity. They created the first effective vaccine against Congo River virus. That disease was once the scourge of Equatorial Africa, but it's fading into history thanks to the vaccine, which some have called the Holloman vaccine in honor of its creator. Furthermore, Dr. Holloman's generous gifts to the hospital were an important source of funding for the isolation facility that houses Mr. Fenton. And I am pleased to announce that Dr. Holloman is once again stepping forward in the current, um—circumstances."

Holloman smiled a modest smile for a man so heavily praised. I realized now why he had looked unfamiliar. I had interviewed him during the early startup years of Immune Corporation when the company was small and top brass like him were accessible. But after ImCo's success with Congo River vaccine, he had become hard to reach and the years had changed him on the outside. I had been fooled, not just by his hairline, which had gone all the way over the top, but also by his width, which had grown in proportion to his wealth. The term *fat cat* came to mind. He had shrunk and widened, compared to the taller, thinner, more physically imposing man I remembered. But my last visit to his office had been years before.

Kay Erwin went on to describe Holloman's stature in the international research community and his prominence among the donors who financed the isolation ward. I supposed a small tithe of his Immune Corporation stock holdings could have underwritten the whole facility.

Holloman stood in demurring silence, faintly smiling while Kay praised him. "This morning," she said, "with approval from the Centers for Disease Control, I've agreed to provide a sample of the virus to Dr. Holloman and his coworkers at ImCo. They will immediately begin checking the organism for mutations or altered structure. Along with the CDC and Fort Detrick, Dr. Holloman will field a third team responding to this case, so you should all be reassured that we have triple coverage in the interest of public safety. Dr. Holloman…"

Erwin stepped down and Holloman went to the podium. He adjusted the microphone and thanked Kay for her introduction. Then he swept his gaze across the crowd and said, "I have assigned a team of my best investigators to this project. If I may brag a bit, we have plenty of scientific talent at ImCo to carry out every conceivable analysis of this virus. And if anything unusual is discovered along the way, we'll institute a top-priority project to create a new vaccine to neutralize it."

I made some more notes while Holloman leaned into the microphone and launched into a lengthy rap about the skills of his staff, the wealth of research capability at ImCo, and the company's top-flight biological isolation facilities, which were smaller than the hospital's but equally secure. He droned on until I had made more than enough notes. After some time, I found myself yawning despite the seriousness of the day's news.

Finally, Kay Erwin approached the podium and looked at her wristwatch for effect. Squeezing between Holloman and the mike, she said, "It's good to know your staff can help in the unlikely event that this virus is a new strain. Until then, we really shouldn't speculate on the virus's origins or the need for new vaccines." Holloman stepped aside, and she turned her attention to the crowd. "Now, if there are no more questions—"

"I've got one more," I called out. "You mentioned that Mr. Fenton might have contracted the disease from someone crossing into the U.S. Do you know where that person is?"

Kay's shoulders slumped. "I wish we did. The best I can tell you is we have sent a notice to all hospitals in the U. S. and Canada advising them to watch for people with smallpox symptoms. But Mr. Fenton may have caught the virus from someone who had an extremely mild exposure or was recovering from the disease, in which case the source may never be known. My focus right now is on Mr. Fenton, keeping him isolated and helping him get well." She looked at her wristwatch again. "We've used our allotted time. So, ladies and gentlemen, thank you for coming."

Some more hands went up, but Kay fended them off with a gesture and a promise of more details in another conference to be scheduled soon. The meeting broke up as she led Holloman out through the stage door, followed by the buzz-cut man, who hadn't said a thing.

"Do you know him?" I asked Cameron Phipps, pointing at the man as he vanished through the door behind Erwin and Holloman.

"Vincent Nagumo," Cameron said after a moment's thought. "Special Agent, FBI. Seattle Antiterrorism Unit, I believe."

"I can see why Kay didn't introduce him," I said. "So they *do* suspect something is up."

"Maybe," Cameron replied, closing his notebook computer. "It all sounds pretty scary, but it sounds pretty iffy, too." He got up and moved toward the door. "Are you coming?" he asked. "I'll walk out with you."

I shook my head and kept my seat. "Prerogative of a freelancer. I don't have an editor screaming for my copy. No publication deadlines."

"Poor fellow." He waved goodbye over his shoulder on his way out. Phipps, a reporter for the *Puget Sound Business Daily*, recently scooped me on a story concerning a sunburn remedy made from extracts of jellyfish. It was an ironic scoop, considering Phipps is about the darkest African American I know while my own pale skin, on occasion, cooks up red as Dungeness crab. And he had a point this time around. He would be in print by morning. My story would probably come out later, in a weekly blog or monthly print publication. And I would have to compete with other freelancers for attention.

I tidied up my hastily scrawled notes as the film crews cleared their equipment and the other reporters rushed back to their newsrooms. I wrote parts of a first draft on my notepad until one of the hospital clean-up staff came in to vacuum the stage. I put on my windbreaker and tucked the notepad in a pocket and meandered out, retracing my path through convoluted corridors to the main entrance. I was just in time to spot Kay Erwin, Stuart Holloman, and Vincent Nagumo saying goodbye on the stone steps. I homed in on them, but they went in three separate directions. Kay came in through the automatic sliding glass doors as I was going out. I paused to shoot a quick question at her. "Why tell us anything, Kay? Your job would be simpler if you kept this under your hat."

"Off the record?" she asked.

"Sure, okay."

"News like this is dangerous if it leaks. Fenton's neighbors in Sumas are wondering what's up. It might cause a panic if people knew we were trying to hide something. So, I'm under orders to handle it the way I did today and get the word out as low-key as possible."

"Orders from whom?"

"Let's just say high places."

"High places in Washington D.C.?"

The spooked expression reappeared. "I can't tell you any more."

I disengaged from her with a nod and a quick wave. I had other questions, for other people. I hurried down the steps, but my prime target, Nagumo, had quickly vanished. Holloman was meat and potatoes for me too, and I caught him at the curb just as he was about to get into a silver limousine marked IMMUNE CORPORATION that was waiting for him.

"Dr. Holloman," I called politely. He had already grasped the door handle. He held onto it as he turned to eye me carefully.

"I'd like to get some more detail on your plans," I said.

He thought for a second. Then he shrugged his round shoulders. "I suppose I could give you some time. But not right now. I'm due back at ImCo for a board meeting."

Sensing an interview dissolving like a sea fog, I upped the ante. "I think this story might make *Newsweek*, or at least the cover of *Biotechnology Weekly*. I have their editor's ear."

He read my face for a second, and then responded with a slow nod. "Call my secretary this afternoon. She'll schedule a get-together tomorrow morning."

I let him climb into the passenger seat without further molestation. As the limo drove away I paused at the curb, thinking that I had the makings of a good story coming together. The interview I had just arranged could turn out well for both sides. I would get a scoop worthy of *Newsweek* and Holloman would get what most capitalists want—plenty of people reading about the company's prospects for making money. Holloman could expect some of those readers to buy ImCo stock and boost his net worth a couple more miles into the stratosphere. For me, a story was the payoff—a smoking hot story.

Earlier on that drizzly Seattle morning, I had parked my midnight-blue Mustang in the rattletrap housing-project neighborhood that surrounds Seattle Public Health Hospital and hiked a couple of blocks to the main entrance. I walked back with mixed feelings. Smallpox is a scary thing. The fact that I had never been vaccinated suddenly seemed like a big deal. Just the same, a great story bubbled inside me like strong coffee brewing. I fetched my car and drove back to the parking lot near my writing office in the Pioneer Square District. I bounded up the four flights of stairs, unlocked the green enameled wood-and-glass door of the little garret, and plunked down at my writing desk. As a first order of business I called Dr. Holloman's secretary. She had been alerted, and duly arranged an interview for the only time the next day when Holloman could spare a few minutes of face time, 9 AM.

After that I wandered down to the waterfront and grabbed a quick lunch of fish and chips at Ivar's Seafood Bar. I ate outside on the pier. Enjoying a few sunbreaks that cut the chill of the midday air, I inhaled smells of fried fish, garlic vinegar, and salt air, and listened to ferry honks echoing off the skyscrapers of the Seattle skyline above me. While digesting lunch and the news I had just heard, I flung the last of my fries down to the seagulls riding the green swells of Puget Sound. Then I went back and spent the afternoon at my desk computer, polishing off a first draft of everything I had heard. I figured I would add a lot more detail the next day and have something presentable to an editor by the day after that. I went home that evening knowing the article might just make *Newsweek* if it covered the subject well and they didn't dispatch a horde of their own reporters too quickly.

And I looked forward to walking ImCo's halls again.

But I was clueless as to how personal this story would become.

CHAPTER 2

My full name is Phineus Cornelius Morton. Phineus is after my Greco-American great-uncle Phineus Costas. Cornelius is the whim of my mother, an alumna. Morton, I like to say, is after the grain of salt with which I take most matters. My friends call me Fin. I make a decent living writing articles on medical subjects for the web, newspapers, magazines, and occasional TV or radio reports. Perhaps some of what you have read or heard about Ebola virus, herpes, influenza, and the workings of the human body originated on my writing desk. I don't have much formal medical training, and what knowledge I have came mostly from U.S. Army specialist training as a medical-response Humvee driver. I plied that trade in Baghdad's Green Zone, and later the mountains of Afghanistan. Nowadays, I follow the doctors and medical researchers of the Pacific Northwest. I've got a coyote's nose for news.

The morning on the day of the Holloman interview found me on my normal headings. I drove my Mustang to the Pioneer Square lot where I rent a monthly space. Then, as on many an-other misty Seattle morning, I walked across the mossy, cobbled pavement of Occidental Park and stopped in at Café Perugia for a triple shot of espresso, which I doctored with a pinch of raw sugar. I began sipping my caffeine overdose while scuffing up the steps of the renovated old brick building where I rent my writing office. The fifth-floor garret is an old fashioned cubbyhole of a place with sand-blasted brick walls. Its single wood-framed window is trimmed in chipped, dark-green paint and streaked outside with diesel soot and seagull poop. The old wood-framed, beveled-glass office door is trimmed in the same green paint as the windows. The worn Douglas-fir floor still has dark varnish in the corners. I often leave the door ajar to be accessible to the other top-floor tenants, an old Jewish bookbinder named Rheingau and a gay-and-lesbian marriage counselor named Darlington. They rarely stop by.

I've got a tarnished brass floor lamp with a scorched parchment shade. I clicked it on to banish the gloom of gray daylight, and plunked down at my desk facing the rain- and bird-flecked windowpane. The desk is big, and pretty nice—made of polished oak. It's the only good piece of furniture in the place. In fact, it's just about the only piece. There's an old chair with maroon flower-patterned upholstery in one corner of the room, for interviewees and guests who come by on rare occasions. Three vintage hunter-green metal file cabinets and a small table with my printer on it take up the rest of the space. There's a white-plastic-faced clock on one wall with a white electric cord drooping across the brickwork to a retrofitted metal outlet near the floor. On the opposite wall I've hung my bachelor's degree from the University of Washington, Journalism major.

I didn't start work right away. I hadn't slept too well the night before for obvious reasons. Smallpox and its epidemic implications are not the stuff of sweet dreams. And the dim, wet, gray morning sky hadn't helped me get the day off to a quick start. I let my brain idle for a few minutes in neutral, waiting for the caffeine to kick in. I love the aroma of Café Perugia's coffee—somewhere between macadamia nut and dark chocolate. It is a drug-addiction-like necessity in my morning life. While charging up for the day's big event, I turned on my computer and erased the morning schedule from my calendar. I had nothing interesting planned anyway, except a visit with a UW professor who was studying the psychological effect of sunshine after a long stretch of rainy days. I figured he hadn't had much sun in recent weeks on which to base his work. And I knew he would still be analyzing glum-faced college kids long after my story about Holloman and smallpox was published, and long after I had sipped a thousand more cups of Perugia's sun substitute.

My mental gears began to mesh. I searched the Internet for the subject matter of today's interview, smallpox. I wanted to be up to speed when Holloman talked medical details. I browsed through records on Medline and found some pretty good dope in the Centers for Disease Control's smallpox section. I rechecked a bunch of pages I had already read on U.S. smallpox preparedness, noting the bland assumption that the CDC could handle any anticipated smallpox event. I searched on. A page headed NATIONAL MEDICAL BOARD offered some meaty quotes.

"Smallpox is considered among the most virulent diseases of mankind. The causative agent, variola virus, moves from person to person through physical contact, or through the air when victims cough or sneeze during the prodromal phase of the disease." On another page I found an odd bit—a brief discussion of variolation, the old practice of deliberately scratching the skin with the virus in hope of giving the patient a mild rash followed by immunity. This technique, used in the 1700s and 1800s, sometimes led to a fatal illness that arose more quickly than when patients were exposed normally.

I imagined Kay Erwin visiting these same pages in preparation for her press meeting. If she had, then she would have choked on one note. "In the great epidemics of the past, the virus propagated itself from person to person with extreme efficiency. If one family member came down with smallpox, the entire household might be killed or debilitated."

And another note. "Smallpox scourged the Old World with plagues of mass death first recorded by the ancient Chinese and Egyptians. It was the deadliest of human infections until the end of the 18th century, when Edward Jenner developed the first smallpox vaccine. Jenner instituted a campaign of inoculation that continued for two centuries, culminating in 1977 when the World Health Organization announced the complete absence of the disease on earth. Smallpox was declared extinct. It exists today only in research laboratories."

That seemed like plenty of background. But I went looking for more sensational stuff. I googled into the deep ocean of unofficial crap and turned up a web page yammering about experiments by Australian researchers looking for a way to exterminate a plague of mice. They genetically altered the mousepox virus by adding an immunosuppressive gene encoding the interleukin 4 protein, which upped the lethality of mousepox from 20 percent to 100 percent—meaning that every mouse injected with the engineered virus died. The web site hooted some jaw-dropping questions about what might happen if somebody did that with the human virus.

But you can't trust any old web site, so I clicked off along another link trail. Eventually I hit some gritty stuff about Washington State on a page posted by a member of the Duwamish Indian Tribe, a descendant of Seattle's original native people. It was another jaw-dropper.

"When American settlers first sailed into Puget Sound in the 1850s, a thriving Indian culture existed. The natives lived well in a world of salmon, cedar longhouses, totem poles, elaborate costumed dances, and primitive prosperity. But smallpox came with the Americans on ships from San Francisco and the Orient. Within three years it had wiped out most of the native people, killing ninety percent of some villages in a single year. Corpses lay across the floors of longhouses once filled with the joyous screams of children, now silent forever. The tidal wave of smallpox swept away an entire way of life and left mass graves that can still be seen on the reservations today. During the plague, Old Chief Seattle made his most famous speech, before the governor of the new Washington Territory. In that speech he gave up most of his tribe's lands to the newcomers without much complaint, saying it was fitting the new settlers should use the land because his people had all but vanished from the places they knew and loved. He mourned his people, brought low by an enemy they could not see or defend against. He said, "Your God loves your people and hates mine... he makes your people stronger every day... while mine ebb away like a fast-receding tide."

Queasy thoughts struck me. Could smallpox impact today's society as hard as it hit Chief Seattle's people? Experience told me modern medicine could answer any threat. But my guts told me differently. Hadn't Kay Erwin said something was strange about this virus? Why was that FBI fellow, Nagumo, hanging around?

My window has a pretty good overlook on Pioneer Square. Glancing sidelong, I can just glimpse the bronze bust of Chief Seattle at the base of the totem pole that stands at one end of the triangular park. I imagined him in the depths of depression over what smallpox had done to his people.

Finally something—maybe it was the rising caffeine buzz from the triple shot—clued me to the passage of time. I glanced at the clock and leaped from my chair. *Eight fifty-five!* I was almost late for my appointment with Dr. Holloman.

I clicked off my computer and yanked my windbreaker from the rack by the door, locked up and hurried down to the street. Worried that a major story could slip away, I ran past Chief Seattle's bust and sprinted the dozen blocks to ImCo, which sits in the heart of Seattle's waterfront.

Immune Corporation's research building is short compared to the skyscrapers towering around it. At six stories high, it's a squat concrete-and-brick building shaped like a kid's ABC block—or an ATC block, considering the genetic code on which the company's fortunes were built. Some say ImCo is the preeminent Northwest biotech company and a contender for that honor world-wide. At sidewalk level, its unprepossessing walls are of solid brick, painted a light salmon pink. But the upper stories are lined with wide windows, inside which passers-by can glimpse researchers in long white lab coats busying themselves with the latest in laboratory equipment.

I went to the front desk and signed in with the security guard, who sent me up the elevator to the top floor. When the doors opened onto the penthouse-level executive office suites, I entered the domain of the power elite of ImCo. The landing's floor was of polished green serpentine stone and the walls gleamed with dark cherry-wood paneling. The wall facing the elevators announced IMMUNE CORPORATION in polished-brass letters two feet tall. It looked like the entryway to a Wall-Street brokerage firm.

Through a glass door and inside the carpeted executive suite, a young woman sat behind a high cherry-wood reception desk. Proclaimed SALLY ANN NOONAN by her brass name placard, she looked a little out-of-place. Maybe it was her black-dyed, blond-rooted hair, or maybe her triple-pierced ears. I imagined a pentagram tattooed on her ass as well. I liked her.

"Fin Morton," I announced myself.

"Dr. Holloman is expecting you." Smiling pleasantly, she stepped from behind the desk, long-legged and short-skirted in black nylon. I followed the prance of her black, ankle-high stiletto-heeled boots through a heavy cherry-wood door, brass handled and multi-windowed, into Dr. Holloman's inner sanctum. *Outer sanctum* I should say. It was a broad corner office with a harbor view, well-suited to Holloman's high standing at Immune Corporation and among Seattle's corporate bigwigs in general. Two entire walls were windowed with sweeping views of Seattle's waterfront and Puget Sound glimmering in the near distance. The Olympic Mountains rose beyond that, under clearing skies. A white-and-forest-green ferry plied the waters of Elliott Bay, escorted by a small red Coast Guard gunboat. I had recently read an article in Forbes Magazine in which the outlook from Holloman's windows was described as "a view to kill or die for."

Stuart Holloman himself was almost lost in the vastness of his office and the immensity of his view. He sat behind a cherry-wood desk set off to one side of the room as if to let the visitor be gob-smacked by the imposing vista first. If that was the intention, it worked.

"Hello, Mr. Morton," Holloman said in neutral tones when Sally Ann announced me. As she left us, he stood as if he might shake my hand, but the breadth of his desk was too great. Without the distractions of a press conference, I had a better chance to get a physical impression of him. He was a little shorter than I, and I am of average height. He wore a charcoal gray suit with pinstripes, and looked to me more like a financier than a scientist. The bald dome of his head glinted in light flooding in from the windows.

On the windowed side of his office, a couch of rich crimson velour with matching armchairs and a coffee table beckoned, but he motioned me into one of three guest chairs facing his desk. The chairs were rich too—oxblood leather on carved cherry frames, studded with large pol-ished-brass rivets. He watched my face as I sat, perhaps gauging whether I was suitably awed by his office. I was.

He settled into his high-backed oxblood leather executive chair and his suit parted, exposing a pink shirt with buttons stretched across his gut. His dark gray tie fell to one side of his ample belly. *Fat cat,* I found myself thinking again, despite intending to start the interview without a bias for or against the man. He hadn't given me a reason to dislike him, but an instinct told me that there was something vaguely uncool about him. I hadn't put my finger on it yet.

Leaning his elbows on his desk and rubbing his pudgy hands together, Holloman studied me with small gray eyes—a little on the beady side, I thought. Then he opened his palms wide and asked, "Where should we begin?"

I took my notepad out of my coat pocket and launched into my plan-ned line of questioning. "Supposing this smallpox virus is a new strain, what role do you see ImCo playing in its cure?"

"Central," he replied.

"In what way?"

"The virus will arrive here later this morning, by courier. That means ImCo will be the first commercial organization to get a look at the thing. We'll be in a situation comparable to the one in which we developed our vaccine against the Congo River virus—"

"The product that put ImCo on the map," I remarked while scribbling.

"Yes," Holloman agreed. "Our most successful research project to date and our first major product." Absentmindedly, he patted his belly with both hands, as if anticipating the cat growing fatter. "I foresee the same thing happening again. We'll get early access to information about the virus's DNA, and if anything unusual turns up, we'll be one step ahead of the world. My scientists will have the inside track in the race to develop a vaccine. So we can ace out the competition."

"There will be competitors?"

"There are always competitors in this business. A vaccine can be worth hundreds-of-millions of dollars a year. Virogen in Boston is our main enemy. So far, with the exception of Congo River virus, they've always been a half step ahead of us. But this will be Congo River all over again, another golden opportunity."

I sensed Holloman's mental wheels turning. It was clear he had had profit motives foremost when he agreed to help Kay Erwin investigate the smallpox virus. Creeping across the back of my mind came a ques-tion I didn't ask. How much did humanity figure in his thinking? Or was it all about money? "I remember once reading some rumblings out of Virogen," I remarked. "They said you took unfair advantage of a university professor's unpublished Congo River data. Stole his ideas."

"Sour grapes," Holloman said flatly, staring at me with confidence. "ImCo beat Virogen to the FDA. It's as simple as that. They may have spent a lot of time and money on the project, but we won the race. The first company to file with the Patent Office and the FDA on a new vaccine is always the winner."

I recognized a juicy quote and scrawled as fast as I could write. He was in a talkative mood, so I went after more verbal fireworks. "What do you think of people calling it the Holloman vaccine?"

"It's like the Salk vaccine against polio being named after its inventor," he said. A smile flickered across his face. "I haven't discouraged the practice. Although I would rather see my name associated with a product with, shall we say, a larger profit margin? Not a lot of people need the Congo River vaccine. Mostly just villagers in the African bush."

"And they've got no money to pay for it."

"Exactly. If it weren't for WHO funding, we would have gone broke making it for them."

In five minutes I got several pages of quotes that would make great copy in a magazine or web article. And if they stirred some reaction from Virogen's execs, I'd have an opportunity to interview them. Holloman was in a mood to make a splash, and so was I.

"Back to the case at hand," I said. "If Mr. Fenton's virus is a new mutant, you're confident you can make an effective vaccine?"

"Absolutely," Holloman responded. "In fact, I've assigned a team of our best investigators to start as soon as we get the sample. I am certain we can produce a vaccine in record time."

In record time, I scribbled. "I'd like to hear how you'll do that."

"And I'd like to tell you," Holloman replied. And then he glanced at his wristwatch. "But we only have so much time. I have a meeting with a couple of key investors in fifteen minutes. I'll need to wrap this up before that. I have some reading to do." He patted a thick legal document sitting on one side of his desk.

"All right," I acquiesced. "Perhaps we could finish off with some of the technical details on how you created the Holloman—the Congo River vaccine. Can you describe the actual laboratory procedures? It would make great background material on how you'll tackle smallpox."

A wrinkle appeared in his forehead, just a little crease. "Yes, uh..." His eyes fixated beyond me, as if something on the far wall had drawn his attention. I glanced around, following his gaze, but nothing was there.

When I turned back, his face seemed to have reddened. I got the scent of fresh news, so I pressed him. "Your methods are no longer secret, having been patented and filed with the Food and Drug Administration, right? I'd like very much to hear the details of how you made such a brilliant discovery."

He knit his thick fingers in front of him on the oxblood leather blotter of his desk, flexing them until his dimpled knuckles showed white. His lips drew tight. My journalistic instincts keyed up another step.

"Is there a problem with what I'm asking? Maybe one of your technical people could walk me through the steps of your discovery, if you're too busy."

He cleared his throat softly, as if about to broach a delicate subject. "That's a good idea," he said. He worried one thumbnail with the other as if weighing a difficult decision. Then he inhaled sharply. "The actual work was done by Peyton McKean."

"By whom?"

"Peyton McKean," he repeated with a faint quaver in his voice. "One of our junior scientists. He's the one who made the actual breakthrough, acting on my orders, of course."

"Of course," I responded, jotting McKean's name.

Holloman had gone beet red. Too red, I thought, for a cagey corporate exec who ought to be among the thicker-skinned of interviewees. Just from the look of things, I decided there was yet another story here.

"Could I meet this Peyton McKean, then? If he can give me the details, I won't need to take up more of your time."

"Yes," Holloman murmured, glancing at his watch again. "That would be acceptable. But please keep your questions confined to the Congo River vaccine."

"Okay," I agreed, although I didn't quite take his meaning about limiting my questions.

He pressed an intercom button. "Sally Ann, find Peyton McKean for me, will you please?"

I got only small talk from Holloman after that. Time dragged for more than ten minutes until Sally Ann finally came in with a man following her. He was a tall, thin man of about thirty-five with a long, straight, Germanic nose and the pale skin of someone who spends too much time at work. He had a high forehead and dark brown wavy hair worn a little long and swept back, partially covering his ears and neck with loose curls. He was clean-shaven and a bit thin-lipped. His white lab coat was unbuttoned and the sage green chambray shirt under that was unbuttoned at the collar, and under that came the neckline of a brown T-shirt. Threadbare brown denim pants and brown leather walking shoes gave no hint of formality. *Laboratory Casual*, I thought. I had encountered this near-chaotic appearance often enough before on young, science-absorbed assistant professors at the universities on my beat. The look contrasted strongly with Holloman's corporate, gray-suited uptightness.

McKean's dark eyes had an Einsteinian intensity, as alert and piercing as any eyes I have ever seen. His thin frame and erect, square shoulders gave him a scrawny, schoolmasterly look overall. I rose to greet him, to discover that he stood half-a-head taller than I.

"Peyton McKean," said Holloman, "meet Phineus Morton, medical reporter."

"Phineus?" McKean murmured while shaking my hand with thin fingers that gripped much more firmly than I had expected. "Named after the blind seer of Greek legend?"

"Named after a Greek uncle," I responded. "Nice to meet you, Dr. McKean."

"Call me Peyton." A cordial smile turned up the corners of his mouth.

"Call me Fin," I replied.

McKean looked at Holloman and asked, "What's up, Stuart?"

Holloman glanced at his wristwatch. "We've been waiting nearly fifteen minutes," he said. "Where were you?"

"At the coffee shop across the street." McKean turned to me. "My work requires more *thinking* than *doing.* I like to get away and mull things over."

Holloman raised an eyebrow. "Can't you do your mulling in your office?"

"Answer: no." McKean replied as if the two words were enough explanation.

The crease in Holloman's forehead had reappeared. "When I ask for you, I'll expect you in my office a little quicker next time."

"Then check the coffee shop first," McKean suggested. His lack of tact surprised me more than his gangling, disheveled appearance.

Holloman's eyes narrowed. But he let the issue drop. Waving Sally Ann out the door, he explained to McKean in a measured voice, "Mr. Morton is here to write an article about our work on the smallpox virus from Seattle Public Health."

"I see," said McKean. "An intriguing virus, that one."

"Dangerous," I suggested.

"Safe enough," McKean countered, "once it's in our bio-containment facility."

Holloman cleared his throat. "Peyton, Mr. Morton would like some background information on our laboratory procedures. You have my permission to give him some detail on how we handled the Congo River virus."

"We—?" McKean began, and then stopped. "Yes, of course."

"Don't tell him anything we still consider proprietary, Peyton. But give him enough detail to make him see how we did it."

McKean nodded.

Sensing the introductions at an end, I began to sit down.

"No, don't sit," said Holloman.

I stopped halfway to the chair then stood again. Holloman pointed to the door.

"Take Mr. Morton to your office, Peyton. The two of you can talk these things over while you wait for the smallpox sample. I've got other matters to attend to. And I'm late getting to them, thanks to your tardiness, Peyton."

"Come with me," McKean said, turning quickly for the door as if he felt the less time spent in his boss's office the better. As we went out, Holloman called after us.

"Mr. Morton, I'll be quite happy to have you write about what Peyton McKean tells you, but—" he paused significantly.

I turned in the doorway, waiting for him to finish. He appeared to have shrunk behind his wide desk with distance, seeming now a smaller and rounder man than when I came in. He said, "I want to read your copy before you send it for publication."

"I don't usually let interviewees review or alter what I write—"

"But you will this time," he said, eyeing me stubbornly, "if you ever want to come through my office doorway again."

"My manuscript will be passed by you, sir," I acquiesced.

"Thank you." He picked up the legal brief. The red color that had painted his cheeks while dealing with Peyton McKean was fading. But he watched the two of us turn to go with a hint of anxiety in his pale gray eyes.

CHAPTER 3

McKean seemed chipper as we strolled past Sally Ann's desk to the elevator foyer. He gave her a wave and she winked a gooey eyelash at him, then went back to touching up her blood-black lipstick using a compact mirror. McKean clasped his hands behind his back and strode so quickly on his lanky legs that I almost had to run to the elevator to keep up with him. He pressed the down button with a long bony finger. While we waited, I explained my interest in the origins of the Congo River vaccine.

On the elevator descending to the third floor, McKean seemed suddenly introverted. His brow creased, as Holloman's had. He kept his hands behind his back and fidgeted in a nervous way, rocking a little from heels to toes like a man suffused with more energy than he knew what to do with.

"How long have you worked for Dr. Holloman?" I asked.

"Five years."

"You've seen a lot of growth at Immune Corporation then, haven't you?"

"I was the first scientist hired by Dr. Holloman and his capitalist cohorts."

"You were lucky to get in so early."

He snorted sardonically, and watched the lighted numbers over the door count down while I watched him. He had a peculiar look on his face. There was a hint of something in his eyes. Hostility? No. Frustration? Maybe. But that was not quite it.

"I had something they wanted," he said with an odd tension in his voice, as if he were about to say something better left unsaid.

"What?"

"In my graduate school days at New York Hospital, I discovered some of the techniques used to create the Congo River vaccine."

"Holloman mentioned you had helped him with that."

He chuckled. "One could say I 'helped,' I suppose."

"Such a brilliant success," I said, "must have made ImCo's founders rich."

"Answer: yes," he agreed flatly.

Curious about his odd responses, I pressed on. "With revenues from sale of the Congo River vaccine, ImCo has expanded to—what? —a thousand employees?"

"More like two."

"And the company is now worth several hundred million dollars?"

"More like a billion."

"Promotions all around, huh?"

He leaned back against the elevator wall, frozen like some inner spring mechanism had just locked up. He was a smart one, but he couldn't hide some hint of the negative I sensed in our conversation.

"All you founders," I needled onward, "must have made a killing."

"Technically," McKean said, "I'm not a founder."

The elevator reached the third floor and the door opened. This landing lacked the opulence of the executive suites. There was no polish and there were no frills here, just a narrow hall of speckled linoleum tile, plain sheetrock walls painted off-white, and overhead fluorescent lighting panels.

As we stepped off the elevator, I turned toward the waterfront side of the building. I nearly collided with McKean, who turned toward the city side. I stepped aside and then fell in behind him, hustling down a long hall with office doorways on one side and laboratory doors and interior windows on the other.

I continued fishing for a question that would open McKean up. "You must feel honored," I said to his back, "to be allowed to work on something as impressive as the Congo River virus project."

"Allowed to work on it?" he chuckled without turning. "I proposed it."

I had struck pay dirt. "Sorry," I said sincerely. "Dr. Holloman didn't mention that fact."

"No," McKean said, turning to eye me briefly then continuing on with a cocky toss of his head. "Not likely."

"Tell me a little about the project," I asked, trailing him like a hungry pup begging for a handout.

"To make the Congo River virus vaccine," he said, stopping and turning so quickly that I nearly ran into him, "we dissected the virus at the molecular level and learned which of its many parts were the targets of the body's immune response." His attitude seemed to shift now that science was the subject, and he continued enthusiastically. "Because the whole virus is dangerous to work with, we fragmented the viral DNA and isolated the portions that encode certain proteins—the viral surface molecules. Those are the crucial attack points for the immune system. We mass-produced those surface proteins in harmless bacteria, purified them, used them to make the vaccine, injected it into patients, and the rest is history."

"A biosynthetic vaccine," I remarked.

"Essentially," McKean agreed, seemingly amused by my interest in that detail. "You grow bacteria in the same way beer or wine is fermented, and then you extract the viral protein from the broth."

"Impressive," I said. "A *tour de force* of modern vaccine technology. Isn't the Congo River Virus all but extinct in the wild, now?"

He gave me a wan smile. "So ImCo's public relations people would like you to believe. I was content to save some lives."

"But that's not enough for Holloman?"

"He says there's not enough money to be made curing Congo River disease. He's got a corporate mind set. Saving penniless Africans doesn't pay well enough. Only when you cure a disease prevalent in wealthy nations does your company move into the multi-billion dollar league."

"Still," I resisted, "the success of the vaccine made investors want to gamble on ImCo. The stock price moved up quite a bit."

"Unjustifiably high."

"You seem pretty unenthusiastic about events that must have made you and the founders rich."

McKean chuckled. "You are wrong if you include me with that bunch. My research may have made their company a success, but I'm still just a worker bee. I've got about as many stock options as a Congo River villager."

"Your lab?" I asked, pointing through the wire-reinforced interior windows to a laboratory we were passing when he stopped. Something in the massed ranks of reagent bottles on shelves, the glitter of clean benches and floors, and the sterile glare of fluorescent lighting seemed to suit my new acquaintance's pale looks. Several people in white lab coats like McKean's manned the benches and machinery.

"No," McKean said. "They're on my neighbor's turf. That's the domain of Dr. David Curman, a colleague and competitor."

"An interesting choice of words," I said. "Competitor, within the same company?"

"Science is a contentious endeavor," McKean responded. "Theories and experimental proposals sometimes clash."

I made a mental note to pursue those thoughts if time allowed. We moved on, passing another lab window where my first impression was of sound. From inside came the thump of music, and I spotted stereo speakers on one of the shelves. I couldn't make out the words, but the beat was strong and rhythmic—a blues song.

McKean stopped by the door. "These are my labs," he said, a smile flickering on his thin lips. The previous laboratory had been much more spacious and a lot quieter. This one was noisy and crammed with laboratory goods and equipment. Every surface was either occupied by some piece of apparatus or cluttered with a chaotic jumble of reagent bottles, racks of test tubes, unruly stacks of computer printout paper, glassware, laboratory notebooks, and other odds and ends defying description. There were as many people present here as in the other lab—three people dressed in white lab coats. They were busy at their benchtop labors, each engrossed in some scientific task. I took a mixed impression from the intensity on their faces, the clutter, and the insistent beat of the music. Either I was witnessing the pulse of fast-paced discovery, or the workings of maniacal obsession. Maybe both.

McKean didn't enter the lab. Instead, he led me beyond it and turned into an open office doorway across the hall. It was a surprisingly tiny space. Smaller than my own garret, it was no more than ten feet on a side. Like mine, it possessed a single window. And its view contrasted with Holloman's like night contrasts with day. There was no grand waterfront vista here. Instead, McKean's window looked across the street at an old warehouse with a crumbling brick façade and bleak, dark, and dust-hazed windows.

The office itself was a bit more modern than mine. The retrofitted aluminum framed window was set into a tan-painted wall of wood-grained concrete. The taupe Berber carpet and off-white wallboard interior walls struck me as a rather poor hangout for the architect of the experiments on which ImCo based its fortunes.

"Cozy," I remarked.

"Very." He smiled in his peculiar, tight-lipped way, and motioned me into one of two guest chairs. These were cheap compared to the ones in Holloman's office but comfortable enough, with cushioned backs of dark-green fabric and plain wooden arms.

I scanned the office and found it reminiscent of the over-full spaces of the lab. There were four tall black metal file cabinets and two tall oak-veneered bookshelves, which were crammed with scientific volumes with interesting titles: *Natural History of Congo River Virus, Practical Immunochemistry,* and *Stedman's Medical Dictionary.* A few titles didn't fit my expectations: *Northwest Native Shamanism, Dinosaur Eggs and Babies.* McKean's small gray metal desk was covered with papers, several inches deep, mainly photocopies of scientific journal articles. I glanced quickly at a few titles: "Synthetic chemistry of the peptide bond," "DNA, RNA, and the polymerase chain-reaction," and "Viral mutation mechanisms." These seemed consistent with the interests of a medical researcher but again there were odd ones. "Astrophysics and the cosmological constant," "Songbirds of the Solomon Islands," and "A Neanderthal flute." Every paper had been worked over with a yellow highlighter marking-pen.

A large potted avocado plant thrived by pressing itself against the small window. Its pendulous green leaves had spread toward the fluorescent lighting overhead, taking up much of the office space not already occupied by furniture. On the wall nearest me, a large whiteboard was densely scrawled with four colors of marking pens in long strings of A, T, G, and C code letters. These, I had no doubt, were the DNA sequences of whatever microbe McKean had been discussing most recently. On another wall were large nature photos in oak picture frames. One was of an evergreen forest where huge tree trunks rose from a ferny grotto. The other was of Mount Rainier's icy top bathed in sunrise pink. I smiled. So McKean had a view after all.

He settled into his desk chair, a swivel on five casters, upholstered with the same green cloth as mine. He turned it to face me almost knee to knee, crowded by the close confines of his office. Then he leaned back with his angular elbows on the black plastic armrests, his hands knit and his long index fingers steepled in an Ichabodian schoolmasterly way.

"So," he began. "We have a short time before the virus sample arrives. What questions can I answer for you?"

"It's funny," I remarked. "I've never heard your name mentioned in reference to Congo River vaccine. You would think Dr. Holloman would be justifiably proud of his scientists' inventiveness."

A faint smile crept across McKean's thin face, as if he took a perverse pleasure in my needling. Only at this moment did I realize I was dealing with a much more worldly fellow than I had first judged him to be. My newsman's experience has taught me to spot the faintest signs of guile or deceit. There were none in McKean's dark, earnest eyes.

"Perhaps Holloman *is* proud," McKean admitted. "But I have my doubts he wants all the details of the discovery made known." He watched me amusedly, as if anticipating the thoughts turning in my mind.

"So," —my mental wheels spun— "publicizing the details of the experiments would show the world how great science gets done, but the image of Holloman as the inventor of the Congo River vaccine would be gone."

"Very astute." McKean replied. His smile widened. But the smile faded, and he appeared to be savoring a mixed taste in his mouth. "He warned you he would edit the text."

"Yes, he did," I acknowledged. "But the Congo River vaccine should be considered your invention—is that what you're saying?"

He shrugged and then murmured in a level voice, "I'm not saying that." Nevertheless I detected a contradiction of his words in the hard look of his eyes and the angry-young-man jut of his chin. I wasn't sure where to take the idea from here.

"You see," he volunteered after a moment, "I'm Holloman's *employee.* Therefore, whatever I invent while on his payroll is *his,* not mine."

"I suppose so," I agreed. "But you just now used the words 'I invent.' So the vaccine *was* your discovery?"

His dark eyebrows raised. He sat straighter, as if he hadn't expected to be cornered by the likes of me. "Sure," he said after a moment. "It's all a matter of record. I proposed the project in the first place and led the team that did the lab work." He pointed to several tattered laboratory notebooks on a corner of his desk, half covered in photocopied sheets. He said nothing more.

I gestured at our humble surroundings. "Forgive me for saying this, Dr. McKean, but you don't seem to have gotten much recognition for creating the product that made the company's stock skyrocket."

He turned and stared at the brick wall across the street. "Wall Street is the province of businessmen," he said. "I'm a scientist."

I almost regretted having trodden over such a sensitive subject. He drew his thumb and fingers over his chin, staring outside thoughtfully for quite some time. Then his desk phone rang. He answered, and then covered the mouthpiece with his hand. "It's Janet Emerson, my head technician. The virus courier is down at the loading dock." He uncovered the receiver. "Yes, Janet, go down and sign the sample in. I'll meet you in the containment facility."

He hung up the phone, seeming relieved at the change of subject. "Looks like we'll chat another time. I've got to go to the lab in a few minutes."

"To handle the virus?" I asked.

"Yes," he replied lightheartedly. "You're welcome to watch."

"I don't know," I said. "How dangerous—"

"Hah!" He cut me off. "Don't worry. Janet and I handle pathological materials like this routinely."

"Viruses as lethal as smallpox?"

"Congo River virus was no pipsqueak, and we handled it just fine. Janet and I worked on a hepatitis vaccine in my postdoc years in the Army's chemical and biological warfare labs at Fort Detrick, Maryland. She joined me here shortly after I took this job."

"She's that loyal? Following you across the continent?"

"Answer: yes. We're extremely close collaborators."

"I imagine you're both under constant stress, working with viruses like Congo River or smallpox."

"Not really." McKean rose and began buttoning his lab coat. "Whole viruses may be deadly, but the first thing we did with the Congo River virus was to fragment the viral DNA. After that, we worked with the pieces. Each fragment was unable to grow on its own. There was no need even to keep the pieces in the isolation facility once we separated them from the rest of the viral genome."

"And you don't anticipate any greater risk with smallpox?"

"Not after we break up the DNA, which is the first thing we'll do today. Of course, that sort of preliminary work goes on in strict bio-containment."

"I'm glad to hear that."

"Shall we go to the lab?" McKean asked. "You can have a peek inside our containment facility."

After a brief hesitation I said, "Okay. But I'm not sure how close I want to get to this thing."

"Where's the newshound's spirit of inquiry?" McKean mocked. "You won't be anywhere near the real danger. We've got layer-upon-layer of precautions, following strict CDC guidelines. And this won't be the first time we've had a killer in our bio-containment facility."

We got up and I followed him across the hall and into the lab. The music player thumped an old Chicago blues shuffle while two people in white lab coats, a man and a woman, worked at lab benches. McKean stopped to lean over each one's shoulder, glancing briefly at their experiments in progress. Then he introduced me, first to Robert Johnson, his master's-level biologist, who was making microbial growth medium by combining salts, nutrients, and sterile water in flasks, and then to Beryl Shum, his molecular biology assistant. He explained that she was setting up an analytical run on the lab's polymerase chain reaction DNA synthesizing apparatus. The toaster-sized black gadget sat inside a microbiological sterility-control cabinet, taking up less space than the music player and seeming to have fewer features: a numeric keypad on the front, a small aluminum block on top with about eight dozen holes in it, and a black cable snaking to an electrical outlet. Some of the holes held small clear plastic test tubes into which Beryl, sitting on a tall lab stool and manipulating a micro syringe with blue-plastic-gloved hands, was transferring DNA test samples.

"She's analyzing some new Congo River virus isolates," McKean explained to me. "The virus keeps mutating, but has yet to escape the protection of our vaccine." Then he spent several minutes discussing the details of the experiment with Beryl in scientific lingo that quickly left me behind. I stepped back to take a wider view and observe McKean in his element.

I have already noted that Peyton McKean is a physically striking man. At well over six feet, he overtopped his coworkers and me, but there was nothing intimidating about him. He had an easy-going, graceful way about him that put his lab-mates at ease. Beryl and he chatted amiably while she transferred samples into the tubes on the PCR block. McKean was pleasantly animated as he gabbed in molecular biology jargon. He seemed to have forgotten the frustrations of corporate politics that we had been discussing moments before. The long, angular features of his face bore a good-natured expression. His thin-lipped mouth frequently arched up at the corners in a little smile. A constant twinkle lit his dark eyes. Obviously, the intricacies of research pleased him more than discussing money or status. And I saw in the intensity of those eyes, in the habitual slight frown, and even in the length of the straight nose down which he viewed the world, an uncanny depth of thought and a formidable mental capacity.

His technical talk, full of terms like "nested oligonucleotide primers," "annealing temperature," and "template DNA," was fully comprehensible to Beryl but left me feeling like I was trying to follow a chat in Sanskrit. After several minutes McKean left Beryl and Robert to their work, motioning me to follow him to the far side of the room. There, beyond a second wired-glass interior window, was yet another laboratory, with one person inside, gowned in white and blue from head to toe.

"This," he said with a good measure pride in his tone, "is our bio-containment facility."

It was a bright room with a clean linoleum-tile floor, bare walls and minimal equipment inside. It contained just the essentials for microbiology work: an oven-like microbiological incubator for growing bacteria, a tall freezer, a counter with a sink and gas fixtures, a bench-top centrifuge and other minor equipment. The lack of clutter contrasted to the outer lab where we were surrounded by shelves and benches covered with bottles, flasks, glassware, and dozens of electronic gadgets that evaded my powers of definition.

"It's very nice," I remarked. "Shiny... clean... sterile looking..."

"More than that," he said. "It's a BSL-3 facility."

"BSL-3..." I tried to puzzle out the meaning of the acronym. "Bio... Biosecurity..."

"Bio-Safety Level Three," McKean corrected me. "The national standard for work involving hazardous microbes. It has its own enclosed air supply, filtered so that not even a virus can escape. The entire room is under negative air pressure compared to this room, so any leakage around the sealed doors will go in, not out. We keep the room scrubbed with disinfectant soap, and the whole place is bathed in UV light at night to kill anything that might try to grow on the floors or equipment."

The person inside the facility was a young, smallish, and very pretty woman, wearing a white lab coat, blue scrub pants, blue latex gloves and blue paper booties. Her long hair was knotted up under a blue paper head-cover.

"That's Janet," McKean said. "She's just brought the virus up from the delivery bay." Janet noticed McKean and shot him a quick smile, and then turned her attention back to the counter in front of her. A cubic white Styrofoam box, about one foot on all sides, sat on the stainless steel surface. Janet seemed casual about it, although every surface was marked with biohazard warning stickers: red rectangles with evil-looking black trefoil biohazard symbols on them. I imagined myself holding that box at arm's length and still finding it too close for comfort.

"So those are adequate precautions?" I asked. A chill raced along my spine as Janet undid the clear sealing tape that held the lid on the box.

"Hmm?" McKean looked at me blankly, as if I had disturbed other more important thoughts.

"The package," I said. "Is she being careful enough with it?"

He nodded. "It's very dangerous at the core, but if the people at the hospital did their job properly, there are multiple layers of sealed containment before you get to the virus."

"And if not?"

"Then no amount of gloving or white-coating will keep her safe—or us, for that matter."

My mouth dropped. He began to chuckle. "Really, Fin. Have a little faith in our survival instincts, and our containment facilities."

I took a deep breath to calm my heart rate as I watched Janet lift the lid from the Styrofoam box. Goose bumps rose on my arms as I watched what seemed like Pandora at her big moment. But no cloud of demons arose from the cube when she got the lid off. McKean glanced at me sidelong, and then back at Janet.

"Relax," he said. "She's protected by much more than just that container."

"I hope so."

"Absolutely. The box is only there to protect the viral sample if it should be dropped, and to keep it cooled on ice. The real bio-safety controls are inside that. Hence the relatively casual handling up to this point. There are more layers inside the box, the first of which you are about to see."

Janet reached a gloved hand into the box and lifted out a cylindrical canister of brown cardboard about the size and shape of a one-quart oatmeal box. This carton had a biohazard label where the picture of the chubby Quaker usually goes.

"That's the outer canister of the triple packaging system," McKean explained. "It has a screw cap and more than enough absorbent material inside to soak up the viral sample if it should spill. And we're still not through with bio-containment."

Janet moved to a ten-foot wide stainless-steel-and-glass cabinet on one side of the room, and placed the container inside a small hatch at one end. She closed the hatch door and sealed it with a revolving metal wheel.

McKean said, "You're quite safe now, Fin. That's the last time the virus will be handled directly, and it's still inside three layers of sterile packaging."

Janet moved to the front of the cabinet, where four round holes entered its lower wall. These were openings for two pairs of integral arm-length black rubber gloves.

"That glove box," McKean explained as Janet slipped her arms into two of the holes, "is the only place Janet and I will handle the virus, using gloves that are sealed tightly into the walls of the cabinet. The whole box is airtight and under negative pressure. It's a compact version of the BSL-4 facilities at CDC and Fort Detrick. It's secure enough to contain any microbe, no matter how deadly."

"If you say so."

With her arms up to the elbows in the gloves, Janet looked through a window into the cabinet and picked up something that was beyond my view, presumably the virus in its packaging. She worked quickly, going through motions of unscrewing the cap of the canister and withdrawing its contents. McKean eyed me sidelong as I watched.

"She's taking out the inner canister. It's similar to the outer canister but half its size, with more absorbent in it. Next, she'll take the sample vial out of the inner canister."

"What sort of sample vial?"

"A screw-capped plastic test tube with the virus inside it, in cell culture fluid like what Robert is making. Hopefully, the screw-cap of the virus tube is still sealed tight."

"And if it isn't?"

"Janet will drop everything and rush out here screaming."

I recoiled a step from the window and McKean broke into a broad grin. "You really are a Nervous Nelly," he quipped.

I smiled at my own edginess and McKean's counter-display of professional coolness.

He shrugged. "At this point, a spill would be no great problem. The BSL-4 cabinet's interior is kept sterile by ultraviolet lighting inside its top. Any leaks in there would spill into a virus-lethal environment that we routinely scrub with hypochlorite bleach. The chamber is hermetically sealed off from Janet and everyone else."

I watched Janet closely, happy to see that she continued her work without concern.

McKean said, "Even the packaging won't come out of that cabinet until it's been immersed in a bath of chemicals that kill microbes, basically bleach plus detergent. The virus itself won't come out again until we've fragmented its DNA into harmless pieces like we did with the Congo River virus. After that, we can bring the fragments into the main lab here where we have all the equipment we need to do our work. Out here, we put on gloves and lab coats to avoid contaminating the sample, rather than the other way around."

"Really?"

"The human body is covered in microbes, Fin, no matter how hygienic one tries to be. Most of those microbes are beneficial to us. But they wreak havoc if they come in contact with viral DNA fragments. DNA is really quite fragile."

"So chopping the virus's DNA into fragments is the crucial step for safety's sake," I said. "How do you do that?"

"By a complex process," McKean replied. "It involves cloning. The first step, which I will personally carry out in a few minutes, is to extract the DNA from the virus and chop it into smaller fragments of known size with Hind-III."

"With what?" I asked when McKean pronounced the word. I thought he said, "Hindi three," referring to the language of India.

"Hin-dee three." McKean mouthed the syllables slowly. "Suffice it to say it's a protein molecule that cuts the virus's DNA at specific places along its length. We isolate the pieces and splice them together with circular rings of carrier DNA. We put the rings, called plasmids, inside live *Escherichia coli* bacteria where they multiply. We isolate single bacterial cells and grow them into colonies of billions of identical copies, or clones, each of which carries the same circular plasmid with its chunk of viral DNA. We can analyze the DNA as we please after that."

"Complicated," I remarked.

"But in the end," McKean said, "relatively simple and safe. Each fragment of viral DNA ends up in its own separate harmless *E. coli* culture. You can grow it *ad infinitum* to produce as much viral DNA as you need."

"Clever."

"Then, using DNA sequencing techniques similar to what Beryl is doing now, you can read the sequences of the DNA fragments like a series of books."

"How safe are you while you're doing all this?"

"Very," McKean asserted. "Because each clone of *E. coli* carries only a small portion of the viral DNA, there is no chance of the virus escaping. It's like working with a dangerous criminal, but only after separating his head, arms, and legs to study them individually. He wouldn't be too likely to escape and commit another crime at that point. Not even with all the King's horses and all the King's men helping."

"Won't there be a lot of DNA pieces to keep track of?"

"Answer: yes. The smallpox genome is one of the largest of any virus."

"So how will you sort it out after you break it up? What's to keep you from ending up with *E. coli* containing just random bits and pieces of viral DNA?"

"You're pretty smart, for a reporter," McKean said. "The secret is in how the Hind-III enzyme cuts the viral DNA—only at specific segments where the sequence A-A-G-C-T-T occurs. This sequence exists at just a few places within the viral DNA, so Hind-III yields a reproducible set of nineteen sub-fragments."

"I guess that makes sense," I said, "although I'm still a little hazy on how it all works."

McKean smiled as if pleased by the comprehension I had gained of his complex subject. He went on. "The nineteen fragments all have unique sizes. The smallest of them is a string of several hundred DNA code letters. It doesn't contain much that we're interested in. The largest fragment contains over twenty thousand letters. Our analysis of the virus will begin with the larger fragments. How we use them to obtain sequence data or to make a vaccine are stories for another time. I'll be glad to explain when we get that far, in a few days or weeks."

Janet Emerson withdrew a hand from the glove box and waved to catch McKean's eye, and then gave him a come here signal by crooking a blue-gloved finger.

"No more time for explanations," he concluded, moving toward the outer door of an airlock about the size of a closet. Turning the latch on the airlock door, he added, "She's got the virus unpackaged and waiting for the extraction and enzyme treatment. I'll be tied up for some time doing the Hind-III digestion, so I'll trust you to show yourself out. You can watch us for as long as you like. But it's a rather lengthy procedure."

He shut the door to seal himself inside, then covered his shoes with a pair of paper boots. He put on a hair cover and plastic gloves and went into the containment room with Janet. They put their arms in the two sets of glove openings and immediately began working in tight unison, carrying out a series of manipulations of the virus that I could only imagine, my view being obstructed by the walls of the glove box.

I stayed for almost an hour, watching them work and occasionally getting a chill when I pondered how Peyton McKean and Janet Emerson were manipulating a live and deadly virus that had already brought at least one person to the brink of death. As I observed them passing materials back and forth inside the glove box with the harmonious efficiency of two long-familiar labmates, I realized something. Despite my specialization in medical writing, most of the details of genetic engineering were beyond my grasp. It was a phenomenally complex business.

McKean and Emerson's sedate chatting, which I could see but not hear through the safety glass, convinced me the virus was in good hands and would indeed be subdued as McKean intended. I found myself thinking, though, that McKean was a more impressive—and a more peculiar—scientist than any other I had met.

Eventually I decided I was overloaded with facts and had better start typing before the details faded. I tapped on the window glass and waved goodbye to the busy pair, and then did as McKean had suggested and showed myself out. I took the elevator to the ground floor, dropped off my pass at the front desk and went out onto the streets. I inhaled the lush Seattle air freshened by a passing rain squall, and let the tension of the previous hours pass. I felt the euphoria a writer gets when he has great copy in his head. I walked briskly in the dazzling light of an afternoon sun-break, hurrying through Pioneer Square to Café Perugia, where I bought a prosciutto-and-mozzarella sandwich and a triple shot to take back to my writing office. I ate while feverishly typing the day's observations into a nicely expanding manuscript. My mind buzzed with more questions for McKean. Would he be able to determine how the virus had evaded Fenton's immunity by reading its DNA sequence? Could he tell a naturally mutated virus from an artificially mutated one?

There were more dimensions to this story than I had hoped for. Given how things would turn out, that was still an understatement.

CHAPTER 4

I left my office a little after 5 PM. I wanted to catch the evening TV news and see if the local or national media had picked up the preceding day's press conference. So far, Kay Erwin's low-key announcement had made headlines in the Post Intelligencer Online and Seattle Times newspaper, but it had been delivered out-of-phase for the New York Times and East-Coast television media. That wouldn't last long.

I pulled my Mustang off the lot and drove up First Avenue to north Belltown, where the Space Needle's saucer deck hovers overhead like the bridge of the Starship Enterprise. I make my home in an old four-story brick walk-up building called "Denny Heights" by my landlord and "Dingy Heights" by me. I live alone a small studio apartment, a refugee from a recent live-in romance that fell through. All in all, it suits me. Even my solitude is okay. Freelance writing is a lonesome business and a quiet household keeps my productivity high.

I have a monthly parking space in a small garage across the street. I crossed to my apartment building and scuffed up the stone staircase to the second-floor landing. My neighbor across the hall, Penny Worthe, has a habit of coming out her door just as I'm going in mine.

"Have you heard the news?" she asked. "It's just terrible."

"Smallpox?" I replied.

She looked at me oddly. "Haven't you heard about the kidnapping? A girl was taken from the Jungle Gym nightclub, just two blocks from here. I was there last Saturday night. It's freaking me out."

"I'm sure you're safe," I said.

"Meaning I'm not much to look at, right?" she replied. "Mousy brown hair, not tall enough, too round in the curves. You figure a sexual predator would pass me by for someone more interesting."

"I didn't say that."

"But you thought it."

"So you're a mind reader now?" To make her feel better I said in an offhand way, "Okay, Penny, if I were a sexual predator you'd be the first person I would prey upon. Is that better?"

She looked at me coyly. "Tonight works for me."

"G'night Penny," I said, turning my key in the latch.

I let myself in and put the six o'clock news on TV and watched out of the corner of an eye while I cooked dinner. I was waiting for the small-pox news to break, but got Penny's kidnapping story instead. The anchorwoman went into detail about a young redheaded woman who had been missing for four days after last being seen at the Jungle Gym. I started frying a steak on the stove and got some broccoli heating in the microwave while the kidnapping story went on without letup. I cut up some potatoes and put them in a frying pan with hot olive oil. I unbagged a ready-made salad and still the story just wouldn't quit, so I grabbed the remote to flip to another channel. Just before I hit the button, the anchorwoman said something that made me pause.

"Police describe the kidnapper as a dark-complexioned man with a Middle Eastern accent."

Given that terrorists were still mixed in my thinking about the smallpox incident, I watched while the anchorwoman's image dissolved into a tight shot of a distraught woman in her early twenties addressing a street reporter's microphone in front of a suburban home.

"He was very dark and handsome," she said. "He bought us drinks and kept asking Charlotte to dance. He had a neatly trimmed goatee and mustache. Very… Arabic-looking… you know, jet black hair, dark eyes, a heavy shadow of beard on his cheeks. And handsome—did I already say that?"

The scene dissolved to a yearbook photo of Charlotte Keller. She looked young, like her friend, and was lightly freckled, with a head of thick, reddish-blond hair and a beautiful smile. The anchorwoman said, "Police request anyone having information to call them at—"

The sputter of hot grease drew my attention back to the stove. The potatoes were browning to black on one side and my steak was getting way beyond bleu. I rescued them from their infernos and threw them onto a plate and sat down at my kitchenette table to eat. A gardening news segment came on after a commercial, so I picked up the remote and switched channels to try again. I grazed to the next news station while eating, and got more on the kidnapping, but no mention of smallpox. Apparently Kay Erwin's assurances that the matter was contained had had their desired effect. It seemed to be a non-item locally.

At 6 PM, the national news led off with the smallpox story. I was glad of the low-key spin they put on it. "We are told there is nothing to worry about," the anchor announced. "The incident is contained at its source, and the CDC is on the scene to take charge of cleanup. No terrorist involvement is suspected."

So there it was, just as Kay had intended—scary news coupled with copious reassurances to the public. War news on came next, so I switched off the TV and finished my meal. Although Kay's media manipulation had come off beautifully, I still had lingering doubts about how safe we really were.

I transcribed the day's notes onto my home computer, which is cloud-linked to my office computer. Then I decided to turn in early. I was in my loft bed by 9 PM, intending to rise early the next morning and finish off my report. But an uncomfortably odd assortment of thoughts kept me awake for some time—thoughts of viruses, missing girls, Middle Eastern men, and the apprehension I had seen on Kay Erwin's face at the start of it all. I had an instinct that, despite many assurances to the contrary, all was not right. And perhaps far from it.

***

The next morning's writing went well. In an hour had I bashed out the preliminary draft of a segment on ImCo's involvement in handling the smallpox case. I planned to e-mail a submission to *Newsweek* the next day. I hustled off to my writing office, arrived, triple-shot of espresso in hand, and synced the smallpox story from my Internet cloud. Just then, my desk phone rang.

"Fin?" a half-familiar, thin voice asked from the other end. "Peyton McKean here. I called to invite you to see our first results. Janet and I worked late last night. And we've picked up the hint of something interesting."

"I'll be there as quickly as I can!" I gulped the rest of my coffee, hurried down to the street, and jogged the seven blocks to the ImCo building. Once I was seated in McKean's office, I watched while he and Janet discussed DNA data displayed on his desktop computer. "This is a map of the viral DNA from Mr. Fenton," McKean said for my benefit, pointing at the left-hand of two tall ladder-like vertical streaks shown on the screen. "Compare it to a known sample of smallpox DNA, on the right."

I studied the two ladders on the screen. Against a white background, the DNA indeed looked like two ladders with dark gray rungs, standing side by side—except that these ladders were missing many of their rungs and had no side rails at all—just ascending sets of rungs, each rung shaped like a hyphen with rounded ends. Each ladder had more than a dozen rungs, and these were unevenly spaced, as if someone had knocked out half of the rungs in random fashion.

"Do the two ladders look identical to you, Fin?" McKean asked after I had taken a moment to study them.

"Yes, they do," I replied. "The pattern of rungs missing or present in each ladder is the same."

"Nineteen rungs in each ladder," Janet added. "Just what we expect for normal Bangladesh strain smallpox."

McKean took a schoolmasterly, lecturing tone. "These nineteen rungs, or bands as we normally call them, are the expected result of reacting Hind-III enzyme with smallpox DNA."

I said, "Let me make sure I understand what you're showing me. Each of the rungs—or bands—is a DNA sub-fragment molecule?"

"Exactly," McKean responded. "Or to be more precise, each band formed when millions of copies of the same DNA fragment moved together down from a starting point at the top, pulled through a gelatinous material by an electric field which drew them downward at a rate determined by their size. All the DNA molecules in those bands started their journey at the same place, but the smaller molecules moved faster while the larger ones were impeded by their greater size and moved at slower rates."

He pointed at the topmost band.

"The DNA molecules in this band, called Fragment A, are more than ten-thousand code letters long, while the smallest DNA in the band at the bottom of the ladder, Fragment S, has only a few hundred A's, T's, G's and C's in it." He looked at me cagily down his long nose. "Are you sure you don't see any differences between the two ladders, Fin?"

I looked at the screen again. "No. They look identical."

"That's what I thought at first," Janet said, smiling a little smugly.

"But look carefully, right here." McKean pointed a long index finger at the bands that were the second from the top of each ladder. "Do these B Fragments really match?"

I looked more carefully. "Ah! The left-hand one is slightly higher. I see it now that you point it out, Peyton."

"Careful observation is the key to success in DNA analysis," McKean asserted. "Without meticulous thought and observation, many researchers miss much of what's right before their eyes. Here, we see Fragment B from Mr. Fenton's virus has moved just slightly slower than that of the normal virus. That means it's heavier than the normal Fragment B. Perhaps twenty or thirty code letters longer."

"Twenty, out of thousands," I remarked. "Can you really measure such a slight difference?"

"That's one thing we're concerned about right now," Janet said.

McKean explained. "Such a small variation might not be real—just an experimental error, a wrinkle in the gel presented here. But I suspect it's not. I think we should sequence Mr. Fenton's B fragment, don't you, Janet?"

"Sure," she said. "If it will help explain things."

"Is that an easy thing?" I asked. "To sequence the fragment?"

McKean shook his head. "It will take some doing, although I'm sure Janet is up to the task."

He tugged at his angular chin, doing some mental calculations. "Fragment B is the second largest in the entire viral genome. It's too big to fully sequence without sub-fragmentation. You see, Fin, when we determine the sequence of DNA code letters—called bases, or nucleotides—we start from one end of the DNA chain and read as many letters as we can, moving along the chain. However, the reading process is a chemical reaction, which begins to fade out after a few hundred code-letters. We have to start reading again, farther along the DNA, overlapping the first sequence and continuing past the stretch where the first analysis faded out. It can take quite a few overlapping sub-fragments, which we make by cutting the fragment with more restriction enzymes other than Hind-III. It can take a while to read the entire sequence."

"Weeks, or months" said Janet.

McKean raised an eyebrow at her. "Maybe a little quicker, if we prioritize the project high enough."

Janet sighed. "Why do I foresee more late nights in the lab?"

"All for a worthy cause," McKean replied with a fond smile. There was warmth between them that rang of good fellowship, at least.

"Please forgive the fact that I'm still worried about terrorist plots," I said. "But doesn't this DNA alteration confirm that the virus's genetic structure has been tampered with?"

McKean looked thoughtful. "Altered by a human hand?"

"That's what I mean."

He thought for a long moment. "It's certainly not beyond nature's ability to change the virus this way. But a human-generated change might look the same."

"So how will you decide if it's man-made or a natural change?"

"I'm not sure if we will be able to tell that or not. We'll simply have to take a detailed look at the altered genetic sequence and see if there are any telltale signs of genetic engineering. If so, then foul play would indeed be indicated."

"How soon will you know?"

"Tomorrow at the soonest, when the first of the sequencing data are in hand. Maybe not for some time, though, if the mutation is in a hard-to-reach portion of the DNA sequence." He looked at his watch. "There is one thing I would like to do, and now might be the best time. Janet, I think I'll go and have a look at Kay Erwin's data for this virus. She carried out this same sort of restriction-mapping experiment to confirm the diagnosis of smallpox, but she didn't mention any altered fragments. Given how slight the change is, her people may have missed it. After all, they were looking for similarities in the ladders, not differences. I have a hunch their data may record the same subtle alteration. Just a glance at her results would confirm our finding."

"While you go to see her," Janet replied, "I'll make the sub-fragments and set up the sequencing apparatus for the first run."

McKean turned to me. "Fin, would you like to join me in a dash to Seattle Public Health? You might find the isolation ward interesting. Mr. Fenton is still there, still hanging on to life by a thread."

"I'd love to see the place—and Mr. Fenton. That's a rare opportunity for a medical reporter."

While McKean phoned Kay Erwin and arranged a visit, I considered my good fortune. My instincts told me the more time spent with Peyton McKean the better, although I was surprised he wanted me to tag along on such a crucial mission. I suspected the inventor of the Congo River vaccine, who chafed under the dominion of Stuart Holloman, liked the idea that I might provide some press coverage as an embedded journalist.

"Do you have a car?" McKean asked. "I would like you to drive if you don't mind."

"Glad to. My car's just a few blocks from here."

"That will be fine. I'm a poor driver. Too easily distracted by abstract thoughts, I'm afraid."

***

We walked to my Mustang, and several minutes later I drove us into the delivery area of Seattle Public Health Hospital. Using Kay's name, McKean cajoled a security guard to let us park beside the loading dock and board a stainless steel elevator, in which the guard used his passkey and pressed a floor button marked "Restricted Access" and sent us up. When we stepped off, we were greeted by an intern in a white hospital staff uniform. He led us to the end of a corridor where a wall-sized window of wire-reinforced safety glass bared the way. A sign above the window wall read, "Infectious Disease Isolation Facility."

"Wait here," the intern said before taking leave of us. "Dr. Erwin will be right with you."

Beyond the window was an entire hospital corridor perpendicular to one in which we stood, running to the left and right down the length of two opposing wings of the hospital. Spaced at regular intervals along both halls were doorways leading to patient rooms and other facilities. Directly in front of us, in the center between the two wings was an open area with a square nursing-station counter replete with television monitors, phones, and file cabinets. In essence, an entire hospital ward had been sealed off behind the glass wall.

McKean said, "The entire area behind this glass is as securely isolated as the BSL-4 cabinet you saw in my lab. Nothing gets out without being thoroughly sterilized. That includes equipment, supplies, clothing, and, er, other things. Ah, there's Kay."

Erwin stood just inside the open door of a room immediately to our right within the facility. She was dressed in a yellow spacesuit-like isolation suit made of inflatable plastic with a small air compressor on her back. Inside the room were two beds, in the nearest of which I could just glimpse the sheet-covered feet of a patient. McKean rapped a knuckle on the window. Erwin turned and smiled at us through her clear plastic faceplate. She came out of the room, stopped on the opposite side of the window wall, and pushed a button on a desktop console that abutted the window. A small speaker set into the glass at about head height clicked on. Kay's voice came across, distantly, and ringing with the sound of her plastic suit. "Hi, Peyton. Hi, Fin. Sorry, this moon suit makes it hard to talk. Can you hear me okay?"

"Passably," said McKean. I nodded.

She pointed a thumb toward the patient. "I just checked Mr. Fenton's vital signs."

"And?" McKean prompted.

She shrugged inside the bulging suit. "Not too vital. He's comatose. High fever, lungs badly congested. May not last the night."

"Poor fellow," McKean said. "Nasty disease. But we've come to look at your DNA data."

"Yeah. Okay. I'm finished here. I'll meet you in my office once I'm clean."

She moved down the corridor to our left and we tagged along on our side of the window. My reporter's eyes were busy laying down mental notes about everything I saw inside the isolation facility. I felt awed and a little terrified to know the glass wall was all that held an epidemic in check. Kay moved past the on-duty station into the left-hand corridor. The first door on the far side was labeled, "Supply Commissary." As she went down the hall, she passed another door labeled "X-ray," and third labeled "Surgery." I was unprepared for what came next. A closed green doorway with a small rectangular window in it had the ominous label, "Autopsy." The efficiency of the ward, it seemed, ranged almost to ghoulish. Across the hall from the autopsy room Kay spun the wheel latch of a large stainless steel hatch doorway labeled "Sterility Control." She sealed herself into an airlock and then went on to the Sterility Control room proper, which we could see into through a window that faced the outside of the facility. The room was a twelve-by-twenty-foot space with a tile floor and a hanging metal shower ring at the end where she entered. She pulled the ring and the shower sprayed her isolation suit from head to foot with sterilizing solution, which ran off her and into a drain in the floor. She then moved to a dressing area and removed the suit by opening a zipper that ran down its front from shoulder to crotch. She stepped out, wearing green surgical scrubs and paper booties, and hung the isolation suit on a wall next to several others. Then she passed through the hatch doors of the near-end airlock, exchanging her booties for street shoes on the way, and finally stepped out to join us in the outer corridor.

"That's better," she said, smiling. "Being on the ward is about as comfortable as being on the moon. But we follow procedures to the letter with something as deadly as smallpox onboard." She ushered us across the hall and into her office, a typical medical doctor's workspace. It was a neat, tidy place with a large metal desk, framed degree certificates on the wall, shelves of medical reference books, a window with a view of city office towers and sunlight streaming through half-drawn Venetian blinds. McKean and I settled into guest chairs as Kay pressed a button to wake her computer. A minute later she had her results on the screen, which she turned toward us. McKean leaned close and stared at the pair of DNA ladders.

"Have you noticed," he asked Erwin, "how Fenton's Fragment B looks a little heavy?"

"No," Erwin said, turning the computer back to take another look. "But now that you mention it, it does seem a tad higher up the gel than the standard virus fragment, doesn't it?"

"It does," McKean said.

"I'm glad you noticed that," Erwin said. "Too fine a shade of difference for my eye. I don't do a lot of genetic analysis."

McKean nodded. "Understandable. You've got your hands full with Mr. Fenton, and the DNA difference we're looking at is quite subtle. But now I am certain it's real. We'll make a major time commitment to sequence Fragment B and find out how it has changed."

"Good," Erwin said. "Otherwise we're still at a loss as to what makes this strain so virulent."

"Fragment B contains some pretty interesting genes, you know."

Erwin looked at him uncertainly. "The virus has so many genes. I've read about them, but my mind just boggles. It's hard to keep track of them all."

McKean nodded. "One hundred eighty-seven genes, at last count."

"At last count?" I interjected. "I read that the variola virus was sequenced in 1993. Its entire genome is known, isn't it?"

McKean chuckled condescendingly. "Remind me to explain multiple, overlapping reading frames, Fin. The ways in which variola DNA gets translated into proteins in the cell is still being worked out. There may be dozens of virus-encoded genes right before our eyes, of which we are still unaware. The number of genes might still grow."

Erwin asked, "But you've got a favorite suspect gene on Fragment B?"

"Answer: yes," McKean said. "The gene encoding the viral surface antigen, B7R. It's the main target for anti-smallpox antibodies."

Seeing my eyebrows knitting, he explained. "The bloodstream of immunized patients contains antibody proteins, which attach to the viral B7R surface protein in a lock-and-key fit, to aid in its destruction. If this strain of smallpox has an altered B7R protein, then—"

"Then that could explain the virus escaping Mr. Fenton's pre-existing antibodies," Erwin interjected.

"Exactly," McKean affirmed. "A mutated viral surface protein might shake off Fenton's old antibodies. I'll keep Janet busy determining if and how this surface protein has been altered."

"Good," said Erwin. "The sooner we know how this virus has gone bad, the sooner we can take countermeasures."

"By the way," McKean said almost as an afterthought. "Are there any other cases of smallpox yet?"

Erwin's expression clouded. "Yeah," she sighed. "Two members of Fenton's family have come down with fever and congestion. Two co-workers at the border station have come down with fevers. The CDC team's got them all under watch at their homes. But there is worse news. A register clerk at Fenton's local convenience store reported to a hospital with a fever last night. His home is outside the vaccination containment ring."

"If he's got smallpox," McKean said, "we're looking at a local break-out."

"Uh-huh," Erwin murmured glumly. "The CDC team is already setting up a larger temporary isolation facility, expecting more patients. The President just this morning authorized vaccination of the entire town of Sumas."

"The President of the United States?" I asked. "Is that who you meant yesterday when you said you were under orders from high places?"

She shook her head. "Not directly. But I was informed that he wanted to downplay things. It seems he's as worried about panic as about public safety. Says he doesn't want businesses to be hurt if people needlessly lock themselves in their homes. But now I think even the President's gotten the message. Vaccinating all of Sumas tells me he's on the same page with me."

"But the outcome is still in doubt," McKean said. "The old vaccine didn't stop Fenton's virus."

"Let's just hope it's more effective in other vaccinees," Erwin said. "And on the positive side, we've had no reports of smallpox in other cities yet."

"But the incubation period for smallpox is long," McKean countered. "An exposed person might take fourteen days to feel sick, and several more before breaking out in a rash that would give a definitive diagnosis. So a lot more cases could be brewing out there."

"Given Fenton's job as a customs inspector," I said, "couldn't he have exposed people crossing the border just before he got sick enough to go to his doctor? They could be anywhere by now."

Kay nodded. "The CDC is watching carefully for that sort of thing. Nothing yet."

"On the other hand," I said, "if someone was transporting the virus on purpose, then Inspector Fenton might have snooped too deeply into someone's luggage."

McKean raised a finger. "Or he may have contacted someone in a car who had the virus but didn't know it yet."

"I don't like the implication that someone was deliberately transporting the virus," Kay said. "And I'm not willing to declare this a case of..."

"Bioterror?" I asked.

"It's possible, of course," she said. "But who would do such a thing?"

"Remember when one of our units in Afghanistan came across a safe house where Al Qaeda had a makeshift lab and notes on culturing biological warfare microbes?"

"Yes, Fin," Kay said. "I remember. But they didn't have facilities sophisticated enough to genetically alter a smallpox virus."

"You can't do virology in a house, or a cave," McKean remarked.

"I'm certain we'll never face a bioterror threat from unsophisticated terrorists. It would require too much central organization and precision work in a completely modern laboratory."

"Okay," I allowed. "But it doesn't mean such facilities couldn't exist."

"That's all speculation," said Erwin. "But one thing is certain. Mr. Fenton's case is an anomaly. There hasn't been any smallpox in the Pacific Northwest since the nineteen-twenties. It's hard to see how this case could arise spontaneously out of nature. That makes a terrorist attack at least worth keeping in mind." She looked at me thoughtfully and added, "But don't quote me on that."

"Okay... for now," I said.

"But, if there were a plot," said McKean, "it is eminently sensible that the first victim would be a border agent. If someone was deliberately bringing the virus into the country, and if Fenton nearly caught him—"

"Too bad he didn't," interjected a young man in a dark blue suit who had appeared at Erwin's office door. "That would have made my job easier."

Kay nodded at the newcomer. "Let me introduce you fellows," she said. "Peyton McKean and Fin Morton, this is Joseph Fuad, FBI agent."

We shook hands with Fuad, who appeared to be of Middle Eastern heritage, although thoroughly Americanized in dress and hairstyle. His face was clean-shaven, although his cheeks bore a five o'clock shadow despite the hour, which was not yet noon. As he exchanged hellos with us, he used standard, Midwestern English.

Erwin explained, "Mr. Fuad is the FBI liaison to the CIA on this case, assigned by Vince Nagumo. He's a specialist in Middle Eastern immigrant communities on both sides of the Canadian border. If there were an Islamic plot to bring smallpox into the U.S., he would have heard about it. Right, Joe?"

"Actually, we've heard some rumors of that sort," Fuad replied. "But they have turned out to be idle gossip. Rumors are extremely hard to verify."

"Until something happens," I said.

He smiled reassuringly. "We haven't turned up any real conspiracies yet, Mr. Morton." He turned his gray eyes on McKean. "One of my duties is to keep the home office informed on your progress, Dr. McKean."

McKean raised an eyebrow. "No one mentioned you to me. Do you have any virology training?"

"Not much. Just college biology at Rutgers. But I did get a solid B."

"That's a start." McKean eyed him thoughtfully. "You won't hamstring us with a need to explain every detail, will you?"

"No, sir. Just give me the gist of what you find out. That's all I need."

McKean gave Fuad a quick rundown of Fragment B's mysterious weight-gain, and then we left him chatting with Erwin, and departed the hospital. I dropped McKean off at his lab and went back to my writing office to flesh out my notes on my scientifically prodigious new acquaintance.

Toward the end of the afternoon, by prearrangement, I strolled over to ImCo. The guard admitted me and sent me up to McKean's office. I arrived just as Janet was showing him the first of her DNA sequence data files. Her pretty face was lit by a glow from McKean's computer and the excitement of discovery.

"This DNA-sequencing run was a good, long one," she said. "Nearly three hundred steps." On the computer screen, the data appeared as long strings of the code letters A, T, C and G. She said, "I got into the coding region for the B7R surface antigen protein. There's definitely something different about it."

"I see that." McKean focused his dark eyes on the screen. "There is a DNA insertion, just like I suspected."

"Insertion?" I asked.

McKean nodded. "Janet has found the place where the original DNA code of the virus broke open and new code was spliced in." He pointed to a line of code on the screen and counted. "One, two, three, four, five, hmm, hmm, hmmm. Twenty-seven new code letters added."

"Added?" I said. "Added by whom?"

"By nature, or by human hand. We still don't know that."

I pressed him. "Can such an insertion of DNA happen naturally?"

"Yes, it happens all the time. It's one of the major mechanisms of gene evolution. The DNA chain breaks open and new links are added by one means or another. Some of the mechanisms are still pretty obscure."

"Is there any way to tell if humans played a part?"

"Not absolutely. But sometimes there are telltale signs. Investigators often use restriction enzymes to open the DNA. You can spot them by the cut sites they leave behind—short DNA segments like the one used by Hind-III, A-A-G-C-T-T. Such sequences may remain in the DNA chain after it has been artificially altered. That seems not to be the case here, however."

He leaned forward, frowning at the sequence of code letters. "Hmm," he murmured, deep in thought. "There is one peculiarity about the added sequence. It repeats itself."

"I saw that," said Janet. "But I didn't know what to make of it."

McKean drew a finger along the segment of inserted code, emphasizing it for my benefit. It read:

GATATCGAGGATATCGAGGATATCGAG

It was flanked on either side by additional letters with no more meaning for me than the segment he pointed out.

"See how it repeats?" he asked. "Every nine letters, it repeats itself."

"No." I shrugged. "It all looks random to me."

"Count it out, Fin. Read it in threes. G-A-T, A-T-C, G-A-G. See how that pattern repeats three times?"

"Oh, yes!" I finally saw what had been plain to McKean's experienced eye. "But I don't get your point. So what if it repeats?"

"Such repeats are extremely rare in nature, although they do happen. On the other hand, humans might do such a thing easily."

"Why?"

"That is the big question, isn't it?" McKean pondered the sequence a moment more, and then asked Janet, "Is this within the protein-coding segment of the gene?"

"Yes it is."

"Then this insertion alters the B7R surface protein of the virus," he said. "And that is consistent with the virus having avoided Fenton's antibodies by having an altered surface covering. These changes may be the key to how that happened."

"How do DNA changes alter a protein?" I asked. "It's been a while since I studied biology."

"Let me refresh your memory." McKean took a professorial tone. "DNA code does nothing by itself. It is no more than a blueprint for other molecules to follow. The A, T, C and G code letters are read by other cellular molecules and translated into proteins that do the gene's work. Proteins are also long strings of code letters, as you may recall."

"Yes," I said. "Strings of amino acids."

"Very good," said McKean. "There are twenty different kinds of amino acids that are strung together in making proteins. For simplicity, think of them like twenty different colors of beads in a child's pop-it necklace. In your mind, undo that necklace so the string is linear, not circular. That's the best model. Now, the amino acids of any protein are assembled into specific sequences according to the DNA code. To do that, the cell's machinery reads the DNA letters three at a time and then translates them into the protein's amino-acid code. But there is one more critical step. The protein does not remain just a long string of amino acids; it bunches up into a ball, the surface of which is covered with different amino acids—or beads, in my example—in a variety of patterns. Each of the many different types of proteins in your body jumbles up in a unique way and has a unique array of amino acids on its surface."

He entered a command into his computer's keyboard. After a moment of number crunching, the screen blanked and then the DNA sequence reappeared, this time with a second line of code under the first. McKean pointed at the lower line.

GATATCGAGGATATCGAGGATATCGAG
AspIleGluAspIleGluAspIleGlu

"See there," he said, running his finger over the line. "The first three DNA letters, G-A-T, have been decoded into the amino acid, Asp, which is an abbreviation for aspartic acid, one of the building blocks of proteins. Next comes Ile, short for isoleucine, another amino acid; and then Glu, which stands for glutamic acid. Then those three amino acids repeat three times."

"Three repeats of three," I remarked. "I still don't get the significance."

"I can't help noting," McKean said, "that two of the amino acids are unusual in being negatively charged—aspartic and glutamic acids."

"That's important?"

"Only in that the immune system is notable for the difficulty it has in dealing with highly negatively charged surfaces. This altered B7R protein has taken on a very strong negative charge, by virtue of this inserted sequence. That's a pretty drastic alteration to the virus's surface coat."

"An electrostatic charge," Janet suggested, "to push the old antibodies away."

"Quite possibly," McKean agreed. "This viral alteration is a diabolically clever way of evading immunity, no matter how it came about."

McKean remained cool, but my pulse had sped up. "Are you saying this virus is custom-made to cause disease?"

"Answer: yes," McKean murmured. And then he caught his breath. He scowled more deeply at the screen. "Custom-made indeed."

I didn't like a change I heard in his tone. "You weren't sure if this mutation was natural or man-made," I said. "Are you having second thoughts?"

"More than that," he replied quietly, staring at the computer as if he saw something profoundly disturbing. "I'm quite sure now. It is indeed man-made."

"What makes you so sure?" I was deeply shaken by the implications of his calm statement.

He typed in some new commands and made a quick half-explanation. "When in a hurry, molecular biologists use a shorthand to write amino-acid codes. They reduce each three-letter abbreviation to a single letter, sometimes having little connection to the original name. Asp, for instance, is shorthanded to D."

"Just D?" I asked.

"Right. Using single-letter codes allows the twenty amino acids to be written quickly, using twenty different letters of the alphabet. Very efficient."

"But what's your point?"

The computer flashed the sequence in front of us again. A new third line had appeared:

GATATCGAGGATATCGAGGATATCGAG
AspIleGluAspIleGluAspIleGlu
   D   I   E   D   I   E   D   I   E

Janet gasped. Momentarily at a loss, I scanned the sequence until the repeated message came clear.

"DIE, DIE, DIE!" I exclaimed as the realization sank in that this was the product of an evil, all-too-human mind. "I can't believe my eyes."

"Believe them," McKean said grimly. "The probability that nature produced this sequence has just gone to zero."

McKean got on the phone to Kay Erwin while I sagged into a chair, astonished that our worst fear was now a reality. He explained the details to Kay, switching on his speakerphone so we could hear her response. "I just got off the phone with Fort Detrick," she said. "General Moralez had the same news."

McKean glanced at me and tapped a fingertip to his temple. "Great minds run in the same gutter."

"You can't think this is funny," I complained.

He shook his head, but seemed rather unperturbed by the confirmation of my worst fear. He clasped one elbow and tugged at his chin like some thoughtful Brahmin, as Kay replayed her conversation with the general.

"They're increasing Federal activity immediately," she said. "The President and the Secretary of Homeland Security are on this twenty-four, seven now. But they're even more worried about panic than before. I've been ordered to extract a promise of secrecy from my staff, and now I've got to ask the same of you and your people, Peyton. You too, Fin."

McKean quickly said, "You can count on Janet and me." Janet nodded.

I acquiesced reluctantly. "This may cost me a news scoop."

Kay apologized, and then encouraged Peyton and Janet to increase their efforts. After goodbyes, McKean switched off the speakerphone. His office was suddenly, resoundingly silent. He scribbled a note on a yellow notepad, while my mind boggled at his calm air.

"Peyton," I began.

"Hmm?" he responded, still scribbling.

"I'm surprised your reaction is so matter-of-fact. Aren't you scared?"

He eyed me thoughtfully. "Answer: no. Although, I suppose I should be." He glanced at Janet, who stood by his desk like a statue, her face as pale as marble and a tremor working through her thin body. Then he looked at me, and I'm sure I wasn't much better off.

"So," he said curtly. "Two people in this room are having normal reactions to shocking news. That's good enough. I'm busy."

He scribbled on his notepad some more while Janet and I exchanged blank looks.

"Well," I said. "If anyone needs to be cool and collected, I guess it ought to be the person most able to do something about it."

"And I'm that person," McKean affirmed.

The phone rang and McKean hit the speakerphone button again. He said hello while continuing to write. A man's voice said, "Hi, Cousin Peyton. It's Mike, over here in Winthrop. I got a problem."

McKean leaned close to me and whispered for my benefit, "He owns some horse acreage in the Methow Valley, northeast of the Cascade Mountains." He pronounced the word "Met-how."

"Who you whispering to?" Mike asked.

"Two people," McKean replied. "My head technician, Janet—"

"Hi, Janet," Mike said. "Remember me from your department's camp-out last summer? That was my ranch you were on. My horses you folks rode. My cowshit you probably stepped in."

Janet shook herself slightly, mentally shifting gears. "Hi," she said. "I remember you, Mike."

McKean continued the introductions. "—and Fin Morton, a journalist."

"A reporter?"

"Yes. A medical reporter."

"Good," Mike said. "Maybe he can write about what's going on over here."

"And what exactly is that?" McKean tapped his pencil on his notepad, eager to get back to his notes.

"You know my neighbor that breeds Arabian horses? Calls his spread Arabians Unlimited?"

"Yes," McKean said, "I recall seeing his ranch gate on the highway."

"Well," Mike said. "I found out he's doin' a lot more than raising Arabians. I wouldn'ta been suspicious but, well, the guy that owns the place—people call him the Sheik."

McKean raised an eyebrow as if pondering the same uncomfortable thought that immediately came to my mind. Mike went on, unaware of concerned glances the three of us exchanged. "He bought the ranch next to my place a couple years ago. Now, with all this talk about smallpox and terrorists, I just thought—"

McKean frowned. "I don't think you can suspect him of anything just because of his Arab origins. Since 9/11, too many people have been looking askance at perfectly good Arab-American citizens."

"No, you're right," Mike conceded. "There's a Jordanian fellow on the volunteer fire department with me. He's a good guy. I ain't suspicious that way. Or I wasn't, anyways. But there's been a lotta people coming and going at Arabians Unlimited lately. Lots of cars. Lots of SUVs with dark-tinted windows. And some strange stuff happening."

"Such as?"

"Well, I tend to a little weed patch up in the hills behind my house. I usually take my dog up there with me. Now, he's got a mind of his own when he's off leash. So yesterday I had to run him down way to-hell-and-gone across the next ridge. I got to where I could see my neighbors' place. They got a big house and a couple of barns and some stables and stuff. And I saw something that didn't sit too well. A black SUV pulls up and out get two men and they have a girl with them. A red-haired girl, and what gets me is it looks like they've got her hands cuffed behind her. They took her inside this one big building, like a poultry barn maybe, and, well, that's all I know. I don't think she wanted to go in there. They had to sort of pull her along."

"A red-haired girl!" I exclaimed, recalling the news report of the previous night. "One was kidnapped!"

"Damn straight," said Mike.

McKean asked, "Didn't you call the police?"

"Yeah, sure. I called the Sheriff's Office when I got home. And Sheriff Barker stopped by later that day. Said he'd been over to check out the Sheik's place, and I musta been seein' things. He was real curious about where I was when I saw what I saw. Warned me not to trespass on my neighbor's property. Said he'd talked to the Sheik and the Sheik was threatening to press charges if I came around there again. So it turns out I'm the one in trouble. Can you believe that?"

"Um-hmm." McKean murmured, wringing his lips thoughtfully.

"But Sheriff Barker and me, we never did get along. He came to my place a couple years ago with a health inspector. Tried to condemn my well. Nearly ran me off my own property. Come to think of it, that was right after the Sheik moved in. I had to go to court and get permission to pump my own water. You know, Peyton, I really don't like that it was right after the Sheik got here. You'd almost think the Sheriff was in cahoots with them or something. Maybe he's on the take, you know what I mean?"

"Perhaps," McKean said. "But what is it you want me to do?"

"I heard about that smallpox case on TV. They said ImCo was working on it, so I thought of you. I mean, suppose the people messing with smallpox are at the Sheik's place? Ain't you got some connections with the powers that be?"

McKean looked dubious. "I suppose I might."

"Well maybe you could get them to look into this. I got a real strong feeling about it. It ain't too far from here to the Sumas border crossing."

"I know that," McKean said.

"I guess I don't have no proof. But what's he doin' with that woman? That's what I wanna know."

"How far away were you when you saw the girl?"

"Oh, 'bout half a mile. Maybe a little closer."

McKean frowned. "Rather far away to be certain she was handcuffed. But it's worth looking into. I'll pass the word along."

"Thanks," Mike said. "I gotta go now. Dog needs feedin'. Bye."

"Goodbye." McKean clicked off the phone. "Mike's got a Rottweiler," he explained to me. "Between the dog and his shotgun, he's probably quite safe from any foul play. But I wish I knew what to make of all this."

"The missing redhead," I said. "The news said she was abducted by a dark-haired, Arabic-looking man."

McKean paused for a moment, as if weighing an overload of data. Then he reactivated the speakerphone and punched Kay Erwin's number. Within several minutes, he had explained his cousin's news first to Erwin, and then to the FBI man, Joe Fuad.

Fuad cleared his throat, sounding uncomfortable even over the speakerphone. "Listen," he began, "I'll get someone to look into this if you insist."

"But?" McKean prompted.

"But I wouldn't make too much of it. The telephone lines always get buzzing when there's a missing person story. Reports of redheads will be popping up all over the landscape for a few days. Ninety-nine-point-nine percent will be false leads. And just because the neighbor is of Arab extraction, there's no need to stir up any anti-Arab sentiment is there? Your cousin isn't... a skinhead, maybe?"

"My cousin fought along with Saudi Arabian soldiers in the first Gulf War," McKean retorted. "He's got no beef against Arab Americans."

"Just thought I'd ask," Fuad replied. "You never know, with people who live back up in the hills, especially after 9/11."

McKean, Janet, and I looked at each other dumbfounded, until Fuad spoke again. "Don't worry. I'll definitely let the agency know about this. And I'll give the Sheriff's Office in Winthrop a call. We'll go on the assumption that every lead is worth following, no matter how far-fetched."

"That seems prudent," McKean said. He drummed his fingers on the desktop as if he suddenly wanted to be off the phone. "Let us know what you find out."

"Sure thing," said Fuad. "And you be sure to keep me up-to-date on your research, okay? Now, is there anything else?"

"No."

"Then, goodbye." There was a click on the other end and a dial tone. McKean switched off the speakerphone, his dark brows brooding.

"Sounds like I just offended the man," he said.

"But who else were you supposed to call?" Janet asked.

"I don't know. The FBI regional office, I suppose. But Fuad is the man they entrusted to this case, isn't he? He's the logical choice."

I shrugged. "At least we know the matter will be looked into."

CHAPTER 5

What a difference one day can make. I had simultaneously come across my biggest story ever, and sworn not to write about it. I got home that evening around six, dragging with me some take-out teriyaki chicken and a really bad attitude about the future. I picked at the chicken, sipped cabernet and watched the TV news analysts babble about smallpox, terrorists and a bunch of things they knew nothing about. None of them gabbed about "DIE, DIE, DIE" because they didn't know it yet.

I drank two more glasses of cab. Then I climbed into my loft bed and passed out.

In the morning, I called McKean's office from home, wanting information even if I couldn't publish it. ImCo's receptionist told me Dr. McKean had gone to Seattle Public Health Hospital. He would be out most of the day.

I'm not one who is easily left behind. I drove my Mustang to the hospital and bluffed my way into the loading area with the story that I was supposed to meet Dr. McKean and cover his reactions to developments in the case of the customs inspector. The security guard doubted me, but relented when a call to the ward confirmed that McKean was there and willing to see me. Ushered up to the isolation floor, I found McKean with Kay Erwin, who was dressed in turquoise scrubs, standing outside the glass wall of the isolation ward and staring inside. Neither was speaking.

They turned in response to my hello. McKean looked somber. Erwin seemed downright depressed.

"What's wrong?" I asked.

"Nothing unexpected." McKean pointed inside the ward, off to the left, where two men in yellow isolation suits were grappling with a large object on a stainless steel gurney inside the Autopsy Room. My eyes widened when I realized what they were struggling with—*the customs man's corpse.* They were tucking it inside a heavy black-plastic body bag.

"He died at 1 AM last night," Erwin explained. "I oversaw the autopsy."

"Very efficient," McKean said. "The way you arranged this place."

"We can't risk contaminating the morgue downstairs with an infectious subject like this one," she replied. "They're bagging him for removal to a specially outfitted crematorium."

I watched the men with a shudder of disgust. "Poor fellow," I said. "Were any of his family able to come to see him before—?"

Erwin's expression went from bad to worse. "They're all sick with smallpox."

"Every one of them?"

"His wife and two teenage kids," Erwin murmured. "The whole family has been admitted to the Sumas isolation facility. Their prospects aren't good."

The naked cadaver, just yesterday Mr. Harold Fenton, was a pale yellowish, waxy looking husk of what had once been a human being. Its skin was covered from scalp to foot with hundreds of thumbtack-sized white spots, each surrounded by a small ring of reddish inflammation, long-since cooled in death to a purplish hue. The eyes were sunken, half-open horrors. His jaw was slack, his mouth an open hole. His hands, once vital, now terrified me with their too-apparent lifelessness. The signs of the autopsy were more horrific yet. Erwin and company had invaded the body in seemingly too many places. The abdomen was filleted like a fish and the chest cavity had been cracked open, rib-by-rib. Worse, the top of the head had been lifted off. A flap of skin with Mr. Fenton's scalp dangled to one side of an exposed, pink-boned cranium. The head flopped over and I saw to my horror that the brain had been completely removed.

"Intriguing incisions," McKean said. I glanced at him sidelong as he studied the slashed body with no hint of the agitation that ran through me like an electric current.

"You're used to this sort of thing?" I asked him.

"What sort of thing?" He looked at me in vague surprise. "Oh, the cadaver—the autopsy. No. In fact, I can't recall having seen a dead person until today. None of this surprises me, though. Nothing I wouldn't expect."

"You've got a stronger stomach than I do."

"Less awe of death, perhaps."

When the two men got the corpse inside the bag I breathed easier. One of them zipped it up, and up, covering the viscera and then the gaping chest. Finally, with a last tug on the zipper, the poor, brainless head of Mr. Harold Fenton vanished from the sight of the world for good. One of the men put a red biohazard sticker on the chest area. My stomach swirled with nausea as the men moved the gurney through the airlock into the Sterility Control room and began washing the outside of the bag under the shower of sterilizing solution.

Peyton McKean chatted with Kay Erwin regarding the whereabouts of the man's brain and viscera and the nature of her findings among those organs, until I felt like I might pass out. But I recalled the TV news that morning, which had given me another concern to bring to this place of death. So I interrupted.

"Peyton, have you heard any more about the redhead your cousin was worried about?"

"No," he said. "I assume the situation is in good hands with the FBI fellow, Fuad."

"Well, I heard some more on TV this morning."

"I rarely watch television. What did you see?"

"There's another unsolved abduction case. An older one, in Vancouver, British Columbia. The authorities say it's the same M.O. She was abducted from a nightclub."

McKean narrowed one eye. "When did she disappear?"

"Two weeks ago, I think it was."

Though he had been blasé about the cadaver, this news seemed to have more effect. His expression clouded and he shook his head slowly, as if reluctant to believe his own logic.

"A double coincidence," he said. "Statistically improbable."

"What?" I asked.

"The abductions," he said. "Between the Vancouver and the Seattle cases, there is a separation time of one week. That's about the length of time it takes for a smallpox rash to break out on a deliberately infected individual. If I planned to pass an infection from one victim to the next, that's exactly the length of time I would pick." He tugged at his chin. "It may just be a simple coincidence, but—"

"No need to concern yourself," a voice interrupted. It was Joseph Fuad, freshly arrived from the elevator. "I was aware of the Vancouver case before the news people got hold of it. Vancouver's my territory, remember? So far we haven't been able to make a connection between the cases. And just to let you know, I contacted the Sheriff's Office in Winthrop. They sent someone around to investigate your cousin's claims, Dr. McKean. The redhead in question is the ranch owner's wife. Your cousin witnessed—how should I put it? —a domestic situation. She claims there was no harm done. She wasn't under any coercion. She and her husband are getting along just fine now."

McKean and I exchanged glances. I said to McKean, "To hear your cousin describe it, there was more than a household squabble going on."

"But he was looking on from a distance," Fuad said. "Best to leave the investigation to trained professionals rather than nosy neighbors, don't you think?"

"Of course," McKean agreed.

Fuad looked at McKean cagily for a second. "I had a nice long chat with the Sheriff," he said. "A fellow named John Barker. He's a true professional. Believe me, if there was any problem whatsoever, he would have been the first to spot it."

"I suppose so." McKean frowned as if the shadow of a doubt lingered.

"Problem solved, then," Fuad concluded.

McKean and I looked at each other for a moment, and then nodded our reluctant agreement. Fuad made motions as if wiping dirt from his palms. "We'll just chalk it up as a false lead. A coincidence."

"So it seems," McKean said.

"On the other hand," Fuad went on, "your discovery of man-made changes in the virus—now *that's* gotten quite a reaction at the agency. We're running down of every bit of information we can find regarding Mr. Fenton and whoever infected him. We're checking every Customs record entered in the last three weeks—automobile license plates, driver identities, visas, passports. Anything that even remotely looks like a lead is being followed up. We're interviewing one heck of a lot of people that went through Mr. Fenton's checkpoint. The CIA's Antiterrorism Center is sending some experts, the NSA is involved, and the Army and CDC are gearing up to lock down Sumas completely and vaccinate everyone there. Too late to help that one, though." Fuad nodded at the men bringing the gurney out of the airlock, passing us on their way to the elevator with the body bag, which glistened from head to toe with disinfectant solution. Mr. Harold Fenton was on the first leg of his journey to become smoke and ash. I shuddered.

Kay Erwin said, "Let's hope there won't be any more like him."

"Amen," said Fuad.

Erwin and Fuad followed the gurney to the elevator, pausing to carry on a quiet conversation after the elevator doors closed and the men and their gruesome cargo disappeared. McKean and I stood silently in the middle of the hallway, mulling private thoughts about death and small-pox.

A cell phone on McKean's hip made a faint tone and he took it and held it to his ear. In response to his hello, a voice on the other end began talking just below the threshold of my hearing.

"Yes," McKean said. "I did tell the FBI. The fellow is here right now." As the caller went on, McKean's expression darkened and he cast a sudden glance at Fuad, who was still chatting at the elevator with Kay Erwin. He turned deliberately to face away from Fuad and moved along the corridor to get out of earshot, simultaneously waving me to follow. He stopped near the corner of the window wall and motioned me near to listen. I leaned into the phone, glancing at Fuad and Erwin who still chatted, unaware of our actions. The voice on the phone was Cousin Mike. He was speaking in spooked, breathless tones.

"—your office told me to call this number."

"Sorry I've been hard to reach," McKean said. "But what you're say-ing can't be true. Fuad assured us the redhead is the Sheik's wife."

"That's a lie," Mike said. "She's a brunette. I seen her when they first bought the property. Mary and I took some cookies over as a welcome to the neighborhood before they put up the gate and the guard shack. He introduced her as the missus and she took the cookies from us. She's a fat old brunette who wears a scarf or my name ain't Mike."

"Women's hair color," McKean suggested, "sometimes changes."

"Listen!" Mike continued urgently. "I went snooping around and found some kinda lab in that building they took the girl into."

McKean frowned. "How could you tell it was a lab?"

"Lots of machines, gadgets and stuff. Lab stuff."

"And the girl," McKean prompted. "Did you find her?"

"Nope. I heard somebody comin' so I took off. But you should see this lab. I'm thinking it's a virus lab, or something like that."

McKean paused a long moment, frowning. "Perhaps I should have a look at it," he said at last. "It would be pretty obvious to me whether it was set up for virus propagation, drugs, or whatever. I'd better get off the line now. Someone's coming." Erwin had gone into her office and Fuad was headed straight for us.

"Wait!" Cousin Mike cried. "I gotta know something first. Did that FBI dude ever get anybody to look into these guys?"

"He said Sheriff Barker did," McKean whispered. "But now," he spoke away from Fuad, who had quickened his pace toward us, "I'm not so sure."

"I'm tellin' you," Mike said urgently. "The Sheriff is *in* on this. Somebody else has got to check these guys out. Sure as hell they got something to do with this smallpox story."

"I'm beginning to suspect you're right," McKean replied.

As Fuad neared us, I stepped away from the phone, acting as casual as someone caught in the act can be. McKean hastily concluded his conversation. "I'll try to think of something and get back to you. I've got to go. Goodbye."

He clicked off the phone and reslung it on his hip just as Fuad reached us.

"Interesting phone call?" Fuad asked, his eyes darting from McKean's to mine and back again.

"Interesting? Oh, yes," McKean said. "Janet called from the lab. It seems the autoclave—the glassware sterilizer—has broken down."

"You had to come over this way to talk about it?"

"Bad phone reception," McKean countered. "I couldn't hear her over your conversation. Without the autoclave, we'll run into some delays in our analysis of the virus. I told her I'd be right over to fix it."

Fuad cocked his head. "Don't you have repair people to do stuff like that?"

"Answer: yes," McKean vamped beautifully. "But when time is critical, it's advisable to do it yourself." He turned to head for the elevator and I followed.

Fuad tagged along. "Maybe I'll come with you."

"Suit yourself," McKean said calmly. "But all I can promise you is the tedium of a long sojourn inside the workings of a stainless steel contraption."

Fuad stopped in his tracks. "You're right," he said—maybe a bit too thoughtfully. He watched us walk to the elevator, scowling as if he might suspect he had been put off a trail he would rather stay on. "Let me know if anything significant comes up, will you?"

"You can rely on me," McKean said as we got aboard the elevator.

On the way down McKean turned to me. "I smell a rat."

"Fuad's dirty," I agreed.

McKean let his eyes unfocus in deep thought.

"But," I spoke quietly, suddenly wondering if the elevator walls were bugged, "if he's involved with the virus, what can we do? Who can *we* rely on?"

"Ourselves," McKean replied.

"The police," I suggested.

"If they turn around and contact the FBI, then Fuad will get wind that we suspect him."

"Is that a problem?"

"If you don't like getting shot in a dark alley, I'd say it *could* be a problem. He already wonders what we're up to, wouldn't you agree?"

"Yes," I acknowledged. "He was pretty keen to hear that phone call."

We got off the elevator and paused on the loading dock.

"I don't know what to make of Mike," said McKean. "He can be pretty squirrelly."

"So, what are you thinking of doing?"

"Mike suggested we just sneak into the Sheik's barn and have a look around, and he's right. It will be obvious to me if it's a virology lab. If not, then I'll know Mike is out of line. But if there *is* a virology lab in that building—"

"Or a kidnapped redhead," I added.

"Yes," McKean said. "Then somebody ought to do something about it, don't you agree?"

I was surprised by his impetuous decision. "It might be dangerous."

"Let's call it an adventure." A tight-lipped smile crimped the corners of his mouth.

I shook my head. "I wouldn't have figured you for an adventurer."

"Oh? Why not?"

"Just doesn't fit the profile of a scientist."

"You figure I'm too much the geek to just *do* it?"

"No. I only meant that you're already involved in some pretty exciting and critical research."

"True," he acknowledged. "But my actions in the lab for the next few days are pretty much a foregone conclusion. I will create a subunit vaccine. It will be effective or it won't. Time will tell. Other than that, the lab work from this point is mostly a succession of test tubes, incubators and flasks. It can be delegated, and Janet is infinitely reliable. But Mike's problem is something very different, isn't it? It's the chance to travel to a distant place and steal into a bastion of potential danger. Getting the goods on the bad guys, if that's who they are."

"Peyton McKean!" I laughed. "You're a thrill-seeker!"

He smiled. "Let's just say my mind needs stimulation. Too much of what happens in the laboratory is predictable to me. It takes a lot to get my adrenaline pumping. Life is often too sedate for my constitution."

"Even with a new vaccine in the offing?"

"All the more so." McKean lofted a pedagogical index finger and elaborated. "With the project in Janet's capable hands, no time need be lost. If my cousin's story turns out to be nothing, then I will have taken a diverting ride through some spectacular country. My thinking on scientific subjects will no doubt be stimulated."

"How do you figure?"

"I have found it is exactly at the moment I feel compelled to stick close to my work that I must get away and let my thoughts clear. When inspired thinking is what is needed, then it is best to leave the details behind. Hopefully, I'll come back with a refreshed mind and new insights into the vaccine problem. Getting away from one's work is sometimes the best way to get it done."

"A method to your madness," I thought out loud.

He smiled. "We won't be gone too long."

"We? You don't expect *me* to come with you!"

"Yes, I do," he said. "You want to help, don't you?"

I was caught off guard. "I guess so."

He looked at me cagily. "You see, there's one thing I need from you."

"What?"

"I need a ride, Fin. I really am a pitiful driver. I even hitched a ride here in the ImCo courier van this morning. Will you drive me to Winthrop?"

I had been edging toward my car while we spoke. Now I moved faster, but McKean reached the passenger door as quickly as I reached the driver's.

I grabbed the handle. He grabbed his. "You'll drive me, then?" He looked at me like a lost German shepherd puppy.

I swallowed hard. "All right. I will."

"That's the spirit," he said. He got in, but as I sat in the driver's seat, I felt a gnawing worry about what I was getting into. The notion of running up against kidnappers or terrorists—or both—got my heart pounding. I drove out of the loading area considering ways to decline McKean's invitation to adventure. But then my mind suddenly cleared. All my doubts fled, overruled by a drive more powerful than survival— the journalist's instinct for a story. Not only would I be first on the scene of a major news scoop if anything turned up, but I would spend, by a quick reckoning, nearly ten hours in the enclosed space of my car with a man whom I truly wished to know better as a journalistic subject. It all came in a flash of insight. Driving Peyton McKean to Winthrop was both the decent, upstanding thing to do—and my ticket to a professional triumph.

If it didn't get me killed.

As I drove toward an entrance to Interstate 5, McKean tapped my arm with a finger.

"To ImCo first, Fin. I need to attend some details before we leave— the little matter of the vaccine Janet and I are going to create."

PART TWO

IN THE METHOW VALLEY

CHAPTER 6

McKean called Janet to his office and in ten minutes mapped out a strategy for making a vaccine biosynthetically in *E. coli* bacterial culture. They would use the same genetic engineering tricks they had used to create the Congo River vaccine. The details flew past me like a conversation between a Greek and a Roman without interpreters.

A subunit vaccine, McKean called it. Janet would take the DNA encoding the B7R protein with its DIE, DIE, DIE sequence, stitch it into a new DNA plasmid carrier, mass produce it in culture, then purify B7R with an antibody that could grab the molecule via a short segment of added amino acids McKean called a flag, or an epitope tag.

"That's the idea that got me hired here," McKean told me. "Mass-producing viral subunits as flagged molecules and purifying them with anti-flag antibodies."

"The invention you made in New York?"

"Exactly. It simplifies the purification step, which is often a stumbling block. It's like attaching a handle to each B7R molecule—an easy way to grab hold of it. Anti-flag purification can cut weeks off the development time for a vaccine. Let's hope that's enough."

He scribbled on his yellow pad, spelling out two short strings of DNA letters encoding the flag amino acid sequence, and handed it to Janet.

"There you go," he said. "Two synthetic DNA oligonucleotides that we can stitch onto the B7R gene. You can start making them on the oligonucleotide synthesizer right away. Leave it running overnight."

"No problem," Janet replied. "They'll be ready in the morning."

McKean got up. "I'll be out the rest of the day. But I'll be here in the morning bright and early."

Janet nodded. "About the time the synthetic DNA oligomers come off the machine."

"Right," he said. "I'll help you splice them onto the B7R gene. I suppose I should stand around wringing my hands until then, but you know I trust you, Janet."

She smiled.

He said to me, "Even so, we'll be in a real horserace if the virus breaks out of containment in Sumas. The quick purification is the last step. Before that can happen, we'll have to get the microbes to grow with B7R in their guts. They don't always cooperate."

Janet's face clouded and he noticed. "Let's hope we'll only be carrying out an academic exercise," he said, "rather than battling a modern plague."

Her eyes widened. "Things aren't that serious, are they, Peyton?"

He shrugged. "I'm not certain any more." Then he cleared his throat as another disturbing thought came to him. "By the way, Janet, if that FBI man, Fuad, calls or comes around, tell him I went out to borrow an autoclave part from a lab at the University of Washington—you don't know which one, or when I'll be back. That should keep him off our trail."

She frowned. "Why do you need him off your trail?"

McKean and I exchanged glances.

"I can't tell you why, at the moment," he said. "But I'll be counting on you."

She looked dubious, but said, "Okay, Peyton."

"Now," McKean said. "You'd better get to work, and I'd better get going."

Janet went to the lab as McKean gathered an olive green canvas field coat and an olive canvas safari hat from pegs on the wall. He paused as we were about to leave.

"I almost forgot another obligation," he said. He picked up his phone and dialed. After a few seconds he murmured, "Answering machine again."

"Hello Dear," he said. "I'm going to be working late tonight. I'll tell you about it when I get home. Sorry to miss my turn cooking dinner. There are leftovers in the 'fridge."

I noticed a small family photo on the wall next to McKean's whiteboard. A sandy-haired boy of about six sat between McKean and a nice looking blond woman about half McKean's height. The photo was close to McKean's desk so he could see it easily while he worked.

"Say 'Hi' to Sean for me," McKean finished. "Tell him I'm sorry there'll be no bedtime story tonight, unless you want to read him one. Remind him Daddy loves him very much."

He hung up the phone and we headed for the elevator. I asked, "She'll be okay with that?"

McKean nodded. "I've done plenty of all-nighters in the lab. She'll assume it's another one of those. That will keep her from worrying about bigger things. I'll give her the real details after we're back safe and sound. Don't you have anyone to call?"

"Nope. Wish I did."

Within ten minutes I had my Mustang speeding northbound on Interstate 5. McKean sat in the passenger seat in a thoughtful mood. He stared blankly at the traffic as I threaded my way through it, going a bit over the speed limit.

"Thanks for agreeing to drive us to Winthrop," he said after a time. "It's really quite a long haul."

"Don't mention it," I said. So far, it seemed McKean was more interested in my credentials as a chauffeur than my companionship. But that was no problem for the newshound in me.

"So, you're not the world's most reliable a driver?" I ventured.

"Answer: no," he said. "When my mind is full of thoughts, I neglect my steering, signaling, and braking. When I'm obsessed with conflicting data, my eyes neglect to tell my brain the whereabouts of traffic although my foot presses the accelerator down all the harder. That makes for a lot of horn honking and finger gesturing in my direction."

"With a mind like yours, Peyton, that must happen pretty often."

"Too often, I'm afraid. Anyway, with you driving, we have no such concern."

"Thanks for the backhanded compliment about my brainpower," I said. "I'll keep my eyes on the road and my hands on the wheel."

"Please do, and hurry," McKean urged. I floored the accelerator and passed a semi on the right. I began changing lanes too often and, no doubt, offending more than a few fellow drivers as the Mustang flew northbound through busy suburban traffic.

McKean settled in for a five-hour trip on a route that would take us first northbound through the lowland farmsteads and evergreen forests situated between Puget Sound and the Cascade Mountains, and then eastbound across the North Cascade Highway to the ranchlands of the Methow Valley. I started chatting up McKean while slinking past traffic snarls on a two-lane freeway with slow trucks passing slower ones, sanctimonious jerks driving the speed limit in the fast lane, and some aggressive drivers rushing up on the tails of cars ahead of them to make sure there was no room for me to change lanes. Some of them gave me a honk and a finger when I went anyway.

Despite the difficult driving and my misgivings about what lay ahead, I remained true to my ulterior motive in accompanying Peyton McKean. I was going to learn more about him, if it put us both in the ditch. As we passed the Tulalip Casino in Marysville I said, "Explain again why you're doing this."

"Doing what?" McKean shook himself out of deep thoughts.

"Heading off on a what might be a wild goose chase when you've got the hottest project I can imagine going on in your lab."

"I like to go where things don't add up," he said. "In science, and in life. That's my favorite turf, *terra incognita*. To do good science, you've got to spend most of your time at the outer limits. That's where great discoveries are made."

"You've got to spend time there," I said. "I'm not so sure about me."

"Try it."

I shrugged. "Okay. But if this *isn't* a wild goose chase, we could get ourselves killed."

McKean shrugged. "Mike's stumbled onto a little bit of *terra incognita…*" He stared out at the dairy lands and black-and-white spotted cows of Stanwood zipping past, his eyes following details but his mind a million miles off. "I've just got to see what he's onto."

"Fair enough," I said. I had intended to grill him on every detail of his scientific background while we traveled, but I found myself in a weird mental space. Between the hard driving and doubts about what we might find before we saw the farms of Stanwood again, I had trouble concentrating on a proper interview. There were long stretches where neither of us spoke. The sound of my car's tires droning on the pavement was hypnotizing.

South of Mount Vernon, the Skagit River bottomland was covered with fields of red-and-yellow tulips. The colors shook me out of a zombie-like trance I had fallen under.

"Hey Peyton," I said. "May I call you Peyton?"

He smiled a mesmerized smile, staring at yellow rows of daffodils wagonwheeling past. "Call me 'Hey Shit-head,' if you want," he murmured. "I don't stand on formalities."

"I guess not. So why do you think terrorists would attack the State of Washington?"

"I doubt they are interested in Washington *per se,* " he replied. "Think of it this way. The distance from the Arabian Peninsula to the State of

Washington is over seven thousand miles. The two places are a world apart. But to someone from the Middle East, Washington lies invitingly close to any point in the contiguous United States. It's the back door to the U.S.A."

"Why not the Mexican border?" I suggested.

"Ahmed Ressam," said McKean, "was caught with a carload of explosives at the Port Angeles checkpoint. That's the westernmost crossing between Canada and the contiguous U.S. Perhaps he figured our security would be lax at such a far-flung outpost. It's as remote as you get from the major population centers to the south and east. Of course, he made a mistake when he tested the alertness of the home state of Boeing and Microsoft."

"True," I agreed. "But it was only the last in a chain of inspectors that caught him. Los Angeles International Airport nearly got a big hole blown in it."

McKean sighed. "I don't expect to ever live in a world free of terrorism."

"Why not?"

He shook his head slowly. "Terrorism is not a new idea. The biology underlying it is innate, part of our animal character. Terrorism is, quite simply, apish." He leaned back in his seat, folded his hands, steepled his long, thin index fingers together, and touched them to his lips.

"I can't see that," I resisted. "It seems to me terrorism is an outgrowth of civilization, not nature."

"Then you are biologically nearsighted." He took the somber tone of a world-weary visionary. "Terrorism is, unfortunately, a simple expression of biology, like the appeal of a flower to a bee." He scanned the rows of tulips fanning past his side window.

"How do you figure? It seems to me terrorism is pretty complex. It's motivated by political situations like the Arab-Israeli conflict."

A wan smile crossed McKean's face. He let his dark eyes play over the passing rows of flowers. "Politics is the superficial motive, Fin. The deeper motive is boy-girl stuff."

"Boy-girl stuff? You mean sexuality?"

"Answer: yes."

"You think sex motivates terrorists? I think that's the last thing on their minds."

"Before I got my Ph.D.," he said, "I was a biology major at the University of Washington. Like any of the best schools, it's a true universe of ideas. I studied a great many subjects, not just biology and biochemistry, but the social sciences, psychology, sociology, and the like. I see humans as animals first, male and female, and then as higher creatures second. And that's regardless of whether you consider the evolutionary sense or the creationist view. Either evolution or God has given us traits in common with animals. That's what intrigues me more than any other subject—the animal nature of humanity."

"But Peyton, jihadis are religious zealots and adherents of political causes. You're not suggesting their religious indoctrination and military training are unimportant?"

He swept the air in front of him with a hand, as if clearing away an obscuring haze. "I understand that people ascribe complex motivations to terrorists, and terrorists' own opinions of themselves key on themes like revenge and liberation. But that's superficial. Deeper down, they have the basest of motives. Instinctual ones, animal ones."

"Such as…"

"The drive for personal power. The desire for sex."

I shook my head. But McKean glanced at me sidelong with one eye-brow cocked up with smug certainty. "In the human species," he said, "as with most apes, there is an instinctual phenomenon, part of the sexual response, that is best described as 'down with up'."

I neatly whisked past a semi on the right, but I was having trouble getting the connection McKean had made.

"Among the apes," he went on, "the dominant males get all the best. The best feeding spots, the most adoration from younger animals, the attention of a harem of the most beautiful and fertile females. But there is always a group waiting in the wings—the angry young males. These are frustrated young bulls whose desire to get at the females is blunted by the lead male's power and ability to dominate the group. These subdominant males are always on the lookout to find a weakness in the big male. They try to form liaisons with females while he sleeps. They attack him if he shows an infirmity of any kind. Sooner or later, a young male succeeds in challenging the dominant male and the order of things in the tribe changes. All attention now goes to the new upstart. The old dominator is dispossessed and cast out into the jungle to die. It's all programmed instinctually into the apes, from whose mold we were created."

"Terrorists as animals," I said skeptically. "You would have a hard time convincing a radical Muslim cleric of that."

"Yes," McKean agreed. "I'm sure no one is more blind to this than the mullahs who preach hate. But every fourteen-year-old boy who has seen a fourteen-year-old girl look past him to admire a sixteen-year-old boy knows the feeling of subdominance. It's a universal male experience. Females feel it too, looking at more popular girls. But boys feel it the most. No imam needs to teach it. Subvert that teenage frustration with a religious message, and you've got a powerful weapon at your disposal."

"But how does the animal desire to overcome dominance motivate terrorists?"

"In their case, it's the dominant *society* that is attacked, not necessarily an individual. Terrorists desire to bring down that which stands tall or flies high, either by demolishing the buildings of the dominant society, or bringing down its airplanes, which are symbols of how modern society has left them behind. Or, they may simply want to kill people of higher social standing. Depending on how low they themselves started, there are many targets they must look up to. At the heart of the matter, they simply wish to eliminate that which implies their own inferiority. It's just the same as getting rid of the dominant male ape. Down with up, and up with down."

"Astonishing."

"The average terrorist is a young man without influence over events in his life, or over women. Most come from the lower ranks of society. And many women respond sexually to money and power—some more than others, but it's always present as a relict of their female-ape ancestry. Food and protection were the desired commodities then. Nowadays it's money and status. Subconsciously, young male terrorists wish to reduce all of society to their lowly status, hoping that will put them on an equal footing with their formerly powerful rivals. From there, they would have an equal chance to compete for females."

"I still don't see it," I resisted. "Most terrorists die while carrying out their plans. How does that get them a girlfriend?"

McKean chuckled. "Hijackers and suicide bombers. That's where religion comes in to embellish the simple ape instinct with a story. What do the mullahs promise every Islamic martyr? What will he find in the afterlife? Riches? Wealth? Sure. And a six-dozen virgins to marry. That's part of the deal. And it works on the male psyche via instincts that are much stronger than most of us would like to admit. The heavenly rewards promised to suicide bombers are the very things the ape wants— all the advantages of dominant status. Jihad may masquerade as holy guidance, but viewed cynically it simply inflames the ape's instinct to bring down that which is up. It panders shamelessly to the animal desire to breed with as many females as possible. And leaders who send these young men on their missions are, to my eye, calculating schemers who use the classic teenage obsession to subvert new recruits to the cause."

I shook my head in amazement. "So, Peyton, you've reduced the average martyr to nothing more than a sexually frustrated adolescent ape who dreams of asserting his command over females through acts of violence against the dominant members of the group."

"Well said, Fin! Their mullahs' religious doctrines are nothing more than Coke and Pepsi commercials gone over to the dark side, preying on the same aggressive instincts that have made young people rebel since before the Stone Age. A rather common and bestial motivation for holy war, wouldn't you say?"

"But not all terrorists are young, or poor, or male."

"Not everyone fits the mold," McKean agreed. "But by-and-large, angry young males form the core of the 'down with up' group, among terrorists and apes alike. Some may grow older but never grow out of it. Especially those who never find a path to legitimate success. And if those men are rich like Osama bin Laden or the Sheik, they never need to grow up."

I shook my head. "It's sickening to think of terrorists as status seekers in a monstrous, perverted way."

"Exactly," McKean said.

I took the eastbound exit onto the North Cascades Highway. We lapsed into silence as we left the tulip fields behind and rolled slowly through the traffic-choked towns of Burlington and Sedro Woolley. After that, the road narrowed to a busy two-lane country highway as it entered the mountains.

I focused on overtaking and passing cars on the straightaways while McKean placidly studied the mountain peaks looming as a series of increasingly massive rock piles. Though my hands and feet were busy driving, I couldn't shake a nagging ache in the pit of my gut. I had more doubts than ever about the wisdom of our expedition.

The road followed a long, eastward-tending valley whose bottomland was dotted with farms and dairy homesteads. Here and there we glimpsed the beauty of the Skagit River's broad nickel-green waters framed by tall cottonwoods and white-clouded skies. The farm fields gradually vanished into tall evergreen forests checkerboarding the mountainsides in timber lots of old and new growth.

Leaving civilization behind, we entered a deep glacier-cut canyon bounded by pyramidal peaks half-shrouded in cloudbanks and draped with snowfields. McKean exclaimed about one crag after another, babbling about granites, breccias, gabbros, intrusives and thrust faults.

I focused my attention on the steering wheel and the oncoming traffic. Every cliff-side bend heralded another car or truck exploding at us out of nowhere. Several hours into it, white knuckled, I took us over the rainy summit of Washington Pass with wipers beating.

Then suddenly we were in the clear and moving down the eastern rain-shadowed side of the Cascades under blue skies. The road was still tortuous, but traffic subsided and the country opened into long vistas of pine-studded mountainsides.

CHAPTER 7

Fifteen minutes of hard driving brought us out of the mountain canyons and we rolled smoothly onto the open, sagebrush-dotted prairies of the Methow Valley. I cracked a window and took a breath of the balmy sage-scented air, a dozen degrees warmer than Seattle. A road sign put Winthrop just ten miles ahead. After five more miles on the gently winding highway, McKean said, "We're here."

I pulled the Mustang onto a wide, graveled shoulder in front of a wrought-iron-grilled ranch entry gate set against a hilly landscape of dry grass and sagebrush. It was an eye popper. The new-looking asphalted entry road ran between two immense pylons of mortared granite blocks with an overhead cross-member made from a four-foot thick ponderosa pine trunk. A massive oak placard hung on chains beneath the cross-member, engraved with silhouettes of rearing horses and a carved inscription arching across the center in two lines: ARABIANS UNLIMITED — BREEDERS OF FINE HORSES. The asphalt drive curved in an arc that disappeared behind a grassy hillock without a glimpse of the ranch itself. I gawked at the magnificent entry, momentarily wondering how we would get past the closed wrought-iron gate.

McKean tapped my shoulder and pointed.

"Not here," he said. "There." A second gate had escaped my notice, just beyond its posh neighbor. It was a miserable little entry, pitifully constructed of two scrawny, weathered, telephone-pole uprights bridged by a flimsy cross-member of two-by-fours nailed together side by side.

Hanging from the two-by-fours and putting a pot-bellied sag into them was a warped and weathered plywood sign with peeling black lettering that said M&M RANCH.

"Mike and Mary Jenson's place," McKean said, waving me forward. I drove through the un-gated entry and onto a rutted gravel drive that followed a line of barbed-wire fencing strung on rotting wooden posts and choked with dried tumbleweed. The Mustang jostled on the potholed road and high centered a couple of times as I followed a curve that mirrored, in a humble way, the haughty arc of Arabians Unlimited's smooth new asphalt road.

The tumbleweed fence line led around a hillock onto a secluded bottomland where the road surface became no more than compacted dust. A cloud billowed behind us. Sagebrush crowded the road and scraped along the sides of my car, no-doubt marring the pristine midnight-blue paint job. "This place isn't much to look at," I mumbled, "compared to the neighbors' spread."

McKean nodded. "A decade ago, Mike's homestead was the only one here. The new neighbors have what he lacks. Money."

The Mustang rolled past a flat pasture trampled into dust by a herd of rangy-looking Hereford cattle. At a point somewhat less than a mile in, we reached a weather-beaten doublewide trailer home, still on its wheels and parked under a lonesome cottonwood tree that partially shaded it from the hot mid-afternoon sun.

I pulled the Mustang to a halt near an old sun-scorched blue pickup truck whose vintage I could hardly guess, other than thinking it probably predated *me* by a few years. We got out into the pall of dust that had chased the Mustang and walked to the house trailer's front porch, a jury-rigged assembly of pressure-treated two-by-fours and planks, hand-sawn and in need of squaring, covered by a frayed rectangle of green plastic Astroturf. Just inside the open front door of the house I spotted a man in the act of setting aside a shotgun. He stepped out of the dark interior. "Hi, Peyton," he said. His voice was friendly enough, but it had a grim undertone.

"Hello, Mike," McKean said. He pointed a thumb in my direction. "This is Fin Morton."

Mike nodded at me and I nodded back. He was a man of average height or a little less, decently muscled, in blue jeans and dusty cowboy boots and a plaid orange-and-brown western shirt. His close-cropped hair was a medium brown and his eyes, squinting into the harsh glare of the sun, were a medium brown as well. His clean-shaven face was leathery and darkly tanned. Along the sides of his neck were signs of his lot in life, permanent red speckles where the skin was exposed to the sun and elements—a redneck.

He came down the steps and pointed with his nose toward the far end of the trailer home, where a platform of welded angle iron supported two elevated barrels, one of stove-oil to heat the house, the other of diesel for his antique red-and-rust tractor, which was parked just beyond the barrel platform. A shape lay in the shade under the barrels. When I recognized it, hairs stood on the back of my neck. It was a dead dog. A Rottweiler.

Mike let us eye the blood-spattered carcass awhile. Then he let out a bitter sigh.

"Somebody shot him, 'bout four in the morning." He kicked some dust with a cowboy boot toe and swallowed hard, biting on emotion. "I heard him barking. And then comes a shot and I heard him yelpin'. So I grabbed my shotgun. But it was pitch dark outside. He's laying on the drive, just twitchin'. I couldn't see who shot him, so I sent a load of buckshot out in the dark. Whoever it was had a car about a hundred yards or so towards the highway. They tore out of here and I gave 'em another load of buckshot but they got away clean."

"Did you call the police?" McKean asked.

"Nope. I think maybe that's who did it."

"The Sheriff?"

"Damn straight." Mike looked at the dog again and his mouth drew down like he wanted to cry.

McKean wondered, "Why would the Sheriff—?"

"Come snooping around? Trying to get sump'n on me, run me outta here, that's why. Now I got another reason to get over there and see what's going on."

"So," I said. "What's the plan?"

Mike nodded at a grassy ridge and pine-dotted hills grading into the Cascades in the west. "My property runs for better'n a mile up that way, beside the Sheik's. I figure we'll take a little hike over that ridge after dark. Same way I went when I seen the redhead and checked out the lab. If we find anything, we come back and call the CIA, the FBI—I don't know who."

We went inside the trailer to wait for darkness. Kids' toys were strewn on a worn brown carpet, and the place smelled of dirty diapers. "I sent Mary and the kids to her sister's for a day or two," Mike explained. "Till I get this sorted out." We sat down at a square kitchen table with a torn red-and-white plaid plastic cover patched with duct tape, and spent some time sipping Budweiser from longneck bottles. Dusk lingered for more than an hour on a clear early-summer evening. McKean and Mike passed the time by swapping stories about tight spots they had gotten into over the years.

I opened up a little and talked about a firefight in Baghdad from which I had retrieved a couple of wounded children. "But with your dog as a warning," I concluded, "I have a feeling tonight might be the tightest spot any of us has ever seen."

"Oh, I don't know," Mike said, getting up and going to a cupboard. "I seen some pretty tense action in Saudi. Saddam Hussein tried a pre-emptive counterattack, y'know."

McKean pointed a thumb at Mike. "Army Ranger training."

"I'm impressed," I said.

"Can't say I'm a *bona fide* Ranger," Mike said, fishing something off the back of a top shelf. "But I was in the Ranger training program. Bo-loed partway through."

"That happens to a lot of soldiers," I said. "You're still better trained than the average G.I. And a lot better than me."

Mike came back and sat down. My eyes bugged out at what he had in his hands—a baggie of green weed and a small wooden pipe painted with leopard spots. He began to pack the bowl with a heavy load of frosty-white-looking bud.

"Just 'cause I washed out," he said, "don't mean I didn't learn a thing or two. Enough to get us inside that place next door."

He lit the pipe with a butane lighter, inhaled deeply, and passed the pipe across the table to McKean. McKean accepted it without comment and took a strong drag. When he offered it to me, I waved it off.

"Are you guys nuts?" I asked. "Getting shitfaced seems like a bad way to keep safe."

"Live dangerously," Mike said, cracking a wise-ass smile. He took another hit and so did McKean.

McKean held his breath so long that he exhaled clear air. He offered the pipe to me again. "When in Rome," he said.

"When in Rome," I acquiesced. I reached for the pipe but Mike intercepted it and filled the bowl with a fresh bud. He held his lighter to it while I took a little hit for show. That was a mistake. A few seconds later, I felt as if the top of my head were lifting off.

McKean grinned at me. "Killer smoke, eh?"

I nodded.

"Cowshit's the best fertilizer," Mike said with authority. "Totally organic."

Darkness fell outside the trailer windows while Mike and McKean gabbed and guffawed about harvesting buds and drying weed and bongs and joints and roaches and brownies and a litany of other stuff I was too stoned to follow. I seemed to be more profoundly affected than either of them. Eventually, as the clock moved past 9 PM, Mike killed his second beer that I knew of and got up. "C'mon," he said. "Time's a-wastin'."

He put the pipe and baggie away and went to a closet and fetched out a camouflage-green shoulder holster with a small black pistol buttoned into it. He strapped it on, and then pulled a second gun and belt out of the closet. "Either of you guys want one of these?"

I shrugged. "No thanks."

McKean said, "I had a girlfriend whose ex-boyfriend once held a gun on me for a couple of hours until he passed out."

Mike thought about that for a moment. "So, do you want one, or not?"

"No," McKean replied.

Mike put the gun away, and then he put on a camouflaged hunting jacket and led us outside. I followed the two of them out under a starry sky, feeling jittery. I couldn't pin it on fear exactly. Just as likely I was wired on Mike's super-potent marijuana. We followed a game trail up and over the ridge, hiking without much talk through sagebrush country, crossing a series of small rolling hills between Mike's place and the Sheik's. The night had grown starkly black. The stars and quarter moon overhead were shockingly beautiful. After what seemed an eternity of footfalls and no speech, we came to a new looking five-foot wire-lattice fence on some high ground. Mike pointed down into a little valley illuminated by the lights of a cluster of buildings. "That's the place."

The house was huge and brightly lit. It dwarfed most of the surrounding barns, sheds and outbuildings. Mike pointed past it to the farthest barn. "They took her in there."

McKean said, "Rather far for you to see handcuffs clearly."

"I know," Mike agreed. "That's why I went down there snoopin' around. Come on."

Using the wire lattice of the fence for hand and footholds, he climbed over at one of the upright posts. We followed. I got edgy when I set foot on the far side of the fence, knowing we were now trespassers. My pulse quickened as we headed down the slope. Our footsteps, rustling the dry grass, sounded to my heightened senses like an army on the march. "This might be a one-way trip," I whispered, "if we find somebody with something to hide."

"Don't get paranoid," Mike whispered, following up with some marijuana-inspired giggles as he led us down onto a broad pasture made lush by a rolling sprinkler system that hissed and ticked on the far side of the lot. We moved fluidly at double time across the empty pasture. I mimicked Mike's soldier-crouch but McKean tagged along after us with his head high, gazing around as if making scientific observations of the place. We were an odd assortment of THC-inebriated misfits.

We moved into the moon shadow beside a white equestrian fence that ran to the house, which was a massive, modern structure of river stone and pine logs. Like a castle, it barred our way to the other buildings. Its white draperies were pulled back and bright light pierced the darkness for many yards around it.

My paranoia escalated and my heart pounded as we penetrated to the middle of the ranch compound and approached the house. Neither of my companions seemed concerned, but I was intimidated enough to whisper, "What if somebody sees us?"

"C'mon," Mike whispered back. "Didn't you ever sneak around at night as a kid? Anyway, they're making too much noise to hear us. And it's too bright inside to see us out here."

He was right. The place was about as quiet as a discotheque. As we came to where the fence abutted the rear corner of the house, the building's pine log walls were rattling with the sound of Arabian music amplified with a good hundred watts per channel. A darbuka drum rattled a Dervish rhythm, accompanied by the chink-a-chink of a tambourine and the hypnotic jing-jingling of finger cymbals. A thin male voice warbled a high-pitched Arab melody, like a muezzin calling from a minaret. A weird violin-like instrument buzzed a tortuous Middle Eastern scale in counterpoint.

We threaded ourselves through the fence slats and stepped onto a graveled parking area where half-a-dozen cars were nosed in at the side of the house. Skulking our way behind them, we passed two gleaming black SUVs, a new oversized black pickup truck, and a shiny black limousine. Mike paused and pointed at the last vehicle in line with a sour expression. It was a dark emerald green sedan with police lights on top and a tan stripe running along the side. On the door was a five-pointed star emblem with George Washington's head in the middle.

"I told you," Mike whispered. "Barker's in cahoots."

McKean nodded. The night felt a little colder.

We rounded the corner of the house and came under one of the front windows. Across a wide porch spanning the front of the house, the bottom windowsill was head-high for McKean and somewhat higher for Mike and me.

"Maybe our redhead's in there," McKean whispered.

"Yeah," Mike whispered back. "Maybe so."

We went up on tiptoe to catch a glimpse inside. A huge two-story western-style great room with log ceiling beams and a log balcony running around its perimeter, was centered on a massive river-rock fireplace and chimney. A squat, middle-aged woman bustled past the window carrying a silver platter of food, dressed in a dark brown frock with a thick black hijab scarf-and-veil covering her head entirely except for her eyes. We crouched back into the darkness below the porch.

"Sheik's wife, Khadija," Mike whispered.

"Couldn't see her hair," McKean said.

Once she had passed the window, all three of us—in a fit of unhealthy curiosity—grabbed the log porch railings and drew ourselves up for a better look. Seemingly determined to take every stupid chance possible, we peered over the windowsill like three comic idiots in a Hollywood movie.

The house's interior made my mouth hang open. Huge raw timber beams supported a roof forty feet above us, like in a National Park hotel. The fireplace opening was as tall as a man and held a bank of embers that radiated warmth I could feel through the window glass. The rustic beauty of the place was a backdrop for fine Middle Eastern furnishings: silk draperies in Chinese red with black Arabic lettering hung from the balconies. Persian rugs with tan-and-maroon patterns covered much of the wooden floor. Lacquered wooden chests were scattered around, punctuated by polished brass floor lamps with tiffany shades. On the fireplace mantel were gold boxes, jade vases, and an antique ebony clock with its hands showing 10:05. Above the clock, mounted on the chimney was a huge painting in an ornate gilded frame: a harem of semi-naked and diaphanous-veiled pale-skinned Arab ladies frolicking around a fountain, guarded by a huge scowling black eunuch in a green turban, blue vest, baggy pink silk pants and red curly-toed slippers, with crossed burly arms and a scimitar in his right hand.

A heavy, ornate table in a dining area on one side of the fireplace could easily have seated two dozen for dinner. Khadija joined an older and plumper woman at the table, and poured tea from the sterling service. The two women turned their attention to the menfolk, who were gathered in a portico on the opposite side of the fireplace.

There were six men, most wearing turbans and Arabian frocks, sitting on a semicircle of silk floor cushions and smoking an elaborate golden hookah. They talked and laughed and puffed on individual smoke hoses. Mike pointed out a fellow in a green-and-tan sheriff's uniform, with short cropped blond hair and an evergreen smoky bear hat he had set on a pillow beside him.

"Sheriff Barker," he hissed. "In the thick of things."

"Who's that tall fellow?" McKean pointed to a man dressed in a black robe and white turban, facing away from us.

"The owner of this spread," Mike said. "Sheik Abdul-Ghazi."

The Sheik sat erect on a purple silk cushion. He took a deep draw on the hookah, and let it out slowly. He made a remark with thick smoke curling around his head and raised an old fashioned cocktail glass and downed its contents at a gulp. Then he lifted a stubby whiskey bottle and poured another shot of brown liquid.

"Glen Cuiddich scotch!" McKean exclaimed in a whisper. "One of the most expensive brands."

"Nothing but the best for the old Sheik," Mike quipped.

"I thought religious Muslims didn't drink alcohol," I said.

"Or smoke," McKean added.

The Sheik gestured toward the other people in the room—three young teenaged girls dressed in austere brown frocks, who were amusing themselves by dancing on the open floor space between the men and the old women. The dancers made girlish approximations of belly dancers' motions, keeping time to the music, which came from speakers mounted on the fireplace wall. The girls, whom I assumed were the daughters of one or more of the men, smiled in naive enjoyment of their dance, and the men and women watched them fondly.

"What do you think it is those guys are smoking?" I whispered.

"Sheesha," McKean said. "Flavored tobacco."

Suddenly, a dark-haired woman in her early twenties entered the room from a far doorway and walked past the men, turning every head—including ours. She was tall and straight and dressed in a British equestrian outfit minus the jacket and helmet. Her khaki Jodhpur riding pants, black leather jackboots and white shirt hugged a body fit to make any man's tongue hang out. She went for a wooden staircase that climbed to the balcony, but the girls waylaid her and begged her to join their dance.

Tugged by her hands, she agreed with a good-natured smile. Raising her arms over her head, she snapped her fingers in time to the rhythm. Extending a booted foot, she took a small half step forward and swayed her hips to the music. The girls mimicked her moves enthusiastically, while the old women shook their heads in disapproval. The men gawked, and so did we three peeping Toms.

The young woman ignored the attention, dancing only for the girls' benefit. She moved with a grace that emphasized the beauty of her fine curves, which were scarcely hidden by her clothes. Ignoring the leering men, she swayed her torso in a serpentine motion and wove her arms like minaret spires over her head, while the girls did their best to emulate her.

The Sheik tugged at his long grey beard, seeming particularly riveted on the woman's body as she swayed to the music. Then a remark from Sheriff Barker brought rude laughter from the other men. Knowing she was the butt of the joke, the woman stopped and lowered her arms. She eyed the men with sharp disdain, and then spun on a boot toe and went to the stairs, ignoring the girls' pleas that she stay.

I tracked her movements like a radar lock. Watching her long dark hair sway fluidly as she mounted the steps, I understood why Mohammed had urged Arab women to cover their faces and bodies—lest they tempt men to distraction. And I was distracted in the extreme by her beauty—a face of a light tan tone, an oval jaw and small chin that were delicate and haughty at the same time. As she moved up the stairs, she cast another disdainful glance down on the men and I saw her face in profile. Something about her regally sculpted features—something about her eyes, naturally lined by dark lashes and framed by coal-black brows—made me think of Cleopatra. *Could this woman have descended from the bloodline of the Pharaohs?*

She so mesmerized me that I lingered a moment despite McKean and Mike hissing at me to move on with them. Instead, my enthralled eyes followed her boot-steps up the staircase and watched her cross a log-balustraded balcony to a door where she disappeared into a room. When the door closed, I was left shaking my head and blinking my eyes to get my bearings. Bewitched, I had nearly forgotten my risky circumstances. I had gawked at the woman with mouth agape like some country yokel.

Suddenly, the Sheik's wife Khadija reappeared at the window, seemingly out of nowhere, and my enchantment ended in a blaze of adrenaline. Although her face was mostly hidden by her black hijab, her dark eyes peered straight in my direction!

I froze behind the porch rail like a jackrabbit in a car's headlights. My pulse raced. But, immobilized by the effects of marijuana and left hypnotizing by the beauty I had been watching, I couldn't force myself to flee. I crouched, as still as a statue.

Khadija came quite near the window glass. Her eyes seemed to pierce the darkness, seeking me out. She stared intently in my direction, increasing my mesmerization and adding a measure of terror. I expected her to cry out and raise an alarm, but she didn't.

She looked even more searchingly into the window glass. It dawned on me she wasn't looking at me at all. She had seen her own reflection on the inside of the window and was studying her own appearance. I was just an unwilling voyeur.

Appraising herself intently, she raised her hands and pulled down the lower veil panel, uncovering features neither refined nor beautiful. Her nose was long and hooked. Her lips were small, permanently puckered and wizened. She opened them into a smile that was more like a grimace, showing teeth that were uneven and yellowed.

She raised the upper panel of her veil, revealing a forehead that bore two heavy horizontal lines across a lumpy, heavy brow. Her eyebrows were thick, even though they lacked penciling, and merged in the middle.

And the eyes that stared at all this unloveliness were themselves unlovely. Dark, puffy-lidded things, they were yellowed where they should have been white. Her hair, matted, stringy, long, and black with gray streaks, drooped in wispy, snake-like half-curls appropriately framing her Medusan visage. It all had the effect of turning me to stone, almost literally. I was immobilized and scarcely able to breathe.

Eventually, with her eyes glaring in self-contempt, Khadija pulled the forehead wrap down, raised the chin veil, and turned from the window. Released from her awful spell, I tumbled backward from the railing and sprawled on the shadowed ground at the base of the porch near a mock orange bush. I drew in a deep, gasping breath as a flurry of fragrant white mock-orange petals settled over me. My heart pounded in my throat. My head spun dizzily, full of Arabian drums rat-tattling and cymbals chink-chinking and the loveliness of the young woman and the horror of the old witch. As I watched Khadija move away from the window, the thought crossed my mind that, for some women at least, Mohammed might have had another reason to demand the wearing of the veil—to hide such ghastly features from human sight.

Someone touched me on the shoulder, and I jumped about a foot. It was Mike. "C'mon, dude," he whispered. I scrambled after him, only too glad to get away from the window. The three of us crawled along the front-porch shadow and then crept past a second house, a two-story, rectangular, bunkhouse-like structure that might have been the ranch's main residence back in homesteader times.

"Did you get a look at her hair?" McKean whispered over a shoulder to me.

"Uh-huh."

"Was it red?"

"Uh-uh. Black snakes."

He looked at me peculiarly as we pressed on, following Mike past a parked semi truck with a white box trailer. Ahead of the semi were three white vans with no windows on their sides or backs. We moved past them and slunk across the driveway toward a pair of barns connected by an equestrian fence.

The first of these buildings was a modest-sized horse stable, white-washed and thirty feet on a side. We moved in front of its double barn doors and slipped into the moon shadow under an eave. Mike pointed to the next building, a long, white, barn-like structure.

"They took her in there," he whispered. "That's where the lab is, too."

We moved to the corner of the horse barn, preparing for a dash to the next building. Suddenly, a horse's loud whinny ripped through the night. We ducked back into the shadows.

The source of the noise made itself known just inches from us. Where the barn connected with the equestrian fence, a black Arabian horse jutted its head over the top fence rail. The whites of its eyes were wide in anger and its nostrils flared to take in our unfamiliar scent. Its hooves pounded the ground.

Mike, who was nearest the animal, pressed himself against the barn doors in a vain effort to disappear from the horse's sight. I followed his example, squashing myself as flat as a bug on a windshield. Not so, Peyton McKean. He stepped away from the barn and moved toward the horse.

"What are you *doing?*" I hissed.

He ignored me. "Whatsa matter boy?" he crooned to the horse in a low voice. "Did we upset you? How 'bout a treat?" He pulled a paper packet of coffee-shop sugar out of a coat pocket, shook it twice from the corner to settle its contents, and ripped an end off. All the while he edged closer to the stallion. The horse ceased its agitated movements and eyed the sugar packet with interest. McKean poured the packet's contents into the palm of his left hand and held it out. There was a moment of absolute silence and immobility, but the animal's curiosity gave way to fear. It bolted from the fence and trotted away with ears pinned back and tail high, letting out another loud whinny.

"They *must* have heard that inside," I hissed.

"Yeah," Mike agreed, eyeing the houses nervously. So far, however, no one had come to a window to see what the trouble was.

"Ah," McKean said a moment later in a soft, reassuring voice. "And how about you, my lady? Sugar?" He held out his hand again and a second, slightly smaller horse stretched its muzzle out of the darkness—a pure white Arabian mare. She thrust her pink nose tentatively beneath the top slat and sniffed the sugar in McKean's hand. She began to nibble. As she did so, the stallion standing behind her settled down, growing curious about the favor being given to his more docile mate.

The mare's eyes mellowed, enraptured by the treat. Her ears swiveled calmly as she nibbled the sugar from McKean's hand with her dainty pink muzzle. The stallion's agitation bled off and soon he was crowding her, stretching his head over the top rail to make it clear he expected a similar favor.

Mike and I came away from the barn and approached McKean and his new friends. McKean reached his right hand into his coat pocket while still holding his left out to the mare. He pulled out a second sugar packet, which he handed to me.

"For the stallion," he said. I ripped open the package and poured the contents into my left hand as McKean had done, offering it to the stallion. Soon he was as calm as the mare, licking the sweet stuff from my hand. His whiskers brushed my palm softly, his tongue lapped up the sugar gingerly. I calmed down too, drawing a deep breath of sweet pasture air and noticing that these were incredibly fine animals, one black, one white, and both of regal bearing. They seemed like pampered pets. Their coats shone in the moonlight, their long manes and tails flicked like fine silk.

As the horses finish their sweets, Mike chuckled. "What else you got in your pockets, Cousin Peyton?"

"A stir stick," McKean whispered. "And some packets of real powdered milk. You don't know how often I'm offered coffee that is insufficiently light and sweet for my tastes."

When the stallion finished his sugar, he draped his chin across the mare's withers and settled down like he was ready to nap. He made a soft chuggaring noise as if to say that no more alarms would be going up from him. We slunk away to the poultry barn. Mike crept to its double front doors and silently undid the latch. He moved inside in a combat crouch, eyeing every corner of the dimly lighted interior. My heartbeat accelerated as McKean and I followed him in, making no sound whatsoever. Just inside the double doors was a white, plywood-screened wall situated to hide the building's interior from any eyes that might peer through the front entrance. An inscription was painted on the wall in black Arabic lettering with an English translation below it.

ENTRY STRICTLY FORBIDDEN WITHOUT SHEIK'S PERMISSION

My pulse edged up a notch as we rounded the barrier. But there was nothing beyond except the wide, dim, empty space of a poultry-raising facility. Low feed troughs of stainless steel ran the length of the floor— an empty floor, glistening clean and bare, where a thousand chickens may once have fattened for market. The area was spotless and free of any smell of livestock. Instead, I caught a whiff of disinfectant. Along the far wall were several laboratory benches. Mike led us to them, signifying by pointing that these were the source of his suspicions about a virology lab. The equipment covering the bench tops defied my powers of identification, but McKean examined everything quickly and turned to Mike with a wry look on his face. He pointed to each piece and whispered its identity, "Feed mixer, refrigerator, chick incubators, egg candling light." He shrugged his shoulders and opened his hands wide. "Haven't you ever seen this sort of stuff before, farm boy?"

Mike looked embarrassed. He shrugged. "I seen a meth lab once."

McKean shook his head. "Nothing but animal maintenance equipment. If it's a genetic engineering facility, it's not like any I've ever seen."

Mike went red enough to see even in the dim light. "I guess I didn't have time to get a very good look."

McKean and I exchanged perturbed glances.

"Maybe we should go," I suggested.

McKean nodded. We turned for the door, but Mike hissed, "Wait! I still want to know what happened to that redhead."

McKean paused, and then cocked an ear. He raised a cautionary thin index finger to his lips. "Listen."

A low murmur could be heard at the far end of the room. The three of us went dead silent. Straining my ears, I made out two masculine voices carrying on a conversation in Arabic. Mike moved swiftly and silently toward the source of the sound, which was a large side room fifty paces from where we had entered the building. Its door was ajar. Strong light from within streaked the floor. In fact, this light was the sole source of illumination by which we had been observing the room and its contents. I suddenly got a panicky urge to scurry back the way I had come. Instead, I tiptoed behind McKean silently, following Mike as he made what seemed like a big mistake. Mike pressed his back against the wall beside the doorway. As we stole to his side, he crouched low and peeked around the doorjamb.

The voices droned incomprehensibly in Arabic, while Mike scanned the room for a few seconds. Then he motioned with a couple flicks of his fingers for us peek around him. McKean bent and peered over Mike's head. I went up on tiptoe and looked over McKean's shoulder. As I did so, the thought struck me that we must look comical, all peeking around a doorframe, one face above another, like three Hollywood idiots again.

But what we saw inside that whitewashed room wasn't funny. In a space that had once been the office of the animal facility, stood two men in long white cotton thawb robes with white ghutra scarves on their heads. Their backs were toward us. They leaned over a third person, who sat in a heavy wooden chair—or rather lay in the chair, because the person, a woman with bright red hair, had collapsed so utterly that I thought she must be dead. Her head lolled on the wooden back of the chair at an impossible angle. Staring at her, all doubt fled my mind. *This was the kidnapped woman! These men were her captors! Mike's story was true!* Every hackle on my neck went up when I focused on what commanded the men's attention. The girl's arms were strapped to the arms of the chair, and the back of her left forearm bore a long slash that was splotched hideously with dried blood. Worse, the skin of her arm was swollen and dotted with thumbtack-sized white spots.

McKean mouthed one word almost inaudibly. "Smallpox."

Suddenly, my mind boggled at how far I had allowed myself to be dragged into jeopardy. *Kidnappers! Terrorists! Mad schemes with deadly viruses! All were suddenly real beyond question.* A new, panicky notion made every nerve in my body tingle—we would be discovered instantly if either of the men turned in our direction.

But I didn't have more than a moment to worry about that.

A shrill cry came from behind us. It was a woman's voice, screaming an alarm in Arabic. I turned to find the beauty in the riding outfit ten paces behind us, calling to the men in the room. Although she was screaming, she showed no fear of us. Her eyes glared to match the stallion's rage a few minutes before. She was like a she-devil, warning not only the men inside the room, but anyone else within a hundred yards.

I glanced back into the room. The men had turned to stare at us in confusion and surprise. As a group, the three of us stepped away from the door to get out of their view, but now a third Arab man appeared almost beside us, bursting from the previously closed door of an adjacent room. Dressed in a tailored dark gray suit, he leveled a pistol at us. "Stop where you are!" he shouted in Arab-inflected English.

We straightened up, caught between the raging she-devil, the redhead's captors, and the pistol man. Mike had reached for his gun, but too late. The Arab aimed at Mike's heart and shouted, "Don't touch it!"

Mike's hand hovered over his holster for a moment, and then he raised his hands along with McKean and me.

The man muttered a long string of curses in Arabic, while covering us at chest level. He yanked Mike's gun from its holster and put it in his coat packet. Then he stepped back and his face lit with a cruel smile. "Infidels in our midst," he said haughtily. He eyed us narrowly for a moment, pointing the gun from one chest to the next as if shooting us was his first impulse, but something restrained him. A smile rippled across his lips, which were framed by a trimmed black mustache and goatee, set on a chiseled face with refined Levantine features. He was as handsome as the woman—who had ceased shouting and now joined him—was beautiful. He flashed a triumphant, perfectly white smile at her. Then he frisked us, one-handed, and waved us inside the room with the pistol.

As we went in, the woman spoke to him in Arabic-inflected English. "I came from the house, Massoud. I wanted to see what was upsetting my horses. I saw these men go in here and I followed them."

"You did well, Jameela," Massoud replied.

We stopped near the unconscious redhead and her captors. Jameela's dark, Cleopatran eyes burned angrily into mine for a moment, and her dark brows drew into a scowl of hate. Somehow, the great beauty of her features made her anger seem all the more diabolical.

As we stood in the full light of the room, the two robed men looked us over carefully. One of the two was slightly taller, hefty, fat-cheeked, and wearing a full but short-cropped black beard that covered a receding chin. The shorter of the two men was a small, weasel-like, hatched-nosed man with beady black eyes and a naturally jittery manner to match his weasel looks. His beard was sparse and cropped in such a way that gray hairs bristled around his mouth, giving him a scruffy, thuggish look despite his white ghutra and thawb gown.

"Thanks be to Allah," he said to Jameela, "that you ignored the sign, which warned you to keep out of here. You have caught these infidels before they could ruin our holy mission."

Now the woman glanced around the room more carefully, and her expression changed. Those pharaonic eyes grew wide with shock when they fell on the redhead. She went to take a close look at the unconscious woman and then turned to the weasel-like man with a look of disgust and horror. "What are you *doing*, Dr. Taleed?" A quavering note of fear now colored her voice.

Taleed raised both hands in a calming gesture. "That girl is immaterial," he said.

The momentary fear that had gripped Jameela seemed to leave her, and the Cleopatran scowl returned to her face. "What sort of evil do you do here, Dr. Taleed? This American woman is sick."

"Sick indeed," the doctor affirmed, puffing like a bantam rooster. "She carries my smallpox virus, which will bring this nation to its knees!"

Jameela gasped as if comprehending a great horror for the first time. Far from appeased by the doctor's statement, she flushed red with anger. Her sense of horror changed to outrage as the meaning of Taleed's words sank in.

"But I will not stand for this!" She stamped a booted foot. "This is Satan's work!"

The doctor smiled reassuringly at her. "On the contrary," he said in an accent inflected with a hint of British. "It is Allah's work."

"You must stop this!" Jameela exclaimed. "It is murder." She spoke with such conviction that I was almost mesmerized by the fire flashing in her dark eyes.

The doctor shook his head condescendingly. "It is not the place of women to question the doings of men. And now that you have seen what we do here, Jameela, we must make sure that you, too, will keep our little secret."

"Keep your secret!" She glanced around the room. "What will you do—?" Massoud took a step toward her, as did the doctor. She shrank away from them. "Will you imprison me here in this barn? I am already as good as a prisoner on this ranch!"

"The Sheik will decide," Massoud said coldly.

A look of disdain spread over her face. "If this is the Sheik's idea—" she pointed emphatically at the captive woman, "—then he is a monster. Only a monster could think of something so cruel."

Massoud had heard enough. "You will not speak of the great man that way!" He slapped her hard across the face with the back of his left hand. The force of the blow knocked her off her feet.

As I saw her tumble to the floor, a change happened in me. Something in the bestiality of the man's act, the violence toward a woman, the stunned expression on her face when she looked up—*and the Arabian beauty of that face*—caught me unprepared. Adrenaline surged. I lost my head and leaped at Massoud, roaring like a lion. I grabbed his gun with my left hand and closed the fingers of my right around his windpipe. I squeezed with all my might, choking off his breath. The gun discharged and a slug smacked into the ceiling. But I grappled a thumb into the trigger mechanism to stop him from firing again. I pressed my fingers into his throat until his eyes bugged out. His cruel sneer gave way to a misshapen grimace. We struggled against each other silently as his face went purple. I gained the advantage as his strength faded, and I pried the gun from his grip. I had every intention of using it on him, but an instant after I got the pistol free, the doctor swung a club-sized piece of wood at my head. So intent was I on finishing my opponent that I failed to dodge the blow. When the club hit my temple, my vision exploded in a burst of white light. My consciousness blanked and I collapsed to the floor beside the woman I had tried to defend.

CHAPTER 8

When I woke up I was strapped into a heavy chair like the one holding the redheaded girl. Mike was strapped into a chair on my left and Peyton McKean was shackled beyond him. The effects of the marijuana had faded, replaced by heart-pounding fear pulsing through me. Groggily, I looked around for the woman, Jameela, but she was gone. Nearby, our three male captors were conversing quietly in Arabic. Dr. Taleed, at the center of the conversation, eyed us as he spoke, but he didn't afford us the dignity of humans. He discussed us arrogantly, as if we were cattle to him, lambs ready for the slaughter.

I leaned forward, looking down our short row of chairs at McKean. "Is your adrenaline pumping yet, Peyton?"

He turned his head to me sharply, as if snapping out of a deep reverie. "What's that?"

"You said lab work didn't get your adrenaline pumping. How's this doing?"

"Oh," he remarked thoughtfully. "Quite nicely."

Dr. Taleed approached us and inspected McKean's face for a moment. "Did I hear the name, Peyton?" he asked. "You look familiar, but I can't quite place you. What is your surname?"

"McKean."

"Ah," Taleed said. "A coworker of Dr. Holloman, the maker of the Congo River vaccine. You attended him at his lecture at Cambridge University, did you not?"

"I *wrote* his lecture," McKean muttered. "And he brought me along to cover any questions he couldn't answer."

"I was in England, looking after some, er, virological matters there," Taleed said. "Rafiq," he gestured at his assistant, "and I met you and Dr. Holloman at the reception after the lecture. We spoke about epidemics. Do you recall? Your opinion that smallpox is the most dangerous of organisms helped me make my choice."

McKean stared at him disdainfully. "There were hundreds of scientists at that reception. I'm afraid your face is not familiar, nor your name. Taleed, is it?"

"Ibrahim Taleed," the doctor replied. "A humble researcher, unworthy of your notice. Like most who work for Allah, I have labored in obscurity. Recognition for my work will come on the Day of Judgment."

McKean pointed his long nose at the sick woman's arm. "From the looks of it," he muttered, "you'll be bound for Hell on that day."

Taleed chuckled forbearingly. "Believe as you wish, Dr. McKean. I see myself doing Allah's will in jihad."

"This is barbaric," I interjected.

Neither man acknowledged my statement. McKean said, "I'm mystified, Taleed. Why not cultivate the virus in cell culture? Why use humans?"

"A wise question," the weasel-faced man admitted. "As you have guessed, we would rather grow the organisms in culture. But sadly, that is impossible."

"Why?"

"It seems Allah has guided my work too well. You see, Dr. Peyton McKean, my genetic alterations of the virus have created a super organism. As with all prodigies—perhaps yourself included—the virus has weaknesses directly related to its strengths. The virus is now so well adapted to human victims that it no longer can grow in cell culture. It has become, through the grace of Allah, perfectly adapted to its holy mission. It must grow in living human flesh. It will not grow anywhere else. This blessing has caused us some difficulties in transporting and passing the virus along."

"Forgive me," McKean muttered, "if I'm unsympathetic."

Taleed ignored the remark. "This virus is my crowning accomplishment. See how it spreads outward from the inoculation wound?"

McKean glanced at the girl's arm, as did I. The rash of spots was thickest near the gash.

"It always grows that way," Taleed said. "From the wound outward. Are you familiar with the concept of progressive vaccinia, Dr. McKean?"

"Answer: yes. Some individuals contract the condition from a dose of the standard smallpox vaccine."

"Yes." Taleed's eyes lit like a vampire's in sight of blood. "In a normal vaccination, a single pock appears on the arm and heals with the coming of immunity. In progressive vaccinia, that one pock multiplies, spreading across the body until the victim is literally eaten alive."

"A perverse outcome," McKean murmured. "The vaccine consumes the very person the it was meant to protect."

Taleed observed McKean closely. "You are well versed," he said. "What caused you to take such an interest in smallpox?"

McKean's face remained deadpan. "Let's just say I like to stay current in all things virological. Smallpox is… intriguing."

"Yes, most intriguing," Taleed replied. "In my humble engineering experiments with this virus, I found that all the prisoners we inoculated suffered this outcome, which you have called perverse. They died like this girl is dying. Even those already immunized with the old smallpox vaccine. None were safe."

"That explains Fenton," McKean said.

"Ah, yes," Taleed agreed. "The unfortunate customs inspector. I was in that car, as was Rafiq, and Massoud, our driver. Our smallpox carrier, one of Massoud's many girlfriends—was in the back seat, heavily sedated."

"The missing Vancouver woman," I said.

"Yes," Taleed confirmed. "We told the inspector she was dead drunk. He was suspicious, of course, but he had no other reason to detain us. He searched the automobile thoroughly, but found nothing. Our only cargo was the girl herself, and the virus growing within her arm. But the wound was carefully bandaged and covered by the sleeve of her coat. Clever of us, don't you think?"

"Diabolically so," McKean growled.

"Diabolically? You suggest Satan was on our side?"

McKean stared at him without comment. After a moment of meeting McKean's steady gaze, Taleed's beady weasel eyes glanced to the floor. Then he muttered, mockingly, "It is a pity I cannot let you return to your laboratories. Perhaps you could save yourself from this virus before it consumes you. It would amuse me to imagine you trying."

McKean said nothing, sitting tight on information that would have shocked the doctor—that an attempt to make a vaccine was already underway. After a long moment, McKean said in measured tones, "Someone will come up with a vaccine sooner or later."

Taleed laughed sardonically. "Later, Dr. McKean. Much later. Too late for you—and America." He leaned near McKean's face and hissed like a cobra, "Do you wonder why my companions and I have no fear of the virus?"

McKean answered coolly. "I assume you've made some sort of vaccine for yourself. Formaldehyde-killed virus, unless I miss my guess."

"You guess well," Taleed concurred. He straightened and threw the tails of his white Arab headdress over his shoulders. "When I first engineered the virus two years ago I made a small amount of vaccine from it. That vaccine now protects those of us who work for Sheik Abdul-Ghazi."

He was about to say more, but hushed when two other men entered the room.

The first swept in with a flourish of black-and-white Arabian robes. Scowling, gray-bearded, and wearing a white turban, he had an imperious air.

"The Sheik," Mike muttered out the corner of his mouth.

Taleed bowed and remained half-bent as the Sheik approached. Rafiq and Massoud showed even greater humility, bending so low I thought they were about to throw themselves at the man's black-sandaled feet.

I had seen only the Sheik's back at the window of the house. Now, I got a better look at his face. His untrimmed long beard of stringy black hair was flecked with gray and blazed with a white swath of chin whiskers. A small mouth and deep clefts at each side of his hooked, crooked nose gave him a permanent sneer. His eyes met mine briefly and a chill ran through me. His bottomless black pupils glowered under beetling dark brows. Stray hairs on his cheekbones gave a bestial look to his face. His coal-black eyes were sunken and underlain by baggy pouches of dark, wrinkled skin. The whites of his eyes were stained a sickly brownish yellow. His lower lip drooped, a purplish, soft, mushy appendage, while the rest of his mouth seemed pinched. His jaundiced and waxy yellow skin, stretched tautly across protruding cheekbones and hooked nose, convinced me he was an unhealthy man.

He made a motion with upturned palms indicating that the bowing men should rise. The fingers of both hands were decked in multiple jeweled rings. His wrists were circled by gold and silver bracelets so numerous and weighty that I was surprised he could lift his arms. The gold rattled as he folded his hands piously in front of his white thawb gown, over which a gold-faced belt held a curved jambiya dagger at the center of his thin belly. The knife handle and scabbard were inlaid with dazzling jewels.

The other newcomer was Sheriff Barker. Hatless and clean-shaven, dressed in his green-and-beige uniform, he was a stark contrast to the Sheik. His pale, freckled faced was a standout among his Arab companions. He came near and leaned over Mike, his blue eyes lit with cold delight. "You had to stick your nose where it didn't belong, didn't you, Mikey?" he said softly. "I tried to warn you off, but you just didn't get it. Now I'll have to watch you die." He straightened, resting his fists on his hips in a tough-cop stance. His jaws worked continually on a piece of gum. The temple muscles rippling under the blond bristles of his close-cropped, military-style hair, disgusted me.

Mike glared at him. "You're a whole new kinda pig."

The Sheriff grinned. "Hey, Mikey!" he hissed, leaning closer and working his gum harder. "You s'pose your wife will mind having a gentleman caller after you're gone? If she survives the epidemic, that is?"

Mike strained at his shackles. "If you touch Mary—"

"You'll what?" the Sheriff sneered. "You'll be dead, that's what. And I'll be rich."

Mike growled like an animal. He struggled to raise his arms, but straps held his wrists and elbows tightly to the chair.

The Sheik took an interest in the exchange. "Please, Sheriff Barker," he said in Arab-inflected English. "Don't provoke him. He needs his strength to produce for us."

"Produce what?" Mike muttered.

"Smallpox virus," the Sheik replied, smiling with long teeth that were yellowed by smoking. "You see, my unfortunate, nosy neighbor, you and your friends are part of our plan now."

"You snake!" Mike growled, unafraid of the Sheik's penetrating gaze.

"Snake indeed," the Sheik replied. "I am a cobra whose venom works Allah's will. I will poison America until she crumbles to dust." He turned and clapped his hands twice, clattering his jewelry. In response, Taleed and his assistant went to a wheeled tray-table that was covered with a blue absorbent pad, on which were an assortment of bottles, vials and medical gadgets. From among them, Taleed lifted a jambiya dagger much like the Sheik's but lacking jewels, and drew it from its sheath. As he came toward us with the knife, he purred, "Why use a syringe, when jihad is best accomplished with a weapon?"

Rafiq pulled back the sleeve from the unconscious redhead's left forearm, exposing the full length of the gash, and Taleed drew the flat of the knife-tip across the sores several times, as if using a whetstone. Smears of yellowish liquid from the smallpox pustules beaded on the blade.

The Sheik was pleased. "Allah sent you to us, in his all-seeing wisdom."

"How do you figure?" McKean muttered.

"Look at this girl." Abdul-Ghazi approached the redhead and stroked the matted, sweat-drenched hair on her temple. She responded with a faint, gurgling moan. "Poor little harlot," he said to her in mock sympathy. "Massoud picked you up in a blasphemous nightclub, where alcoholic drink was served and men danced with women. You were too weakened by your debauched life to last as long as we expected. You are already dying, too soon, too soon, my dear." He stroked her cheek in mock sympathy, and then turned to us.

"We feared the virus would die with this woman. But see what Allah has provided?" He spread his bejeweled hands to indicate the three of us. "New vessels to carry forward my army of viruses."

Dr. Taleed inspected the blade's moist tip. "A nice inoculum," he said. He turned to me first, because I was nearest to the girl. Rafiq rolled back my left shirtsleeve, exposing the skin of my forearm. I struggled, knowing what was coming. As Taleed slowly brought the blade down, I tried to wriggle my arm away, but tight leather straps at the wrist and elbow held it securely. As the tip of the knife touched my skin just above the wrist, sweat broke over my brow and a chill ran the length of my body.

With a practiced hand, Taleed drew the sharp tip of the dagger along my forearm, incising a sinuous gash from my wrist almost to my elbow. I cried out through clenched teeth at the pain of the wound. Blood welled up along the undulations of the cut and trickled down my arm, dripping onto the chair and the floor. The two men paid little attention to the blood or my stifled cries. They returned to the girl and Taleed whetted the blade again on her pocks.

"So much for sterile technique," McKean murmured as they approached Mike with the blade.

"A medical man?" the Sheik asked McKean, as Rafiq bared Mike's arm. "You have some knowledge of the healing arts, do you?"

"He is a scientific researcher," Taleed said.

Abdul-Ghazi grinned. "You have done your last research," he said. "Instead, you will be the experimental animal."

Mike grimaced but kept silent as Taleed inscribed a serpentine gash along his forearm.

"Dr. McKean," Taleed said when he finished with Mike. "See how easily we pass the virus from one person to the next? Soon—" he eyed McKean cruelly as he drew another inoculum from the girl, "—you will produce legions of new viruses for us. In you will grow the smallpox we will use in a second wave of our attack."

McKean bore the slash of the blade stoically.

Taleed cleaned the knife and as he put it back on the table, another man entered the room.

The newcomer looked more African-American than Arab. His face was freckled, his skin a deep tan, his wavy black hair pomaded and combed back flat over his head. He had a blaze of white hair on one side. He wore a chestnut-brown double-breasted silk suit, and a black-and-silver striped necktie with matching handkerchief tucked in his breast pocket. The toes of shiny brown wingtips peeked from under the razor sharp creases of his suit pants. He seemed too suave, clean-shaven, and smiling for his austerely gowned company, and yet he was obviously an integral part of the conspiracy.

Approaching the Sheik, he placed his hands together in front of him and bowed deeply. "Holy one," he said softly. "Your jihadis are ready."

"Excellent timing," the Sheik exclaimed. "Mullah Shabab, my good friend, you have prepared well."

He and Shabab embraced and kissed each other on both cheeks. Shabab was built like a basketball player, and stood somewhat taller than Abdul-Ghazi.

"The timing of your arrival is most excellent," the Sheik said, holding Shabab by both shoulders. "Bring the soldiers of my first wave, immediately."

Shabab exited by backward steps punctuated with small bows. He reappeared several minutes later, leading a group of young men, who followed him in single file. He shepherded the recruits' movements like a soft-spoken drill sergeant, guiding them to stand in line near the redhead. The young men wore American style T-shirts with sport or fitness logos, or hoodie sweat shirts, or casual coats of leather or nylon, and most wore sport or fitness pants, shorts, and footwear. Some appeared to be of Middle Eastern origins, but others seemed more like Shabab—Americans of African ancestry. Still others were of European or Asiatic extraction. All, as McKean had anticipated on our drive to Winthrop, were quite young. The entire lot of them ranged in age from about eighteen to early twenties. All wore facial hair in one pattern or another, although some appeared to have been clean-shaven up until a week or two previously. Some even seemed hard-pressed to grow much more than peach fuzz on their chins.

Shabab spoke a few words, and the youths rolled up their left sleeves and prepared to file past the redhead. Taleed inoculated each one with the same dagger he had used on us, repeatedly daubing the dagger tip on the pocks of the unconscious redhead. Each youth offered his forearm and took the slash without complaint. Taleed's assistant bandaged the wounds with gauze, and then Shabab directed each young man back out the door.

The Sheik stood near the door while the grim procession moved past him on the way out. He smiled beneficently and put a hand on the shoulder of each young man, whispering words of encouragement.

"You see, Dr. McKean," the Sheik crowed between blessings, "how prepared these young martyrs are for battle with your evil nation? The virus will surely kill them all. Yet each one is quite prepared to die." He paused to offer another soft-spoken benediction and then resumed. "They shall see Paradise soon. And there, as martyred believers, they will live at the right hand of Allah amid riches untold, with the attentions of so many women—"

"Every teenage boy's dream!" McKean interrupted loudly. "Why not just give them the keys to your shiny new SUVs and a dating allowance?"

The Sheik stared hard at McKean as if he were not a man who tolerated interruption. He said, "My jihadis have their eyes focused beyond the temptations of this world. Driving fast cars and chasing fast women is the American way, not the way of the righteous. These young warriors have been drawn from your polluted cities and drug-infested streets by Shabab and his followers. They have turned their faces away from this profane land and they now look to heaven, not earth. But before they leave this mortal realm, they have pledged to send a great many of your fast-car drivers and loose-women chasers to Hell, where they will burn forever, their faces dragged through hot coals—"

"You can spare the details," McKean growled.

The Sheik blessed several more boys, glaring at McKean in between. "These brave warriors are but the first wave of our attack. A white truck and three white vans will carry them and the virus across the land, spreading it to every place your people congregate. Consider what will happen when they touch their sores to people, or door handles in hotels and stores, or faucets in lavatories, or escalators in shopping malls? Touching even the doors of schools where your children begin learning your evil ways?"

"A monstrously perfect plan," McKean grumbled.

The Sheik laughed out loud. A diabolical glow lit his eyes. "Allah guides us in everything, Dr. McKean. The truck looks like a white moving van, but inside will be a cargo of warriors who bring death to every major city in this land. And another truck will arrive soon, bringing more Americans recruited from among your country's poor and dispossessed, and more of our own young men, whom we have smuggled into your ports in cargo containers from the far corners of the earth."

"You've thought of everything, haven't you?" McKean said in an oddly a smug tone that made me think of Janet, two hundred miles away, carrying out procedures that might neutralize his threat.

"Allah," said Abdul-Ghazi, "guides the righteous."

Peyton shook his head slowly. "Regarding religious matters and jihad, I don't believe either side can claim title to righteousness."

Sheik jutted his goat-bearded jaw. "Allah will guide me in destroying America, the home of the CIA, which strikes blows against my family."

"Do you really believe God will help you or anyone else murder millions of people? I don't believe God is so cruel. What I believe is that he will oppose to you—and your jihad virus."

"Brave words from a man who will die soon."

After about fifty men had been inoculated, the repeated daubing of the knife on the redheaded girl's swollen arm drew her out of her torpor. Lifting her head, she went into spasms of coughing and gagging. Struggling uselessly against her restraints, she seemed to wilt as the last young man received his dose. She gasped one last time, and then slumped in the chair like a deflating balloon.

The Sheik saw this and blessed the last jihadi perfunctorily, sending him on his way. He came and leaned over the dead redhead and smiled cruelly. "You see, American harlot, what your whoring ways have brought you? Death, and soon, damnation. Allah be praised." He nodded to the handsome Arab, Massoud, and the man began unbinding the body from its chair. I looked at him closely as he worked, recalling the young woman on TV describing a handsome Arabic face with neatly trimmed goatee and mustache.

"You're the nightclub kidnapper," I muttered.

His face lit with pride. "Yes, I am the one. My power over women is a blessing."

He caressed the redhead's matted hair the way the Sheik had done. "When I made love to you that night," he said into her dead ear, "you cried out in pleasure. When we brought you here and cut your arm, you cried out in pain. Now you will join the other infidel slut in the hole in the ground behind this barn. There you will await the Day of Judgment. When it comes, Allah will cause you to cry out for eternity—in the burning fires of Hell!"

He lifted her limp body in his arms, and carried her out a rear door.

Abdul-Ghazi turned to us and said mockingly, "I would ask for Allah's mercy upon her, but she is surely damned for failing to follow the True Prophet. Allahu akbar."

"What are you going to do with us?" I asked.

He smiled at me wickedly. "Your arrival here has been quite timely. In your arms, we will grow the virus for the second wave of warriors. I had intended to hold back several of the first wave as carriers of virus for the second. But now it is you who will provide the virus for the next inoculation—out of your own dying flesh. Do you see how perfectly

Allah guides my work?"

The sound of booted footsteps on the floorboards of the barn broke the fix of the Sheik's malignant gaze on my eyes. He turned as the woman, Jameela, came to within a few paces of him. She glared at him fiercely. A red welt had risen on her cheek where Massoud had hit her, but contempt for them all was written in her haughty scowl.

"Jameela!" the Sheik said with a paternalistic smile. "My wayward little lotus flower."

"What you do here is—is evil."

"Ah," he smiled. "Your eyes are as lovely as a lamb's. They should not be permitted to see such things."

"But I have seen—"

"And now," the Sheik interrupted, "your childish mind cries for these people."

"I'm no child."

"But you are a woman, and Allah grants women no strength—"

"He granted me the strength to tell right from wrong."

"No, my child. He did not. If he had, you would not go among men in such clothing." With a gesture, he swept the curves of her blouse and pants. "So revealing. On such a desirable a body. Do you presume to explain Allah's laws to me? You, who have not learned even to cover your head with a scarf and your body with a modest robe?" His gaze lingered on her breasts.

"I'll cover my body with a thong bikini," she hissed, "if I choose."

His thick dark brows narrowed. She stared back at him haughtily, her chin jutting out and her lips pursed in repudiation. Their eyes locked.

"The Prophet!" the Sheik roared, "dictated that women should avert their eyes from men's! Can you not obey even that small teaching?"

"Mohammad said no such thing," she replied coolly, despite the way he puffed with rage. "Such behavior is called for only in women who live among *righteous* men, which I see you are not." The glare in her Cleopatran eyes could easily have faced down a hungry lion.

"You insolent—!" The Sheik choked.

Trembling in rage, he hurried to a whitewashed wooden post and took down a strap from a peg. It was a wooden-handled leather flail, about two feet long. He approached Jameela, gripping the handle in his right hand and letting the strap dangle at his side as if he were accustomed to wielding it. He locked eyes with her but she held her ground. He stopped several paces from her and slapped the flail against his left palm. "We have used this strap to silence our captive, when her tongue became seditious. Perhaps you need a taste of it too."

Jameela drew a braided black-leather riding crop from her belt and stood tall. "If you strike me," she said, "I will defend myself. —And you too!" She wheeled and slashed the crop at Massoud, who had come back and approached her from the side. It caught him on the cheek with a sharp *snap!* He staggered back and put his fingers to his cheek. Then he doubled his fists and looked like he was about to charge her.

"No, Massoud!" the Sheik ordered, holding up a hand. "This is no time for such matters."

Massoud unclenched his fists, and Jameela lowered her crop.

The Sheik tossed the flail back against post, where it dropped to the floor. "We are not here to debate the misbehavior of one women, or to punish it."

He turned to McKean. "In my country, a woman was recently stoned to death for the wearing a thong bathing suit at a public beach." He looked at Jameela and chuckled. "But you, my little lotus flower. You are high-spirited, like my horses. When the time comes you will bear me fine sons."

"I will never bear you a child," she growled.

"We shall see, my fiery one. Need I remind you that your father and mother are under my father's protection in Kharifa?"

"In his custody."

"As Allah wills. They are well cared for."

"Allah wills this! Allah wills that!" she seethed. "Your sanctimonious words mean nothing to me. What do you care for the words of the Prophet? I have seen you drink. And I have seen you smoke. And this—" she indicated us with a wave of her hand, "—is *your* plan, not Allah's!"

The Sheik's expression went from forbearance to anger. "Do not flout me with such insolence!" he bellowed. "I follow the laws of the Sharia, handed down from the companions of the Prophet—"

"The Sharia," she shouted back at him, "was written long after the death of the Prophet, by men like you."

"It is a holy scripture," the Sheik muttered, "written by holy men inspired by Allah."

"Some of them were cruel men," she shot back at him. "Men who misinterpreted the words of Mohammed—who delighted in war—who oppressed their women."

"Oppressed?" He cocked his turbaned head. "Oppressed?" He held out his jeweled hands in a gesture of conciliation. "Search your heart, Jameela." He approached her closely, looking down into her face. "Are you not well taken care of? Allah gave men dominion over women, just as he gave them dominion over beasts."

"Beasts!" she cried. "I am no beast! You will *never* have dominion over me!"

A hint of smile tightened his flaccid mouth. "We shall see."

"You'll never shut me inside your house like a hen in a coop, the way you keep your wife."

"My first wife," he corrected. Then he bent toward her slightly as if to kiss her on the lips.

She turned her head aside but held her ground. He kissed her on the cheek, straightening to look down his hooked nose at her. "I know," he soothed, "that you will never submit to me the way Khadija has done. You are like a wild horse, a mare that I shall—" he leaned close to her face again, "—take great delight—" he leaned closer, "—in riding, one day."

Jameela uttered a half-choked cry of exasperation, and then turned and stalked out of the room. As her boot steps faded in the dark toward the front of the barn, he let his laughter follow her—cool, calculated and augmented by the chuckling of his men.

"She is a whirlwind of impiety," he said to Massoud. "But Allah is oft forgiving, most merciful." He suddenly glanced around as if his exchange with the woman had made him forget the business at hand.

The last jihadis and Mullah Shabab had disappeared while he sparred with Jameela. Now he noticed Sheriff Barker leaning over Mike again, muttering in his ear. "Hey, Mikey," Barker hissed. "Too bad about your dog."

"You!" the Sheik called gruffly to the Sheriff. "You take too much pleasure in all this. I do not wish to see you gloat so. Therefore, take this man," he pointed at Mike but spoke to Barker and Rafiq. "Bind him, and put him aboard the truck. He will carry the virus to New York City. By the time he is delirious and is cast out on the streets there, our other warriors will have dispersed in the vans to other targets." Rafiq took up a bottle of clear liquid from the table and poured some on a white cloth. Then he moved quickly to Mike and put the cloth over his nose and mouth. Mike struggled, but in a moment he was unconscious. Unstrapping him from his chair, Rafiq and Barker laid him on the floor and bound him hand-and-foot with ropes.

"Take him to the truck," Abdul-Ghazi said. "And, Sheriff, swallow your false pride at his death. You will not witness it, for he will be three thousand miles away."

The Sheriff looked disappointed, but lacked the backbone to complain. He and Rafiq lifted Mike by the armpits and dragged him out with his cowboy-booted feet trailing on the floor. The Sheik turned to go, but paused at the door. He contemplated Peyton McKean once more.

"American Doctor," he said. "How does it feel to be the agent of your own people's destruction?"

McKean locked eyes with the Sheik. "Don't be so sure of it," he muttered. "This isn't over yet."

The Sheik burst into a yellow-toothed smile. "Sadly, for you," he said, "I think it is over." He left with a swish of his black robe.

That left only Dr. Taleed. He wiped the knife blade with an alcohol swab, put it back in its scabbard, and placed it on the tray table.

"Taleed," said McKean.

"Yes?"

"I have been trying to recall your work. You studied the Dengue virus, didn't you?"

"Indeed I did, at the Rockefeller Institute, New York City, long before the twin towers fell."

"You determined the Dengue virus's killing mechanism and how to neutralize it. You were a fine medical researcher before you went bad."

"Before I found Sheik Abdul-Ghazi. His father's money has built me a fine research institute in Kharifa."

"I see," McKean murmured.

"The Regime," Taleed went on, "has made me a prominent research director, as I have always wished."

"Abdul-Ghazi's money has twisted your soul," McKean muttered. "This new smallpox virus—why would you create such a thing? You could do so much good with your scientific knowledge."

"The Qur'an," said the doctor, "tells of a Day of Judgment when Allah will sweep away all the ills afflicting the righteous. We will have no need of doctors, no diseases to treat. Until that day, disease is our weapon of war. The young men you saw will die soon, but they are prepared for this. They will go to safe houses across the land, transported in the truck, the vans, and in the cars of sympathizers who will meet them on the highway. The warriors will secretly disperse in the last days before the fever strikes them down."

"And then?" McKean asked.

"After spreading the virus as the Sheik told you, they will go to public places and show their wounded arms, thus striking terror into every American heart. Each has been taught the role he must play at the end of his life on earth."

McKean stared into Taleed's beady weasel eyes, momentarily silent as if letting the whole scheme sink in. "You're insane," he muttered at last. "All of you."

Taleed turned to go, but hesitated near the doorway. "We shall see," he muttered venomously, "who is insane."

He vanished, and we sat for a long time in silence. I glanced at a wall clock and was surprised to see only a half-hour had transpired since our apprehension. The time-dilating effects of the marijuana had made it seem as though an eternity of rapid-fire events had transpired.

I drew deep, slow breaths, trying to calm my shaken nerves. But the gash on my arm and thoughts of the virus filtering deeper into my flesh kept panicky thoughts foremost in my mind. *Could a vengeful Allah really be bent on destroying America? Was the Sheik a holy messenger, as he claimed?* The thoughts were preposterous, but they echoed around my rattled brain like the tolling of a death knell.

Meanwhile McKean craned his neck to inspect our prison from floor to ceiling. His calm, contemplative manner made me realize that if the Sheik had had an inkling of the danger Dr. Peyton McKean posed to his plans, the dagger would have slit McKean's throat, rather than inoculate him.

I strained at the straps holding my arms, but they wouldn't budge. "I wish you would use that brain of yours to get us out of here," I said to McKean, "before we end up like that redhead."

He made no immediate reply. He stared upward through the whitewashed rafters as if his eyes, and his prodigious mind, were fixated on some celestial object a million miles away.

"Sometimes," he murmured, "the simplest problems are the most insoluble."

CHAPTER 9

Apart from aimlessly staring at the whitewashed slat walls of the room, there was nothing to do but watch the clock as the minutes and hours progressed slowly toward a dire future. We had been captured sometime just past 10 PM, but midnight came and went while we passed the time in sporadic, pointless conversations or long bouts of silence. Peyton Mc-Kean talked more about the virus than he did about escape. Maybe he was right to do so. Our position seemed hopeless. Our fate seemed sealed. As time progressed through the small hours of the night, my despair grew by tiny increments each time I glanced at the gash on my forearm. The blood dried to cracked streaks of blackish red, but my imagination painted pictures at the cellular level. I could almost feel the viruses percolating through my flesh, moving into my bloodstream like miniature terrorist infiltrators, each little speck of DNA-and-protein able to proliferate into a thousand identical copies after sabotaging just one of my body's cells. It appalled me that I would produce a new legion of viruses just as the dead girl had, and spawn another truckload of terrorists. Already, I could imagine thousands of viruses tumbling out of dying cells in my wound, moving into the fluid spaces under my skin, attacking new cells, and co-opting my substance into theirs.

Our captors had bound us tightly with heavy leather horse straps that constrained our chests, pressed us flat against the backs of our chairs, and kept our upper bodies from moving side-to-side or forward or back. Pinioned as I was, the view of my injured forearm was inescapable. I am sure that if I could have bent my head low enough, I would have tried to chew my own arm off at the elbow, so great was my fear of what was incubating under my skin.

Sometime past 4 AM, my head slumped forward. I fell into exhausted sleep.

"Wake up!"

The voice was feminine, melodious, angelic—and concerned. "Wake up!" I lifted my head and blinked my eyes. Long dark hair fell on either side of my face, smelling faintly of jasmine. Two dark eyes, incredibly beautiful, loomed incredibly near. A thrill raced through me.

"Jameela!" I croaked hoarsely.

"Shhh," she cautioned under her breath. "Massoud and Dr. Taleed may be nearby." Her fingers worked quickly to undo the buckle of the horse strap holding my chest. As she loosened the shackles on my arms, I watched her in dumb wonder. The she-devil had become a dark-haired angel coming to my rescue.

I didn't fully awaken until she had freed both my arms and unbound my ankles. I stood, shakily, as she unshackled McKean, keeping a nervous eye on the front door as she worked. "If they come now," she whispered, "we are lost."

McKean watched all this in his detached, academic manner. "It must be near sunrise," he said as he stood up. "If we don't get away quickly we'll be in broad daylight."

"I have thought of that," Jameela said. "Come."

We followed her out the door of the office, through the poultry facility, and out into the dim, pre-dawn light. She made for the horse barn and McKean and I followed, keeping a tight watch on the houses, which were in direct line-of-sight now that the white truck and vans were gone. I expected someone to discover us at any moment.

"You can't leave by the main road," Jameela said as we approached the barn. "The guard near the highway would spot you for sure."

"Whichever way we go," McKean said in a hushed voice, "we had better hurry." He nodded toward the eastern horizon where the sun would break across the ridges within minutes.

"I have a plan," Jameela said as she opened the doors of the horse barn.

"But why are you helping us?" I asked as we followed her in.

"Right is right and wrong is wrong," she said, moving to a tack post between two of the stalls and taking down two bridles. They were no ordinary bridles, but the expensive trappings of pampered pets made of polished black leather with silver studs bearing what looked like real diamonds and emeralds.

"Which of you rides best?" she asked. McKean and I exchanged blank glances.

"I've ridden before," I said.

"Can you handle a stallion?" She held a bridle out to me.

"I think so."

Her dark eyes searched my face as if she were looking at me for the first time. "You will take Majid. He is hardest to control."

She led us through a side door to a gate that bordered the roadway in front of the barn. The black and white horses calmly watched her swing the gate open.

She went to the mare and stroked her pink nose. "Zahirah, my jewel," she said. "You look content this morning."

Jameela bridled the mare easily, but I had trouble with the stallion. He tossed his head when I tried to put his bridle on, refusing to allow me to put the straps over his ears.

"Majid," Jameela crooned in a melodious voice. "You must let this man ride you." She took the bridle from my hands and completed the job with easy fluid movements. She set the bit in Majid's mouth and said to him, "These men need our help. Be a good boy for me this morning, please?"

Her sweet intonations calmed the black stallion. He stopped tossing his head, but he eyed me warily as if he wanted to resist what was coming. She stroked his neck several times, and he seemed compelled to behave by his mistress's touch.

"What about saddles?" I asked.

"No time," Jameela said. "You won't need them if you get away without being spotted." She pointed across the road and the pasture beyond that, to a ridgeline in the west. "There is a gate high up beyond that hill. You can get through the fence there and go to your friend's house."

She looked at McKean, who stared at the mare's back as if uncertain how to get on. "You *can* ride, can't you?" she asked.

"Answer: uh, yes," he replied. "I've sat a horse on several occasions."

"Zahirah is gentle," Jameela said. "She will mind you."

She knit her fingers and offered McKean a leg up. He straddled the mare's back awkwardly on his belly before righting himself.

Impatient to get moving, I grasped the stallion's shoulder, kicked my leg high and vaulted onto his back, propelled by adrenaline. As I sat upright, Majid reared and let out a whinny. I tugged the reins to settle him, but he pranced and snorted until Jameela came to his head with a few more soothing words. He calmed as he became accustomed to my weight, but he chomped noisily at the bit.

Suddenly, there was a shout from the direction of the bunkhouse. The handsome man, Massoud, came off the front porch and sprinted toward us.

"We have been seen!" Jameela cried, suddenly terrified.

Massoud called out in Arabic to warn the others inside the big house. Then he raised a pistol and a loud *crack* and puff of smoke made his intentions clear.

Jameela grasped the mare's halter and led McKean through the gate. "Ride, quickly!" she said, slapping the mare's rump to make her bolt forward. "The whole household will be after you in seconds!"

Majid followed the mare through the gate, his hooves clattering on the asphalt drive. As Massoud approached at a dead run and fired another shot, three more men appeared on the porch of the big house and hurried down the steps, drawing handguns.

"Hurry!" Jameela urged, spanking the stallion on the rump. He lunged forward, but a sudden thought made me rein him back.

"What about you?" I called to Jameela. "They've seen you helping us. You're not safe here!"

She looked as though that thought hadn't occurred to her. Her eyes widened. Gauging her stricken expression, I didn't hesitate. I reined Majid around in a tight circle and leaned down. "Here!" I shouted, holding out my right hand. "You're coming with us!"

She stood frozen for a moment. She stared into my face with an astonishing mix of emotions filling those dark eyes: fear, doubt, and panic. And then came resolve, and—I thought—maybe even a hint of attraction. She reached out her hand.

Massoud's pistol sounded again and a bullet scuddered past my ear.

I took her hand, clenched hard and pulled her toward me with all my might, just as Majid bolted. Propelled by the stallion's power and the tug of my hand, Jameela came free of the ground. Her body swung in an arc that somehow set her onto Majid's back behind me. She threw her arms around me as the stallion broke into a full gallop. With hooves clattering the pavement louder than the pistol shots, Majid thundered across the road and onto the grassy field, where he quickly caught up to McKean and the mare. As the two horses raced toward the ridge, Massoud's shouts and shots grew fainter.

I glanced over my shoulder. "We're not out of this yet!" I cried. The four men were sprinting toward the cars parked beside the house.

In seconds, the two black Jeep Cherokees were racing up the slope after us. Our head start was no more than a quarter mile at best. One Jeep came straight after us over the uneven ground, while the other followed a fence-line road angling away to our left.

We galloped over the top of a low rise, losing sight of both Jeeps. But one came airborne over a low hillock a second later, hot on our tails.

The passenger in that Jeep leveled a handgun and fired. A bullet whizzed past us. An odd thought flashed across my mind. *To die right now would be an incredible way to go*—my horse's black mane dancing high with each lunge of his gallop, a beautiful woman pressing herself to me, her dark hair flowing like the horse's mane. The sensation of our bodies moving together in the cadence of the gallop thrilled me, despite all. With her body so close to mine, a single bullet could have pierced both our hearts, sending us together into the hereafter—a far better death than what the Sheik had planned.

But the beauty behind me was a better reason *to live* than to die. All fear suddenly fled and I rode confidently, slapping the reins against Majid's neck, urging him to greater speed. I searched the land ahead for the best route, but two paths seemed to diverge. A small ridge ran ahead of us with swales on the left and right. Majid had the bit in his teeth and his feet tore up the ground. He would quickly dictate our path unless I made the choice for him.

"Which way?" I called to Jameela over my shoulder.

"To the left," she cried. I lay the reins over and guided Majid up the leftward swale. Zahirah and McKean followed. The Jeep tailing us was falling behind as the land became more uneven. The horses flew over the rugged ground with agility born of their breeding, but the Jeep bounded erratically. It bounced across a gully and then tumbled, rolling over in a cloud of dust.

"Hah!" I cried. "Where did he learn to drive?"

Majid was lathered from the exertion of galloping uphill with his heavy load, but I pressed him hard with heels to his ribs. "We're getting away clean," I shouted.

"Don't be so sure," Jameela cautioned. "Where is the other car?"

We had our answer when Majid cleared the top of the swale. The other Jeep was a hundred yards away on the left, slightly ahead of us and paralleling the wire lattice fence we had crossed to get onto the ranch. The gravel fence-line road leveled the rough terrain that had wrecked the other Jeep.

As our mounts raced onto a flat pasture above the ridge and galloped toward the gate, I gauged the Jeep's speed. It was closing on the gate faster than our horses. We would all meet at the point where Jameela intended for us to escape. The race was already lost. "They're cutting us off," I called over my shoulder. "What now?"

The passenger in the Jeep stuck a machinegun pistol out his window and opened up at a hundred yards distance.

"To the left," Jameela shouted over the gun's roar, "behind them." I reined Majid hard to the left and Zahirah followed. We raced for a point on the fence that we could reach before the Jeep could turn and come after us. I scanned the fence for a gate, but saw none.

"What's your plan?" I called back to Jameela.

"Ride there!" She pointed to a place on the fence line where a hummock of boulder-strewn ground rose alongside the fence, short of overtopping it by only inches. Beyond the fence lay another hummock of slightly lesser height.

"You want to *jump* that?"

"You have a better idea?" She wrapped her arms around me tighter.

The Jeep, now behind us, skidded to a halt. Then it began a turn that sent it lurching over the rough ground beside the road. The machine pistol rat-tatted, but the jostling of the Jeep ruined the gunman's aim. As our mounts raced up the near side of the hummock and sprinted to the brink, I heard a shout of frustration from the shooter. Our horses vaulted one after the other, their black and white bodies arcing above the fence and touching down on the far hummock with easy grace. Neither Jameela nor I so much as lost our balance. McKean's lanky body lurched far forward, but he stayed in place. As the horses clattered down the rocky surface of the far-side hummock, I let out a loud "yee-haw!" of triumph. I reined my mount toward a stand of stunted pine trees and we thundered behind their cover as the machine pistol sounded again, now hopelessly distant.

I reined Majid behind the cover of the trees and down the far side of the ridge. In seconds we were out of sight of the Jeep and its occupants. I slowed Majid to a canter and then to a walk.

"We did it!" Jameela called out in disbelief. "We got away."

"But not for long," McKean cautioned, coming alongside us as we descended a dry wash. "We've got to get out of this valley on something faster than horses. No offense, Zahirah." He patted the mare's lathery withers.

We loped our mounts downhill under cover of a sparse scrub woodland. A lack of pursuing engine noise assured us that the Jeep was unable to follow directly. A dry streambed soon led us to Mike's trailer.

Jameela slid off Majid's back and I dismounted after her. McKean dropped to the ground and took his cell phone from its clip. He tried keying it, but shook his head. "Reception is… non-existent."

"Mike might have a land line," I suggested.

"No time for that."

"Why?"

McKean nodded toward the driveway.

Following his eyes, I saw a car barreling toward us on Mike's drive and throwing up a cloud of dust.

It was Sheriff Barker's squad car.

CHAPTER 10

"Quick, Fin!" McKean called, dashing to the Mustang. "Get us out of here!"

Jameela hesitated. "My horses—"

I grabbed her hand and pulled her toward the car. "They'll have to find their own way home," I said, opening the door and shoving, more than helping, her into the back seat. I got in behind the wheel just as the squad car scratched to a halt on the gravel, nose-to-nose with the Mustang. The horses reared and bolted away. I jammed the key in the slot and cranked the ignition. I jerked the shift lever into reverse and floored it.

Any notion that the Sheriff's intentions were less than deadly vanished when both he and his passenger, Massoud, threw open their doors, drew their handguns, and came at us. The Mustang's rear wheels chugged on the gravel, clattering rocks against the undercarriage and fishtailing away from them. When the two men leveled their weapons, I shifted into low on the fly and the scuddering tires reversed their spin, propelling the Mustang forward. Knowing the men were near enough to pick us off easily as we moved past them, I tried a desperate maneuver.

"Get down!" I shouted. My passengers ducked below the level of the dashboard as I steered for Barker with the engine wrapping up and the tires sending out a spray of rock and dust behind. Both men managed only one shot. Massoud's went wide. The Sheriff's punched a hole in the center of my windshield. By then the Mustang's front bumper was nearly at his knees. He leaped to the side to escape being hit and the Mustang fishtailed between him and the squad car as he fell, spraying him with gravel and dust. I glanced in my rear-view mirror as we hurtled along the driveway. Massoud fired two more ineffectual shots, and then Sheriff Barker arose in the pall of dust and pulled off several more. But these missed their marks as well, as we gained distance.

As we approached the highway, I asked McKean, "Which way should I turn?"

"Help is closest in Winthrop," he said, sitting up. "Take a right."

Just then, a huge black pickup truck barreled out of the gate of Arabians Unlimited and skidded to a stop, straddling both lanes of the highway on our right and blocking any chance of getting to Winthrop. The driver rolled his window down and drew a handgun. Simultaneously, a second man stood up behind the cab with a shotgun.

"Look out for those guys!" McKean called, but I was already in motion. I had slowed only momentarily where Mike's driveway met the highway. Knowing the Sheriff must already be in his car and on our tail, and with our escape to Winthrop blocked, there was no need to second-guess. I shifted into low and cranked the wheel to the left.

The man in the rear of the pickup leveled his shotgun. Knowing his blast would be concentrated enough to kill at short range, I floored the gas pedal, dumped the clutch, and we jumped forward with tires screaming on the asphalt. I heard the shotgun's blast, but it had gone high or wide and there was no impact of buckshot. The Mustang's tires painted black stripes on the asphalt and threw up a cloud of blue smoke that momentarily screened us from the gunmen.

As we gained speed, the black vehicle burst through the smoke and came after us. Keeping one eye on my rear-view mirror, I saw the shotgun man fire his second barrel over the top of the cab, and I heard the clatter of buckshot on the Mustang's metal skin. But we had pulled away enough that the shot had no effect. I held the steering wheel straight and shifted through the gears in a furious acceleration that quickly widened the distance between us and the pickup. Silently thanking the Mustang's outsized engine for leaving our pursuers behind, I tore along the highway westbound toward the North Cascades at more than eighty miles an hour and gaining speed.

Jameela sat up, and I was glad to see in the mirror that she was unharmed by the flying lead. She turned to watch the pickup fall behind us.

I heard McKean say, "Hello, operator?" He had his cell phone to his ear. "What's that? Operator, you're breaking up. We have an emergency."

"We're too far off the beaten path," I said. "There's probably no cell phone tower out here."

"Then we'll have to ride this one out on our own." McKean clicked off the phone and put it away.

In the mirror, I spotted the Sheriff's car following the pickup. Its lights weren't flashing. "The only worse thing that could happen to us," I said, "is if that cop calls in another cop to cut us off."

McKean shook his head. "I doubt Sheriff Barker wants any other police knowing what he's mixed up in. Did you see who his passenger was?"

"Yes," I said. "The kidnapper."

On a straight stretch of highway, I pushed the Mustang to just over one-hundred miles an hour and the pickup fell behind rapidly. But my hope of a clean escape faded when the Sheriff pulled out and passed him, quickly reaching a speed that matched our own. The highway entered a series of winding turns, which I took at the limit of control. The patrol car took the turns smoothly and soon was not far off my tail. A glance in the mirror sent a jolt of adrenaline rippling through me—Massoud had opened his window, put his arm out, and aimed his pistol at us.

We rounded a forested bend and raced through a homestead valley, heading into the mountains. The only witnesses to our deadly chase were cows and horses grazing behind barbed wire fences. I heard the crack of the pistol over the sound of air rushing through the hole in my windshield.

"I'm no James Bond," I said. "I'm not trained for this."

"You're doing well," McKean said. "And you only need to get us to a safe stopping place. Somewhere with too many witnesses."

I cast my memory back over the unpopulated country we had seen on our trip from the west. I wasn't optimistic about our chances. I held the car on the road through another sweeping turn with my speedometer pegged at one-hundred-ten miles an hour. McKean got a map out of the glove box. He said, "The first settlement of any size is Marblemount, on the other side of Washington Pass. It's seventy-five miles from here."

The Sheriff hadn't lost any ground. "I can't hold these guys off for long," I protested.

"Seventy-five miles it will have to be," McKean said simply. "I have utmost confidence in you, Fin."

A bullet shattered my side mirror.

"I'm glad you feel that way." I tightened my grip on the wheel and gritted my teeth when a sharp mountain turn came up suddenly. I tried to ease into it, rotating the steering wheel as precisely as I could, but the Mustang's tires cried and it heeled over hard to the side. The loss of traction brought it up close to the guardrail and gave me a glimpse into a deep and boulder-filled stream gully. I wrestled the car back in line, white knuckled, but felt the traction getting more squirrely with each twist of the highway. The Sheriff's car seemed immune to the centrifugal force of the turns. Somehow, despite my speed, he drew near my rear bumper.

"How does he drive like that?" I cried out in frustration.

"Ah," McKean said, as if the answer had just struck him. "He probably has a gyroscopic stabilizer mounted in this trunk, or reactive suspension, or both."

McKean's thoughtful assessment of the Sheriff's vehicular superiority was cold comfort. As we raced higher into the mountains, the crags towering around us moved past at an unreal speed, as if we were in a low-flying jet. I tried to pull ahead of the Sheriff by taking outrageous chances. On an upgrade, I caught up to a slow-moving motor home and shot around it without checking for oncoming traffic.

There was a Volkswagen minivan coming at us around a bend.

I didn't flinch, squeezing in ahead of the motor home at the last split second. The VW driver hit his brakes and sounded his horn like a mad bee, buzzing ee-ee-ee-oo-oo-ooh as we went by. On a short straightaway I glanced into the mirror, hoping my chance-taking had paid off. It had. I was leaving the motor home behind and the Sheriff was stuck behind it. But my moment of joy was brief. The next curve opened onto a long uphill straightaway with a passing lane. The Sheriff passed the motor home easily and accelerated after us again.

The North Cascade Mountains rushed past like a Disneyland ride while I kept the gas pedal floored and gripped the wheel with sweaty hands. My passengers silently watched the squad car out the rear window. I steered through each turn at the limit of my ability, often over one-hundred-miles-an-hour and frequently with all four wheels screaming and drifting toward the shoulder. The centerline was no more than a neglected reminder that I crossed freely, straightening every curve. Coming around one hairpin with my view obscured by a sheer rock wall, I met a deadly surprise—an oncoming semi truck. Its big, square cab filled the lane I had strayed into. I jerked the wheel to get back to my own side, but reacted too hard and the Mustang went into a four-wheel drift. I pawed the wheel right, left, then right again, pulling us through several fishtailing turns by willpower more than skill. I held my breath until we were back on a straight course. Jameela stifled a scream.

McKean cried, "Nice moves!"

A glance in my mirror told me the Sheriff had had more time to dodge the semi. He had moved smoothly back into his own lane and kept his momentum intact while mine bled away. I floored the gas and accelerated up a straight stretch of road, but he caught us with speed to spare. He pulled out into the empty oncoming lane and came side-by-side with us. "I don't like this one bit!" I cried.

Massoud hung out the passenger window and pointed his pistol at me. His dark hair blew flat sideways in the wind and he had trouble framing a level shot. My heartbeat accelerated to panic level. Before I could react beyond that, he jerked the trigger and a bullet shattered my side window, showering everyone in the car with glass particles—but the slug missed me, somehow.

At that instant, with tiny glass shards peppering the side of my face, I expected to die. I didn't guess or wonder about it. I knew it. My hands trembled on the steering wheel until I could barely keep it in my sweaty grip. I had no James-Bond training, no license to kill, nothing close to the preparation one needs to deal with such an overwhelming threat. Jameela screamed loud enough to make my ears ring. At first she cried out in terror but in mid-shriek, her tone changed to rage.

Suddenly she was hanging out the window behind me, shouting profaneities at Massoud in Arabic. And she wasn't content with mere words. The back floor of my car had an odd collection of things I had meant to clean up or use someday. Jameela hadn't failed to notice. As Massoud drew a second bead on me, she leaned far out the side window brandishing, of all things, a can of Pringles Barbecue Potato Chips. She pitched it at him along with a curse in Arabic. The can burst open against the elbow of his pistol arm and a flock of chips flew to the rear like chaff from a jet fighter. Massoud was distracted, but only for an instant. He turned his attention back to me, trying to square a shot but finding it hard to hold the gun steady in the wind. Jameela rummaged across the back floor again and came up with a full one-quart sports bottle of Talking Rain drinking water, which she chucked hard at his head. He ducked, giving up his aim. He lost his aim again when she tossed one of my hiking boots, and again as she tossed its mate.

"Hey!" I protested without thinking. "Those boots cost a lot of money—"

"How much is your life worth?" Jameela roared.

"You're right," I said. "Use anything you can find."

She grabbed a loaded litterbag and threw it at him. As its contents strewed along the highway, McKean muttered inanely, "The Sheriff will give us a thousand-dollar littering ticket in addition to killing us."

That got a nervous laugh out of me. But Jameela was single-minded. She kept up her barrage, following the litterbag with an individual-sized Domino's Pizza box, which spun like a Frisbee and winged off Massoud's right shoulder. Then came another Pringles can, regular flavor this time, empty and crushed from having been stepped on. It flew past his face a little high and to the left. Jameela followed it with a fresh curse but there was a lull in her barrage of flying objects.

On a straight stretch, drag racing the Sheriff at over a hundred miles an hour, I glanced at her in the mirror. Her dark hair blew in the wind that roared in through the shattered window. Her dark eyes were lit with an animal rage that surprised me. *And, she looked more beautiful than any woman I had ever seen.* A chill tingled along my spine. But she scowled at me, turning the scorn she had heaped on Massoud on me. "Is that all the trash you've got?" she demanded. "I'm out of things to throw."

"Sorry," I apologized, wishing I had let the Mustang accumulate a mountain of junk.

My would-be murderer, Massoud, had finally found the time he needed to frame a shot. Grinning triumphantly, he aimed at my face. But the squad car hit a pothole and his shot thumped into the metal of my door, stopping inches from my heart.

With Jameela out of ammo, I knew Massoud would get a clean shot if I didn't do something quickly. To the right, the road edge vanished over the brink of a canyon. That gave me only one option. I wrenched the wheel toward the Sheriff. The Mustang swerved within inches of the patrol car, causing Massoud to draw his head and arm inside for fear of having them crushed.

I had no intention of colliding with the patrol car. But, as I had hoped, the Sheriff swerved to avoid what seemed like an imminent collision. As the squad car lost momentum, I floored the gas pedal to give the Mustang a narrow lead. Another oncoming semi forced the Sheriff back into the lane behind us.

McKean, so often a man of eloquent commentary, sat bolt upright, silent, muzzled by too many rapid events and whizzing bullets.

We entered another hairpin turn. As the Mustang heeled sideways and her inner wheels left the pavement, I clenched my teeth and gripped the wheel with knuckles long-since gone white.

But the Sheriff's sedan seemed to hug the road more tightly every time my car got squirrelly. Barker had no intention of letting us reach a safe haven on the far side of the pass, which was rapidly nearing as we covered miles in seconds. As we exited that particularly treacherous turn he made a fresh move, pulling up tightly on the left side of my tail. When he didn't advance further, McKean muttered, "He's going to try the PIT maneuver."

"The what?" I asked, but I found out immediately. The patrol car's right-front bumper contacted the Mustang's left-rear bumper. Simultaneously Barker turned his wheel and accelerated against us, putting a rightward momentum into the Mustang's rear end. We began a sideways sliding motion that I sensed would become a fatal spinout. Gripping the wheel with all my might, I steered out of the spin—but just barely.

"P—I—T," McKean spelled out the initials, raising a long index finger to accentuate his remarks. "Pursuit Intervention Technique. Sheriff Barker surely trained for this at a police driving academy. The efficacy of the PIT maneuver depends, not so much on the impact, but upon the sideways momentum imparted to the target vehicle. He'll use it again to push your rear end sideways, initiating a spiral motion that will spin you off the highway. Unless—"

"Unless what?" I cried. The Sheriff was coming up on my left rear quarter again for another try.

"Unless you provide a counter-momentum," McKean replied. "You must impart an equal-and-opposite rotation to your own tail."

"What? How—?" I had no time for lengthy explanations. The Sheriff's bumper was within inches of the Mustang's rear end again.

McKean's lecture faltered as he saw how immanent catastrophe was. "Er, a fishtail... In the opposite direction..."

I reacted by gingerly swinging the wheel twice, back and forth, just as Barker was about to make contact. The Mustang responded to my dicey steering and its tires floated loose of the pavement.

McKean continued, "...causing a counter-impact..."

The Mustang took on the sort of counter-rotation McKean had called for, just as Barker accelerated into my left-rear quarter.

The two cars banged together much harder this time, and my counter-momentum amplified the PIT maneuver's impact. Suddenly all four of my tires were screaming on the pavement in a corkscrew slide. I yanked the wheel this way and that, but we went into a full spinout, rotating over the highway surface at nearly ninety-miles-an-hour as the mountains swirled dizzily around us.

Jameela screamed. I shouted in frustration, expecting to hit the ditch and tip into a fatal rollover. But then my mind cleared. All panic fled. I chose the only course of action left—I kept my foot off the brake and let the car's momentum carry us in slow revolutions straight ahead along the highway. The scenery seemed to glide past almost serenely, through three complete 360-degree pans, while the car's speed bled off.

When I finally was able to apply the brakes and bring us to a halt, we were still in the westbound lane but facing eastward.

Filled with adrenaline, I gasped like a guppy out of water. My passengers were no better off. McKean's eyes flicked from side to side as if the landscape were still spinning past him. Jameela had sunk into the back seat until she was almost lying down. She sat up slowly, as if she couldn't believe she was still alive. She and McKean looked at me with such wide-eyed expressions of relief that I burst into hysterical laughter.

"Well done, Fin," McKean crowed.

My giddiness lasted only until Jameela exclaimed, "Where is the Sheriff?"

I looked around, expecting to see the patrol car screech to a halt and hear the roar of gunshots. But nothing was there at all.

After a moment, Peyton McKean pointed a long finger past the cracked front windshield, back in the direction we had just come. "Look there."

A second set of tire marks, interwoven with ours, painted a braided trail that led off the highway. The guardrail had a new gap about thirty feet long. A trace of dust rose over the fallen rail and flattened barrier posts. Beyond that, nothing was to be seen except a forested canyon, beyond which craggy Snagtooth Ridge rose in the distance.

McKean raised his finger and restarted his aborted lecture. "So we see that your counter-thrust against the Sheriff's PIT maneuver had the desired effect. Your reversed momentum imparted a counter-spin to the front end of Sheriff's car with the net effect that it was Barker who went off the highway rather then you."

"Are we truly safe?" Jameela asked. She had a hand on her chest. Her neck veins pulsed.

"Safe for the moment," McKean said. "But we had better get away quickly. They might get out and start shooting if they are uninjured."

I restarted my engine, U-turned the Mustang, and raced away westbound, jamming the accelerator down to put plenty of distance between us and them. As we moved up an extended switchback curving beneath the granite tower of Liberty Bell Dome, nearing Washington Pass, I could look back and see where the Sheriff had crashed. Beyond the broken guardrail was a cliff that dropped seventy feet onto a lower rock outcrop. The patrol car had pancaked upside down, crushing the passenger compartment. Dust billowed around the wreck, but there was no sign of the occupants.

"Fatal," McKean remarked as we sped around a turn that, which eventually hid the scene from us.

"No doubt you're right," I agreed. A peculiar emotion arose in my chest as I drove on at a slower but still speeding pace. Somewhere in my heart was a turbulence, a soul-deep unease.

"I just killed a man," I said.

"Two," McKean corrected me. "And very well done."

I shook my head. "I'm not cut out for this."

"Apparently," McKean countered, "you are."

My hands trembled on the wheel from pent up adrenaline. I murmured, "What a hell of a way to go."

Jameela put a hand gently on my shoulder. "It could have been us, Fin."

"I suppose so." But I was haunted by a crawling discomfort along my spine, a nagging sense that no man's death is a good thing. I glanced at Jameela in the mirror and noticed tears streaking her cheeks. Little tremors moved through her.

I said, "You were very brave back there."

She nodded. But she looked too much in shock to feel proud of what she had done. That was something we had in common.

There were no other signs of pursuit as I drove over Washington Pass and headed west down the valley of the Skagit River. I kept just over the speed limit, cruising swiftly for Seattle. McKean pulled out his cell phone again. But then he looked thoughtful, and put it away without trying a call.

"Best not to contact the authorities just yet," he said. "Given these infected gashes on our arms, I think it's better to turn ourselves over directly to Kay Erwin at Seattle Public Health Hospital."

PART THREE

HOSPITALIZED

CHAPTER 11

Eventually the North Cascades Highway merged onto Interstate 5. As I drove south past the tulip fields at Mount Vernon, McKean placed a call to Kay Erwin. He explained our situation and suggested she get the isolation ward ready for three new customers. There was a brief discussion about our turning north and going to Sumas, where the CDC was setting up a makeshift clinic for additional smallpox cases in the gymnasium of the Nooksak Valley High School, but McKean successfully argued that he was needed in Seattle to oversee the vaccine work. Clicking off the phone, he said, "She'll be waiting with a dose of the standard vaccine for each of us."

"I thought it didn't work," I said.

"Not well, perhaps," McKean said philosophically, "but it's the only option. Janet cannot have made much progress on the new vaccine in a day. It might be weeks before she can coax her *E. coli* cultures into making even a trace of subunit."

"If you're deliberately trying to freak me out," I said, "you're doing a good job." The door to the autopsy room loomed in my imagination.

"Sorry, Fin. Just being realistic."

As I sped down I-5, McKean dialed a number Kay had given him, that of Vince Nagumo, who was now the senior FBI agent in charge of this case. He described our experiences in the Methow Valley to Nagumo, who took down detailed information and promised to investigate as quickly as possible. But when McKean tried to explain the likelihood of

Fuad's involvement, Nagumo resisted. "He's a proven asset and a reliable man," I heard him say.

After Nagumo, McKean called Janet at the lab. He urged her to pull an all-nighter, without fully explaining our circumstances. After good-byes, he clicked off the phone. "No need to upset her just yet," he murmured, eying his oozing wound.

The return to Seattle was a high-speed freeway drive punctuated by occasional carloads of people pointing and gawking at the bullet holes in my ravaged Mustang as we went by. Just North of Everett, McKean turned to Jameela, who had been silent the whole time.

"May I ask how you got involved with these men in the first place?"

I glanced at her in the mirror and saw regret tinge her beautiful, pharaonic eyes.

"I am a veterinarian," she said. "A specialist in Arabian horses. When I came here from Cairo, I had no idea what the Sheik was doing. He lives like a sultan of the old times. He has absolute power over everyone, his servants, his guards, his helpers, and their wives, and their children. No outsiders ever got past the guards at the gate, except that awful Sheriff. When the Sheik leaves the ranch, he travels in a limousine with dark windows. When he visits outsiders, he dresses in American business clothes. But on the ranch he is highly traditional."

"He mentioned marrying you," I said.

"Hah!" She rolled her eyes. "He already has one wife, whom he treats like a slave. But he wants more. He is fond of quoting the Qur'an's advice on how a man should manage many wives at once. The holy book has old, out-of-date passages that explain how to keep one's wives sexually satisfied, and under what conditions it is appropriate to marry your slave girls. I think he considers me one of those."

"A slave girl?"

"Yes. I am a middle-class Egyptian by heritage. That means I am far below Abdul-Ghazi's royal bloodlines. Within days of my arrival he sent me an invitation, via Massoud. I was to join him in his bedrooms, which are in a separate wing of the house from his wife's. I refused, of course. But since then he has confined me to the ranch, as he does all the women of his household. He treats us like cattle—his wife, his daughters, me. He insists that all his women wear traditional veils and shawls."

"But you don't," I said.

"I refused," she replied in the same haughty tone she had used with the Sheik.

"He threatened to beat you."

"He beats the other women if they dress improperly, or show too little respect for him, or speak too loudly. But I must wear riding clothes to exercise Majid, Zahirah and his other horses."

"So he made an exception for you?"

"*I* made an exception for me."

"He has never beaten you?"

"He would not dare."

"But if he is so horrible, why not escape him before now?"

"Because of my beautiful Zahirah," she sighed. "I could not bear to leave her. And, lately I have learned my father and mother are detained in the court of his father, the Sultan of Kharifa."

"Kharifa," McKean said. "A tiny Sultanate on the south coast of the Arabian Peninsula, between east Yemen and western Oman."

"That is the place. Smaller than Monaco, but much richer."

"Your parents are prisoners there?"

"They are comfortable, but they may not leave. The Sheik has warned me that things could go poorly for them if I did not obey him."

McKean asked, "You had no inkling something evil was afoot? The virus, the victims?"

"He kept those things secret, even from those who live on the ranch. You saw the sign warning people not to enter that building. I never made trouble for myself by disobeying that warning—until last night, when I saw you go in. I only wish I had not called for help."

"You and I both." I looked at my wounded arm.

"Only once did something odd happen," she said. "One day about two months ago, Dr. Taleed insisted all who lived on the ranch be immunized for tetanus. He gave us the shots himself."

"Including Sheik Abdul-Ghazi?" McKean asked.

"Yes. The Sheik, and Dr. Taleed himself. We all got a shot."

"That was no tetanus shot," McKean asserted. "It was a dose of Taleed's smallpox vaccine, unless I miss my guess. If so, Jameela, you're already immune. You have no fear of catching anything from Fin or me. The Sheik has laid his plans well."

"What a monster," I muttered.

McKean looked thoughtful. "He sees himself as a holy warrior."

Jameela cursed in Arabic. "The Sheik is a Muslim the way Hitler was a Christian."

I glanced in the mirror. She looked deeply upset.

"It was brave of you to help us," I said. "You risked your life."

"And you," she said, smiling. "You saved my life twice today. Once, in this car. And before, when you took me up on Majid. Massoud would have killed me for helping you."

Her eyes met mine in the mirror, and we shared a soulful connection, until I got squirrelly as I often do with a beautiful woman so near. I searched my mind for something lighthearted to put us both at ease. "I used to date a girl who was part Arab," I said, hoping to spark the idea in her mind.

McKean cut in. "What part?"

"What?" I said.

"What part of her was Arab? Her hands? Her feet? Her...?"

An assortment of my ex-girlfriend's body parts flashed across my mind. Jameela looked away. The moment had fled.

CHAPTER 12

The trip to the Methow Valley had been fast, but this morning's return was faster. I kept the Mustang well above the speed limit. Conversation was sparse. The tall evergreen forests and mountain vistas along the highway lost their beauty, given our dismal situation and the exhaustion of a long night.

Just south of Everett we picked up an escort of two police cars. They stationed themselves one in front and one behind the Mustang, with their lights on. I took our speed up a notch. Around noon we arrived at the hospital's rear delivery area. It was cordoned off with yellow police tape. A clear plastic canopy covered one of the loading docks. I pulled in under the canopy, and the escort cops parked in such a way as to block the entrance to the loading area. They stayed in their cars with their windows rolled up. Other than them, there was no one at the entrance. Word had no doubt spread about who—and what—was coming. As we got out, three men in yellow isolation moon suits came to meet us. One of them took my keys with a promise to clean and disinfect my poor mangled Mustang and store her in the hospital garage. The other two accompanied us to the stainless-steel freight elevator, now also covered in clear plastic, and we ascended to the isolation facility.

When I stepped off the elevator, I looked around for Joseph Fuad. McKean and I had already discussed tackling him and disarming him. But he was nowhere in sight.

One of the two yellow-suits was an intern with dark blond hair, wary blue eyes, and DAVID ZIMMER MD on his nametag. He ushered us toward the airlock, but I stopped outside the window wall, rooted to the spot where I had watched the same two men who accompanied us now, zippering up the body of Harold Fenton.

"You're sure about this?" I asked McKean.

"Absolutely." He turned with Jameela to follow the intern. I went along despite a certainty that bad times waited on the other side of the glass. We went through the airlock in pairs, and then the second moon-suited guy followed us and wiped down every surface from floor to ceiling with disinfectant-soaked towels.

Beyond the sterility control room and the second airlock, Dr. Zimmer showed us to the same room in which Harold Fenton had died. McKean chose the bed on which Fenton had lain, apparently unafraid of its history. I took the other, where no one had died that I knew of. While I sat on the bed, making peace with my new surroundings, Zimmer showed Jameela to a second room just beyond ours.

The other isolation-suited fellow came along after he had swabbed the stainless steel surfaces of the inner airlock. He was a huge black fellow with mild eyes, cornrowed hair, and the body of a football lineman. His yellow plastic suit was wrapped tightly around his thick torso, biceps, and thighs. His nametag read JOHN HAWKINS RN. He brought us hospital gowns and then drew the curtains separating McKean's bed from mine, so we could change out of our street clothes. After Hawkins disappeared with our clothes, Kay Erwin showed up in her own yellow pressure suit.

"Let's have a look at that," she said, motioning for me to lie down and swinging out from the side of the bed a small platform on which to rest my arm. Zimmer joined her.

She clucked her tongue. "That's a nasty cut. It will need some stitches." She asked Zimmer, "What do you think, David, would debridement help?"

"De-what?" I asked. My fear level kicked up a notch at the unfamiliar term.

Zimmer eyed the wound. "I don't know. The virus could already have filtered pretty far into the surrounding tissue. We would have to take a lot."

"A lot of what?" I asked. "What's this thing you're talking about? De—"

"Debridement," Erwin finished for me. "It's the...um, cutting away of infected flesh."

I felt dizzy. There was a medical tray table beside the bed that reminded me of Dr. Taleed's table. I eyed a scalpel among the instruments laid out on it, and it seemed like a fountain of cold water had started running in my guts. Erwin said, "I don't know how much good debridement would do. The trauma would hinder the healing process. And it probably wouldn't eliminate the virus entirely."

McKean came to watch the proceedings. While fidgeting with the rear ties of his gown, he added his two-cents-worth. "Just one escaped virus is enough to propagate an infection."

"Thanks, for that," I said. "Any more kind thoughts?"

"Just being realistic," he said. "Go ahead Fin, have the debridement if you wish."

"Whoa!" I said. "I'm not saying I want it."

Erwin sensed my panic. "All right," she said. "No debridement, just a thorough scrubbing. I don't want you getting gangrene while you're supposed to be fighting off smallpox."

I gritted my teeth as Erwin took a large hypodermic syringe, filled it with lidocaine, and injected a dozen shots of the anesthetic inside and around the wound. Once it was numb, she used a disinfectant-soaked sponge to scour the wound to get at whatever virus and contamination she was able to reach. I gritted my teeth again and closed my eyes while Zimmer finished off with a set of black stitches that pulled the swollen edges of the gash together. I got dizzy while he worked. One moment I was nauseous, the next I felt palpitations in my heart. I sweated from start to finish.

Finally, when Zimmer had wrapped my arm in gauze, I thought my agony was over.

"Now, then," Kay Erwin said. "We'll need a baseline exanthema assessment."

"A what?" I looked at her nearly cross-eyed with apprehension and exhaustion.

"Skin manifestations," Kay explained. "I want to know about any preexisting marks on you, so we can keep an eye out for pocks."

"That's a good idea," I said. And then I thought twice. "Now, wait a minute. On *what* part of me?"

"Every part."

I opened my mouth to protest, but Kay was done with formalities. She drew the curtains to shut out McKean and went for the drawstrings of my gown. "This won't take more than a minute," she reassured me.

I felt myself going red. Hadn't I wondered, at one press conference or another, what Kay herself might look like naked?

She got the gown off me quickly, working with practiced hands despite the heavy rubber gloves and squeaking plastic pressure suit. I tried covering strategic parts of me with my hands, but she motioned for me to lie down on my back and then pulled my hands to my sides. I stared at the ceiling, concentrating on the lights and electrical conduits, to keep from going a deeper red. She inspected my face, flicking away a couple of glass window fragments and daubing the holes with a bit of gauze soaked in disinfectant. Then she scrutinized my neck, chest, belly, navel, and groin, moving parts around with cold, gloved fingers, squinting at the top, bottom and sides of everything. I squirmed. When she moved on to inspect my legs, feet, and the spaces between my toes, I breathed easier.

"Roll over and lie with your hands at your sides," she said. I did as she asked, staring at the wall as she made her way up from my feet to my thighs.

"Spread your legs please."

Stationed at about butt level, she said, "Wider."

I closed my eyes and tried not to imagine her gazing into nooks that I myself had never seen. At least she didn't touch anything. She came up over my back, briefly pointing out a bump, a mole, and something she thought might be a small pimple to Zimmer. She fingered her way through the hair at the nape of my neck and on my head, and then she was done.

"You can get dressed," she said, handing me my gown.

I put it on slowly. What was the point of hurrying? I would never have a secret from Kay Erwin again as far as my body was concerned.

After they drew some blood from my good arm, Kay and the intern left me, closing the green curtain after them.

"Come on Peyton," I heard her say. "Same procedure for you."

I put on a new gown and blue bathrobe Hawkins had brought me. Then I lay down flat on my back, letting the heat and blush drain from my face. Erwin gave McKean the same cleaning, stitching, and full-body meat-locker inspection she had given me.

McKean bore his flaying and examination more stoically than I did, perhaps because he understood the purpose of it better. He even went so far as to make remarks about the depth and condition of his wound as they worked on him. But he wasn't entirely inhuman. When Erwin got to the whole-body exam he said, "I can assure you I've already looked down there and found nothing remarkable—"

"I'll be the judge of that," said Kay. It got quiet for a minute or two. And then she was done. Once McKean was in his gown and bathrobe, Zimmer pushed the curtain back. While McKean and I lay recovering from our ordeals, Erwin went to give Jameela the same treatment, minus the pain and stitches.

"Why bother with all the cleaning," I asked McKean, "if only one virus needs to get beyond the edges of the wound?"

"What else can they do for us?" he said. "Would you prefer amputation at the elbow?"

I laid my head back on my pillow and thought about that prospect. "I guess that was a stupid question."

"Not much point to amputation," McKean said. "Any escaped virus has already entered your bloodstream. It could be anywhere inside you."

"Thanks for the comforting thought," I muttered. I put my good hand over my eyes and rubbed the lids, imagining myself typing at a keyboard without a left hand. Erwin and Zimmer came back, accompanied by Jameela, who was dressed in white pajamas and a blue robe. The docs busied themselves with their next task. Erwin took up a small vial of standard smallpox vaccine and dipped a tiny metal lancet into it. She asked Jameela to roll up her sleeve, and then swabbed her shoulder with an alcohol wipe and gave her an inoculation of a half-dozen pricks of the lancet. My turn was next. I bared my left shoulder and she swabbed a spot and needled some new holes in my skin.

"It's the old vaccine," she said, putting a small dot-shaped Band-Aid on it. "It's nothing like what Dr. McKean's working on, but it ought to help a little."

"What about that progressive vaccinia Dr. Taleed was talking about?" I asked her. "What happens if I get that?"

"Then," McKean interjected, "you'll die twice."

"Very funny," I grumbled.

"Let's keep a positive attitude," said Kay.

McKean smiled and quipped at me again, "You'll positively die twice, Fin."

She gave McKean his half-dozen pricks while I rubbed my vaccinated and Band-Aided left shoulder.

When Erwin and Zimmer went to the duty station to write up our charts and discuss what they had done so far, I lay back and closed my eyes. But the thought of the autopsy room down the hall soon had them open again.

Jameela came and put a hand on my good shoulder. "You should sleep, Fin. You've had so little rest. Even Dr. McKean dozed while you drove us back from the ranch. Close your eyes."

I obeyed. Soothed by her sweet tone, and lulled by that hint of jasmine, I succumbed to a bone-aching fatigue that weighed me into the mattress. I fell asleep.

Several hours later, I awoke, having regained a small amount of the strength that events had sapped from me. I would have slept all night and into the next day, but an unfamiliar male voice jarred my mind into consciousness.

"—the right to remain silent. Anything you say can and will be used against you." I got up and pulled back the curtain that had been drawn around my bed, shaking off a wave of dizziness. I could see Jameela in the corridor outside the room, facing the window wall. A man stood outside, addressing her through the intercom speaker and holding up a wallet with a detective's badge for her to inspect through the wired window glass. His dark blue suit, emerald eyes, and buzz-cut bristling black hair were familiar.

"Vince Nagumo," I muttered. I went out to stand beside Jameela and decided I didn't care too much for the Special Agent. "What's going on?" I demanded.

Jameela turned to me. "Oh, Fin," she said with a desperate appeal in her eyes and voice. "He's arresting me!"

A ripple of anger ran through me. "On what charge?"

"No charges, at the moment," Nagumo replied. "In fact, she's not under arrest. She'll be held as a material witness."

"Is that any better?"

He didn't answer. Instead, he smiled at me palliatively. "You must be Phineus Morton."

"Yeah, that's right. And I know who you are. Special Agent Vincent Nagumo, FBI Counterterrorism Unit, Seattle."

"Very good," said Nagumo.

"I've got one question for you," I grumbled. "You're Joe Fuad's boss. So where's Joe Fuad right now?"

Nagumo made a blank face. "Gone missing."

"Missing? What's that supposed to mean?"

He raised a hand. "Hold it. Hold it. I'm the one asking the questions here."

"No, you're not." I stepped closer to the window. "I think Fuad's in with these terrorists."

Nagumo nodded. "So I heard again from Dr. McKean while you were sleeping. But Fuad might be under deep cover at the moment. He might have hit upon something important and can't communicate right now. We'll watch the situation carefully, I assure you."

I opened my mouth to say more but Nagumo cut me off. "I've already passed along everything Dr. McKean told me about the ranch. Don't think we aren't working hard on this case. That's what brings me to this window. I want to know what Miss Noori knows. And she's going to tell me, aren't you ma'am?"

"Of course," Jameela said. "Anything I know, you will know."

"That's good," Nagumo replied.

"But why read her her rights?" I asked. "If she's not under arrest?"

"Let's call it protective custody," he said insincerely. "She stays here as long as she's under quarantine. But after that, she comes with us."

"Listen!" I said. "I'm sure she's not involved in this. I'll vouch for her."

"We'll figure out who's involved in what as we go along," Nagumo resisted. "Until then, we'll make sure nobody tries to escape." He pointed at a uniformed police officer, a woman seated in a chair near the elevator and reading a pocketbook. She wore a pistol at her hip.

"Right now we've only got a few leads to follow. And your girl-friend's one of them."

Girlfriend. Jameela and I exchanged surprised glances.

Nagumo turned and walked toward the elevator. He called back to us, "I've got plenty to pass on to D.C. for now. But I'll be back."

I wasn't paying attention to him. I was studying Jameela's eyes. An emotion worked behind her expression, something hard to define. A mixture of hope and fear perhaps, or attraction and reluctance. Or all of those things.

"I did not expect you to defend me," she said. "Thank you for being so kind."

"Of course." I said. "You risked your life for Peyton and me. Why wouldn't I speak up for you?"

"Because I am of the Middle East," she said, casting her eyes downward. "And Middle Easterners did this to you." She pointed at my bandage.

"Don't underestimate me," I replied. "I can see the difference between you and the Sheik's kind." She smiled. I put an arm around her shoulder and gave her a reassuring hug. I let the embrace last a moment longer than I should have, smelling the sweet fragrance of jasmine that had followed her into this grim place. She pulled away.

"In Egypt," she said, looking at the floor, "among my family's circles, unmarried women and men don't get so close, especially dressed like this."

"I'm sorry," I said.

"No," she waved a hand. "Don't be sorry. This is America. Men and women are free here to—" She paused.

"To—?" I prompted.

"To comfort one another." She suddenly turned to me and threw her arms around my chest and hugged me tightly. I wrapped my good arm around her and she rested her cheek against my chest.

"You're trembling," I said.

She didn't reply, but wept softly against my shoulder for a time. Perhaps not until that moment did I realize how deeply affected she was by all that had happened. *Of course. Who wouldn't be?*

I held her tightly and caressed the hair at the back of her head. She sobbed quietly.

The replacement of her riding outfit with hospital pajamas and bathrobe made her seem more frail. Although she had shown plenty of spunk against Sheik Abdul-Ghazi and Massoud, she now brought out an instinct in me to protect that which is dear. I hugged her for a long moment, until she seemed to have had enough. She pushed away from me gently and wiped tears from her cheeks, wearing a faint smile. She turned her back to me and cinched up the belt of her robe. As the blue garment tightened around her thin waist, my eyes were drawn to the flair of her hips, with inevitable consequences. Jameela's beautiful curves sent a jolt of excitement through me.

My thoughts muddled up. I wanted to protect her, and ravage her at the same time. Unable to decide how to act, I stood rigid as a marble statue.

She turned after a moment and looked into my face. Those glorious, pharaonic dark eyes seeming to read something there that she understood. A crooked smile played across her lips and she arched an eyebrow.

"What are you thinking, Phineus Morton?"

I was in awe of her feminine power. "Uh—" I faltered, confused by a welter of thoughts.

She smiled more.

I glanced away to collect my thoughts. But my eyes landed upon something that shattered my concentration—the stainless steel door labeled 'Autopsy Room.'

Ice water flooded into my veins again. I shook my head. "I don't know what I'm thinking," I mumbled.

A rap at the window diverted us.

Kay Erwin was outside the glass wall, dressed in her office clothes. She looked upset. McKean came out of the room and joined us at the two-way speaker.

"More bad news?" he asked.

"Mr. Fenton's physician, Dr. Adams, has come down with smallpox. The CDC team admitted him to the new quarantine ward they've set up at the high school."

"What's the condition of Fenton's family?" McKean asked.

"Very serious. All three cases—the wife, the son, and the daughter—have high fevers and pocks starting to appear. That's understandable in the kids. They've never been immunized against smallpox. But the wife was immunized as a child and is gravely ill anyway—the same lack of resistance as her husband. And three of Fenton's neighbors have developed fevers. They've been admitted to the school clinic as well. And there are a couple dozen other suspicious fevers in Sumas."

"The virus is highly contagious," McKean murmured.

"Yes," Erwin agreed. "We've declared a state-wide public health emergency. We're still trying to keep the virus confined to Sumas, but meanwhile the conventional vaccine is being distributed throughout the state. We will have immunized everyone in Sumas in the next day or so, but everything takes time. Precious time."

McKean rubbed his vaccinated shoulder. "And it all may be a worthless gesture."

Erwin sighed. "I've been thinking about that. We've got enough cases among formerly vaccinated people to know we've got a significantly altered organism. I sure wish we had your new B7R vaccine in hand."

McKean nodded. "And tested for efficacy. There's no guarantee that *it* will work, either."

"Don't say that, Peyton. If it isn't any better than the old vaccine, then we're very quickly out of options."

McKean drummed his thin fingertips against the glass. "This barrier is now the worst obstacle to my participation in finding a cure."

Erwin shook her head. "It's a shame, Peyton. We need your help right now."

Kay went back to her office, and Peyton wandered to the duty station to make a phone call to his wife. I felt a need for exercise, so I began pacing up and down the long ward hallway. Jameela tagged along. We inspected the row of patient rooms, making few comments. Walking the other direction, I looked over the ward's emergency resuscitation equipment with new eyes. At the autopsy room's small window, I glanced in, thinking how cold its stainless steel table looked. Rib-cutters hung on a wall like a pair of gargoylish brush loppers. On a counter were foot-long stainless steel needles attached to clear plastic hoses for sucking fluids from body cavities.

Jameela grasped me by an elbow. "Come away from here, Fin. You won't be in there, ever—God willing."

She led me back to the far end of the corridor like a therapist coaxing a man recovering from a stroke. There was a window at the end of the hall where we could watch city traffic passing below us.

"How did Abdul-Ghazi become so diabolical?" I asked her.

She shrugged. "He is blessed with great wealth, but he misuses it."

"They say money is the root of all evil."

"And he has too much of it," she said. "His family comes from a line descended from Mohammed, so they say. The old Sultan of Kharifa, his father, controls gold mines and oil pipelines from the Gulf States to the Indian Ocean. He charges a small tax on every barrel of oil, and so they have become fantastically wealthy. In a land of desert mountains and few people, this wealth is without use. It is what tainted the Sheik. The Sultan divided his money among dozens of sons and gave half the amount to his many daughters, according to custom. Even though the wealth was divided, it still made Abdul-Ghazi rich beyond most men's dreams. But he had a reputation as a playboy, a womanizer, an aimless young man and a child of idle wealth. His only interest was raising Arabian horses. He lived in Hollywood for a while. But when his father was struck by an assassin's bullet, he appeared to have a conversion, at least on the surface. He was no longer clean-shaven. He no longer dressed in western clothes. He gathered to him men like Massoud—angry young men, Muslims enraged against America. Men committed to jihad."

"Attracted by his money," I said. "Just like it was with bin Laden."

"Yes," Jameela agreed. "My father says oil breeds wealth, wealth breeds piety, piety breeds intolerance, intolerance breeds war. Allah sometimes bestows wealth in order to test a man's soul. To see if he will work righteousness or wrong."

"I guess Abdul-Ghazi has made his choice."

"Indeed," she agreed. "But he portrays himself as the Mahdi."

"Mahdi—?"

"In Islamic tradition, the Mahdi is a holy man who will come and right the wrongs of the world. A messiah, a savior of Muslim people, and —some say—a great warrior."

"Abdul-Ghazi thinks he is this man?"

"I have heard Massoud call him Mahdi. But the Sheik is a man of so many vices, he cannot possibly believe it himself."

We strolled back to the ward's central on-duty station. McKean had taken a seat and was talking into a small video camera mounted on top of one of the computers. On the screen was a live video image of Janet Emerson. "You would tell me if you were in real danger, wouldn't you?" she asked.

"Of course," he lied smoothly. "We're getting the best care we could possibly get. Don't worry."

"Okay." Her voice sounded thinner than just the effect of the computer microphone. "If you're sure."

"Absolutely. But I'll be under observation here for some time."

Janet was at her lab desk, one elbow on a pile of computer printouts. Her shoulders sagged. Her eyes were underscored with dark circles. But a faint smile colored her pretty face as she looked at Peyton McKean on her own screen. I leaned down until I was within range of the video camera. "You look tired," I said to her.

"I worked most of the night," she replied. "I've got the B7R gene spliced into the carrier DNA. I'm ready to put it into the *E. coli* cells. In a few days I should be able to grow up a small culture with a little of the product."

"Not enough for immunizations," McKean murmured. "I want you to turn the subunit vaccine project over to Robert and Beryl."

"What—?" Janet exclaimed in surprise.

"They can keep it moving along," McKean explained. "But I've got a new idea for you to try. I want you to make a synthetic vaccine."

She looked at him dubiously. "Chemical synthesis, you mean?"

"Answer: yes."

"But synthetic vaccines don't work."

"They don't work well," he agreed. "They're just tiny fragments of the virus. Too small to stimulate much immunity."

"So, why—?"

"Because they're fast. You can have a large batch ready in two days. And a little immunity quickly is better than a strong reaction that comes too late."

She looked horrified. "I thought you said you weren't in danger."

He laughed, perhaps to disarm her. "Don't worry about me. It's those folks up in Sumas I'm thinking of. The clock is ticking. Now, have you got the B7R sequence handy?"

"Right here." She held up the computer printout I had seen in McKean's office.

"Hold it close to the video camera," he said.

She did, and the screen filled with DNA sequence. McKean took a pad of yellow lined paper and a pen and wrote down the crucial segment:

DIEDIEDIE

"We'll focus on the genetically-altered sequence of amino acids. It's got to be a key target of immunity or Taleed wouldn't have bothered changing it. These amino acids will form the center of a slightly larger epitope."

"Epi—what?" I asked.

"Epitope" McKean repeated. "Greek for 'on-the-surface'. This segment of amino acids is probably located on the surface of the B7R protein and therefore a prime target for binding by antibodies. To make certain we've given the immune system a sufficiently large target, I'm going to include three more amino acids on either side. That will make the chain long enough to be grasped by several different antibodies at the same time—always a good idea with a vaccine. The more antibodies the merrier."

"Nothing is merry about this situation," I said.

McKean looked at the printout and added more amino acids at the ends of his hand-written sequence:

VPKDIEDIEDIEAYT

"But I'm still not finished," he said. "We need to add something that will encourage the immune system to sense this small molecule as something much larger and more threatening. If this peptide were injected into a patient as it is, it would dissipate from the injection site and be cleared from the bloodstream in minutes. Being small, it would be filtered out of the blood by the kidneys. To make it stay where we inject it, and also to make it appear threatening to white blood cells, I'll need to make it bigger. I'll attach a molecular anchor."

"A what?" I asked.

"Let me elaborate," McKean said with slow, professorial diction as he scribbled more letters on the left:

dpKGVPKDIEDIEDIEAYT

"The dpKG stands for dipalmitoyl-lysyl-glycine," he said.

"Are you dreaming this up as you go?" I asked.

"Essentially," McKean said. "Anyway, dpKG is a rather bulky, oil-soluble substance, like a fat molecule. With it attached, the peptide vaccine is no longer water-soluble. Instead, one vaccine molecule aggregates with the next to build up globs of vaccine peptides all stuck together. White blood cells react to these large globs as if they were whole viruses.

The body's natural process of inflammation is triggered and a proper immune response results."

"Ingenious" I said. "But will it work?"

"Theoretically," McKean said. "Though I've never tried anything exactly like this before."

"Then how can you be sure?" I asked.

"We'll test it on experimental animals," he said. "Us."

He held up the yellow pad so Janet could copy the sequence.

She had grown more flustered and red as he casually discussed what she had now figured out was a life-or-death test.

"If this works," McKean said, "it will be the fastest vaccine synthesis ever."

"If it works," Janet repeated.

"Yes," he said. "And I'm sure it will. As long as it's synthesized correctly."

"As long as—!" Janet went purple. I guessed she had just figured out how *on-the-spot* she was.

"Now," McKean continued calmly. "Regarding vaccine doses, you have the chemicals on hand to synthesize about a gram of this material. A gram is just a fraction of an ounce, but it will be enough to vaccinate several thousand people if necessary." He got a starry-eyed look. "Imagine! A whole new vaccine created in just two days, given nothing more to start with than a computer printout of the virus's DNA sequence. How does that strike you, Fin?"

I shrugged. "Great, if it works."

McKean went on without acknowledging my doubts. "Janet can scale up her synthesis to make enough vaccine to immunize ten-thousand people, just a few days later."

"Great, if it works," I repeated.

"If it works," McKean finally acknowledged, deflating a little.

"And if not?" Janet asked. A quaver had developed in her voice.

McKean shrugged. For a moment he had nothing to say. Then he looked her in the face. "I wish there were someone in the lab who could spell you for a while. But chemical peptide synthesis is a rather specialized technique. There is no one else I would care to rely on at ImCo. If I weren't, er, busy here, I would take your place at the bench myself."

"It's all right," she said. "Sally Ann has been a doll. She's kept a steady flow of caffeine and food coming from the executive kitchen. I'll be okay."

"Good," McKean said. "There's still plenty of time to get the first dose of vaccine in our arms before the virus takes hold. We'll be immune to the virus days before its growth rate accelerates to dangerous levels."

Janet now went ash white. "But you said you weren't in danger."

McKean shrugged his angular shoulders. "Let's stay optimistic about that. For now, don't let me keep you any longer. We'll chat again soon."

After goodbyes, McKean turned off the video feed. He turned to us with a philosophical look on his face. "Janet is incredibly good at what she does. I doubt things would move much faster if I were there. The vaccine should be ready for injection within forty-eight hours."

"Barring any unforeseen problems," I muttered.

"We've worked together on a few other chemical synthesis projects. It's fairly straightforward. She'll chemically link the amino acids, one by one, onto microscopic plastic particles, by a process called Merrifield synthesis. Sometime tomorrow when the vaccine is finished, she'll remove it from the beads by simply extracting with hydrofluoric acid."

"Extraction with hydrofluoric acid is simple?" I asked.

McKean smiled and dismissed the question. "From there, just one last treatment yields a product pure enough to go into our arms—the vaccine must be freeze-dried. It's the same process that turns instant coffee from a liquid to a solid. You freeze the liquid as a shell of ice inside a glass jar, and then subject the jar to a vacuum until the ice sublimates to dryness. Whatever remains in the jar is freeze-dried. In the case of our vaccine, I expect a fluffy white powder with the consistency of cotton candy."

I was dubious. "I've never heard of anyone making a vaccine overnight. Doesn't it usually take years to develop one?"

"An old notion," McKean said. "The potential of chemically synthesized vaccines has scarcely been recognized, but I've puttered with the technique for years. It's good to finally get a chance to put it to the test. And I'm confident we'll have this vaccine in hand very soon."

"In arm," I said, pointing at my shoulder. We all forced a laugh. And then I noticed that the gauze on my wrist was stained with orangish fluid that had seeped from my wound.

"Yes. In arm," McKean said. "And the sooner the better."

CHAPTER 13

Janet reappeared on the computer screen at the duty station several hours later and we gathered around.

"What is it?" McKean asked.

"There's someone here who would like to talk with you."

A hefty body in a gray suit and pink shirt appeared over her left shoulder. She moved aside and the owner of the body plunked into the chair. It was Stuart Holloman.

"Sorry to hear about your, uh, bad luck," Holloman said.

"Thanks for the concern," McKean replied.

"You seem to have a way of winding up right where the action is, in the lab or out of it. But you took off without official leave from work." Holloman glared across cyberspace. Veins stood out on his bald head.

"A last-minute thing," McKean answered unapologetically. "I would have told you, but it seemed more important to get where we were going as soon as possible."

Holloman was unappeased. "I'll overlook your unexcused absenteeism, given how important your escapade turned out to be. But I've got to say, Peyton, you're not regular guy, not a team player."

"I don't suppose I ever will be."

"No," Holloman agreed. "But you can't flout my authority forever. Just a friendly warning. You've got to toe the line sometimes, no matter how brilliant you think you are. Other people's opinions matter, too."

"I'll take that into consideration," said McKean.

Holloman sat silent and sour-faced for a moment, obviously not getting what he wanted out of the conversation. Then he got up and walked off-screen without a goodbye or a backward glance.

McKean sat tugging on his chin, uncommunicative. Janet took her seat again and watched off-screen for a moment. "He's gone now," she said.

"Good," said McKean. "Let's get back to work, then."

"Okay."

"Once you've set the freeze-dryer running," he said, "you'll have at least an eight-hour wait while the vaccine peptide dries. You can go home and get some well-deserved rest."

In the next few minutes, Janet and Peyton focused their attention on the work at hand, discussing the synthesis without remark or reaction to what Holloman had said. Jameela and I drifted away as they discussed Merrifield synthesis in too much detail for my overstressed brain to comprehend. But I paused, a few paces off, to note how casually McKean chatted into the computer video camera, laughing and making small talk with Janet.

Jameela whispered, "He gets along well with her."

"Yes," I agreed. "He's quite pleasant with his coworkers. But he and his boss—"

"—hate each other," she concluded for me.

McKean's videoconference concluded when Hawkins came in in his isolation suit bringing a dinner of roast beef, mashed potatoes and green beans. The three of us took our meals at a small table in McKean's and my room, which had become a central meeting place for the three of us. After dinner and some animated discussions of international politics, epidemics, and jihad, McKean got up and stood in the hallway on our side of the glass as if waiting for someone's arrival. He was.

Shortly past 6 PM two people got off the elevator. A trim blond woman dressed in a tan business suit led a sandy-haired boy, a child of perhaps seven, dressed in blue jeans and a green coat, by the hand. She brought him with her to the window.

Peyton approached the window closely. There was an odd silence, as if no one was prepared for this moment. The boy said, "Hi, Daddy."

"Hi, Sean," McKean replied warmly. He bent down to exchange smiles with the boy. Then he stood and addressed his wife more coolly, "Hi, Evvie."

Overwrought-looking, she shook her head slowly. "Peyton..." she began, but seemed at a loss for words. "I think maybe you've gone too far this time."

"Perhaps I have," he agreed.

"You—" she began in a harsh tone, but stopped herself. "It wouldn't have hurt you to think about us before you got into this."

He nodded. Then he knelt by the window glass to be near his son. "How's my boy?" He asked with a smile.

"Fine, Daddy," Sean replied. "When are you going to get well?"

"Soon," McKean said. "Just a few days."

"Good," the boy said. "Mutley wants to play with you, Dad. He doesn't wag his tail very much. He misses you." He put a small hand against the window glass.

McKean covered the same spot on his side of the window with his own hand. "I miss you and Mutley, both," he said. Their gazes joined and their hands communed through the barrier, reaching out through glass, quarantine, time, evil, hate, and desperation to take comfort in their nearness.

Jameela and I moved away to give the family time alone, walking to the end of the hallway while McKean and his loved ones discussed their private concerns. McKean's wife seemed argumentative, but the boy and McKean kept their hands together on the glass. Eventually, an orderly came and spoke softly to Mrs. McKean. She took her son's hand from the glass and led him to the elevator. When Sean waved goodbye, McKean's face took on an uncharacteristically remorseful look. He waved back, and then the elevator doors closed and they were gone.

He stood at the window wall for some time before returning to his bed. There, he seemed to take solace in a medical journal, marking it prodigiously with a yellow highlighter he had appropriated from the duty desk.

The visit by McKean's loved ones reminded me I had people, too. But I didn't call my folks in Phoenix. I didn't want to hear my mother cry, or take my father's chiding about harebrained schemes. And if I died, somebody else could call them.

Confined to the ward as we were, time slowed to a crawl. My only relief came from chatting with Jameela. In the evening, she and I played chess on a table in our room. She trounced me and then provoked McKean into a match. I watched them play from my bed. They played several slow-paced games that went on for a long time. By the time they were tied at a game apiece, I had grazed through every channel on the room's wall-mounted television set without news of smallpox or kidnapped redheads. All I got was CNN reports on Middle-Eastern fighting, and then a local late-night news story about a man shooting his neighbor over the noise his wind chimes made. Sometime past 10 PM, after a narrow loss to McKean, Jameela bid us both goodnight and went to her room. McKean went back to his bed and his medical journals and his yellow highlighter.

I dozed until Peyton McKean raised the sound volume on the TV. I opened my eyes to see a female reporter under camera lights on the shoulder of a dark county highway. The road behind her was the one we had roared along that morning in the Methow Valley.

"Details are sketchy," she began. "But officers of the Okanogan County Sheriff's Department, acting in concert with the FBI, have surrounded a ranch not far from us here on the North Cascades Highway. We are barred from the area until it is declared safe by the Sheriff's Department. All we know at this time is that the incident is somehow connected to the smallpox cases reported in Sumas. Apparently one or more persons of interest in that matter are being sought by agents here."

Beyond that, the reporter had little information.

"She should be here," I said, when the segment came to an end. "I bet she'd like to interview us." We watched the station for half an hour but got only a sports note about a Seattle Mariners' pitcher with tennis elbow, the weather forecast, which unsurprisingly called for rain, and a long feature about West Seattle High School in an uproar over changing their mascot from the Indians to something less ethnically offensive. Surprisingly, several members of the Duwamish tribe, the original West Seattle Indians, weighed in in favor of *keeping* the Indians name.

"Times are screwy," I said.

"Hospital confinement," McKean observed, "is a bore punctuated by bad news." He switched off the TV. I killed the room lights and drew the green privacy curtains around my bed just after eleven.

I tossed on top of the covers for hours, drifting in and out of sleep.

Dozing, I dreamed I was riding the black stallion again, this time with slack reins, in Mohammed's vast garden of date palms, moseying along a peaceful sand-banked stream. Beside me, Jameela rode the white mare. Looking smart in her riding outfit, she smiled at me. Her dark Cleopatran eyes seemed to beckon me closer.

"Jameela," I began, but the twittering of a bird high among the date clusters made her turn and look away.

I raised my voice and spoke to her more loudly.

An odd noise interrupted the dream. It wasn't a sound you would hear in a garden of date palms. It was the clatter of curtain hangers sliding on an overhead track.

"Fin?" The voice was Jameela's, but she had vanished from the dream. The scene dissolved as I sat up in the dim light of the hospital room. The green hospital curtains around my bed were parted. Standing over me was—

"Jameela!" I exclaimed. "Where—?"

She looked at me with one eyebrow raised like a beautiful teacher who had caught a schoolboy up to some mischief. "You were talking in your sleep. You called my name."

She was dressed in pajamas and a blue robe. I had expected the riding outfit, but it had vanished along with the dream. Momentarily confused, I blinked at her stupidly.

An inscrutable smile crossed her beautiful face. She leaned close and cooed, "You said more than just my name. Don't you remember?"

The warmth of a red flush crept over my face. "You've got me on that one. I don't remember exactly what I said."

"But I do," she whispered. "And I am... flattered."

"You should be flattered," Peyton McKean chuckled from beyond the curtains. "To be paid such compliments by the wordsmith, Fin Morton. And in such... graphic detail!"

My face must have gone from red to purple. Jameela watched my discomfort and laughed melodiously. "Fin!" she teased. "You are embarrassed?"

McKean showed no mercy. "You talk most charmingly in your sleep, Fin. But you had better make such suggestions in private, next time."

"I could not sleep," Jameela explained. "I came to see if I could borrow one of your books. That's when you... said what you said."

"What did I say?" I demanded.

McKean laughed outright. "That is not a suitable topic for mixed company."

Jameela laughed too. But she seemed to think I had suffered enough. She leaned near and whispered softly, "My answer, Fin Morton, is—maybe."

She chose a book from the pile and then went out, pulling the curtains closed after her. She paused a moment by the doorway and whispered, "Goodnight, Fin." Then she was gone, leaving me sputtering and Peyton McKean chuckling.

"What the hell did I say to her?" I asked.

"Nothing I care to repeat. You'll have to get it from her."

"Thanks for the help," I muttered. "I'll be embarrassed to see her tomorrow."

"Humiliation goes with the territory."

"What territory?"

"Masculinity. Being the aggressive gender. We males are instigators. Half the time we make fools of ourselves."

"That's supposed to cheer me up?"

"My point is, she's sure you're interested in her now, isn't she? However lamely you did it, you've got her thinking."

"You wouldn't know by her reactions."

"You wouldn't," McKean said. "But *I* would. She's shy. Easily embarrassed. She's gone away to think it over."

McKean was sitting on the edge of his bed silhouetted on the curtain divider by the dim glow of his reading light. "I think she likes you."

"You really think so?"

"Oh, I don't know." McKean arranged the covers over his legs. "It's just a theory. A hypothesis I'm working on. I could just as easily be wrong as right. But I advise you to proceed on the assumption I am right."

He lay down and snapped off his reading light, darkening the room. "Goodnight, Fin."

"Goodnight, Peyton." I shook my muddled head, lay down and closed my eyes.

CHAPTER 14

The next morning Jameela joined Peyton and me for breakfast at the small table in our room. Over ham and eggs, orange juice, and toast, we talked awhile and watched Nurse Hawkins in his isolation suit changing the sheets and blankets on our beds. He put the old ones in a black plastic bag marked INCINERATOR and left us.

To break the long silence that followed, I asked Jameela, "Is this food all right for you? I mean, do you usually eat some other kind of food?"

She looked at me thoughtfully. "Halal, you mean? Do you expect me to be so different?"

"I just meant— I don't know what I meant."

"I have eaten Big Mac hamburgers at McDonalds in Giza," she said. "I buy Levis blue jeans at the shopping mall in Cairo. I learned to drive my father's car at sixteen. I got drunk on wine at seventeen. And at eighteen I lost—" She stopped.

"What?"

"Never mind. There are rock concerts in Cairo, you know. I watched American movies and TV shows dubbed in Arabic. My life there was nice. Not so different from America."

"I'm sorry," I said. "I didn't mean to imply anything."

She still looked mildly offended, so I tried to explain myself. "You know, Jameela, beneath this coarse, rude exterior lies a very delicate—"

"—posterior," McKean finished for me.

Jameela laughed. I got red and clammed up. But McKean took over.

"A little more family history please, Jameela," he said.

"I was raised in good circumstances," she said. "My father is a physician trained at Oxford. We lived in one of Cairo's best suburbs. I was one of three children. I have one older brother and one younger one. My eldest brother is in England, training to be a doctor like my father. I was studious too. But, above all, I loved horses. I learned to ride at one of the finest Egyptian riding academies while my father was treating the director's arthritis. I studied at the American University to improve my English. I got my master's degree in veterinary science from Cairo University and went on to the National Arabian Horse Stables in Giza, in the shadow of the pyramids. I learned the care and training of Arabian horses there. And it was there I met my beloved mare, Zahirah."

"And Sheik Abdul-Ghazi?" McKean prompted.

"My life," she replied, "has taken some unhappy turnings."

"How so?"

"Sheik Abdul-Ghazi arrived from America one day to look over horses for breeding stock. He purchased Zahirah the same day for cash money, a large amount. I was heartbroken. When the director told him this, he instantly offered to take me to America. I agreed, thinking only that he wanted me to tend to Zahirah. Soon after I arrived, however, he made his real intentions known. When he told me he wished to make me his second wife, I refused, of course. But then my father was arrested in Kharifa. He was lured there by a request to tend the crippling back injury of the Sultan. But his passport was taken and he is held there now without charges. They forced him to call and urge me to marry Sheik Abdul-Ghazi. I still refused, but my dear father remains under house arrest in the court of the Sultan. My mother joined him there of her own free will. She is a loyal wife."

McKean nodded thoughtfully. "You risked a lot when you decided to rescue us."

Jameela sighed. "I hoped not to be discovered. And now my parents may be in mortal danger because of my choice."

"A brave choice," McKean said. "And your brothers, where are they now?"

"My elder brother is safe in England. But my younger brother, I do not know. He has disappeared. He is an angry young man. He expressed sympathy for Islamic radicals. In the Arab Spring demonstrations, he marched with them. I am afraid he will follow a man like Sheik Abdul-Ghazi. I have heard him quote the Qur'an's most warlike words."

"An unfortunate emphasis," McKean said sympathetically. "There is as much in the Qur'an about peace as about war."

"You have read the Qur'an?" she asked.

McKean nodded. "I have delved into all the great religions of the world, although not as deeply as I know the scientific literature."

"Then you know Islam is not fundamentally a violent religion," she said.

"Yes," McKean agreed. "It says, 'Requite evil with good and he who is your enemy will become your dearest friend.' That is clearly a call to peace over war. And its third verse acknowledges the importance of the Laws of Moses and the Gospel of Jesus. I take it you subscribe to the voice of moderation in the Qur'an, Jameela."

"Yes," she said emphatically. "My family history requires it. You see, my father is a Muslim, but my mother is a Coptic Christian. In our home, we learned a simple faith. Like Jesus, Mohammed's message was peaceful: believe in one God, Allah ar-Rahim, a God who is merciful; Allah ar-Rahman, a God who is compassionate. I don't believe Allah wants anyone killed for any cause."

"Allah as-Salam," said McKean.

"Exactly," Jameela replied, "Allah is the bestower of peace."

"And you're Coptic Christian as well," McKean remarked.

"I celebrate Christmas and Easter, and other Christian holidays, as well as Muslim," she said. "Do you know that the celebration of Easter continues a forty-five-hundred-year-old springtime festival from the times of the Pharaohs, Sham El-Nessim, celebrated by Muslims too?"

"I did not know that," McKean admitted.

She smiled. "Are you a man of faith, Dr. McKean?"

He smiled in return. "Suffice it to say, I have no doubts."

"Really? I would expect a scientist to have many doubts about matters of faith."

"But I am not in doubt." He smiled obscurely. "I am absolutely convinced that I *don't know*. I'm as pure an agnostic as a person can be. There may be a God and an afterlife, or there may not, but I am sure I don't know the answer. I hold closely to the Greek origin of the word agnostic, which means, quite simply, not knowing."

"I have never doubted," said Jameela. "And you, Fin?"

I adjusted the gauze of my bandage. "I hope that Allah, or Jesus, or somebody, will get us out of this mess."

"God will save you," Jameela said, "if you have faith. Do you?"

"A tough question," I replied. "I go back and forth. One day I'll look at a glorious sunrise or the simple joy of a child, and I believe there must be a God who made it all. But then I see people committing mass murder, torture, genocide—and I can't believe there is a God sitting on the sidelines while it happens. Let's just say I'm confused."

She turned to McKean. "But is there nothing you believe unconditionally, unquestioningly?"

"Very little," McKean said. "Although I do have a deep and abiding belief in Santa Claus and the Easter Bunny."

Jameela laughed.

"I'm serious," he said. "American Christianity is a lesson for the world. The fact that our most widely celebrated holidays are such great fun, and that we exalt children and indulge them with gifts, probably says more about the good nature of Americans than anything else we do."

"Bravo!" Jameela cried.

"But what's this?" McKean turned to the TV set, which we had neglected during our breakfast conversation. On the screen was the same female reporter we had seen the night before. Illuminated by morning sun, she stood near a Humvee marked FBI, parked by a familiar stone gate, now crisscrossed with police crime-scene tape. I grabbed the remote and turned up the volume.

"We have just been briefed," the reporter said, "by Special Agent Vincent Nagumo, on events that transpired overnight here at the Arabians Unlimited horse ranch. Police and FBI units detained two men in this black truck." She indicated a familiar large black pickup, pulled out behind the gate. Its front windshield was smashed and bullet holes riddled its fenders. "They then entered the ranch about midnight. Many shots were fired. Two suspects were critically wounded, but no injuries were reported among law enforcement personnel. Seven people were taken into custody at the ranch's main house."

"Seven?" Jameela said. "But more than a dozen lived there."

"These were transported to the FBI's Seattle facilities for interrogation. All were of Middle Eastern origins, but none was the reputed owner of the property, Sheik Abdul-Ghazi. The Sheik eluded capture, but his family was detained, including his wife and four children. Three other men arrested on the property claimed to be recently hired help who cared for the Sheik's horses."

"That's not true!" Jameela protested. "I cared for the horses myself."

The reporter walked to an equestrian fence beside the gate and held out a hand with upturned palm. A horse thrust its pink muzzle under the top slat, nuzzling in vain for a treat.

"Zahirah!" Jameela cried, her face lighting with joy. A moment later, the black stallion reached his head over the fence to nuzzle the same empty hand. "Majid! Oh, my beauties found their way home."

"Police and FBI agents," the reporter went on, "were responding to reports of a clandestine operation here, said to be infecting victims with smallpox. However, no evidence of such an operation was found, nor any sign of a pit full of bodies that had been rumored to be here. There were no signs of captives, no smallpox, and no bodies. Just a herd of Arabian horses, including these two—and they're not talking."

"That's impossible!" I exclaimed.

"Authorities say their investigation is at a standstill. However, they consider their sources of information credible, so the search will continue. The three arrested men were in violation of immigration laws and will be held along with the Sheik's family pending his apprehension."

The reporter signed off, and when a man shouting about a furniture warehouse sale came on, I lowered the volume.

"I don't get it," I said. "We weren't *seeing things,* were we? The redhead, she's one dead body for sure."

McKean drew his fingers over his chin. "The Sheik must have cleared out right after we escaped. He surely knew a response by the authorities was likely. He must have retrieved the bodies and dumped them elsewhere. And then he absconded with any other evidence."

"Including that damn virus," I said.

McKean looked at me closely. "You know, Fin," he said, "you don't look too well."

"You're so pale," Jameela remarked, looking into my face.

A chill ran through me. Suddenly I felt as badly as they said I looked. I broke a sweat as McKean continued eying me carefully. "Your pallor might be an early manifestation of illness. I feel okay, myself."

"But you were vaccinated when you were young, and I wasn't."

McKean nodded affirmatively, continuing to observe me closely. "A fever arising in you, first, would be consistent with our immunization histories."

My heart began to palpitate. There was a long moment of silence.

And then a tone came from the computer at the on-duty station. McKean hurried out, sat down and said, "Hello, Janet."

He smiled, but as Jameela and I followed him, his smile faded. "What is it? What's wrong?" he asked.

Looking over McKean's shoulder, we saw Janet sitting at her laboratory desk as before. But now her eyes were damp with tears. She held in her hands a large glass jar with a blue plastic lid, from which protruded a short length of stainless steel pipe—a freeze-drying flask. She held it up so we could see that there was no white vaccine powder inside. It was empty.

"Someone—" Janet's voice cracked with emotion, "—got into the lab last night. We can't figure out how they got past security. They took the sample jar from the freeze-drier and washed the vaccine down the sink." She hung her head and sobbed.

"Who would do such a thing?" Jameela cried.

McKean sat in silent thought for a moment. And then he shook his head. "That's it, then," he said. "They've beaten us." He looked at his bandaged arm. "Time is running out."

Janet sat bleary-eyed and trembling. "I stayed up half the night. I finished it! I put it on the freeze drier and went home to get some sleep. If only I had stayed—"

"Don't blame yourself," McKean said to her softly. "You'll just have to start all over again, that's all."

"Of course I will, immediately. But will it be too late?"

"Answer: probably—for us. But for America: no."

Tears streamed down her cheeks. "But I want to help *you,*" she sobbed.

"I'm afraid there's no help for us," McKean said, "except our own innate immunity, and that's in serious doubt given the death of Fenton and the illness of his family. Fin's already showing some signs..."

A wave of dizziness washed over me. I felt myself trembling. Fear was part of my reaction, but the bigger part was rage. I slammed a fist on the duty-station counter. "Who did this? How *the hell* did someone know what to look for?"

McKean shook his head. "I don't know. I'm out of ideas." He looked brittle.

"Our security guards were on the alert," Janet said.

"Not alert enough," I growled.

"Dr. Holloman has increased security," Janet replied. "He's brought in two Seattle police officers to patrol the halls."

"Now that it's too late," I muttered.

"It will have to do," McKean said. "The next batch has got to be completed as soon as possible. You know what you have to do, Janet. You had better get to work."

"Okay." Janet leaned forward to switch off her computer. "Goodbye, Peyton." She took a long look at him.

McKean nodded a silent farewell and clicked off the video window.

"Who would do such a thing?" Jameela asked.

"An inside job?" I suggested.

"It's easy to think that," McKean agreed. "No one has ever gotten past security at ImCo. But it's hard to imagine anyone inside ImCo wanting the vaccine to fail."

"The ones most immediately hurt," I suggested, "would be you and I. Maybe this is directed at us. How about Holloman himself?"

"Answer: no. He may be angry with me, but not enough to jeopardize human lives—or ImCo's profits."

"Then who?"

"I'm drawing a blank. It does seem like someone wants us dead."

He got up and wandered away down the hall, absorbed in thought.

After a few moments of silence, Jameela put a hand on my shoulder. "You are so pale," she said. "You should get back in bed."

McKean came back and stopped in front of the counter.

"More depressing news," he murmured.

I shrugged. "Okay, hit me with it. What could be worse than what we just heard?"

"This." He laid his forearm on the counter and pulled the gauze away from his wound. The gash looked better, already healing around the black stitches. But the surrounding skin had reddened for several inches. And on one side of the red area was a single, small, white dot.

I gasped. "Is it...?"

"Answer: yes," McKean confirmed. "It's a pock, classic in form. Note the pus-white color and the outline of bright red inflammation around it. It's my first pock, but I am sure it's not my last."

I tugged the gauze back from my wound. A half-dozen white spots surrounded it.

"Oh, my God! I'm worse off than you!"

McKean nodded. "Again, Fin, you're the more susceptible one. The virus hasn't disseminated throughout our bodies yet, but these spots are the first steps along the way. The infection will gain momentum with time. The old vaccine clearly is not working."

CHAPTER 15

Never in my life have I hit a point as low as the hours following the discovery of the pocks. I lay down on my bed and Jameela sat near me, offering comforting words. But she couldn't sooth away the obvious fact that the disease was gaining ground. McKean wandered the halls in a manic mood, muttering to himself in polysyllabic scientific jargon and occasionally shouting out in exasperation.

He came back into the room mumbling vitriolically about traitors and turncoats. And then he abruptly stopped. He pointed up at the TV on the wall and asked, "Hey, what's this?"

A late-morning news bulletin had interrupted a cooking show that Jameela and I had been ignoring. The camera view showed a freeway stretching over flat, shrubby grassland dotted with cattle, and a mountainous horizon. A white semi truck was overturned in the median, its cab crushed and the trailer's sides crumpled. The ground around it was strewn with dozens of bodies covered in bloodied white sheets.

The camera panned past the vehicle to a black-haired female reporter, identified as Andrea Winchell in the logo line at the bottom of the screen. She held a microphone to the mouth of a uniformed state trooper with a tan smoky bear hat. As I turned the volume up, the trooper said, "The ones that weren't killed in the crash came out shooting. They had pistols, shotguns, automatic weapons, you name it. We backed off and called in a SWAT team. It was a real bad scene for a while, but they couldn't get away. Country's too open. We had 'em pinned down from the start.

There's a good fifty dead men there."

Winchell faced the camera. "There you have it, from the Colorado State Trooper who was involved from the start of the chase. Apparently, there were no survivors among the occupants of the truck. All of the men chose to die in what has been described as a fierce gun battle with police and the SWAT team. But the men didn't go down easily. Several hand grenades were thrown from the truck. One destroyed a state patrol car in the early minutes of the shootout." The camera swung to show a squad car, windowless and blackened by flames, still smoldering. "But in this open country, the men had nowhere to run. Correct, Trooper Harris?"

"That's right. We held them down until a SWAT team of sharp-shooters came in by helicopter. They were able to stand off a safe distance and set up sniping positions. And they used the helicopter as a fire-point too. The perpetrators kept shooting, so we had to kill them all, one-by-one. None of them wanted to be taken alive."

Winchell said, "The pursuing officers, including Trooper Harris here, are being called heroes by the Governor. The chase that led to the shoot-out began near the Utah border and continued for twenty miles before police used spike strips to blow out the truck's tires, sending it off the pavement at high speed. The gun battle lasted several hours, during which traffic on this busy east-west freeway was halted by authorities and backed up for miles. Other details are sketchy right now. The purpose of so many young men traveling in the back of a truck remains unknown."

"Not to us," I said.

"One thing is certain," the reporter went on. "No one here has lived to tell about it." The camera panned across the grassy landscape and the dozens of bloody, sheet-covered corpses.

"Mike!" McKean exclaimed in anguish. "I he must have died in the crash."

"Or was shot by his captors," I said.

"I'm sorry," Jameela commiserated.

The news station went to a commercial and I turned the volume down. None of us had much to say. When the computer beeped again, McKean hurried to the on-duty station and we followed. Janet was on the screen with a smile lighting her face.

"You won't believe this," she bubbled as McKean sat, and Jameela and I crowded over his shoulders.

"Try me," McKean said.

"They dropped one of the analytical sample tubes on the floor. I found it."

McKean jumped visibly in his chair. "How much material?"

She held up a tiny plastic test tube in her rubber-gloved hand. "A routine sample at the last step of synthesis, taken to monitor the completion of the final reaction. Maybe two milligrams. Just a speck."

"That speck is enough to hang a hope on," McKean exclaimed. He leaned back in his chair and his face blanked like a computer screen doing massive calculations. "It might be enough!" he finally said. "Enough vaccine for a bare minimum immunization of three people. Fin, Jameela, and me!"

"That's exactly what *I* thought," Janet agreed. "I'll detach the vaccine from the beads with hydrofluoric acid, and dry it in a little flask on the freeze dryer. I can get it to you by mid-afternoon."

"Excellent!" McKean replied. "Meanwhile, have Robert keep moving on the new large-scale synthesis to replace what's been lost. I have a hunch many people's lives may depend on it."

"He's already working on it," Janet said.

"Perfect!" McKean's face was lit by new hope.

Sometime past 3 PM, Janet arrived outside the window wall, white-coated and delighted to see Peyton McKean on his feet and still showing no general signs of illness, though chills had driven me to my bed several times. Janet held up her precious cargo of vaccine. It was a small, clear-plastic test tube about two inches long. In its pointed, conical bottom was what looked like a tiny half-drop of milk.

"That's it?" I asked.

McKean nodded. "She simply suspended the dry powder in a drop of saline. It's not much, but enough for three if we're careful."

I said, "I can't believe it's that simple to make. Are you sure there's nothing dangerous about it? Nothing toxic—?"

McKean laughed. "Under the circumstances, do you really care?"

"I suppose not."

He turned to Janet. "You brought the adjuvant?"

She held up a second tube containing a drop of off-white, slightly yellowish oil. She swirled it and a smutty yellow-white material rose from the bottom.

"Adjuvant?" I eyed the foul-looking material. It had an unpleasant, pus-like appearance.

"The second component of our vaccine," McKean explained. "The term *adjuvant* means, literally, to make young, or to boost the vigor of the immune response. Our adjuvant has a few more ingredients in the mix than other investigators use. In that yellowish suspension are various extracts of killed bacteria, molds and fungi, materials the body naturally tends to react against. We've concocted a blend of microbial body parts, you might say, and we add to that an assortment of immune-stimulating hormones, which cause white blood cells to roar with activity. Mix this adjuvant in equal parts with the vaccine peptide and the combination causes a dramatic immune reaction."

"Is this a secret recipe of yours?" I asked.

"Not really a secret. We've published our findings in scientific journals. But our work has been ignored by the scientific community."

"Ignored?" I said. "Why is that?"

McKean shrugged. "NIH syndrome."

"NIH," I said. "National Institutes of Health—"

McKean shook his head. "Try, 'Not Invented Here'."

"'Not Invented Here' syndrome?" I puzzled. "Are you saying scientists would ignore a perfectly good product because they didn't invent it themselves?"

"Answer: yes. They're all looking for their own claim to fame."

"But wouldn't that slow down scientific progress?"

"A shame, isn't it?" McKean pointed again at the tube in Janet's hand. "But I'm confident this vaccine will make our white blood cells produce what we need right now—antibodies."

"But why wouldn't the antibodies be targeted against the adjuvant, instead of the vaccine?"

"An astute observation," McKean said. "But our immune systems will see the entire mixture as the enemy. Our immune cells will react to everything, including the vaccine peptide. Have no doubts on that, Fin— we have tested this technique on hundreds of albino mice."

"That's fine," I replied. "But I'm not an albino and I'm not a mouse. Are you sure it will work on us, against this virus?"

"You've got me there," McKean admitted. "We've never tried this particular approach on humans."

"Great," I muttered. "So my life depends on an untested bit of yellow scum."

McKean shrugged again. "If this vaccine is inadequate, Fin, then what else would you like to try?"

I shrugged.

Kay Erwin came from her office and took the test tubes from Janet. She entered the airlock and while she dressed in her pressure suit, McKean conversed quietly with Janet. "Don't let anything delay your new synthesis," he said. "Thousands of lives may depend on you—maybe many more than that. And if this belated dose of vaccine doesn't work, you won't have me to consult with."

McKean voiced the thought with academic coolness, but it was not received that way. Janet's eyes widened, her face reddened, her brow creased, and her jaw dropped. Tears welled in her eyes. "Don't talk like that!" she pleaded. "Don't tell me what I'll do when you're gone. You're not going to..."

"I only meant," McKean interrupted, "that if the worst should happen..."

"The worst won't happen!"

"We don't have to discuss these matters right now," McKean said. "But there is one more thing. Despite the urgency, I think you should find time to get some sleep."

She looked even more surprised. "But, I can't waste time..."

"Every step in the synthesis is critical, Janet. I don't want you making errors due to exhaustion. You look well beyond fatigued."

He was right. Her teary eyes were surrounded by dark circles and her cheeks had a porcelain-like pallor.

"I'm not that bad off," she insisted. "I got some sleep while the main batch of vaccine was freeze-drying. I only wish I had stayed awake to watch it."

"When you get the chance," McKean went on adamantly, "between stages of the synthesis, please find time to lie down on the couch in the staff lounge. Sleep is the best way to assure you don't make a serious mistake along the way. We can't afford a single error."

Kay Erwin came into the ward from the airlock, isolation-suited and carrying a metal tray with the two vaccine components on it. She set the tray on the countertop and picked up a syringe wrapped in sterile packaging. Her black-gloved hands made tearing the paper-and-plastic laminated holder difficult.

"Darn this moon suit," she said.

"Allow me," McKean said. He took the syringe package from her and opened it deftly with his long fingers. "Now, Fin," he said in a lecturing tone, "allow me to demonstrate the final preparation of a synthetic vaccine."

He picked up the test tube containing the milky vaccine peptide solution and drew the liquid into the syringe, half-filling it. He then took up the tube of yellowish adjuvant and squirted the syringe's contents into it, making a 50-50 mix of vaccine and adjuvant. He drew the mixture into the syringe and expelled it back into the tube several times until it congealed to the consistency of mayonnaise. It had a horrid, yellow, mucinous appearance.

"That looks good," McKean said, raising the test tube and eyeing it carefully.

"Looks bad, if you ask me," I retorted.

"Let's hope our immune systems agree, Fin. Now, I'll divide it into thirds."

"Into halves," Jameela said. "You know I am already immune."

"Maybe Dr. Taleed really did give you a tetanus shot," McKean countered.

"No," she replied. "It was Taleed's smallpox vaccine. I am sure of it now."

McKean drew the syringe plunger back to the one-half cc mark, and then raised the needle in front of his face and carefully pushed out a small amount of the emulsion, which slid down the barrel of the needle like the mucus trail of a slug.

"It's ready," he said. "Fin, please turn up your sleeve."

The syringe needle was of a large gauge to allow the viscous liquid through. As I watched the droplet of vaccine make its sluggish way down the needle's shaft, I wasn't so sure I wanted that needle or its load of slime in my arm. But I did as he asked. I lowered my bathrobe sleeve and pulled up the short sleeve of my gown. Kay Erwin wiped the side of my shoulder with an alcohol swab.

With the hint of a smile crossing his face, McKean pinched the flesh of my shoulder and jabbed the needle deep into the muscle. I grimaced as he slowly forced the thick goop through the needle and into the flesh, nearly an inch beneath the surface. The swelling sensation inside the muscle was nauseating. McKean withdrew the needle and Erwin rubbed a fresh alcohol swab over the skin. The eerie, over-full feeling in the flesh made sweat break out on my temples. My chin tightened in a suppressed gag reflex.

McKean observed me as if I were an experimental animal. "Not too severe a reaction," he observed.

"I've seen worse," Erwin concurred. She took a second syringe out of a package, drew the remainder of the vaccine from the test tube, and gave McKean his dose. He flinched at the injection, but quickly recovered.

I rubbed my shoulder, which had developed a new and annoying sensation. "This itches," I said.

"Be glad," McKean said. "It's a sign your body is reacting. The itch represents the first wave of white blood cells already coming in contact with the vaccine. They're responding by pumping out interleukins, histamines, prostaglandins, and a dozen other immune-system alarm signals. Your body is already on the attack. Welcome the itch, Fin. And the painful throbbing you will feel later. They are harbingers of a good immune response."

"So you think I'm already getting immune to Taleed's virus?"

"Theoretically. I'm sure the vaccine is stimulating a response. Let's hope it's not just against the adjuvant."

"How long before we know the answer?"

"A few days. A week."

"But the virus is already growing."

"It does have a bit of a head start." He turned to Erwin. "Do you suppose the government might be interested in producing this vaccine?"

Kay Erwin shifted uneasily, squeaking her moon suit. "I've just heard some unfortunate news on that subject."

"Unfortunate? What news?"

"I was on the phone to General Moralez at Fort Detrick before I came in here. I suggested this vaccine to him, but he has already committed their resources to the same approach you started with, producing the whole B7R subunit in bacterial culture."

McKean shook his head. "It might take weeks to get a culture growing, and months to produce enough of the product."

"They claim to have new ways of accelerating the process."

"I hope they do. Otherwise they're just stuck in the rut of routine. They've been making vaccines that way for years. What about the CDC? Any greater interest there?"

She shook her head and looked at McKean apologetically. "They've appointed a new head of what they're calling the Jihad Virus Group— Roger Devon. You know him, don't you?"

McKean's eyebrows raised high. "Of course I do. He's the former CEO of Virogen, one of ImCo's competitors and the harshest critic of my Congo River vaccine. He almost blocked its FDA approval. Even went before a panel of congressmen to testify against it. Said my Flag molecular handle would interfere with immunity—which it didn't."

Erwin nodded. "So you know exactly who he is. But did you know he had his own version of a Congo River vaccine under development when yours was approved? You wrecked his plans. He was on the brink of getting rich off Virogen's vaccine."

McKean smiled ironically. "Big-time scientists like Devon don't forget easily. Or forgive."

"Having talked with the man, I would say he wants to spit on the ground every time your name is mentioned."

McKean sighed. "But that's still no reason not to try our vaccine. You told him I would give him the formula, no strings attached, no patents filed, for the good of the nation?"

"I did," said Erwin. "But I think he would do anything to make sure you don't invent a second successful vaccine before he creates his first. He's got his entire vaccine division going almost directly opposite what you're doing. They're trying the classic procedure—viral attenuation."

"What!" McKean cried. "He's leading them backward in time, decades into the past. There are a dozen ways to make a vaccine more quickly."

"Attenuation?" I asked. "What's that?"

McKean explained for my benefit. "You grow the whole, live virus in cell culture, infecting human cells over and over again and picking out mutated viruses that grow more slowly. Eventually you get a strain of virus that grows extremely slowly, so the immune system has time to react before the virus spreads throughout the body."

"It seems like a good strategy," I said.

"But that's a much longer timeframe to develop the vaccine. Months before they'll have something attenuated enough to test in animals, and years before they would dare try it in humans. Roger Devon is taking his team out of the running, as far as I'm concerned. It's NIH syndrome at the CDC."

Erwin said, "He just can't stand that the synthetic vaccine is your idea, Peyton."

McKean shook his head. "How many researchers in his group?"

"A whole department. An entire building on the CDC campus. Sixty or seventy people."

"What a waste of manpower at a critical time," McKean muttered. "And what an exercise in futility. It's a matter of foolish pride, rather than scientific reasoning." He looked through the window wall. Janet stood watching the conversation with disbelief on her face. "And what have we've got?" He smiled at her affectionately. "Just you, Janet, with Robert and Beryl to help. That's what it comes down to."

She replied, "Suddenly, I feel awfully small."

"Don't worry," McKean said. "It doesn't take an army to make a synthetic vaccine. In fact—" he turned back to Erwin, "—while Janet carries out the second synthesis, Robert and Beryl will be idle part of the time when their assistance is not needed."

"That's true," Janet agreed. "We don't need three people for one synthesis procedure."

"I would like them to fill up that time with another experiment I've been considering. It might prove quite timely. I would like them to sequence another part of the viral DNA, the fourth invariant segment."

Janet looked surprised. "Why? There's no gene there, no protein encoded there, and no useful antigens. What would you expect to find?"

McKean smiled deviously. "I'm not willing to say at the moment. It's just a hunch, but please put it on a second-highest priority level for Robert and Beryl, just below helping you with the new synthesis. I would really like to see that DNA segment."

"Okay," she said. "If that's what you want."

"I do. Now, don't let us delay you any longer. Hurry back and get things moving!"

As Janet was leaving, she gave McKean a fragile smile as the elevator doors closed.

Kay Erwin cleaned up the syringes and swabs, and then left us to go to the airlock.

When the three of us were alone again, McKean gingerly touched the lump on his shoulder. "This is the first time I've ever been comforted by an irritation," he said.

PART FOUR

A NATIONAL EMERGENCY

CHAPTER 16

Jameela wandered off as McKean and I discussed our shots. Twenty minutes later she came back from her room, showered and looking radiant with her hair knotted behind her head. She had gotten a pair of silk pajamas from Kay Erwin and, even in the blue terrycloth bathrobe and slippers, managed to look elegant. She joined us at the small table in our room just as Hawkins arrived with dinners of pork roast, seasonal vegetables, mashed potatoes, and gravy. My appetite was thin, thanks to a dull aching pain in my shoulder and a queasy stomach. After just a few bites I gave up on the idea of eating and made small talk with Jameela and Peyton. Suddenly, McKean grabbed the remote and turned the volume up on the news again. It was a female CNN anchor, with a picture of the wrecked white truck beside her on the screen.

She said, "For more detail on how this incident started, we go to our local affiliate, Andrea Winchell, in a segment taped six hours earlier in the location where the chase originated."

The view shifted to Andrea with a microphone, standing near an aid car beside another stretch of wide-open freeway. The vehicle's lights were flashing, its rear doors were open and two crewmen were loading a stretcher into the back with a man strapped on it. Although the victim's face was scraped and bleeding, McKean recognized him immediately.

"Mike!"

"This is a very confused scene," said the reporter as the aid men pushed the stretcher inside. "There are three police cars here in addition to the aid car, and they're not willing to tell us much. But so far we've learned this incident may be linked to the smallpox scare in Washington State."

"They've got that right," said McKean.

"Unfortunately, the man who could tell us the most—" she nodded toward the aid car, "—is unconscious and is not expected to live. He apparently jumped from the van while it was moving at seventy miles per hour. Colorado State Trooper Dean Westfall saw it happen."

She held her microphone up in front of the Trooper.

"I think he jumped on purpose," Westfall said. "I was following the truck because its rear door was cracked open a bit, which is illegal. And suddenly both doors flew open, and this guy came flying out. I had to swerve to miss him. And I saw a number of other people in the van. I hit the lights and siren and stopped to assist the victim. But the truck kept rolling, so I called in a fugitive report while rendering assistance. He's pretty banged up. And lucky I didn't run over him."

The screen shifted back to the news anchor. "That footage was filmed six hours ago," she reiterated. "And that incident led to the chase, and the overturned truck situation we have been following. Back to that scene now, where Andrea is waiting."

The scene shifted to the truck location, where Winchell stood waiting with her microphone at the ready.

"Go ahead, Andrea," the anchor prompted.

Just as Winchell was about to speak, someone off-camera called to the reporter briefly. She took on a shocked expression and then turned to the camera again.

"The entire first-response team here, including our film crew, myself, and Officer Westfall, have been ordered to a Public Health Hospital in Grand Junction. We're to be quarantined and treated for smallpox exposure."

A man in an orange hazmat suit came from off-camera and began giving orders. "All right folks," he called. "Shut off the cameras. Let's wrap this up and get you all somewhere safe."

The reporter made a hasty sign-off and the program cut to the newsroom, where the flustered anchorwoman segued to a commercial break.

"Those poor people," Jameela said.

McKean didn't respond immediately. He slowly shook his head. "And poor Mike. I would have saved part of the vaccine if I knew he was still alive."

"Your cousin is a brave man," said Jameela.

"A hero," I agreed. "I'll bet he jumped out when he saw the police car."

"Quite possibly," McKean said. "I'll keep my fingers crossed for him. He's in a terrible fix. Even if he survives his injuries, he's still got to survive the virus. And if he gets a shot of the next batch of vaccine, it may be too late to do him any good. It looks like Mike is an unwilling guinea pig, the negative control on our little vaccine test."

"Negative control?" I puzzled.

"The experimental subject who gets a dose of the disease without any help from the vaccine. In animal studies, he would be the one expected to get sick and die while the vaccinated ones lived."

"Mike's got spunk," I said. "He'll make it."

"Let's hope so." McKean stroked his chin. "I've been thinking. One way to follow developments is to consider the vehicles we saw at the ranch. Mike's heroism has eliminated the white truck and most of the terrorists. We ourselves accounted for a black SUV and the Sheriff's car. The FBI got the black pickup truck. That leaves those three white passenger vans."

"Don't forget the other black SUV," I added.

"And Sheik Abdul-Ghazi's limousine," said Jameela.

***

An hour later, while Nurse Hawkins sweated in his tight-packed yellow isolation suit, clearing away our picked-over dinners, the computer at the on-duty station beeped. We went to the video screen, where Janet was waiting. "Dr. Holloman wants to talk with you again."

McKean hrumphed as Stuart Holloman plunked his hefty body in the lab chair.

"Hello Peyton," Holloman started coolly. "Seems you've beaten everyone to the punch again."

"How so?"

"The President contacted me on the phone. He's gotten wind of your synthetic vaccine through Dr. Erwin and her Fort Detrick connections."

"That makes sense," McKean replied.

"He wants us to scale up to the largest batch we can make. And now I find out Janet's already doing that."

"Right, again," McKean replied.

Holloman stared hard at McKean across cyberspace. "Didn't you think you should keep me informed?"

McKean's eyebrows rose as if his breach of company protocol hadn't dawned on him. "I assumed you wouldn't have a problem with that."

"You're right, I don't have a problem with the vaccine. But it makes me look stupid when the President of the United States calls and I'm in the dark about what you're doing."

"Good point," McKean admitted. "I hadn't thought it through."

Holloman paused like he was waiting for an apology. McKean didn't deliver. Holloman drummed his fingers on the bench top, squinting sharply from the screen. "Next time, try to remember who you work for, will you?" Veins had come up on his temples. "In fact, I'll handle the details of what gets done with your, er, ImCo's vaccine from here on out, is that understood?"

"Yes, it is." McKean sounded cool to the idea.

"Why do you have a problem clearing things with me?"

"Because getting your approval might slow down the decision-making process."

Holloman scowled harder. His bald cranium took on a red glow. He said in a level voice, "Let's just accept that risk. I don't want to be embarrassed again."

McKean seemed about to say more, but he kept his mouth shut.

"The President," Holloman went on, "asked me to keep things quiet, but go ahead and mass-produce the synthetic vaccine. He doesn't want a general alarm to go out just yet. But the virus appears to be getting out of control in Sumas. He wants to immunize everyone who gets exposed, using both the old vaccine and our new one. If this virus spreads, ultimately the entire population of the U.S. might need a dose."

"Yes, of course," McKean said. "Janet's already started our end of the deal."

"So I have just learned," Holloman muttered. "That's why I congratulated you on beating everyone to the punch. Are you sure she's making as much as possible?"

"Yes, I am. She's maxing out our production capability. If the President wants more, he can send some folks to look over her shoulder. They can start another syntheses, in parallel, at their own facilities. Meanwhile, our vaccine batch ought to handle immunizing up to ten-thousand people. That should be sufficient to get immunizations started where they're needed most."

"Yes, Peyton, I'll pass that along to the President. You've done an admirable job of planning ahead," he said grudgingly. "I'll make sure credit is given where credit is due when this is all over. For now, of course, not a word to anyone. The President is worried about a nationwide panic. Can I tell him he can count on you to keep your mouth shut?"

"Answer: yes."

"And your reporter friend there?"

"Yes," I said. "I'm getting too sick to type, anyway."

"I will be silent, also," Jameela added.

Holloman's face lightened when she leaned near enough to our computer's minicam to show up on his screen. "Well, well," he said. "Who is this lovely lady?"

McKean made the introductions.

"The pleasure is all mine," Holloman said. He exchanged some brief pleasantries with her. And then he became stern again. "Just remember, Peyton. I'm in charge from here on out. I don't want *anything* to happen before I hear about it."

He got up and walked away from the camera without a goodbye.

***

That evening we watched the stories evolve on the cable news channels.

One reporter appeared on the stone steps of the Public Health Hospital in Grand Junction, Colorado. He said, "We've just learned the identity of the man who threw himself from the back of the terrorists' van on the highway north of here. He is Mike Jenson, who disappeared from his home near Winthrop, Washington, several days ago in an incident that is under investigation as possibly linked to the smallpox outbreak in Sumas. Details are sketchy," he went on, "but FBI and Homeland Security personnel are said to be on the scene here in Grand Junction now. Nobody is saying very much."

When the news went to a commercial, Jameela said, "If Mike dies, he'll be the first martyr on our side."

McKean said, "I wish I had tried harder to get the authorities involved before we went to the ranch."

"Fuad had us stymied," I reminded him.

McKean thought a moment. "I can't believe Mike had the guts to throw himself out of a truck on the freeway."

"He has made a big difference twice already," Jameela said. "Things would be a lot worse if he hadn't led you to the Sheik in the first place. I would not have found out what the Sheik was doing if I hadn't seen you go into that building. Now he's sacrificed himself again to destroy the men he was riding with."

We talked for a while about subjects for which we had no answers, like the uncertainty of Mike's fate, injured and infected as he was.

McKean and Jameela started another chess match, but I felt a fresh wave of fever coming on and went to bed to ride it out.

CHAPTER 17

I woke the next morning shuddering with a full-blown fever that came and went in surges, as if the virus were unsure whether to claim me now or save me for later. McKean was watching the TV news, which reported Homeland Security raising the national terror threat level from orange to red in light of the Colorado incident. The entire town of Grand Junction was under smallpox quarantine.

Nurse Hawkins served breakfast about 8 AM, but I had no stomach for it beyond a few nibbles of fruit cocktail. I lay down again while the TV coverage repeated the stories from Winthrop and Grand Junction. But I only heard half of it, if that. A crushing headache kept my head on my pillow. Chills shook my entire body. Sweat drenched my forehead and the chest of my hospital gown. No one tried to deny that smallpox had me in its clutches.

McKean came to my bedside several times and made clinical speculations on the progress of the virus inside me, which I rebuffed as not being particularly interesting or helpful in my present condition. Jameela came as well, offering words of sympathy and encouragement. McKean remarked that he guessed his own temperature had increased, although not as much as mine. Dr. Zimmer came around with a thermometer and confirmed McKean's assessments, adding that he was worried that I might go into shock. He insisted both McKean and I should stick to our beds. That was easy for me.

McKean was much less affected. He sat up in bed and filled much of my waking time with discourses on viruses, medicines, and his peculiar observations on humanity and world events. But I spent most of my conscious moments wondering about my fate, which was unknowably linked to viruses and vaccines and white blood cells moving through my veins.

About 10 AM, the television delivered a new breaking story on CNN. The anchor, Connie Leong, popped my eyes wide open when she said, "We have videotape of Sheik Abdul-Ghazi, released earlier on a public access channel."

I propped myself up on two pillows and watched as a poor-quality videotape began playing in an inset box beside Leong. The now-familiar, sallow, bearded face of Sheik Abdul-Ghazi lectured sanctimoniously in Arabic in a shaky, hand-held camera shot. He sat in his black-and-white robes, cross-legged on a prayer rug on what appeared to be somebody's concrete basement floor, waving a lax hand with an index finger raised as he made his points.

Leong talked over the videotape. "Sheik Abdul-Ghazi is believed to be the mastermind behind the outbreaks of smallpox in Washington State and Colorado. Although he acknowledges the Colorado incident was a setback to his cause, he now calls upon his remaining jihadis not to despair, and to attack at the appointed times and places. Although he does not specify the nature of the attacks, our government sources clarify they are anticipating some form of biological attack at one or more population centers, using the smallpox organism now being referred to as the jihad virus."

Behind Leong's voice-over, the Sheik could be heard lecturing in harsh, emphatic Arabic. I watched his eyes. They wore the same sanctimonious glint as when he had overseen our inoculations.

The other side of the screen went to a tight shot of Leong's face. "While it is the policy of this station, in the interest of public security, not to air such calls to action, this case is different. Because this video-tape has already played several times on the public-access channel that first released it, and has aired on Arabic TV stations around the world, we assume any terrorists awaiting the Sheik's message have already received it.

"Reactions have been mixed in other nations. Islamic radical regimes have praised the Sheik; friendly Islamic governments have issued statements of support for the U.S.; Al Jazeera, the Arabic TV news station, issued the tape without comment.

"According to a preliminary translation by the Department of Home-land Security, the tape also calls for stepped up attacks on U.S. and Israeli interests around the world, and urges all Muslims to rise up once the Great U.S. Satan is stricken. At this point, what he means by 'stricken' is unclear."

The Sheik concluded his speech with a slight bow of his white-turbaned head. As Leong finished her voice-over, I stared at Abdul-Ghazi's sanctimonious expression. Behind those dark irises lay a mind of inestimable cruelty. I silently wished him a death as horrible as the one he intended for me.

The tape ended, and Connie Leong turned to a pundit seated at the side of her news desk. "Our Mideast correspondent and news analyst, Benjamin Lesser, has been following this situation closely. Can you please give our viewers some background on the Sheik and his followers?"

"Certainly, Connie. Sheik Ibrahim Abdul-Ghazi al-Kharifi is an extremely wealthy man, who comes from the tiny but rich Sultanate of Kharifa located on the south Arabian coast, between the Al Mahrah region of eastern Yemen, and the Dohai region of western Oman. Its long-reigning Sultan, Ahmed bin Husayn al-Kharifi, has several dozen wives, and is the father of Abdul-Ghazi and fifty-five siblings. The Sultanate has a single city of the same name, Kharifa, in a valley watered by several desert springs. Traditionally, the Kharifi sultans controlled the world's largest stands of frankincense trees, and operated an inland gold mine. The wealth from these assets enabled the current Sultan to build an oil pipeline from the Gulf Emirates, with a terminal on an offshore island in the Indian Ocean. Over the years, tariffs on the oil exports have made the Sultan an even richer man."

"What about terrorism?" Connie asked. "Has it surfaced there before?"

"No. Kharifa has recently been a quiet and placid place, with a docile population and a generally beneficent ruler. Nevertheless, Kharifa is somewhat of an anomaly in the modern world. The Sultan can trace his lineage to the Prophet Mohammad and has declared it is his God-given right to rule over his people. And his enforcement of Islamic law has been seen as among the strictest interpretations short of Afghanistan's Taliban, or al Qaeda itself. For example, a young woman who wore a thong swimsuit to a beach was stoned to death by his decree. Several state-authorized beheadings for major crimes have been reported. The entire judicial system is embodied by the Sultan alone. So, while his country remains a quiet place, he reserves for himself the ultimate authority over life and death."

"And his relationship with his radical son, Abdul-Ghazi?"

"Strained. The Sultan claims he has disowned his son, but the Sheik was seen coming and going at the Royal Kharifa Airport in recent months. So there is a little ambiguity there."

"Turning to the taped message," Leong said, "what do you make of it?"

"I'd say it probably was hastily made in the cellar of a safe-house somewhere in the U.S. It's unlikely Abdul-Ghazi could have gotten past airport security to leave the country."

"Good!" I exclaimed. "Then I can still hope to strangle his scrawny neck before I die!"

"In a related development," Leong said, turning to the camera again, "two men have been arrested in connection with the tape. They are the licensees who ran the public-access TV series that released the Sheik's tape. The program, entitled 'The Way of Jihad,' has long held radical Islamic sympathies. The two men have refused to cooperate with authorities regarding the origins of the videotape, citing their first amendment right to keep their sources confidential. They are currently being held in Federal jail on charges of aiding terrorism. Now, in other news—"

McKean picked up the remote beside his pillow and switched off the television.

"So, you'd like to choke the Sheik," he said to me.

"Damn right. I'm astonished anyone could think himself holy while calling for death and destruction. I'm allowing myself something I haven't allowed in years. I'm allowing myself to hate another human being with every ounce of me, every pulse of my heart, every breath, every bone, every muscle. I want to feel my fingers around his yellow-skinned, scraggly-bearded throat."

"Well!" Jameela interjected. "Such emotions!"

"He's trying to kill me," I said, "and a lot of other people too."

"I hope you get your chance, Fin," said McKean.

At noon, Nurse Hawkins brought lunch. I joined Jameela and Peyton McKean at the room's table, and while they ate with good appetites, I found myself hard-pressed to take down more than a few spoonsful of chicken-noodle soup.

Peyton McKean was in a philosophical mood.

"Why can't people see the commonality of most religions?" he murmured. "Especially the monotheistic religions of Judaism, Christianity, and Islam? I would go one step further and suggest that even the many gods of polytheistic religions could fit into the same scope, if their gods were equated to the angels and holy spirits of monotheistic religions. That done, then there would be precious little to divide one religion from another."

"And precious little to fight about," Jameela agreed.

"Good luck teaching that to the Sheik," I said.

"He's a hard case, I'll admit," said McKean. "But I remain optimistic that someday all religions will be reconciled. The simple means to do that is to tolerate other people's terms for the divine, and not fight over semantics. Most of the strife between religions boils down to words. If I can't accept your definition of God, or Jesus, or Holy Spirit, then we must go to war. It all could be solved by agreeing that each religion is entitled to its set of words for what is considered divine. Fighting only breaks out when someone takes an inflexible stance."

"So much trouble in the world," Jameela said, "all because of a few words."

"Exactly," McKean concurred. "And you are in a interesting position, Jameela, with one foot—so to speak—in each of two religions. I'd be interested to know how you see these things."

"I believe the jihadis are the biggest blasphemers of all," she replied.

"How so?"

"They are trying to tell Allah what he can and cannot do. They say God could not have a son like Jesus, because God is not human. But isn't God capable of all things? They say Allah wants to destroy all other religions. But where is the proof of that? Being all-powerful, Allah could sweep them away in a minute. But why has he not chosen to do so? I think Allah is happy to allow the religions to co-exist. So, why do jihadis see it differently? And how is it that Allah wishes women to be second-class citizens? If he created our bodies, why should we hide them under clothing and stay locked in our homes? That made sense in medieval times, when the streets were dangerous. But now they are safe in most places—except where radical Islamists rule! I think jihadis want Allah to live in the past, not in the present. But it is not their place to dictate to Allah."

"What can be done to change their minds?" I asked.

Peyton McKean shook his head. "I fear the world may have to endure as much as a thousand-year war with jihadis. They are as persistent as they are bull-headed. But decency will prevail. Their medieval views will always be a small minority, until at last they fade away."

"But a thousand years!" I remarked.

"Give or take a couple hundred."

"Are you sure our society can last that long?"

"Even the worst terrorist attacks are mere pinpricks on our culture. They haven't had much real impact, despite all the news-show talk to the contrary."

"But they'll have their way this time—if the virus gets out of control."

"That's a big 'if,' Fin. They're using a medieval virus to fight for a medieval cause against modern medicine."

"So far," I said, touching my sweat-drenched chest for emphasis, "I think the bad guys are winning this round."

***

About 1 PM, after Jameela went back to her own room, Kay Erwin appeared at our door in her pressure suit, announcing that she had come to check McKean's and my vital signs and change our wound dressings. Nurse Hawkins loomed behind her like a huge, yellow-plastic-covered Goliath.

Kay is a bit pinch-nosed. It's the only flaw in her otherwise solid prettiness. It gives her expression a hint of toughness and her voice a nasal sharpness. She was all business this time around, checking Peyton McKean's and my heart rates, blood pressures, reflexes, and temperatures.

My fever was one-hundred-and-one Fahrenheit. McKean's was just ninety-nine degrees. She made notes on our charts and then checked our wounds. Starting with me, she cut away the bandage on my left forearm. As she lifted the gauze, there was a general drawing in of breath. Hawkins' mild eyes widened in surprise. The infection had spread out from the edges of the stitched-up gash. Most of my forearm was a purplish-red mass of swollen flesh. Several dozen whitish spots surrounded the cut. Erwin counted them and noted them on my chart.

"Let's hope the vaccine is working faster than the virus," she said.

"Amen to that," I said, eyeing my arm with cold terror.

Erwin put her black-gloved hands on her yellow-plastic-covered hips, squeaking in her rubbery suit. "Now, don't get embarrassed, Fin, but I've got to inspect your whole body again for spots. You understand, don't you?"

"Of course," I muttered. "I think you're starting to like this. Go ahead."

She hesitated. "Er, Fin... I can't very well inspect you with your gown on."

I grudgingly rose to sit on the edge of my bed, untied my gown, and allowed Nurse Hawkins to take it. He put it in an incinerator bag.

Erwin went over me minutely. "You've got two pocks on your shoulder, and three on the right side of your chin. Turn over, Fin and lie down. All right. The only mark I see is one suspicious little swelling on your left butt cheek."

I closed my eyes, waiting for the moment to end. As she scrawled a note on my chart, a startled gasp announced another witness to my humiliation—Jameela!

She stood in the doorway, eyeing my naked butt. When our eyes met, she burst out laughing and turned to shield her eyes with a cupped hand.

"Is there anybody," I moaned, "who hasn't had a good look at my private parts?" My voice sounded whinier than I intended.

"Not a real good look," McKean said. He sat up to get a closer look at my butt-cheek blemish.

"That's enough," Erwin snapped at both of them. "I'm done. Fin, you can cover up—"

I pulled my sheet over me before she finished the sentence. Hawkins handed me a fresh gown and I put it on under the sheet.

Kay said, "Jameela, I'll check your vital signs in a moment. But I can see right now you're just fine."

Jameela uncovered her eyes and pointed down the hall. "I'll wait in my room."

She left us as Erwin began to examine McKean. His forearm was much less swollen than mine.

"Seven spots," she said after inspecting the wound. "You're better off than Fin. Now, let's have a look at the rest of you, please." As he undid his gown strings, I turned away. My curiosity went only so far.

Kay had counted a total of twenty-nine spots on me, but she found only seven on McKean, and all those on his forearm. She finished her notes and went down the hall to Jameela's room, her isolation suit swooshing. As Hawkins dressed my wound, I asked McKean, "How did you get so lucky? I'd swap my twenty-nine spots for your seven any day."

"The answer," McKean said, "is not a matter of luck. You and I and Jameela make a nice group of experimental subjects."

"How's that?"

"Our symptoms correspond to our vaccination histories. Jameela has had plenty of exposure. She should be showing signs by now. But she is the one who received a dose of Dr. Taleed's vaccine against this specific virus. She seems fully protected. I, who long ago received a dose of the old smallpox vaccine, am partially protected. You on the other hand, who never received any form of smallpox vaccination until two days ago—"

"Don't say it!" I interrupted. "Your cold academic detachment is *way* beyond irritating. Let me complete your lecture for you. I'm completely unprotected."

"Well stated, Fin. You're what's called an 'immunologically naïve subject'." He paused as if my desperate condition—and my humanity—were sinking into his too-intellectual consciousness. He added, "Regrettably."

I stared at the icy blue linoleum floor. "Will I die?"

"Perhaps we'll *both* die," he said. "It's too soon to be sure. It's up to the virus, really."

"That doesn't help much." A tremor came over me, so powerful and bone-rattling that I laid back on my pillows until it subsided. "Is Jameela really safe?" I asked.

"Answer: yes."

I closed my eyes and swooned into a feverish half-sleep.

CHAPTER 18

Both McKean and I went in and out of consciousness during the afternoon. Jameela visited us whenever we were lucid, but then retreated to her own room to read a thick book on Arabian horses that Kay Erwin had brought for her.

About 3 PM, I awoke from one of my swoons with McKean poking my shoulder.

"We've got a visitor on the video link," he said. "Janet Emerson's got the DNA analysis of that odd little corner of the viral genome."

I rose and followed McKean unsteadily, blinking away a crushing headache. Although McKean seemed less feverish than I, his thin face was pallid and his dark hair was matted on one side of his head. I knew my own appearance was far worse.

Janet sat at her desk with her white lab coat on. As we sat, she watched McKean's gaunt face with an expression of deep concern. When she looked at me, she gasped. "Oh Fin, you poor man! Do you feel as bad as you look?"

"Worse."

McKean picked up some sheets of paper from the duty-station printer. Pointing a lean finger the topmost, he asked, "Good sequence data?"

She nodded. "Excellent, although I'm still not quite sure what you're looking for."

McKean laid the sheets along the counter so they made a continuous trace of data that reminded me of four electrocardiogram lines drawn on graph paper. The horizontal traces ran the length of five sheets, one line drawn above the other. Each line recorded a series of upward blips from a flat baseline, so that each trace looked like a comb with many teeth missing. The arrangement of upward jutting teeth seemed random to me, but McKean eyed the traces with familiarity, running his finger over the peaks and flats. He mumbled to himself as he interpreted, several times voicing an excited "ah," or a mystified, "hmh." I sat by, bone weary but determined to see whatever McKean saw.

"You'll note," he said to me, "how no trace has a peak in the same position as any other trace." He moved from the left end of the chart toward the right, touching each peak with the tip of his long index finger.

"There's an A," he said, touching a peak on the top trace. "And then a C." He touched a peak on the bottom plot, and then on to the next peak, which was on the same line. "Another C." And then on to a peak on the second line. "And then a G. You will note, Fin, that the computer has printed the corresponding sequence along the bottom of the sheet, one letter for each of these peaks. The end result of the analysis is one long string of A's T's C's and G's across all five sheets. Do you see how a DNA sequencer works?"

"I see it," I said. "But it all looks pretty random to me."

"Oh, no," McKean said. "The order is not random at all. He eyed the alphabetic results carefully.

Janet watched his face closely, as did I. Jameela, attracted by McKean's bemused utterances, came to join us, putting a hand gently on my shoulder.

"Here!" McKean exclaimed after a moment. "This is what I was looking for." He ran his finger over a segment of lettering that seemed to please him greatly. A smile lit his callow, sweaty face. He took a black marking pen from his pocket and scribbled above one of the T's, making a tall vertical bar of black ink. Beside the T on the right was an A. He blackened the space above it as well, making another thick line and merging that side-to-side with the first to create a fat, vertical black bar. He skipped the next letter, which was a G, leaving the space above it white. But he scrawled another dark a bar above the next letter, another T. "All one has to do," he explained as he continued working his way along the sequence, "is to put a dark bar where there's an A or T, and leave the white space for a C or a G."

After a few more scribbles he sat back to survey his handiwork.

"It looks like a bar code," I said, surprised at how easily McKean had transformed one code into another. "Am I right?"

"Answer: yes." McKean grinned. "It is indeed a bar code. Just like you see in the supermarket. Undetectable to a scientist who's not in on the secret, because he is not looking for such a thing. But easy to create in DNA code and easy to decipher again, as you have just witnessed."

Janet looked mystified. "But what does it say?"

"Bar codes," McKean replied, "are nothing more than numbers, determined by the thickness and spacing of the lines. Now that I have created a series of thick and thin vertical lines, it is a simple matter to extract the numbers that the lines represent. Let's see..."

He studied the bars and slowly called out numbers as he proceeded along the sequence. "Zero, nine, one, one, zero, one. Yes indeed." He smiled brightly at Janet. "Now I'm sure."

"Sure of what?" She frowned, as perplexed as Jameela and I. "Do those numbers mean something to you?"

"They have meaning for all Americans," McKean replied. "September 11, 2001." He ran his finger over the entire sequence. "And there are more numbers here, all specified by a CIA operative and encoded in DNA by me."

"By you?" I asked. "You're saying you had a part in engineering a deadly virus?"

McKean shook his head. "Not the part that is deadly. But this short segment of identifying code? Yes indeed!"

"But," Janet interjected, "how could you possibly remember the numbers?"

"For most of this sequence," said McKean, "I haven't the foggiest recollection. But the 911 segment—" He tapped the left end of the bar code. "That bit is common to all the viruses we marked. It's not a number any American is likely to forget. We put it in as a quick check. The rest of the sequence has meaning only for the CIA officer who put me up to this project."

"But what were they planning to do with this?" I wondered.

"Unless I miss my guess," McKean said, "the rest of this number is a serial number, identifying the strain and origin of the virus. They were tagging smallpox with tracer numbers like the automobile identification numbers you see stamped on a car's chassis and engine block, to identify it if stolen. They had me make quite a few of these codes, hundreds, which I assume they used to tag different batches of smallpox virus. That way, the viruses could be traced without their possessors knowing there was a trace being done. Very ingenious. Typical of the CIA, wouldn't you say?"

"Now wait," I said. "The bad guys would get onto this, sooner or later. They would read the code themselves."

"They might read the DNA code," McKean smiled. "But it's meaningless to a virologist. It was slipped into a segment of DNA that is of little interest to scientists, one with no genes for surface proteins or key viral enzymes. So it seems to be only a few random, insignificant mutations. But from the CIA's perspective, it is a clear-cut way to trace the source of the organism. In fact, I plan to get in touch with my old CIA contacts and see if anyone at Fort Detrick has found this sequence yet. I'll bet they have—probably went straight for it. If not, then I'm sure they'll be quite interested to know of it."

Janet gazed in awe at McKean. "Then what?"

"Unless I miss my guess, they'll use this label to lead them back upstream until they find out who handed this virus to the Sheik. Iran, perhaps, or Iraq... or Russia. I can't decipher who received this particular strain of virus—it was my job to make the code, not deliver it. Making sure the tagged viruses ended up in research labs on the other side of the world was a job for CIA spooks, not me."

"But why would they want to give out samples of the smallpox virus to anyone?"

"It wasn't a matter of giving it out. There was a time when quite a few labs had legitimate access to smallpox virus for vaccine research. But the viruses they received from the World Health Organization's Infectious Disease Unit were suitably marked in anticipation of just such a day as this."

"Incredible," I said.

"No great feat, really," McKean said. "My part, that is. I just created the DNA segments with identifying codes at Fort Detrick. The CIA handled the toughest job. You don't arrange for a WHO lab to deliver bar-coded viruses, without some skill in the spy game."

There was little else to be said. Janet signed off to continue her vaccine synthesis. Jameela went to her room to continue reading about horses. And I went back to my bed to continue shivering and sweating. McKean stayed at the on-duty desk, making some phone calls.

***

In the afternoon, the television news reminded us that the President would address the nation at 6 PM. As the hour neared, McKean joined Jameela at our table, picking over a fresh dinner plate of turkey, mashed potatoes and gravy. I was too weak and nauseous to even make an effort. The most I could do was to prop myself up on my pillows while the CNN news crew made some introductory statements. Then the President appeared, sitting at his desk in the Oval Office with the Presidential and American flags behind him.

"My fellow citizens," he began. "I am here to tell you about a grave threat facing our nation. We have reason to believe that a terrorist group is planning biological attacks with smallpox within the borders of the United States. We are not sure exactly how or where they will strike, but we are sure the threat is real."

"So now everybody knows what we already knew," I said.

The President continued. "Law enforcement authorities in Washington State detected the plot, following leads from vigilant citizens near the town of Winthrop."

"That's us," McKean quipped. "And Cousin Mike."

"Authorities responded swiftly, but unfortunately not quickly enough to intercept all of the terrorists. There is reason to believe that a several small groups are loose within America's borders and are themselves infected with a new strain of smallpox, which they intend to spread to American citizens. The truck that carried many of them from the ranch at Winthrop was stopped in Colorado, and as you probably know, all the men aboard were killed. However, authorities are still seeking three white passenger vans that disappeared from the ranch at the same time, carrying an unknown number of terrorists.

"Earlier today, I directed the Department of Homeland Security to raise its Terror Threat Level warning from High to Extreme, Condition Red. And, because we do not yet know the terrorists' exact plan, I am requesting your help. I need every American citizen to do what he or she can do to bring this threat to an end, and to minimize its impact. To do this, I will need citizen cooperation on an unprecedented scale.

"I have, immediately prior to this broadcast, issued an executive order activating all state and federal law enforcement agencies, including the National Guard, to a state of maximal readiness to counter any activity of this group. But such an order, I realize, could have substantial economic repercussions."

"That's an understatement," McKean murmured.

"Our economy might be severely impacted if Americans were to shutter themselves in their homes. Therefore, I am asking the American people to go about their business as usual, despite the mobilization. I ask only that people avoid any unusual congregations, such as demonstrations, where terrorists might come in contact with them. On the other hand, it is important that people continue going about their normal activities. We must not allow a terror threat to shut down our businesses, schools, universities, shopping centers, movie theaters, grocery stores and other places where we carry out our daily activities. The economic impact of such a shutdown could be drastic. If the terrorists can bring America's economy to a halt, then they will win a victory in terms of hardship and job loss on a massive scale.

"On the positive side, we are certain that most of the terrorists have already been killed or captured, and the remainder cannot hold out forever. In fact, they cannot wait more than a few days. By infecting themselves, they have set a clock ticking. Their own infections will kill or disable them within the next several days. Any who survive and recover will lose their infectiousness. We can, and will, wait them out if they hide, or catch them if they attack. I have officials at all levels, both military and medical, prepared to counteract their plans. Hospitals and health clinics are being prepared as I speak, to treat and isolate any citizens who come in contact with infected persons. The next few days will be challenging, and the measures taken extremely complex, but we will prevail.

"I urge you not to purchase more or less than your normal amounts of supplies. What we need more than anything is business-as-usual."

"But what if people panic anyway?" I asked.

"I trust the American people to avoid panic buying," the President said, as if in answer to my question. "On the other hand, please support your local businesses. Don't stay at home. Buy groceries and medicines as you normally would, in normal quantities, and on your usual schedules. Go to school, attend the theater, attend religious services. Consciously make an effort to pursue those activities in your normal way, but remain extra vigilant at all times.

"Let me reassure you. Smallpox cannot be transmitted through municipal water supplies, food, or other goods. It is spread entirely by physical proximity or direct contact between people. The terrorists have been inoculated on their left forearms, so be on the watch for individuals with wounds or bandages. Report any suspicious persons to the police immediately. Bear in mind that, while many of these men are of Middle-Eastern descent, others come from all ethnic groups, so don't be watching for any one particular facial type."

"I have been assured that our nation's public health community is already on the highest state of alert. Local police precincts are assigning special bio-hazard teams to respond promptly. The Centers for Disease Control have instituted a readiness plan that prepares clinics to take in and isolate infected patients. There are no less than three major national institutions working on new vaccines to counteract the virus, including the National Institutes of Health, the CDC, and the U. S. Army Research Institute for Infectious Diseases at Fort Detrick, Maryland."

McKean snorted. "I hope the public is more reassured than I am, considering the buffoons who are trying to make those vaccines."

"Now, before concluding this announcement," the President said, "I would like to offer some very good news. Acting on information extracted from the terrorists captured in Winthrop, FBI agents today intercepted what was to have been a second truckload of terrorists at a westbound freeway rest area near Bismarck, North Dakota. None of the several dozen men on board the truck had been inoculated, and all have been taken into custody by the FBI and the Department of Homeland Security. We believe these men intended to become a second wave of virus carriers. All appear to be foreign nationals or American Islamic radicals. All will be imprisoned in our South Carolina interrogation facilities. In what I am sure is an extremely difficult time for all Americans, we have now had two great successes against those who would harm us. I expect more success soon."

He signed off with, "God bless you, and God bless America."

As a group of newscasters began a lengthy commentary, McKean turned the TV volume down.

"The terrorists still have the element of surprise," I said.

McKean nodded. "But the President's plan is a good one. And round three of this fight may be more important than rounds one and two, which he just described."

"Round three?"

"Stopping any outbreaks of smallpox before they spread uncontrollably. The experience in Sumas has been a mixed result. They may have it controlled, but only by expanding their ring of containment vaccinations with the old vaccine to the surrounding towns. Let's hope they can hold the line there. I hope the President's public health countermeasures are sufficient, and I hope the new vaccine-making efforts aren't awash in cronyism and political decision-making. If so, then the virus itself may have the last word."

"Why do you say that?"

"Dr. Taleed seemed confident he had engineered an extremely lethal organism. Presumably he tested it on human victims before this plan was hatched. If his jihad virus is substantially more virulent than the Bangladesh strain, then all bets are off on controlling its spread."

"Do you mean its spread within the individual?" I pointed to my bandaged arm. "Or between people?"

"Answer: both."

Throbbing pain under the bandage made me imagine the viruses consuming my flesh—*consuming me*—like a spreading terrorist army. I looked to McKean for some sign of commiseration, but he sat calmly with his eyes unfocussed and his expression placid as if he were pondering subjects infinitely far from our personal concerns.

I shook off a tremor. "How soon will we know if your vaccine is working?"

McKean raised one eyebrow and glanced at me. "Answer: unknown."

"What?"

"Immunity is not something that can be measured precisely, Fin. One can measure levels of antibodies in the bloodstream or cellular responses in a test tube, but protective immunity—" he sighed as if in awe of the concept, "—is an essence that's hard to measure. Only by surviving an infection can anyone truly demonstrate immunity. You and I are the crucial experiment, Fin. We are the laboratory animals. As we live or die, so go the fates of a great many people."

He lapsed into thoughtful silence, and I sank back on my pillows. My stomach was a pit of dread. My mind was a racing engine of horrific images: viruses, pocks, Taleed's gloating weasel face—and the jaundiced, hate-creased, sanctimonious face of Sheik Abdul-Ghazi.

CHAPTER 19

I dozed fitfully. After a while, Jameela went to her room for the night. McKean busied himself with reading. In a wakeful moment, I watched him highlight text in a scientific article with his yellow marker. I found myself getting irritated.

"Aren't you afraid of dying?" I asked him.

"I am afraid my vaccine won't work."

"What's the difference? You'll be dead if it doesn't work."

"My own death is trivial in the big scheme of things. But my vaccine may be all that stands between a great many people and death. I'll never forgive myself if I engineered it wrong. You saw the arbitrary process by which Janet and I constructed it. What if we made a bad call? What if a single amino acid change could have made it work better? That would be agony."

"But you'll be dead in that case."

"True. If I fail, then death will have its merits. It will release me from a vast sense of guilt."

"Guilt—?"

"Given time, I could create a hundred synthetic vaccines from different segments of the B7R protein. Given enough time, I'm sure I would find one that stimulates a maximal immune reaction. But time is not a luxury I can buy. I had my reasons for picking the amino acid sequence I chose—but I may have chosen wrong."

What little comfort I had drawn from McKean's track record with the

Congo River vaccine vanished. "You're that uncertain?"

"Answer: yes," McKean replied. "I am that uncertain." His gaunt, long face expressed more than a shadow of doubt. He turned away from me, laid the article on his night table, and put his head on his pillow. He turned off his reading light. Soon, his regular breathing told me was asleep.

A heavy feeling in my chest kept me awake for some time—a reaction to the pain of my swollen arm and fever chills creeping over my skin. I spent the night in alternating bouts of fitful sleep and insomnia.

By morning, a high fever had me solidly in its grip. I don't recall much that transpired that day, just vague images of McKean spending a lot of time flat on his back with fever; a chessboard, depleted of men, on a small table by his bed with the white king checkmated by a black knight and bishop; Jameela in a chair beside my bed, feeding me broth with a spoon; TV news showing a white van shot up and burned out on a freeway north of Portland with six jihadis dead inside. But mostly I remember fever, sweat, heat, chills, and a sense that Sheik Abdul-Ghazi had won. He had killed McKean and me, and we just didn't know it yet.

Kay Erwin appeared in her isolation suit to examine us. She checked my forearm, which had gone purple and was riddled with more spots than she cared to count—she made some notes on my chart and spoke to me. I recall her lips moving, but I didn't hear what she said.

The isolation ward seemed to me like Death Row. In my imagination, the long hall outside our door led only one place: the autopsy room. I sank deeper into a downward spiral of sweat, chills, and tremors.

Late the next day, Jameela shook me gently, waking me to the Six O'clock News.

"Federal officials," said the anchorman, "report a mixed reaction in cities across America. Most communities remain calm, but some have experienced rushes on food and other essential supplies. A few cities have experienced riots. The number of attacks by infected terrorists remains limited, but a series of incidents continues, striking terror wherever one occurs. The most disturbing report comes from San Francisco, where a crowded BART train was attacked last night. For more, we go to our affiliate there."

A reporter in an overcoat, positioned outside a BART station began, "Commuters aboard the train were assaulted by two men shouting *Allahu Akbar* and waving bloodied arms. According to witnesses, they moved through the length of the train, wiping the blood on people who had no way to escape them. When the train arrived at this station, they attempted to escape. One was subdued by transit police with tasers. The other was shot dead by city police summoned to the scene, as he attempted to escape in a white van. Public health officials have quarantined all commuters who were aboard the train as probable smallpox exposures. Authorities estimate the men may have contaminated as many as two hundred people."

The screen image returned to the anchorman at his desk with staff hustling in the background.

"Another incident occurred last night at the Capitol building in Olympia, Washington, where the State Legislature was meeting in an emergency session. We go there for a report."

An Olympia affiliate reporter with matching short Afro and black microphone ball stood in front of the floodlit Capitol Building.

"Details are sketchy," he said. "This is what we know so far. A young Caucasian man, possibly an infected terrorist, was shot in the entrance foyer of the Capitol Building as he tried to run past the security checkpoint. The man died at the scene after having possibly contaminated several Capitol guards. The rotunda entrance has been cordoned off for decontamination. A white passenger van being sought by police was found parked nearby with three other men inside, apparently already dead of the disease."

McKean, propped up by pillows, said, "Four more pawns taken off the chessboard."

Jameela was in a chair between the two beds. "It *is* like a giant chess match, isn't it?"

"With the fate of civilization in the balance," McKean replied.

I lay back and stared at the ceiling for a time, prostrated in a pool of sweat. It occurred to me that I would soon face the most ancient question asked by mankind. "What do you think happens after you die?" I mumbled.

"Don't talk like that, Fin," Jameela implored me.

McKean said, "I'll give the agnostic's reply. Answer: I don't know."

"Thanks for the comforting thought," I muttered. "Suppose the Sheik's right? Suppose Allah is guiding him, not us?"

"Fin!" McKean scoffed. "The fever has got you talking nonsense. The Sheik is all too human, and therefore subject to error. I'm confident his guiding principles are wrong. If there is a God who is the focus of good in the universe, then he must be on our side."

I shook my head. "But suppose God is as wrathful as Abdul-Ghazi says. Suppose the Sheik has his ear. We might burn in Hell for lack of faith in the right incarnation of God."

"I can't help you with that concern," McKean said.

"You should rest," said Jameela. "The fever has got you talking nonsense." She wiped my brow with a moist cloth. I closed my eyes and soon sank under the full weight of the infection.

Consciousness gave out completely. Time ceased to move. My only sensations were of heat and agonizing pain in every part of my body. My bones were tunnels of volcanic heat. Every muscle burned like a stream of fire. My skin crawled with clammy sweat and wave after wave of body-racking chills.

In the middle of this blind, dull agony, I sensed, more than saw, Nurse Hawkins bind my right forearm to a rigid armrest and place a needle catheter into a vein. Through this intravenous line—I was told later—I was fed fluids to keep me from sweating myself to death.

Beyond that, I have little memory of conscious thoughts or even my physical existence in a human body. Instead, I recall distorted echoes of voices half-heard, sounds indecipherable, as if there were disembodied spirits talking and moving around me. At times, the sounds were more dreamt than heard. And some of those dreams were nightmares.

In one fevered vision I lay on a stone ledge in a Mohammedan hell-scape lit by the glow of molten rock. Sulfurous flames lapped at every inch of my skin with scorching, agonizing heat. I looked up to see Jameela descending toward me as if bourn by a whirlwind. She was naked. Her long dark hair spiraled about her face and shoulders. Buffeted by the maelstrom, she tumbled helplessly in pirouettes over my head. She shrieked so shrilly and pitiably that rage overcame my immobility. I forced myself to rise and threw my disintegrating arms around her, trying to protect her, but beyond any hope of protecting. I felt myself melting into one-ness with her, uniting in eternal hellfire…

That I was comatose, that my agonies lasted more than two days, I was unaware. That medical personnel attended me in their isolation suits, I have no memory. That Jameela was near, leaning over me, soothing me, I only vaguely recall. Once, the haze lifted enough for me to sense her sitting beside me, holding my right hand in hers, and weeping softly.

All else was agony, sweat, and heat.

CHAPTER 20

I opened my eyes. Soft morning light came through the window of our room. I drew in a deep breath of cool hospital air. My fever had dissipated with the night. My heart, not longer palpitating, beat slowly and steadily.

Jameela was away and Peyton McKean was asleep. The ward was silent. The TV was off. The wall clock read 6:48. I lifted the bandage on my forearm. The pocks were changing from angry white points of pain to small dark scabs. The swelling and redness had subsided around the gash, which was almost healed. Someone had removed the stitches. I lifted the neck of my gown and glanced at my chest. The skin was clear. The rash hadn't spread.

"Hallelujah!" I exclaimed.

McKean sat up and eyed me groggily. "What?" he asked.

"Your vaccine worked!"

"Oh, yes," he replied. "It did work, didn't it?" He stretched and yawned.

I took a small hand mirror from my nightstand and inspected my face. I watched my own expression of relief grow as I verified that my face had been spared any more pockmarks other than the three on the right side of my chin, now scabbed over.

Jameela appeared at the door, wearing her silk pajamas and robe. Her hair was tousled and she looked sleepy-faced. "Don't worry, Fin," she smiled. "You're still handsome."

I put the mirror back in its place. Jameela came near.

"You suffered so." She lifted my good hand and kissed my fingers. We looked into each other's faces like comrades reuniting after far-flung, desperate adventures.

Dr. Zimmer came squeaking into the room in his moon suit. He took my pulse. "Sixty-five," he said. "Normal." He cut away the bandage and examined my arm, nodding positively. "How are you feeling, Fin?"

"Fine," I replied. "Although that might be an overstatement."

"Good," he said. "You should be getting a clean bill of health soon, along with Jameela and Dr. McKean. Everyone is coming along great."

"Except for this damnable lethargy," McKean muttered.

"That's understandable," said Zimmer. "You've been through four days of fever."

"Four days!" I exclaimed. "Has it really been that long?"

"Yes," Zimmer said, his eyes no longer wary. "You've been seriously ill, Fin, more so than Peyton, but things are looking up now."

McKean raised an index finger. "It seems our little experiment had the expected outcome. Jameela was fully protected by Taleed's vaccine. I myself represented an individual with partial immunity to smallpox, thanks to my vaccination years ago with the old vaccine. You, on the other hand, were the most susceptible of the three of us. Your disease was the most profound. I half expected you to die, Fin. I am sure a man of lesser constitution would have."

"I— I'm flattered, I guess."

"On the other hand," Zimmer interjected, "we've measured the antibodies in each of your bloodstreams. You, Fin, are now producing more protective antibodies than anyone."

McKean nodded. "Such are the vagaries the immune response. It's precisely because you had such a serious infection that you now are the most immune. The body reacts strongly to strong attacks."

Zimmer scribbled a note on my chart and then left us.

Drained of strength by my long fever, I lapsed into fitful sleep through the morning. Eventually I awoke fully at the sound of Jameela's voice.

"Fin!" she whispered urgently. I opened my eyes and found her leaning close. I sat up and blinked at her groggily.

"I must say goodbye," she said in a stricken tone. "They are taking me away."

I swung my legs over the side of the bed and stood shakily, facing Jameela and Nurse Hawkins, who hovered just over her shoulder in his overstuffed pressure suit, observing me curiously with his mild dark eyes.

A man's cheerful voice came through the intercom out in the hall, "Good morning, Fin." Outside the glass wall I spotted Vince Nagumo in his blue suit. He said, "I'm here to escort Ms. Noori to our offices for some questions and… a little time in our custody."

"Custody!" I growled, still trying to regain full consciousness. I followed Jameela and Hawkins out to the window wall. "I won't let you take her."

"Won't?" Nagumo chuckled. "You don't look like you're in any shape to—"

"That's enough!" I shouted. To my less-than wakeful brain, Nagumo and his over-friendly smile suddenly seemed as evil as the Sheik. Without a fully conscious thought, I pushed Hawkins away from Jameela. He didn't budge much. On the counter of the nursing station, I spotted the scissors Zimmer had used to cut away the dressing from my arm. I snatched them up and pointed them menacingly at Hawkins.

"If you try to take her," I growled, "I'll cut your suit open."

Hawkins took a step toward me, his eyes no longer mild. He stared at me hard, suddenly much more like a football lineman than a nurse.

I held my ground and waved the scissors at him. "You want a case of smallpox?"

That put a little fear into Hawkins' eyes. He stepped back and raised a hand to parry any move I made with the scissors.

Jameela intervened by stepping between us. "Fin, no. I will go with them. I only wanted to say goodbye."

I lowered the scissors.

"Besides," McKean called from his bed, "it wouldn't do to get arrested for assaulting a man with a blunt instrument."

I looked at the scissors. They were the kind with bulbous ends to avoid flesh cuts while snipping gauze. I put them back on the counter.

"That's better," said Nagumo.

Hawkins sigh with relief. Then he said, "You best git yo' ass back in bed."

He looked down and behind me, and I followed his gaze. The back ties of my gown were undone and my butt was in plain view. I clutched the gown to cover myself and backed away into the room.

McKean chuckled as I got back in bed. "Anyway," he said, "Dr. Erwin's about to declare this ward free of smallpox. We're all healthy again. You couldn't infect him if you wanted to."

I called out to Nagumo. "I am sure Jameela is completely innocent. I'll testify—"

"I'll keep that in mind," he replied. "Don't be too upset. She's only being held as a witness. She's not charged with anything right now."

"I want to hear about it immediately if she is," I fumed. "Do you understand?"

"Yes, sir." A wise-guy smile rippled on Nagumo's mouth. "We'll keep you informed." He turned to Jameela and motioned toward the airlock. "Come on, Ms. Noori. We'd better get going."

"Where to?" I asked as Hawkins led her down the hall.

"The Federal Building," Nagumo answered. "She'll be held there in very comfortable quarters."

I tied my gown and put on my blue bathrobe while Jameela went through the decontamination shower and dressed. She reappeared outside the glass wall in the riding outfit she had worn when we escaped the ranch, freshly laundered and pressed. I went to the window and she came to stand opposite me near the speaker. Nagumo waited near the elevator.

She looked at me fondly. "I have enjoyed getting to know you, Fin Morton."

"I hope I didn't offend you too much with whatever I said in my fever."

She smiled. "You are a romantic man. You spoke your heart."

"Miss Noori?" Nagumo called.

"I must go," she said. "I will miss you."

"Don't worry," I said. "I'll come and find you as soon as I get out."

"Miss Noori?" Nagumo called more insistently, waving her to the elevator.

She left me at the wall and went to join him. We looked at each other one last time as the elevator doors closed.

Feeling morose, I wandered back into the room. McKean watched me curiously.

I sighed. "I wish there were more I could do."

McKean started reading another medical journal, but his gaze moved between the page and me as if the article were not quite compelling enough to make him ignore my emotional state.

I sat down on my bed, my shoulders slumping. "I'm afraid I'll never see her again."

"She's a remarkable young woman," McKean mused. "We'd be dead a couple of times if she hadn't been there."

"She's a pretty good shot with a can of Pringles," I said. "Remember the car chase?"

"Of course, Fin. And it strikes me she is lucky to have you to look out for her. I've noticed something about you, my friend, over the course of the last few days."

"What's that?"

"You are a very caring fellow."

"Caring, huh?" I wasn't exactly sure what he meant.

"Some people care deeply about other people, and about right and wrong. I see you're one of those, Fin, and I am proud to know you. Jameela should be glad."

"Thanks, but I'm feeling just a little useless right now."

"You'll find a way to help her. I'm sure of that."

"I'd go after her right now, if I weren't stuck in here."

McKean paused to make yellow mark in the journal. "That won't be an issue much longer. I anticipate we'll be free within the hour. Kay Erwin is meeting with the hospital's medical board as we speak. She proposes to lift our quarantine, based on our recovery and our impressive antibody levels. I am sure the board will agree. I've already called my wife. She and my son will be here soon to pick me up. I would be packing my toothbrush right now, except I want to finish this article."

"We can leave that soon?" I could hardly believe what he was saying.

"Um hmm," he murmured absentmindedly, his eyes playing over a data graph. "We've done our service as guinea pigs and we're on the way to full recovery. After Kay's meeting, we can be gone as quickly as they bring our street clothes."

"I'm going straight after Jameela," I said.

McKean smiled. "I foresee much time spent in bureaucrats' offices."

PART FIVE

ATTACK AND COUNTERATTACK

CHAPTER 21

Within two hours, Kay Erwin signed our release papers. An orderly brought our clothes to the decontamination chamber. I showered and dressed and went out, stopping briefly to say goodbye to McKean at the window wall. He was up and about, having finished his reading. As I headed to the elevator, the doors opened and McKean's wife and son stepped out, Sean rushing ahead of his mother. Father and son reunited at the window wall, placing their hands together through the glass as before.

"I got a sore shoulder," Sean said. "They gave me a shot of your vaccine, and it hurts!"

McKean smiled. "But it will keep you from getting sick. That's a pretty good deal, right?"

"Yep."

McKean broke into a grin. The elevator doors closed as the family chatted at the window.

I made my way out through the hospital's main entrance and gladly took the sunshine of a clear Seattle morning. I walked quickly to the hospital's parking garage and reclaimed my Mustang. I was pleased to find her washed and detailed. When I got in, I noticed a faint aroma of disinfectant, but the blown-out side window provided more than adequate ventilation. The punctured front windshield was patched with duct tape.

I drove out onto the streets of Seattle, jazzed at the sight of bustling lunchtime crowds. I heard people conversing at street corners, saw them going about their business without fear. Joy filled me nearly to bursting. But I still had a serious matter to deal with. I drove to the Federal Building, parked on a nearby Diamond Parking lot, and put twenty dollars into the pay machine—enough money to last all night if necessary. Then I hurried inside to start my quest for Jameela.

I took an elevator to the floor where the FBI's Regional Directorate was located. Nagumo's office was at the end of a hallway paneled in honey oak. Inside a scalloped glass door, his receptionist, a bleach-blond middle-aged lady, sat behind an oak bureau wall with scalloped glass sliding panels that could be closed and locked. No, she said, she couldn't tell me when I could see her boss. And ditto for his witness, Jameela Noori. She directed me to have a seat in the small waiting room outside her windowed bastion.

I sat on a worn old taupe couch, idly pawing the magazines piled on the coffee table. I went through the motions of reading about movie stars as the wall clock, a formerly modern one with dark brass hands mounted directly on the wood of the wall, moved slowly past two, then three, then four o'clock. My stomach growled. I groaned when one or another of my joints throbbed with a dull echo of my fever. I realized the disease had ravaged me more than I wanted to acknowledge. Weariness added to the frustration of my continuing neglect by Nagumo and his receptionist. I inquired at the reception window regularly, but was told repeatedly, "No. They're not ready for you to see her yet."

As I sat with little to occupy my thoughts, an image recurred in my mind—that moment on the North Cascades Highway when I had looked in the Mustang's mirror and saw Jameela's eyes, so wide, frightened, beautiful, and brave, framed by her dark hair blowing in the wind. In that instant when our eyes met, I had felt a timeless connection, as if I were looking back two millennia to glimpse Cleopatra's regal, tragic beauty.

Something had occurred in that instant, on that highway, in those desperate circumstances, that now tore at my heart.

As the wall clock neared 5 PM, the receptionist made noises with her purse that suggested she was about to leave. I cursed under my breath, *"I'm not going to let the federal bureaucracy have you, Jameela!"*

Frustration turned to rage. Rationality fled. I stalked to the window and smashed my fist down on the ledge. *"Right now!"* I demanded in a madman's voice. Blondie had fished some keys out of her bag. She dropped them back in and stared at me with wide, pale blue eyes, but said nothing.

"Did you hear me?" I smashed my fist on the ledge again. A flowerpot of primroses jumped off the edge and smashed on the floor. Terra cotta shards and potting soil scattered across the carpet.

"Sir," she said harshly. "You can't—"

"Yes, I can!" I shouted. "I'm going to see her right now or there'll be hell to pay." I smashed my fist down harder and the ledge snapped in two like a board in a karate demonstration. The halves tumbled to the floor and one landed on my foot. A jolt of pain shot from my toes to the top of my head. I bellowed in a rage and kicked the board across the waiting room. When I turned to the secretary again, her right hand was under her desk. She was pressing a button to summon help. *"Go on!"* I shouted. *"You can put me in a cell right along with Jameela!"*

As soon as I had said it, I thought better. The last thing Jameela and I needed was to be jailed separately. Then, I would be no help to her at all. My best choice was obvious. I wheeled and went to the hallway door. As I threw it open, an alarm bell went off somewhere down the hall. I turned in the doorway and pointed a finger at Blondie, who was peeping over the bureau top. "I'll be back," I growled. Then I slammed the glass door, putting a crack in it, and rushed to the elevator. Fortunately, it arrived quickly, and empty. I went down, hurried out onto the street, and all but ran to my car.

I drove home, muttering that my vigil had been a waste of time, anyway. I tromped up the stairs to my apartment, puffing from the unaccustomed exercise after my long bed-ridden confinement.

Penny Worthe was waiting at our mutual landing. She was dressed in a blue skirt suit, white silk blouse, white hose and incongruous silver-and-lime-green jogging shoes. Her mousy brown hair was pulled back in a bun. She had probably just gotten home from work and paused when she heard me coming. She looked me over with a quizzical expression.

"Hi, Penny," I mumbled.

"You're not infectious, are you, Fin?"

"No. Not anymore."

"I was so worried about you! You were on the news, you know."

"No. I didn't."

"That isolation place sounds scary."

"It is—was." I unlocked my door and opened it.

"I got the Super to loan me a spare key," she said. "I let myself in and watered your plants."

"Thanks. I guess I expected them to be dead."

"No. They're fine."

I went in and closed the door. I shambled to my loft bed, shedding clothing onto the floor along the way. I climbed the ladder and flung myself down on the mattress naked, planning to pass out as quickly as possible. I stared at the ceiling, by degrees admitting to myself that my chances of seeing Jameela Noori again hinged on people over whom I had no influence.

Eventually, my eyelids came down like curtains. I fell into an exhausted sleep.

A short time later, loud thumping jolted my eyelids open in the evening darkness. Someone was pounding on my apartment door. I climbed down from my loft bed, slipped on the T-shirt and boxers I had shed on the floor, and then went to the door.

"Who is it?"

"Penny."

I opened the door and found her standing there in the frumpy, quilted, pink housecoat and fuzzy pink slippers she habitually wears. She clutched the housecoat together at the neck.

"Have you heard?" she asked excitedly.

"Heard what?"

She flew past me and went for the TV remote on the coffee table, navigating the dark room like an echolocating bat.

"Channel 44," she said, switching on the television and plunking down on the couch.

Irritated, I closed the door, went to the couch, and sat down beside her. "Heard what?" I repeated.

"Just listen!"

A combat-helmeted reporter stood, floodlit against a dark sky, with streams of tracer fire arcing above him into the night. Covering his earpiece with one hand and holding his microphone near his mouth with the other, he hollered over the rumble of bomb detonations in the background.

"This is Jerald Rivers reporting from the Sultanate of Kharifa." Beyond him, red cordite flashes silhouetted a mountainous horizon.

"I am embedded with a U.S. Marine expeditionary force that is in action here, reacting on a massive scale to information tracing the DNA of the jihad virus to this small country on the Arabian Peninsula. Air strikes are pounding the hills around me. A full-scale invasion is underway by air, land, and sea. Somewhere offshore lies a task force including the aircraft carrier Kittyhawk and several dozen support and assault ships."

Three transport helicopters woofed loudly overhead, silhouetted black against red smoke and tracer fire and moving toward a distant city, which could be seen by the glow of several burning buildings.

"Kharifa has only a small military force," the reporter continued breathlessly, shouting over the noise of the chopper blades, "but that force has been under assault by B-2 stealth bombers and cruise missiles since just after nightfall, about six hours ago. I came ashore with an amphibious force of Marines, and now a wave of troops is going in on helicopter gunships. This is the second flight of transport helicopters we've seen heading for the capital in the last fifteen minutes. The Marines are using overwhelming force. This tiny sultanate's defenses are expected to fall by dawn, which is not far off.

"A major objective is the only hospital here, the Saqadat Hospital and Research Center near the middle of the capital. It is there that the original stock of smallpox virus used to produce the jihad virus, is said to be housed. Back to you, Heidi."

The scene segued to an Atlanta news desk. "Recapping," said a red-headed anchorwoman. "Government researchers used DNA evidence to trace the source of the jihad virus to a sample given to Saqadat Hospital for vaccine research purposes. Our sources tell us there was a time when Kharifa was considered friendly to the U.S. and such laboratory work with smallpox was viewed positively."

"A prime target of tonight's invasion is the ultra-modern Kharifa Medical Research Institute, located in Saqadat Hospital. We take you there now, where our Mariah Brahmaputra is embedded with the troops. Mariah?"

A dark-haired woman stood with microphone to mouth as soldiers in dark-green rubber combat suits with hoods and gas masks moved past her into the front doors of the hospital. She held her own gas mask and hood under one arm. "Good evening," she said. "Actually it's almost dawn here in Kharifa. The troops behind me are storming the hospital, where resistance has so far been, well, nonexistent. I am told that the objective is to seize and destroy anything related to biological weapons and to capture the head of the institute, a Dr. Ibrahim Taleed, who is rumored to have returned here just yesterday. The troops plan to destroy any biological agents with chemical disinfectants, confiscate micro-biological equipment, and leave nothing of Dr. Taleed's institute but empty rooms."

She turned to watch the action behind her. Squads of soldiers with assault rifles moved unopposed into a new looking five-story flat roofed research laboratory with Arabic lettering above the main entry.

The reporter turned to face the camera again. "It appears the situation here is well in hand. Back to you, Atlanta."

The frame shifted back to the anchor desk again. "Thank you, Mariah," said Heidi. "We have more, regarding the link between the jihad virus and the Institute. For that, we take you to Fort Detrick, Maryland, where reporters caught up with General Vincent Moralez of the U.S. Army's Biological Warfare Division earlier today."

The scene shifted to a marble staircase outside a government building, where a uniformed general was surrounded by reporters. One asked, "Tell us, General, about the DNA code that enabled you to identify the source of the virus. How was it discovered and by whom?"

"Sorry," the General replied. "That's classified information. If I told you, I would have to shoot you." Smiling at his own chestnut, the general walked away. The reporter turned to face the camera. "Apparently that's all we're going to get from military sources, an acknowledgement that a DNA code was involved in the identification of the virus, but no further detail."

I murmured, "So Peyton McKean has once again been passed over where credit is due."

As the broadcast paused for a commercial break, Penny asked, "Are you hungry Fin?"

"I hadn't thought about it, but, yeah, now that you mention it."

She bustled across the hall and came back with a New York steak about the size of Manhattan. Acting on my instructions, she cooked it bloody rare and dished it up with broccoli and potatoes and gravy. I sat at the kitchenette counter and gulped it all down in big bites, even though I would have guessed my appetite could be satisfied by a cup of chicken soup. Afterwards, I flung myself on the couch like a python curling up to digest a water buffalo.

The TV sound had been down while I ate, but now Penny sat down on the other end of the couch, grabbed the remote from the coffee table, and turned the volume up.

Another a reporter with microphone was standing in front of an airport drop-off zone that looked distinctly American.

"Recapping," he said, "a man identified as Sheik Abdul-Ghazi was arrested here today at Chicago's O'Hare International Airport while trying to board a plane for Yemen."

"Abdul-Ghazi's the man who infected you, right?" Penny asked.

"Yeah."

The scene changed to a shot of another reporter standing at the side of a courthouse corridor, as armed bailiffs brought a man past the camera, one officer grasping each of the man's elbows. The man was handcuffed and in an orange prisoner's outfit. He had dark eyebrows and a dark stubble on his recently pig-shaved scalp, as well as on his bare cheeks and chin. The reporter did a voice over. "The Sheik was captured at the airport this morning while checking in under an assumed name."

"The Sheik?" I asked. "That's not him."

"You're sure?"

"I'll never forget his face. That man's skin isn't yellow enough. No dark circles around his eyes. Not enough hate lines on his forehead."

The man sneered at the cameras as he was led past.

"Teeth are too straight," I said. "No way that's him."

"So who have they got?"

"One of his henchmen? A decoy? I don't know."

Penny turned the sound down as another commercial started, and began questioning me about everything that had happened to me. She dragged details out of me about the ranch, and about what the fever was like. She wanted to see the scabs on my arm. She made sympathetic noises about them, crowding me on the couch and gabbling over me like a pink Mother Goose from hell, until I stood up suddenly.

"Goodnight, Penny," I said.

"Hmm?" she responded.

"Goodnight!" I went to the door and opened it.

As she walked out she said, "If there's anything you need…"

"Thanks." I closed the door after her.

I went to the phone and called Nagumo's office, hoping I could find someone there after-hours to tell they had the wrong man. Instead, I ended up listening to a "your call is important to us" message interspersed with muzak for ten minutes.

I hung up, turned off the lights and TV, and climbed back into bed. I lay awake for a while, wondering where Sheik Abdul-Ghazi had gotten to.

***

The next morning I awoke rested and feeling a lot healthier. I opened my blinds and got an eyeful of clear blue sky above the buildings across the street, and the Space Needle's saucer deck looming above. The sun was radiant. I moved around the bright spaces of my apartment with the joy of redeemed life in me. The TV buzzed about the overnight capture of Kharifa, and recanted the story of the Sheik's capture. While I plied my espresso machine for some caffeine, the captured man was described as an accomplice of the Sheik, but Abdul-Ghazi himself remained at large. Then I learned, from a report filed in Washington D.C., that the CDC and the Department of Homeland Security had distributed ImCo's synthetic vaccine nationwide within twenty-four hours, and a mass immunization program was being readied. The contagion at Sumas had been halted within a ten-mile radius of town after claiming only 26 victims. Those exposed at Grand Junction, and all other Sumas residents, had already received doses of the new vaccine.

I put on sweats and sneakers and went to a corner restaurant and ate a big breakfast of eggs, bacon, hashed browns, toast, and cantaloupe, while their TV aired a series of positive news reports from around the nation. Terrorists arrested. Terrorists shot dead. Their attacks in Olympia and San Francisco countered by quick quarantines and the new vaccine.

But all the good news didn't temper my concern for Jameela. After breakfast, I went home and called the FBI offices again. I reached Nagumo's secretary and extracted a vain promise from her, that she would call me with any news of Jameela's situation. Meanwhile, the newscast on my TV showed a scene in San Francisco, where people from the BART incident were lined up to receive the synthetic vaccine.

At a loss as to what else I could do, I sat down at my computer nook and began fleshing out my own all-but-forgotten news article. I paused when the TV coverage switched to Olympia, where state congressmen and women were lined up in the foyer of the Capitol building to receive their inoculations.

I got a phone call just past noon from that newbie newspaper reporter, Melinda Coury.

"How *are* you, Fin?" she said in her hard R-ed Northwest accent. "I heard you have been through some exciting times."

"You've got that right," I said, at the same time realizing my list of eligible females no longer included Melinda, having shrunk to just one person. "I've seen a lot more excitement than I ever want to see again."

"We should get together and talk about it, Fin. Over coffee after the press conference?"

"What press conference?"

"At ImCo. Today. In an hour."

"I hadn't heard about it."

"We just got the e-mail a few minutes ago. Very last-minute. I'm about to rush out the door."

"Thanks," I said. "Me too."

CHAPTER 22

I got off the phone and into high gear. I shed my sweats, showered, shaved, and dressed within minutes. I went out and hurried across the street to my car, and drove downtown. I parked across the street from the ImCo building at the end of a row of satellite vans, went and signed in at the front desk, hurried to the first floor auditorium and settled into a chair in the last row with my usual timing—right at the appointed minute. A glance around the room showed me the news from Seattle wasn't being neglected any more—at least not news from ImCo. A mob of television and print journalists filled the place, seated shoulder-to-shoulder. A dozen cameras crowded the sides and back of the place. A forest of microphones jammed the podium. News of the jihad virus was prime-time, headline stuff.

Kay Erwin was seated in the front row, but not the master of ceremonies at this show. She looked around and gave me smile and a thumbs-up. I waved back. She was off my eligible females list, too, and for more than one reason.

"Well, I'll be... Fin Morton!" Cameron Phipps called out from one row in front of me. His eyebrows rose almost to the top of his high ebony forehead. He grinned a wide, toothy grin, and reached out and shook my hand with one of his thick paws. "I heard you were in the hospital with this disease."

"Yeah," I said. "It wasn't much fun."

"You're lucky to be alive," he said, while surreptitiously wiping his hand on a pant leg. "You're not contagious, are you? I just got my shots."

"Just look at this crowd," I said. "It didn't take the national media long to find out where the action is."

"Eee-nternational meedia," remarked my neighbor on the right, a tall blond fellow. "Eet's alvays thees vay vhen someting beeg happens. Vee all catch the next flight from vherever the last beeg event vas. I've chust now come from Japan, ver der vas a volcanic erooption."

"Oh," I said. "I wasn't aware of one."

"Many people killed."

"And yet you came here."

"I go vhere I am assigned." He pointed to his press pass. It read LARS ALMASSEN - OSLO TIMES.

Our conversation was cut short when an ImCo functionary, a young, tidy, dark-haired buck in a black pinstriped business suit, took the podium to announce Stuart Holloman. While the man dished the expected chatter about the eminence of his boss, I studied the podium's round emblem of polished brass. In the center was a large, stylized, thick letter I, and the words "Immune Corporation" circled the edge. Below it on the podium was a line of smaller brass letters that I could barely see. I craned my neck to read them over the sea of heads in front of me. *Toward a healthy...* I stood momentarily to read it all. *Toward a healthy return on investment.*

I sat down and pulled out my note pad as the eminent Dr. Holloman began with a few statements regarding the danger still posed by the jihad virus. He was puffed up like a bantam rooster, his pink shirt and gold tie almost bursting out of his buttoned gray suit.

"I am proud," he stated the obvious, "to tell you ImCo's scientists have made progress even beyond my high expectations of them. Three days ago, the President of the United States personally asked me to produce 100,000 doses of our synthetic vaccine. I assured him ImCo would do so, and today I am happy to announce that we delivered the full 100,000 doses and we're finishing 100,000 more. Not only that, but I've passed on to the President and the Centers for Disease Control our formula for the vaccine."

"He means Peyton McKean's formula," I whispered to Cameron Phipps.

Holloman went on. "The President is gearing up government labs to produce hundreds of millions of doses before the virus has any further chance to spread. Our investors need not worry about us giving this one away, however. The President promised me Congress will approve payments that will net this company's investors almost a billion dollars."

He then summoned another man in a pinstriped suit to the podium—the Undersecretary of Homeland Defense, to whom he ceremonially handed a vial of vaccine while cameras flashed. "Undersecretary Smith," Holloman said, "will personally carry this vial of vaccine to Washington D.C. to immunize the President himself."

The Undersecretary took the podium and praised Holloman, vowing that every man, woman and child in the United States who wanted a dose of the vaccine would get one. "They tell me you have modestly resisted naming the Congo River vaccine after yourself," he said to Holloman. "Perhaps you'll consent to calling this one the Holloman Vaccine?"

Holloman smiled with feigned humility.

I looked around for Peyton McKean and Janet Emerson but didn't find them, or any other recognizable ImCo personnel other than Stuart Holloman and his dark-haired sycophant. I took some half-hearted notes, but the story didn't interest me that much. There were plenty of pressmen and women to carry the details of Holloman's triumph to the world. I realized I wouldn't need to bother.

After the Undersecretary finished, Holloman took the podium again. He droned on about his role, neglecting to mention anyone else by name. Eventually I got irritated at his studious lack of reference to the two people who had created the very thing for which he now took credit.

"He's leaving out the key players in all this," I whispered to my Scandinavian neighbor.

The Osloite's response was to put an index finger to his lips.

I fumed as I watched my neighbors complacently write down every word of doggerel from Holloman, while the television cameras mindlessly took in every word and gesture. I raised my hand. Holloman glanced my way but didn't acknowledge me. "I am very proud," he continued, "of the hard work and dedication of a large staff too numerous to mention by name. I couldn't have done it without their help."

"I've had enough," I muttered. I stood and blurted out, "Isn't it true that Peyton McKean and Janet Emerson played key roles in all this?"

Holloman eyed me with surprise, and then disdain. The room fell silent. Reporters turned and scowled at the upstart interrupting the presentation. After a moment of thought, Holloman smiled at me condescendingly. "The individuals you mentioned certainly played a role, sir. But there were quite a few others involved. I don't want to single out any of my helpers for more credit than they deserve."

"He refuses to even say McKean's name!" I grumbled under my breath.

He opened his mouth to make another point but I cut him off in a loud voice. "For the benefit of my fellow press people, I'll spell the key names. Peyton McKean, P-E-Y-T-O-N—M-C-K-E-A-N, and Janet Emerson, J-A-N-E-T—E-M-E-R-S-O-N."

Holloman rolled his eyes while I completed my little drill. His forehead went bright red. But he wasn't intimidated. As I sat down he said, "Thank you Mr. er, What's Your Name, for that. But let me finish what I was saying…"

Few of my colleagues wrote down the names I had spelled out. Not until Holloman restarted his self-serving harangue did they begin writing in earnest. I settled down in my chair, deflated, as Holloman detailed the rapid production of the vaccine under his direction—so he claimed—and its shipment around the nation by courier and military transport. I could understand, if not accept, my colleagues' fixation on Holloman. He was enough story for them, dishing up all the drama, urgency, and factual detail they needed to sell a ton of newspapers and hours of internet and television time.

I quit listening after a while. I knew the facts better than Holloman.

During the question-and-answer period, I felt a twinge of exhaustion from the ordeals of the last few days. Holloman fielded the inevitable questions about the logistics of producing the vaccine—additional batches planned or in progress. None of it surprised me, or interested me.

Cameron Phipps shot me a quick thumbs-up and a half smile. "Chin up," he said. "McKean will get his credit. I'll work his name into my next piece, if my editor allows me enough column space."

"Great," I mumbled, knowing how it would be. No column space for secondary characters. I got up and wandered out, feeling tired and disgusted.

The thought struck me that I was not so far from Peyton McKean. He was probably just two floors above me, in his lab. I went to the elevator, but a security guard was stationed there, an old leather skinned man who smelled of stale cigarette smoke.

"Front door's that way," he said in a sandpapery voice, pointing down the hall to the entry foyer.

I held my ground. "I was hoping to see Dr. McKean while I'm here."

He shook his head. "Not today, sir. I have orders to make sure all the press people leave the building." He glanced at my pass. " 'Specially you, Mr. Morton."

Outmaneuvered and aching from the aftereffects of the virus, I allowed myself to be sent toward the door. As I turned a corner and neared the entry, a "pssst" sound came from a hall branching to my left. I turned and was surprised to see Janet Emerson leaning against a wall in such a way that she was out of sight of both the front desk and the elevator guard.

She waved me to her and I ducked into the side hall.

"Want to see Peyton?" she asked in a low voice.

"Sure," I whispered. "How?"

She motioned for me to follow her along the hall. "My ID card will get us up the freight elevator."

On the third floor, we found McKean sitting at Janet's lab desk pouring over some data sheets, while the boom box played some down-and-dirty delta blues. He smiled when he saw me and stopped reading for a moment to say hello. His lab coat was wrinkled and he was gaunt.

"You look tired," I said.

"I have been essentially living in my office," he said. "Janet and I are putting in long hours at the lab bench double-checking the quality of the second large batch of vaccine."

"Ironic," I said. "Holloman is downstairs taking credit while you're up here doing the work."

McKean shrugged. "So what's new?"

"Your attitude amazes me," I marveled. "So, Holloman's coupe is complete? He owns the credit, lock, stock and barrel?"

McKean turned back to his data without saying more.

"Sooner or later," I said, "I'll get your name into print. I've missed the deadline for the next issue of *Biotechnology Weekly*, but there's another deadline next week…"

"It doesn't matter," McKean murmured, scanning his data sheets as if they had suddenly become irresistible to him.

"Oh, really?" I resisted. "Thousands of Americans, if not millions, owe their lives to this vaccine, Peyton. But they're saying it's a product of Stuart Holloman's brilliant mind."

The trace of a smile crossed McKean's narrow face, but he didn't look up. He highlighted several data lines with his yellow marker.

"Don't you care at all that you're being overlooked?" I asked.

"Answer:—" he said without taking his eyes off the data sheet, "I suppose. But the big fish of science always swallow the little ones. Bosses claim credit for the labors of their subordinates more in the sciences than anywhere else."

"It's not fair," I said. "If I hadn't been sick with the virus, I would have gotten an article out first. And it would have been about you, not him. I'm sorry."

"You're forgiven." He highlighted another line.

I wasn't satisfied. "There's something I've been wondering about, Peyton."

"What's that?"

"Why the devil do you stay at ImCo, cooped up under the shadow of

Stuart Holloman? Why not get out and be your own man? You've clearly got what it takes…"

"Get out?" He sighed as if the subject was an old and boring one to him. He turned on his lab stool to face me. "Where to? You don't just go out on a street corner and set up a lab."

"No, of course not. But there must be a better place for you somewhere. How about finding a wealthy patron? Your talents deserve the sponsorship of a modern-day Medici—"

He cut me off in mid-suggestion with a wave of his hand. "Every public and private charity already has a long list of applicants for funding. They've got so many requests they need a fulltime staff just to read the proposals. And it's hard for them to tell the good from the bad. Usually, the ones telling the tallest tales get the money, even if their proposals make exaggerated promises—in fact, precisely because they do. My more sensible proposals have been lost in the shuffle more than once."

"It sounds like you were fated to obscurity from the start. But that's not true for every young scientist, is it?"

"The normal pathway is to append yourself to a big researcher like Holloman, serve him loyally for many years, and hope you will be chosen as his replacement when he retires or dies. It's a feudal system of liege and successor."

I shook my head. "That's ridiculous. By the time it's their turn, most people must have left their best years behind them."

McKean smiled ironically. "It's a well known fact that scientists make most of their breakthroughs in their twenties and thirties."

"So, things are arranged so that only old, hard headed has-beens make it to the top?"

"For the most part, that is true. The occasional young investigator breaks out of the pattern and finds a university departmental chair with no heir-apparent, or gets in on a biotechnology company startup before all the choice positions are taken. But, for most of us, our place in the sun just never opens up."

"But you have done incredible things! You just haven't gotten credit."

A wan smile spread across McKean's face. "Yes," he agreed. "I have excelled, and have not been given credit. But please realize my single most important motive in life has been satisfied. My abhorrence of disease, my hatred of viruses, and my distain for infections that kill and disable people, that part of me has had a wonderful catharsis. And it pleases me very much. Every day I make progress against disease, is a day well spent. If overlords like Holloman hog the credit, so what? I've still done what I set out to do when I got my Ph.D. I've fought human suffering—

and won."

"Duly noted," I said. "And admirable. But you're taking altruism to an extreme. Maybe in the future I can correct the public misperceptions by writing about whose work this really was."

"I wish you luck," McKean said. "And there will no doubt be another adventure of this sort to amuse us both very soon."

"I hope not!"

"Hope as you please," McKean said matter-of-factly. "But anticipate realistically. I wouldn't be surprised if something like this happens again tomorrow. It's part of the times we live in."

"Horrid times, if that's true," Janet said.

"Perhaps," McKean allowed. "But times in which I believe good can still win out over evil."

"Are you so sure?" I asked. "Those ape instincts you mentioned could reduce society to rubble. Down with up."

McKean shook his head. "No, Fin. They won't prevail."

"Why not?"

"The math is simple," he said. "Although evil springs eternally from the young male ape's primitive desire for dominance, there is a powerful counterbalancing force. In fact, I believe, a stronger one."

"Let me in on the secret," I said, "before I give up on humanity."

"We have other instincts. Better ones. The instinct to protect other members of the species is built into apes and us. So is the instinct to share, to care for each other, to foster the young in positive ways—to teach them right from wrong. But most important is the instinct to band together and drive away anything that would do us all harm. Chimpanzees will unite to drive away a leopard. They have an instinct to co-operate in mutual defense. And we humans share that instinct."

"But if there are enough terrorists—"

"Never," McKean said with assurance. "There are always many more people who want to defend society rather than tear it down. Outrages will happen from time to time, but inevitably, the majority—the great, caring mass of humanity—will rouse themselves and put the evil ones in their place. Good prevails in the end by sheer numbers."

"I hope you are right," I said.

"I am sure I am right," McKean replied.

McKean's cell phone rang and he put it on the bench. By habit never one to need a private conversation, he hit the speaker button.

"Hello," he called at the phone, simultaneously jotting a note in a laboratory notebook.

A husky voice said, "Hello, Peyton McKean? This is Roger Devon."

"Hello, Roger." McKean shot a smart-ass smile at Janet and me,

"Dominant ape," he whispered. Then he spoke into the phone. "How's your vaccine coming?"

"Slowly," Devon replied. "In fact, I'm about to cancel the program. I heard you're shipping your second lot of vaccine today. Is that true?"

"Answer: yes."

"Then we'll be getting some of it here in the next day or two to administer to our staff, including me. Looks like you've won another round."

McKean shook his head. "I don't consider it a matter of winning or losing. We all win when a new vaccine is created."

Devon paused for a long time. McKean energetically dotted I's and crossed T's in his notebook until Devon said, "I wonder if you would consider coming to work for me?"

"Answer: no," McKean said without a moment's thought.

Devon paused a moment, and then said, "Can I get you to move from Seattle to Atlanta with the promise of a large office suite, your own secretary, and a bigger and better-staffed laboratory? How about a dozen people working for you?"

"No thank you."

After another, longer pause, Devon said, "Just be aware, Peyton Mc-Kean, I won't always sit by and watch you and your boss claim all the prizes. You might regret this choice."

"I doubt it," said McKean.

They said goodbye and McKean sat back in his chair, steepling his fingers and thinking deeply for a moment after Devon hung up.

"I'm surprised you're not interested," I said. "It sounds like he's offering a big step up for you."

McKean smiled. "Don't forget that Devon is a man who rejected my concept for the synthetic vaccine and steadfastly pursued the old, slow methods. Imagine where we would all be if he were my boss."

"Dead."

"Exactly. Janet and I would have gotten resistance at every step. He might have even forced us to stop and try it his way. I've worked for stodgy old bosses before. They take exception to every new idea and come up with an alternative from their own obsolescent bag of tricks. They're forever trying to prove themselves smarter than me."

"And that's impossible." Janet said, smiling. "We are talking the greatest mind since Sherlock Holmes, here."

McKean let the compliment roll off him unacknowledged. "Here, at least I know Holloman is too dumb to come up with another idea. I get a lot more done that way."

"But he hogs the public recognition."

"Better for humanity that the work gets done. I would get no credit under Devon, and there would also be no vaccine. Holloman is the lesser of two evils. My top priority is curing disease. Let someone else niggle over who gets credit."

"It seems you have nowhere to turn, then."

"Not if I want to get anything done. Speaking of which, Janet and I have just begun a new phase of our work. There is an additional protein-coding segment of viral DNA that can be translated into a second vac-cine, for a booster shot to reinforce people's immune responses to the first. While Holloman and his government buddies mass-produce the first, Janet and I will work up another. I'm sure you will want to be the first journalist to get a look at it."

"And a dose of it," I said.

"This virus will keep us busy for months," McKean said. "Not to mention you, writing a chronicle, if you're interested."

"Of course I am."

"Janet used an electrophoresis procedure to separate the protein shell of the virus into its component parts so we can study them individually." He pointed to an apparatus near him on the bench top. It was a clear Lucite box about half the size of a car battery, with red and black elec-trical wires attached to it. It was open on top, and there was a clear, foamy liquid solution inside its transparent reservoir.

"We've picked out a second viral surface protein, B16R. That will be the target of our second vaccine. By the way, it's got another very inter-esting DNA sequence in it."

He pointed at the data sheet he had been so busy scrutinizing. On the page filled with long lines of DNA and amino acid codes, he had yellow-highlighted a short region with three lines of code, as before. These read:

GATGAGGCTACGCAT
AspGluAlaThrHis
D   E   A   T   H

"I think this sequence will do nicely," he said to Janet with a chuckle, as I gasped at what I saw.

"Another of Taleed's too-clever alterations," she explained.

"He likes to harp on that death-and-dying subject, doesn't he?" I said.

"True," McKean agreed. "He expected his virus to spell death for America. Instead, this second vaccine will doubly protect us against it."

"Peyton McKean," I said, "allow me to tell you how impressed I am by the methodical and thorough way in which you have neutralized Dr. Taleed's biological warfare weapon. You are indeed a modern-day Sherlock Holmes, disguised as a biotechnologist!"

He glanced at me with a humorous twinkle in his eyes. "There's a difference between me and Holmes," he said.

"What's that?"

"Sherlock Holmes' methods were fictional. Mine are real."

"But you still have one thing in common with Sherlock Holmes," I said.

"Oh?"

"An utter lack of humility."

McKean smirked, but otherwise ignored the remark. He and Janet leaned closely over the data sheet, like a enthusiastic co-conspirators.

"Do you want three extra amino acids on either side?" she asked.

"Answer: yes."

"And a glycine spacer?"

"Exactly."

"And dipalmitoyl-lysine on the end?"

McKean sat back in his chair. "You've got it exactly right, Janet. One day, you'll make me redundant in my own lab."

"Then," I said, "*you* can start taking credit for *her* work."

We all laughed. Then McKean said, "You know, there's something to that, Fin. While you and I have been discussing who gets credit, we've overlooked Janet." He put a hand on her shoulder and looked her in the face. "You worked a miracle while I was locked up in the isolation ward, Janet. You probably saved both our lives. And many more. Perhaps millions."

Janet flushed red, beaming a modest but proud smile.

I added, "You probably did more to ruin the Sheik's plans than anyone else."

Suddenly, a low, sinister laugh came from the back of the laboratory. The three of us turned. Two men stood near the fire exit doorway.

CHAPTER 23

"Sheik Abdul-Ghazi!" McKean murmured.

There, impossibly, stood the Sheik, eyeing us as venomously as a cobra. The white turban was gone, as were the flowing robes, exchanged for a black business suit. But the scraggly beard and hateful scowl remained.

McKean rose slowly. For once, his normally taciturn face registered astonishment. "How could you possibly be here?"

"Allah works many wonders," the Sheik hissed. He came toward us, shadowed by the second man, who was dressed in a black business suit as well.

"Joseph Fuad!" I cried. "So you've finally shown your true stripes."

Fuad held a snub-nosed pistol at waist level, covering us. "Now you know for sure," he gloated. "I am an agent in the service of Abdul-Ghazi."

The Sheik stopped about five feet from us. He pointed at Janet with a bejeweled hand. "So, this little woman helped her master overcome my holy plan."

"Master!" Janet cried indignantly. "He's not—"

"Silence!" the Sheik roared. He drew a small, gold-plated pistol from under his coat and pointed it at her. She cringed, but faced him.

"How did you get in here?" McKean demanded.

The Sheik smiled. "Your security system was no problem for my nephew, Yousef, here. He was trained in such matters by your own FBI.

No fire escape is safe from his tricks. Especially when smokers prop certain doors open."

Janet's eyes flashed angrily at Fuad. "It was you who destroyed the first batch of vaccine!"

Fuad smiled proudly and nodded.

The Sheik drew near McKean and fixed him in his beady black-eyed gaze. "You are a brilliant man, Peyton McKean. But it seems I have checkmated you in the end. Before we leave here, we will destroy more than a vaccine. We will destroy its makers."

McKean stood to his full height, looking down on Abdul-Ghazi even though the Sheik himself was a tall man. For a moment not a word was spoken. They glared into each other's eyes, taking each other's measure. The Sheik hissed, "So says the holy Qur'an, 'The plots of the unbelievers will end in nothing.' "

"In the same surah," McKean countered without hesitation, "it says 'He that works evil will be requited with evil.' "

The Sheik paused to consider McKean's statement. A hint of a smile crossed his face, and then disappeared. "I knew you were a learned man, Peyton McKean. But I am surprised to hear you have studied our holy scriptures."

"I am rather widely-read," McKean replied.

The Sheik waved his gun hand, dismissing McKean's comment. "The Qur'an cannot be understood in English. It was inspired in the heart of the Prophet in Allah's language, Arabic."

McKean suddenly rattled off several lengthy lines in Arabic—angrily, gutturally and emphatically. I didn't understand a word of it, but the Sheik's eyebrows raised.

"Most impressive. You quote our scriptures in their original words."

"And I know them well enough to know you have misinterpreted them."

"Ah hah hah hah! You are so wise, Dr. McKean?"

"Enough to see you wrapping yourself in lies that Allah commands what you do. By that logic, whatever cruelty you devise is a divine necessity. Convenient, isn't it, how your interpretation of Sharia law gives all power to a strongman, namely you? I am sure that suits your personal need for greatness. But your vision of Sharia is the same one that inspired brutal dictators like Moammar Ghadafi and Bashar Assad."

"It will not matter what you think, when you are dead," the Sheik said.

"That's the strongman's answer to all disagreements, isn't it?" McKean said. "Anyone who disagrees with me dies! Violence is your ultimate recourse. Violence is what you prefer!"

"As Allah wills."

"No. As *you* will. It gives you pleasure to see others in pain."

"Enough!" He lifted the pistol and aimed it at McKean's heart. "You are a wise man, Dr. McKean. It is too bad your wisdom has no further purpose on this earth. I am afraid it must die with you."

McKean stood remarkably calm before immanent death. Steel-eyed, he hissed another Arabic quotation. And then he added in English, "You know as well as I the Qur'an forbids murder."

"I do not murder," the Sheik said. "I fight a holy war!"

All this conversation took some time. As it transpired, Janet surreptitiously moved to the bench, inching a hand toward McKean's telephone. Now Fuad turned his gun on her. She froze.

The Sheik motioned for her to step away from the bench. "No calls for help, little woman."

She stepped away, and Fuad's gun hand tracked her closely.

The Sheik's eyes narrowed. "It is not the place of a woman to challenge men's doings. And this one has helped destroy my virus—truly Satan has worked his ways through her."

Janet trembled, but doubled her fists and returned the Sheik's scowl, venom for venom. He leaned close and muttered into her face, "In my country, an immodest woman like you would be stoned to death. But today a bullet will have to suffice." He straightened, and said to Fuad, "She is yours to kill, nephew. But first, I claim the honor of killing her master, Peyton McKean."

"Master!" Janet growled. "That's the second time you've said that!"

"It is the way of Allah," the Sheik said blandly, "that men should lead and women follow. You could never have prevailed with your vaccine without a man's instructions."

Janet sputtered in rage.

McKean said, "If you really believe she, by herself, was unable to defeat you, then let her go. I am the one you need to kill. I am the one who created the vaccine."

Janet scowled at McKean. "What do you mean, *you* created it? Didn't I stay up three nights in a row making it?"

McKean turned his head and half-whispered to Janet, "I'm trying to get you out of this. Will you at least play along?"

The Sheik was momentarily diverted by their bickering, and held his fire.

But as McKean bickered, he moved a hand to the lab bench. Suddenly he grabbed up the Lucite electrophoresis apparatus and splashed the liquid into Abdul-Ghazi's face, dousing both his eyes in the frothing solution.

The Sheik cried out in pain and clasped both hands to his face, including the one holding the pistol.

"It's acid!" McKean shouted loudly enough for the Sheik to hear over his own cries. "You'll be blinded unless you wash it away with water! Drop the gun and I'll help you."

Instead, the Sheik fired a shot blindly at McKean. It went wide of McKean's shoulder and shattered glassware on a shelf behind him.

McKean sidestepped to get out of the sweep of the gun.

"Kill them!" Abdul-Ghazi shouted to Fuad.

Fuad raised his gun. But I had edged closer to him as he watched the argument. Now I lunged and struck his arm upward just as he fired. The bullet went over McKean's head and shattered a fluorescent light in the ceiling. There was no second shot. I swung my fist with every ounce of strength and caught Fuad's jaw with such force that he lifted off the floor and flew backward through the air. The first part of him to touch the linoleum tile was the back of his skull, with a loud *crack!* He lay spread-eagled, limp as a dead man. His gun spun away across the floor and stopped against a wastebasket.

The Sheik stood with one hand covering his face and the other out-stretched, waving the pistol blindly in search of McKean. Unable to see his target, he held his fire, shaking with rage and pain as the liquid seared his eyes. I picked up Fuad's gun and pointed it, fully intending to kill him. But McKean raised a hand and I held my fire. He then reached out and deftly disarmed the Sheik, seeming unconcerned about the liquid frothing on the gun.

"Peyton," I cried. "The acid! Your hand!"

Blinded but undaunted, the Sheik reached beneath the other side of his coat and drew out his jeweled dagger.

Janet was standing close beside him. She grabbed a heavy glass Ehr-lenmeyer flask from the counter and swung it hard at the side of his head. It shattered on his temple, knocking him nearly senseless. The dagger dropped from his hand. He staggered in a circle, his jeweled fingers clutching at the air like the claws of a cornered panther. His chest heaved. His eyes were shut tightly against the pain of the foaming liquid.

McKean watched him wheel and turn for a moment. Then he grabbed him by both shoulders and forced him down onto a laboratory stool.

Abdul-Ghazi didn't try to get up. Instead, he rubbed his burning eyes, moaning in pain.

After a minute, he paused. And then he forced one reddened eye open. Squinting, he looked from one to the other of us. His expression, so imperious a minute before, was now confused.

Fuad lay spread-eagled and motionless. I straddled him and glared down into his unseeing, half-open eyes. I trembled with an animal passion, wanting to know for certain he was as dead as he looked. Instead, I saw that he still breathed, spasmodically, in deep, unconscious gasps.

"What teamwork!" McKean exulted.

I turned my attention to the Sheik. I expected to see the skin peeling off his face and hands. Instead, he had managed to get both of his reddened eyes open. He stared supplicatingly at McKean, who covered him with his own golden handgun. When he began daubing at the liquid on his cheeks with his fingertips, McKean's face registered unrestrained glee. Janet broke into a chuckle, wearing grin to match McKean's.

The Sheik looked at his moist fingertips. "This—" he stammered, "this is not acid."

"Quite right," McKean agreed. "The liquid in the electrophoresis apparatus is relatively harmless. Nothing more than a sodium dodecyl sulfate solution."

"Sodium...what?" Abdul-Ghazi blinked his red eyes at McKean.

McKean picked up the container and gazed through one of its clear sides at the suds streaming down the wall. "Dodecyl sulfate," he repeated. "Detergent. A common ingredient in shampoo, also known as lauryl sulfate. It's quite harmless, although it can sting when it gets in one's eyes. Can't it, Sheik Abdul-Ghazi?"

The Sheik cursed under his breath in Arabic. He reached inside his coat, and I pointed Fuad's pistol point-blank at his face. But he wasn't going for a weapon. Instead, he drew out a neatly folded white handkerchief and began gingerly wiping the corners of his eyes.

"Now then," McKean said. "The tables have turned one last time. You won't be killing anyone today, or ever, Sheik."

"You have my gun!" the Sheik pleaded in a voice trembling with emotion. "Kill me! Give me martyrdom! Do not condemn me to rot in an American prison!"

"Sorry," McKean replied. "But I like the idea of you languishing in a cold cell. You'll grow old, realizing that every day is another day Allah has seen fit to leave you sitting there. Until the day comes when you die, and learn the true nature of Hell. Janet, would you mind making that phone call now?"

"Yes, Master," she said with a chuckle.

CHAPTER 24

Janet quickly had 911 directing the police to ImCo. A moan from Fuad announced that he was coming to. As he sat up, and then groggily got to his feet, I covered him with his own gun.

The Sheik sighed in bitter resignation. "The checkmate is yours, Peyton McKean. But jihad will not end here. It will never be over. Another plague, may it please Allah, shall come to these shores. And on that day, I pray you will not be here to foil Allah's will."

"Allah's will!" McKean exclaimed with a laugh. "I think Allah is on our side, not yours."

"Do not blaspheme," Abdul-Ghazi muttered.

"I'm quite serious," McKean replied.

I glanced at McKean and saw a light of righteousness in his eyes. The Sheik saw it too. He bowed his head in defeat.

"One thing I never understood about you, Sheik," I said, still holding Fuad's gun on him. "For a man who quotes the Qur'an regularly, you strike me as having a lot of vices. Tobacco, whiskey, women—"

He smiled ironically. Keeping his eyes on the floor, he murmured, "It is true, I am not a religious man. My piety is a charade I play, to attract religious fools to do my will. It is their belief, not mine, that leads them to their deaths. I have used these fools for my own purposes, not Allah's."

McKean took an interest. "And those purposes were?"

"Revenge. You see, my father the Sultan was shot in an assassination attempt. A sniper's bullet found him while he was riding his horse in the desert. It left him paralyzed from the waist down. He is convinced it was your American CIA that did this, and I have sworn revenge. And I came... so near." He choked on these last words.

Footsteps drummed in the hallway as the policeman assigned to building security belatedly arrived. Officer Jones, a young, handsome cop, came into the room with gun drawn. But he holstered it when he saw things were well in hand. He bound the Sheik's and Fuad's wrists behind their backs with plastic ties. Minutes later, two officers responding to the 911 call led Fuad and the Sheik away for a ride to the police precinct. McKean and I retreated to his office to escape a crowd of coworkers and "competitors" from Dr. Curman's lab who came to gawk at the broken glass and spilled electrophoresis liquid, and listen to Janet retelling the story of the Sheik's capture. Officer Jones came with us, taking statements from each of us and jotting them on a note pad. McKean leaned over his desk and looked out the window to the street below.

"I think you'll be adding one more to your list of captured suspects," he said to Jones.

The officer and I went to the window and pushed aside some avocado leaves to glance at the street. A tall hefty Arab in a blue jeans and a brown shirt stood spread-legged with his hands on the hood of a black limousine. The arriving squad cars had boxed him in at the curb, where he had been waiting for the Sheik in a passenger-loading zone in front of the coffee shop. Two police officers stood with drawn service pistols while a third officer frisked the man and cuffed his hands behind his back.

"Tally up another missing vehicle," I said.

McKean nodded. "The dark-tinted windows explain how they've been getting around without being spotted."

One of the officers led the prisoner to a squad car. Before getting in, the man looked up at our window, as if he knew exactly where Peyton McKean was. He scowled venomously. But whether he saw us or not, I couldn't tell.

"I remember his face." I said. "The last time I saw him, he was spraying my car with buckshot."

The officer put a hand on top of the man's head and guided him into the back seat. When the door was shut, McKean said, "I have a feeling we've seen the last of the Sheik and his henchmen."

Someone rapped a knuckle on McKean's doorjamb. We turned from the window and there, to my astonishment, stood Vince Nagumo.

"May I come in?" he asked.

"Certainly," McKean said, but I was already in motion. I charged Nagumo, doubling a fist.

"Where's Jameela!" I shouted.

Nagumo raised a hand to fend me off. "Easy, easy," he said to me, and then to McKean with a smirk, "Hide the scissors."

His casual reaction sent me ballistic. With a choked cry of rage I raised my fist, intending to smash those grinning teeth down his throat. But a hand grabbed my arm from behind and stopped it in mid swing. I wheeled like an animal at bay, but Officer Jones contorted my wrist into a painful submission hold. I stopped struggling and glared at Nagumo.

He smiled and said, "Relax, buddy." He waved Officer Jones off and I straightened up, still fuming.

"There's no need to get excited, Fin. I can tell you exactly where she is."

"Where?"

"At the Sheik's ranch."

"What? Why?"

"As I told you, she's a material witness. And Arabians Unlimited is in U.S. custody. Basically, it's FBI property now. But managing livestock isn't our business. Her credentials as a horse trainer checked out, so I figured we needed someone with experience to oversee the place."

I rubbed my sore wrist. A profound sense of relief flooded through me. "You mean she's not under arrest?"

"Never was. Now she's free on her own recognizance. We don't consider her a flight-risk, although we still need her as a witness."

I sighed like I had been holding my breath for three days.

Nagumo grinned. "She's one of the good guys, as far as we're concerned."

McKean watched my reaction with a good-natured smile. "Then all is right with the world," he said.

Nagumo pointed toward the lab. "I'm sorry about all that," he said. "I always had my doubts about Fuad."

"How did he manage to fool you?" McKean asked.

Nagumo shook his head as if he were about to tell an embarrassing story for the thousandth time. "His credentials at FBI Central were clean. He's a naturalized U.S. citizen. Immigrated as a child. We have a crying need for good Arabic speakers to infiltrate terrorist cells. That means someone who not only looks Arab, but can speak an Arab dialect like a native—and someone whose loyalties can be trusted. It turns out Fuad only had two of the three requirements. Every now and then a bad guy slips in among the good ones. That's how it is in this business. Screwups happen. Can't be helped. But thanks to you folks, it ended well. Fuad and the Sheik will be logged in at my office and then shipped to the Federal Interrogation Center in South Carolina for some intensive, er, confessions. They'll spend quite a while there. Then they'll move on to the criminal justice system."

"Never to walk free again?" I asked.

"Absolutely."

"But they will no doubt go public with their claim that the CIA shot the Sultan, Abdul-Ghazi's father."

"Let them. Our people in Kharifa have long since gathered good information on that story. The Sultan has been ruthlessly suppressing a mountain rebel group for years. It was a rebel team that took him down, not us."

Nagumo looked at McKean and me with genuine fondness. "You know, things didn't turn out half bad. Thanks to the Sheik's call to jihad, a whole bunch of baddies came out of the underground. We can now account for 89 American-based sympathizers and terrorist operatives. Some are dead of smallpox, some were arrested, some were killed. We've got to thank the Sheik for that. Add it all up and we took out more than half the suspects we knew of in America. Terrorists may not be gone forever, but we set back their American efforts by years, if not decades. We're still following up and arresting the contacts of the dead and wounded men from the truck. The ones we haven't caught yet are on the run, which exposes them to being captured. That's pretty good for a few days' work, wouldn't you say? We ought to thank the Sheik for drawing them out. Oh, and by the way, we found an interesting fellow among the dead from the truck in Colorado. Went by several names. James Washington, Elijah Williams... Recognize this guy?" He handed me a photo of a corpse with a familiar African-American face.

"Mullah Shabab," I said, looking at the natty brown suit, the freckled, deep tan skin, the pomaded hair with a blaze of white up the center.

"He was at the ranch," McKean said, "leading the jihadis around."

"I'll need you to testify to that," Nagumo said. "He was the leader of a radical American group called the Islamic Army—but you would think he was working for us. He had already rounded up a bunch of his homeboys in Detroit and Chicago and had them on a second truck heading west, presumably to the ranch. Forty-seven of them arrested at a rest stop in North Dakota without a shot fired."

"Incredible," I said.

"We've frozen the entire assets of the Islamic Army. Within a few weeks we'll bring a lawsuit forward on behalf of the people of the United States, alleging complicity in terrorism. Shabab's organization is estimated to be worth around $100 million. We hope to take it all as punitive damages."

McKean tugged at his chin. "Just when things seemed darkest, a ray of sunshine."

"The light of justice," said Nagumo. Then he chuckled. "I'm sorry if I was a bit of a bungler at times. But sooner or later us good guys finally get things right."

"And Dr. Taleed?" McKean asked. "What has become of him?"

"A slippery fish," said Nagumo. "We thought he returned to Kharifa, but just yesterday he was spotted in Vancouver, BC. Got across the Canadian border somehow. But the Royal Canadian Mounties have an all-points-bulletin out for him. He won't elude us for long. And even if he does, he's a man without a country. The marines found his genetic engineering operation at a gold mine in the Kharifi desert last night. They're demolishing it right down to twisted steel and concrete dust."

"He might start another," I said.

"Without the Sheik's money?" said McKean. "Not likely."

"Good point. Lab work is super expensive."

"Money truly is the root of all evil in the world," McKean said. "It was only Abdul-Ghazi's money that made him able to carry out his plans. Without money, no labs, no Taleed, no virus. And no young men attracted to his cause like subdominant apes following a new leader. But you know, in some ways I can almost sympathize with the young jihadis."

"What!" I exclaimed. "How could you?" Nagumo and Jones' faces registered the same shock written on my and Janet's faces.

"Consider the plight of the great majority of young people every-where on the planet today," McKean said. "Most are impoverished, some are middle-class, but essentially all are barred from the amenities of the rich. In an overcrowded world, there is negligible hope for personal advancement. And the rich seem intent these days on solidifying their hold on power. Think of the frustration young people feel at seeing the children of the wealthy inheriting great wealth themselves, without the need to work for it. But no avenue to wealth, worked for or not, is open to most young people."

"In a free society," Janet countered, "everyone has a chance to suc-ceed—through hard work."

"A slim chance," McKean rejoined. "And, meanwhile rich kids just get it handed to them on silver platters, like the Sheik did."

"Life is not fair," I said.

"If it's not, then you should not be surprised the terrorist apes are intent on down-with-up. I for one, don't really blame them for being angry."

"But killing people," Nagumo said. "Surely you don't condone—"

"Of course not. My sympathy stops well short of murder. But on the other hand, I am convinced we will see no end to terror until the iniquities of wealth distribution are eliminated. In essence, it is the very existence of rich, privileged classes that breeds rebellion and terror. Even the Arab Spring protestors were calling for an end to privileged classes that ruled over them economically as much as militarily. Eliminate the control of wealth by the few, and those who now want to overthrow society will join in happily, working hard for their share of prosperity."

"Do you think that day will really come?" I asked.

"Answer: yes, indeed I do," McKean replied. "And while I have no sympathy whatsoever for the Sheik, I note that he himself is prone to the same apish down-with-up fixation."

"How do you figure?"

"Consider his lot in life. He is fabulously wealthy, to be sure. But he is also destined to remain the son of a sultan, but never be a sultan himself. I read somewhere that he is 14th in line to the throne. That is, he has no chance of achieving it at all. Just like Osama bin Laden, he must have rankled at his inferior family standing, compared to the heirs in line ahead of him. So he felt the same subdominant-ape motivation that his terrorist supporters felt. But from his already high position, he felt compelled to kill many, not just a few, in order to make himself grander than his brothers. It really was all about sibling rivalry with him—which is another rather apish concern."

Nagumo and Officer Jones left us, wearing befuddled expressions McKean's discourse had put on their faces. We returned to the lab and looked over the scene of our showdown. A forensics team was measuring bullet hole trajectories and taking photographs. The cell phone still lay on the bench. It rang, and McKean put it on speaker.

"Hi Cuz!" the caller said brightly.

"Mike!" McKean cried. "How are you?"

"I'm doin' just fine. Home in my trailer with Mary and the kids."

"Last time we saw you, you were being dragged off with a truckload of jihadis."

"Y'know," Mike said, "them terroristas was a buncha amateurs. The way they tied my hands, I had the knots loose about ten minutes after the truck rolled outta the ranch. Down in Colorado it got hot, so they opened the back door for some air. I expected that might draw some attention from the cops. So as soon as I saw that squad car tailing us, I made my move. I slipped my hands free and grabbed an AK47 that was just sittin' there. I emptied it—and whacked a bunch of 'em. But some of 'em came up with more guns, so I bailed out."

"They said you hit the pavement at seventy plus."

"Felt like a hundred'n seventy."

"Are you really okay?"

"More or less. I got casts all over the place and a couple pockmarks on my forehead. I had a dose of the old smallpox vaccine back in my Special Forces training days, so the jihad virus didn't hit me too hard."

There was a pause.

"Hey, Peyton."

"Yeah, Mike?"

"C'mon over sometime. Y'gotta see the new puppy Mary got me. A Border collie. We named him Larry, after Lawrence of Arabia. And bring Fin along. It'll be harvest time soon. Maybe we'll do a little more... fffffwwwttt."

"Maybe so." McKean smiled at me.

After goodbyes, we were shooed away by the forensics team. McKean was chipper as we walked back to his office. "Things all seem to be working out according to Allah's will," he said.

I laughed. "You have a way with words, Peyton McKean."

He eyed me thoughtfully as we sat. "So what about you, Fin? What will you do next? Write a chronicle of all that's happened?"

"That's on my list. I've got to start writing before any of the details fade. But there's one more important thing I've got to do first."

"A trip to Winthrop?"

"How did you guess?"

McKean smiled. "Thank Jameela for me, from the bottom of my heart."

"I'll do that."

"Tell her I'm proud to know her. She understands all that is best in Islam. The Qur'an's many words of kindness and caring are understood best by the female gender, wouldn't you agree?"

"Absolutely," said Janet, who had followed us across the hall.

"I have a sense," McKean said, "that Muslim women are on the brink of a breakthrough. They have the power to make Islam blossom into a religion of open-heartedness and light."

"A tall order," Janet replied. "They're so oppressed by their men."

"But Jameela showed us how insuppressible the female spirit is," McKean said. "Women like her are mankind's greatest hope of salvation."

"Right now," I said, "I'm most concerned about just two people. How can things work out between Jameela and me? We come from such different worlds."

Janet put a hand on my arm. "It will be fine if you love each other. Do you love her, Fin? Does she love you?"

"I— I don't know," I responded. "I guess I've been making some pretty big assumptions about her feelings for me."

In the quiet that followed, McKean turned to some data sheets on his desk and began pouring over the rows of A, T, G, and C code letters. He took a highlighter from his pocket and made a yellow mark. His prodigious mind had moved on without offering an answer to my question.

I got up and walked out the door, waving a silent farewell to Janet.

CHAPTER 25

The streets of Seattle were wet with drizzle, but the sky was clear and the air was clean. I fetched my car and drove to my office, knowing what I was going to do, although I couldn't guess the outcome.

Walking from my parking space, I paused in Pioneer Square at the base of the totem pole and communed for a moment with the bronze bust of old Chief Seattle. I gazed into those sculpted sad eyes and care-lined face, and felt a connection across centuries. I touched the three pockmark scars on my jaw, feeling the texture of a common experience. I remembered a line from his speech. *The dead are not entirely powerless.* The Duwamish had shown us all the awesome power of a virus by the very fact of their deaths. Their near annihilation was a warning to us all.

And I realized another thing. Old Chief Seattle had it right. Faced with catastrophe, he dealt fairly with the very people who had brought disease to his shores. He saw that the best chance for his people to survive and recover was understanding, not hate and war.

"Maybe that applies to both sides in this conflict," I murmured. "I see what McKean meant. If the world is to be destroyed, it will be at the hands of hateful strongmen like the Sheik. But if the world is to be saved, it will be by women who finally speak with their own voices, expressing their loving, caring nature. Maybe you knew that, too, huh Chief? Maybe your wife counseled your heart."

Sunshine glinted on Seattle's bronze brow, convincing me that, among those not-so-powerless dead, he was nodding his head and smiling.

I continued to my office, grabbed my laptop and a few other essentials, locked up, and then went back to fetch my car from the lot. I drove to my apartment building and, leaving the Mustang in a three minute loading zone, raced up the stairs and into my apartment, stuffed an armload of clothes into a duffel bag, locked up, left a sticky note on Penny Worthe's door entrusting my peace lilies to her, charged back down the stairs two-at-a-time, and fired the ignition before three minutes were up. I raced to the northbound freeway entrance with a patch of corrugated cardboard flapping over the missing side window and the X of silver duct tape still covering the hole in my front windshield. I drove north nearly as fast as when I escaped the Sheriff, and crossed the North Cascades in less than four hours.

I arrived at the ranch as the sun sank toward the mountains. The wrought-iron spans of the Sheik's main gate were open and the police tape was gone, so I drove up the drive past the empty guard kiosk and the bullet-riddled pickup. I pulled up in front of the house and shut off my engine. As I got out, I suddenly wondered if I were a colossal fool to come so far without asking Jameela if I was welcome.

"Hey there!" a cheerful feminine voice called from behind me. I turned and spotted Jameela at the horse barn, dressed in her English riding jacket, khaki jodhpurs, and black jackboots, which fit her as gloriously as on the first day I had seen her. I hurried across the fifty yards between us, and then stopped several paces from her, drinking in the dazzling Cleopatran charm of her face, the glint of sunlight on her dark hair, and the poise of her straight shoulders—while doubting such perfection was attainable by the likes of me.

"Hello, Fin Morton!" she said fondly.

A soft noise from behind made her turn. The pink muzzle of a white horse had been thrust between the fence rails.

"Zahirah!" Jameela cooed. "Perhaps you need more oats."

She turned to me and smiled. "They have been breeding off and on all day, for hours at a time."

My imagination went on a wild ramble with the horses, as Majid put his head over the top rail and chuggared at me. As Jameela petted the mare's muzzle, I held my hand out to the stallion. Majid nuzzled and sniffed my hand, but tossed his head, refusing to let me pet him. Jameela said, "He remembers you fed him sugar, Fin."

"I wonder if he remembers that crazy ride through a hail of bullets?"

"I do."

The time had come to say something more important, but my mind blanked.

She looked at me expectantly. I felt a flush of embarrassment creep up my neck. Her huge dark eyes unnerved me. Suddenly I felt as dumb as the stallion, craving her touch. A smile tugged at her lips, as if she had read my mind. She put a hand on my arm. An amused, sphinx-like expression came over her face.

"I am alone here," she said. "A dozen FBI agents went through every nook of the house and every scrap of paper. But they are gone now. Before they left, they gave me good news. My mother and father were rescued by American soldiers in Kharifa. They are safe at home in Cairo."

"I'm glad," I said. My mind whirred with unspoken thoughts. Above all else, I couldn't let her think my visit was just a friendly one.

"Jameela—" I said abruptly, and too loudly.

Her chin went up. She looked along the fine line of her nose at me with pharaonic solemnity. "Yes, Fin? What is it?"

Thoughts chased themselves around my brain. My heart pounded until I felt dizzy. After an eternity of wordless hesitation, I had no choice but to act. I stepped near and put an arm around her waist. I pulled her gently to me. She resisted for a moment, and then yielded.

I kissed her. She held back at first, but warmed and put her arms around my shoulders. We shared a tender, delicate first kiss of mixed curiosity and fulfillment, long overdue. She drew me tightly to her. We hugged for a long time, as the mare wandered off and the stallion followed her.

Jameela pulled back slightly and looked into my face. A new joy danced in her beautiful Cleopatran eyes. "Will you stay here with me, Fin?"

"If you'd like me to."

She smiled. "You are welcome here as long as you like."

A thought came back from fevered memories. "What did I say, when I was talking in my sleep?"

She disengaged herself from my arms.

"What was it?" I asked again.

"Just one kiss, Fin. You asked for just one kiss. And now you have had it."

"Wait!" I protested. "I didn't mean just one... forever."

"Oh?" A sparkle came into her eyes. "Perhaps you would like one more?"

"More than that," I said.

She didn't respond immediately. "You said many things to me, in your fever. What you wanted did not stop at a kiss."

"What else did I want?"

A smug little smile crept across her face. "Let's go inside," she said.

Starting for the house, she motioned for me to come along.

I followed her, the way Majid followed Zahirah.

###

ABOUT THE AUTHOR

Thomas Patrick Hopp was born in Seattle, Washington. He lived his earliest years in a housing project on the banks of the Duwamish River. Despite a tough start in life, good grades at West Seattle High School and the University of Washington plus a perfect score on the Graduate Record Examination got him into the Ph.D. program in biochemistry at Cornell University Medical College. He studied protein chemistry there, and genetic engineering at Rockefeller University, and went on to help found the multi-billion-dollar Seattle biotechnology company, Immunex Corporation. There, he cloned the two genes for the human immune-system hormone, interleukin one, and advised the team that created Immunex's blockbuster arthritis drug, Enbrel. He created the world's first commercially successful nanotechnology device, a molecular handle called the Flag epitope tag. He plays guitar and bass and has performed onstage with blues legend John Lee Hooker and rock supergroups The Kingsmen and The Drifters. He has lived in San Diego and on Manhattan Island but currently resides near Seattle. To learn more about Thomas Hopp's science, books, and stories, visit him online at http://thomas-hopp.com/blog/.

ACKNOWLEDGMENTS

I am grateful for the help of Pamela Goodfellow, a fine editor and mentor with the writing program at the University of Washington. My thanks also go to the editors and production staff of iUniverse, who helped me produce the first edition of this book. Its revision into a second edition is entirely my own doing and I take credit and blame for all that has been changed in it. I thank Amr Diab for wonderful Egyptian music, which set the backdrop for many long hours at my computer keyboard. I also thank my former co-workers at Immunex Corporation, who provided models for several characters in this novel, some nice, some not-so-nice. Thanks as well to the soldiers, police, firemen, and first aid responders, who do much more than most of us realize to keep us safe in a dangerous world. And lastly, a sesquicentennially belated thanks to Chief Seattle, who witnessed the devastation of a smallpox epidemic first-hand, and whose commitment to non-violence was as great as Mahatma Gandhi or Martin Luther King, Jr.

Books by Thomas P. Hopp

The Dinosaur Wars Science Fiction Series

EARTHFALL
COUNTERATTACK
BLOOD ON THE MOON
DINOSAUR TALES

Peyton McKean Medical Thrillers

THE SMALLPOX INCIDENT
THE NEAH VIRUS

Short Stories

Saving Pachyrhinosaurus
Riding Quetzalcoatlus
Something in the Jungle
Hatching Alamosaurus

The Treasure of Purgatory Crater

A Dangerous Breed
The Re-Election Plot
The Ghost Trees
Blood Tide

Visit the Author's Web Site

www.thomas-hopp.com/blog

Made in United States
Orlando, FL
09 May 2022

17680354R00157